THE
ANDOR

THE
ANDOR

BOOK ONE OF THE LEGENDS OF TIRMAR

MARK DAME

FutureLine Press

Print ISBN: 978-1-946298-20-1
E-book ISBN: 978-1-946298-21-8

First Edition

1 3 5 7 9 10 8 6 4 2

For Michael – Never give up!

Every once in a great age, when the world needs him most, a hero is born.
– Ancient Ranjer proverb

CHAPTER 1

On an island barely thirty-five leagues across, with a population of a few thousand people, a boat in the water would seem to be a normal sight, even an expected one. For Trygsted, however, that was not the case. In fact, there were almost no boats on the island at all. It's not that boats were strictly forbidden. There were no official laws against building or using them. But those few who chose to risk the ocean waters tended to be shunned by the rest of the Andor clan, sometimes even being driven from their homes to live out their days in isolated shacks, far away from the rest of the population.

Flynygyn Geirrsen had often wondered why. Beyond the myths and superstitions, anyway.

Everyone knew from childhood the story of how people had come to Trygsted. And while some thought the story was just a myth, made up by their ancestors to explain the origin of life, few publicly questioned it.

According to the stories, life started when Andor the Great brought the first people to Trygsted from Vahul. They had traveled on great wooden boats and when they had arrived, they had used the timbers from the boats to build the first houses. Andor swore he would never leave Trygsted and so the first people followed his lead.

For as long as anyone could remember, the only purpose a boat served was to send the dead back to Vahul. Their faith taught that the Mithar Ocean was the barrier between the living and the dead. Before the souls of the dead could pass through the gates to the afterlife, they would be separated from their bodies, which would then be returned to the sea by the Guardians of Vahul. This was why the water of the ocean was salty: it was filled with the sweat and tears and blood of the deceased. At least, that was the belief.

The common belief was that if a living person tried to cross the ocean to Vahul, he would be turned away and doomed to roam the ocean for eternity, a lost soul. Those who tempted fate by building boats and riding them on the ocean were seen as reckless at best, though some were labeled as heretics and banished.

And since there were no other bodies of water big enough for a boat, the only official boat builders in Trygsted were the undertakers. The families of the recently deceased would choose a boat to take their loved one to Vahul and the undertaker would prepare the body for its journey. Then priests would use special rafts to tow the boat out beyond the surf zone and set it on its way.

Flyn had always wondered where the boats went, which was why he had built his own boat when he was still a boy, in spite of the superstition. He had never gotten up the courage to go very far, but over the years, he had discovered something else: his boat made him free.

Free from the confines of the island. Free from the day-to-day drudgery.

He loved the boat and being on the water. He had even learned to swim, something almost no one else did. If it wasn't in a glass or in their washtub, most of the Andor clan refused to have anything to do with it.

Even Kelby, Flyn's best friend for as far back as they both could remember, thought Flyn was out of his mind. And yet, he still climbed aboard every time Flyn went out.

They had been fifteen when Flyn built the boat. Kel had helped some, but mostly because there was nothing else to do. He had never actually intended to get in it. So, when the boat was finished, Flyn had gone out by himself to test it. Kel had refused to join him.

That entire summer, Flyn had hidden the boat from his parents, but the next spring, his father had found it while cleaning up brush from the winter. Flyn had pleaded with him for days not to destroy it and finally his father had relented, but made him promise to never go farther from shore than he could throw a rock.

Geirr had also made his son swear not to talk about the boat to anyone. He said it was because he didn't want his son to be an outcast for the rest of his life. Flyn and Kel thought he might be more concerned about how people would look at him, rather than his son. Regardless of his father's reasons, Flyn kept the boat secret, even from his mother—though eventually she found out.

Over the course of that first summer, Kel watched Flyn paddle around in the surf and ride the waves. Eventually, Kel decided he was tired of sitting on the beach while Flyn had all the fun. Although he had been afraid at first, he had mustered up the courage to take a short ride out and back. After that, the pair had used the boat to explore the coast of Trygsted for leagues to the north and south of their home. As they got older, the boys grew bolder and rowed farther out, though never so far that they couldn't see land.

Today though, much to Kel's dismay, they had gone out farther than they ever had before. At least four furlongs from shore.

"Come on, Flyn. Let's go back." Unlike Flyn, Kel had never learned to swim.

"Relax." Flyn was lying back, his eyes closed, enjoying the warm spring sun on his skin. "Try to enjoy yourself."

After the long, cold winter, the sun, the waves, and the salt air were relaxing. He wanted to take a nap. Which he couldn't do with Kel bugging him about being so far from the shore.

"I'm on a boat in the middle of the ocean. How am I supposed to relax?"

"Why don't you try to catch some fish or something?"

"Please, Flyn. At least let's get closer to shore."

Flyn opened one eye to see how serious Kel was. Sometimes he thought Kel made a fuss just to complain. This didn't seem to be one of those times. Kel was staring at him, gripping the sides of the boat so tight his knuckles were white.

"Okay, fine." Flyn sat up and stretched.

The blue water extended to the horizon in every direction except toward the shore to the east. This far out, the water was crystal clear. He could see all the way to the coral reefs that filled the ocean floor below the boat. He had no idea how far below. The clarity of the water made the coral and the colorful fish swimming around it seem closer than they were.

The odd, rocky structures created a magical underwater forest. Red, green, blue, and purple formations, some with plants growing out of them that looked like cabbages, others were like giant fans. All of it swaying back and forth in the gentle current, like grass in a field.

As colorful as the plants and coral were, the fish were even more amazing. Striped and spotted, every color of the rainbow, some so small he could barely see them hiding in the coral. Some nearly as big as a goat. His favorites were the ones colored so bright that they seemed like they might glow in the dark. Occasionally he would even see a ray slipping through the water like some strange underwater bird.

Sometimes he dreamed about swimming with them. He often wondered what it would be like to float through the water with such ease and grace.

"Flyn!" Kel snapped him out of his daydream.

"All right, we're going."

Kel already had one of the paddles in his hands. Flyn picked up the other one and together they started paddling toward the shore. Flyn breathed in the tangy salt air and listened to the gentle slapping of the water against the hull of the boat, the small splashes of the paddles hitting the water. In the distance, seagulls squawked and screeched as they soared through the air, looking for an easy meal.

"You know what we should do, Kel?" Flyn stopped paddling and scanned the coastline.

"Oh, no." Kel kept paddling. "No. Not another one of your grand ideas. You can count me out."

"You haven't even heard the idea yet."

"I don't need to. I can tell by your voice. You've got some big scheme that'll get us in trouble."

"Oh, come on. When do my ideas get us in trouble?"

"What about that time last summer when you talked me into painting Old Man Gaeten's barn yellow? Or the time you were convinced there was an ogre living in the woods and we had to go catch it? We were lost for six hours."

"Hey, that was when we were eight. And Old Man Gaeten paid us to paint his barn."

"Yeah, but he wanted it painted brown, not yellow."

"I think it looked better in yellow."

"He didn't think so. And what about this stupid boat?"

"What are you talking about? We've never gotten in trouble with the boat."

"Just because we've been lucky."

"Come on, at least listen to my idea before you say no."

From the back of the boat, Flyn couldn't see Kel's face, but he was sure he was scowling. Finally, Kel stopped paddling and turned around.

"Okay, what's your great idea?"

"I think we should take the boat around the whole island."

Kel just stared at Flyn for a minute, then turned around and started paddling again.

"So that's a 'yes' then?" Flyn said, laughing.

"No. That's a 'you're out of your mind.'"

"It'll be fun." Flyn grinned at the back of Kel's head.

Kel turned around again.

"No, it won't be fun. It'll be a nightmare. Sitting in the boat all day, paddling, day after day? No thanks. It'll take a month."

"Fifteen days, tops."

"Fifteen days paddling all day, then. No."

"Remember last summer when we went on the boat every day for two weeks straight?"

Kel visibly shuddered. "Yeah. I hated it."

"You did not. You had a great time. Especially when we did the overnight trip down the coast." They had packed all their gear in a watertight box Flyn had made just for the trip, then paddled several hours down the coast before camping for the night. The next morning, they had packed up and paddled back. Kel talked about it for weeks afterward.

"That was just one night. You're talking about over two weeks."

"It'll be like when we were kids and went on that two-week hunting trip with our dads."

"No, it'll be like the worst parts of that and the worst parts about the boat all rolled into one." Kel went back to paddling. "Besides, we have planting to do."

"I know, but the early planting will be done in a couple of weeks. We can go then."

Kel didn't reply.

"Look, we're nineteen years old. This will be the last summer we get to do it. We'll be married next year, then there'll be kids, and work, and responsibilities. It's our last summer of freedom."

"Fine," Kel said, lowering his head. "I'll think about it."

"It'll be great!" Flyn grinned again. He would talk Kel into it. He always did.

It was nearly dinnertime when Flyn walked through the door of his home. The aroma of roasted pork and fresh-baked bread filled the front room that served as a combination kitchen and sitting room of the small house. Steam rose from the pots on the cast-iron stove. Even with all the window shutters open, Flyn started sweating from the heat of the stove as soon as he entered the house.

Helene, his mother, looked up from the kitchen table where she was slicing the bread.

"Hi, Mom." Flyn smiled at her, hoping she wouldn't notice his salt-starched hair and clothes.

"You've been out on that boat again," she said and went back to slicing. He never could sneak anything past her. "Dinner's almost ready. Go wash up."

Flyn hung his head and walked down the hall to the washroom without responding. Even at nineteen, he still felt guilty when she scolded him.

She had never accepted his interest in the water like his father had and she made sure he knew it. He suspected part of her anxiety was because she was afraid of being shunned by the rest of the clan, though he was sure she was mostly worried for his safety. Flyn had tried to convince his mother several times that he was perfectly safe, especially because he could swim. The last time had resulted in a huge argument that led to them not speaking to each other for days. His father had eventually forced them to agree to a truce of sorts. So now Flyn didn't talk to her about it and she didn't yell at him anymore. Although she still made an occasional scolding remark.

Flyn cranked the handle on the water pump, filling the wash basin. One of his father's designs, the pump brought water from the well directly into the washroom. Not having to haul water in from outside was especially nice in the cold winter months. He had made a second pump for the kitchen to supply water for cooking and cleaning.

Geirr had installed similar setups in all of their neighbors' homes in exchange for various goods and services. They mostly offered meat and fruits, or clothing. Occasionally he would receive farming equipment. A couple of years ago, one neighbor had given him a dairy cow. He was even talking about starting a side business after this year's harvest.

Flyn was excited for his father, though he held no interest in participating in Geirr's hobbies himself. That was more his brother's thing. Tyryse was almost nine years younger than Flyn and spent most of his free time tinkering in the barn with their father. Sometimes Flyn wondered if his father like Ty better because of it. Geirr never said anything about it, but the two spent a lot of time together.

Flyn tried to not be envious of Ty's relationship with their father. He knew it was really just a matter of their common interest and that he would be just as close to his father if he liked inventing and building gadgets. Still, sometimes he felt the pangs of jealousy. The pair even seemed to have their own secret language they used when talking about the projects they worked on together.

Most of the time, Flyn was too busy exploring the countryside or paddling up and down the coast in his boat to be concerned about it. He was actually closer to Kel than his own brother. He and Kel had been best friends since well before Ty was born. And while Kel wasn't quite as adventurous as Flyn, he did enjoy a nice hike through the woods, or in the hill country in the center of the island.

If he could just teach Kel to swim, maybe he would enjoy the boat trips too.

Flyn stripped off his clothes and washed off the salt and grime. The cold well water was refreshing after a day on the ocean. A luxury he supposed he wouldn't have when he and Kel took their trip around the island. He put a wet rag over his face and held it there to ease the stinging from the sunburn.

"When you're finished, go tell your father and brother dinner is ready. They're working in the barn."

"Okay, Mom."

Even on a day off, his father was always working on something. After washing up and putting on clean clothes, Flyn walked out to the barn to see what today's project was.

"Hey, Flyn!" Ty waved at him as he walked into the barn. "Guess what we did today."

"Swept out the hayloft?"

"No! We made a mechanical milker for Cow!" Ty had named the cow when he was eight. The rest of the family hadn't thought the cow needed a name, so Ty's name stuck.

"We *tried* to make a mechanical milker," Geirr corrected.

"But it almost worked. It just needs some tweaking."

"We'll try again next week."

"Can we try tomorrow?" Ty was practically bouncing in place.

"Sorry, we have to get back to planting tomorrow." Geirr grinned at his younger son's excitement.

"Awww." Ty dropped his head, the smile fading from his face.

"We'll finish it next weekend, I promise." Geirr turned to his older son. "Did your mother send you to get us for dinner?"

Flyn nodded.

"But can't we work on it a little more now?" Ty pleaded.

Geirr laughed. "Maybe we can do a little more after dinner. Now head inside and get cleaned up."

"Okay!" Ty ran toward the house, yelling for their mother the whole way. "Mom! Guess what Dad and I did!"

Geirr smiled as he watched the boy run as fast as his legs could carry him. Flyn wondered if his father ever looked at him that way.

"Help me put away my tools?" Geirr asked Flyn after Ty had disappeared down the hill.

"Sure."

Geirr cleaned each tool then handed them to Flyn to hang on the wall. He was careful to make sure each went back in its proper place. He didn't have to turn around to know his father was watching.

"So, how was the water today?" his father asked while they worked.

Flyn blushed. "How'd you know?"

"You and Kel leave first thing in the morning and head away from town? There's only one thing you're doing on a day like today." His father smiled at him.

"Mom's mad at me."

"She's just worried about you, son." He handed Flyn the last tool, a small hammer, then started wiping off his work bench with an old rag. "Mothers always worry. At least the good ones do. And you know you don't make her life any easier by going out on that boat. We've had that conversation before."

"I know. I just don't understand why it's such a big deal anyway."

Geirr laughed and wiped his hands with the rag, then tossed it into a basket with the other dirty rags.

"Yes, you do." Geirr put his arm around Flyn's shoulders and led him out of the barn. "You know the story about Andor the Great and the first people just like everyone else."

"But that's just a myth."

"Myth or no, that's just the way things are. If you're going to be a rebel, you have to accept the consequences."

"But you don't believe all that stuff, do you?"

"About Andor the Great being God in human form and bringing the first people to Trygsted on boats? No, that's just a fable invented to explain where people came from. But as for Vahul…"

Geirr was quiet for a moment, then continued in a quieter voice. "Let's just say I believe our souls go somewhere after we die, and what-

ever you call it—Vahul, or the Great Beyond, or something else—
doesn't matter. I believe it's real. Now, whether or not souls reach it by
crossing the ocean on a funeral boat is another story. I suppose I've
always thought it was possible. After all, no one who has tried to find
Vahul has ever come back, so who's to say?"

He turned his head to look at Flyn and smiled.

"Besides, whether it's true or not doesn't make boats any less
dangerous or change the way the rest of the clan looks at them."

"Well, it's a stupid belief."

Geirr stopped walking and faced Flyn.

"Son, don't ever call someone's beliefs stupid. Especially if you
don't have any proof they're wrong."

"I'm sorry, Dad." Flyn looked away, ashamed at his outburst. "I
know. I just like the water. It's relaxing and beautiful. I just wish I
didn't have to hide it. It's not fair."

"Life's not fair, Flyn. You're old enough to know that." He clapped
Flyn on the shoulder. "Just remember this conversation when you're a
father and your son or daughter tells you life isn't fair."

The idea of raising kids of his own was scarier than anything
that could happen in the ocean, but he knew his father was right.
Life was anything but fair. Sometimes the old man actually
made sense.

Dinner was already on the table when they walked in.

"I sent you out to get your father twenty minutes ago," his mother
said, giving them both a disapproving look.

"Sorry, Lene," Geirr said. "It was my fault. I wanted to get all the
tools put away before dinner."

"Well, don't blame me if your food is cold. Now go wash up before
you sit down at the table."

"Yes, Dear." Geirr winked at Flyn before heading to the washroom.

In spite of his mother's warning about a cold dinner, everyone's
food was hot and delicious. Even Ty, a normally picky eater, cleaned
his plate. Flyn and his father both had seconds of everything.

Ty was still excited about the new invention. He explained everything to his mother in minute detail, describing how they had
converted one of the well pumps for the job, and how they had made

the part that attached to the cow out of old steel pipes that they bored out with the drill.

"The problem is it needs to p–pulgate?" Ty looked to his father for help.

"Pulsate."

"Yeah, pulsate! It needs to pulsate so it's more like a baby cow."

Helene smiled and nodded, clearly not understanding half of what Ty was talking about, but feigning interest anyway. Flyn looked out the window to where the late afternoon sun reflected off the ocean in the distance. The water sparkled, diamonds in a sea of blue. No fields to plant, no cows to milk, no wood to gather. The sea was where he wanted to be.

Why wasn't his mother interested in his dreams? In what excited him?

Flyn sighed to himself and turned back to his meal. One thing the sea didn't have: roasted pork.

Dinner conversation turned to the work that lay ahead. Only half the spring fields were sowed. With the cabbages and carrots planted, their next task would be planting potatoes. Flyn cared for farming about as much as he cared for inventing, but the discussion about the planting schedule seemed as good a time as any to bring up his planned trip.

"When we're done planting the potatoes, Kel and I are going to take a trip to Brekkness." Brekkness was a wooded region on the other side of Trygsted.

"For how long?" his father asked.

"A couple of weeks. We're going to hunt boar and deer."

"Just make sure you're back in time to plant the corn and beans." They planted corn and beans in the late spring. If things went according to schedule, they would have nearly a week to spare.

"We will be."

"How are you planning on getting there?" his mother chimed in. He could tell from the way she looked at him that she was suspicious.

"We're going to hike." Flyn didn't like lying to his mother, but he didn't want her worrying about him for two weeks.

"Doesn't Kel's family have horses?" His mother, the practical one.

"Sure, but we'd rather hike."

Flyn noticed his father had stopped eating and was sitting back in his chair, watching him with a raised eyebrow. He knew. Geirr and Helene exchanged a glance. She knew too.

He never could sneak anything past her.

***

"I still don't know about this," Kel said.

The first potato field had been planted and Flyn was enjoying a day off before they started on the second one, the last of the early spring crops. He and Kel were in town to gather supplies for their upcoming trip. His mother had asked him to pick up a few things for her as well. Normally his father and Ty would have been with them, but they were busy working on the milking machine.

They had walked to town with a small cart to carry their supplies. Even before noon, the spring sun was already hot and the young men were sweating from pulling the cart on the half a league trek from the Geirr farm. The heat promised another of the afternoon storms they had been seeing a lot of this spring.

"It'll be fun. When we get back, you'll thank me."

"I doubt it."

Drogave was considered a mid-sized town, with stores that supplied all the general necessities for those living in the surrounding area. The local shops didn't have the selection that was available in the larger towns, though most things could be ordered and shipped. For entertainment, the saloon had music and dancing most evenings. Occasionally a local group would use the saloon to put on a musical, but there was no formal theater.

The Trygsted Messenger Service had a full-service office in town to send and receive correspondence from other towns. As the largest town in the area, Trygsted served as a hub for the smaller towns nearby. In addition to private messages, the office distributed news from other parts of the island. Flyn and Kel had stopped in to check for messages for their respective families and pick up the most recent news flyer.

"Look, they're having a spring festival in Osthorp in two weeks."

Flyn pointed to a notice on the flyer. "That's right about when we'll be there. We can stop for a couple of days and go to the festival."

Kel glanced at the flyer. "We could get there faster by horse."

"Anybody can cross Trygsted by horse. Nobody has ever done it by boat."

"There's a reason for that. And so what if we do? We won't be able to tell anybody."

"We'll know, and that's all that matters. Besides, you already said you would go."

They stopped in front of the Drogave General Store.

"I said I'd think about it. And I did. And I still think it's too risky."

"Okay, just think about it some more. In the meantime, let's just get what we need in case you decide to go."

Kel sighed. "Fine, but I doubt I'll change my mind."

Kel shuffled through the door, his head down. Flyn grinned as he followed his friend into the store. Almost had him.

In addition to salt, eggs, and thread for Flyn's mother, he and Kel each picked up a pack and two waterskins, some rope, work gloves, and a bundle of arrows. Flyn found a fire-building kit with flint and steel and Kel found a hat with a wide brim to protect his face from the sun. It even had a string that went under the chin to keep the hat on his head in the wind. They planned on making bedrolls from old blankets and they would pack cured meat, wheat cakes, and fruits from their pantries at home. Flyn had a fishing pole he would bring to catch fish so they wouldn't have to take food for the whole two weeks.

Their shopping complete, they took the merchandise to the front of the store and laid everything on the counter. Pal Famsen, the store's owner, stood up and crossed his arms, resting them on his large belly. With a round body and an equally round, bald head, he had always reminded Flyn of a snowman.

"Good morning, Mr. Famsen," Flyn said.

"And where do you two think you're going?" He frowned as he looked first at Flyn, then Kel.

Kel was shifting nervously next to Flyn. "We're going on a hunting trip next week when the planting is done." It was always wise to mention that work came first when speaking to an elder.

"That so?" Mr. Famsen eyed them for another moment, then started marking down their purchases on a receipt pad. "I've heard rumors about you."

Flyn and Kel glanced at each other.

"You know what they say about rumors." Flyn tried to laugh.

Mr. Famsen stopped totaling their purchases and looked up at him. "And what would that be, Mr. Geirrsen?"

Flyn felt a lump forming in his throat. He swallowed hard and tried to answer. What had Mr. Famsen heard? Had someone found out about his boat? What would they do to him? Surely that couldn't be it. They had been careful not to let anyone see them.

"That, uh, rumors are like weeds?" Flyn said, his voice dry and weak.

The shopkeeper threw his head back and roared with laughter. Flyn managed a weak smile, his heart pounding in his chest. Kel just stood next to him, trembling. Mr. Famsen shook his head and wiped the tears from his cheeks. His face was bright red from his laughing fit.

"That they do, Mr. Geirrsen, that they do," he said, finally catching his breath. He went back to recording their purchases. "I hear a lot of rumors. Don't generally give them much heed." He finished the receipt and handed it to Flyn, who in turn handed him the money for the goods.

Mr. Famsen leaned closer to the young men, resting his arms on the counter.

"Still, there's some talk going around about you two." He looked around, then continued in a quieter voice so only they could hear him. "They say you have a boat and you've been out on the ocean."

The old man paused.

"Based on Mr. Walensen's reaction here, I would say there's more to this rumor than a weed."

Flyn didn't know what to say. Banished at his age, he would never have a family. He would spend the rest of his life alone. Probably turn into one of those crazy hermits they would sometimes see on the beach talking to seashells.

"Don't worry, son. Your secret's safe with me. In addition to rumors, I hear a lot of secrets. I wouldn't be very good at my job if I didn't. But I make a point of keeping another man's business to myself. Not that I approve of what you're doing, mind you, but I won't be spreading it around. I would suggest you consider reevaluating your choices though. Your poor mother would be devastated if anything should happen to you. And you father won't be selling no more water pump systems if his son is banished for heresy."

The old man stood up and smiled, the firmness melting away, leaving the jolly shopkeeper Flyn had known his whole life.

"Good luck on your hunting trip, boys. Stay out of trouble."

"Thank you, sir. We will." Flyn picked up the package of goods and pushed Kel toward the door.

Once outside, Kel grabbed Flyn's shirt with both hands.

"He knows! Everybody knows! What are we going to do?"

"Calm down, Kel." Flyn pulled away from Kel's grasp.

"But they know!"

"Nobody knows anything. It's just a rumor. Come on, people are starting to stare." He started down the road, pulling Kel after him.

Flyn's mind raced, trying to put together what they had just learned. For rumors to be spreading, someone must have seen them with the boat. But if someone had seen them, they would be hearing more than rumors. Which meant that there was no proof yet, just speculation.

But who? Certainly his parents wouldn't say anything. And Ty didn't know about the boat, did he? No, Flyn had been very careful about that. And no one in Kel's family knew. Kel was far too paranoid to let any of them know about it. And they hadn't told any of their other friends.

He supposed it didn't really matter who had seen them. That someone had was enough. The important question was what to do about it. He had an idea.

"Where are we going?" Kel asked after they had walked for a few minutes.

"The blacksmith."

"What for?"

"I need a new knife for the trip."

"What do you mean? You can't seriously be thinking about still going?"

"I'm very serious."

"After what Mr. Famsen just told us? You're crazy!"

"Actually, I'm not." Flyn stopped and pulled Kel to the side of the road. "I've been thinking about what Mr. Famsen said and that's exactly why I'm still going."

Kel just stared at him in disbelief.

"Look, let's just say someone saw us with the boat. I don't know who, but it was probably a kid. If an adult had seen us, there would be a lot more than rumors going around. So this kid tells his parents and now people are spreading rumors about us and the boat. You know how it'll go. The rumor will keep spreading and pretty soon people will start looking out for us, trying to catch us."

"Exactly! Which is why we can't go." Kel held his hands up and shook them at Flyn to emphasize his words.

"Quiet down or somebody will hear you." Flyn glanced around to make sure no one was paying attention to them. "Now let me finish. Suppose the rumors get to that point. People will start looking for the boat. If they find it, they may or may not be able to prove it's ours."

"You mean yours," Kel interrupted.

"Whatever. The point is even if they can't prove it, the rumors will get worse. The result will be the same. We'll be publicly humiliated and eventually driven out of town. Which means the only thing we can do is get rid of it so no one finds it."

"Yes, exactly." Kel nodded in agreement.

"So that means we need to make this trip more than ever because it'll be the last time we get to use the boat."

Kel put his hands on his head. "You've lost your mind. If people are looking, we'll get caught for sure. Then it won't be a rumor anymore." He shook his head. "No way. It's a really bad idea."

"But don't you see? We won't get caught. Listen, it's perfect. Next weekend, the day after the planting's done, we'll leave early in the morning, before sunrise. We'll be gone before anybody sees us. We'll head north to take advantage of the currents, just like we planned. Except instead of going all the way around, we'll stop near Osthorp and destroy the boat there. Then we'll hike back. We can even go to the festival like normal travelers. When people see us walking back, they'll all assume we did exactly what we're telling everybody we're going to do. There'll be no boat to find."

"You really have lost your mind, Flynygyn."

"No, it's perfect. Even the remains will be all the way on the other side of Trygsted."

Kel just stared at Flyn, eyes wide.

"Admit it, it's a good plan."

"Okay, I can see how that might work," Kel said after thinking for a minute. "But what if someone sees us from the shore while we're paddling around the island?"

"That's why we need to leave before dawn. We'll head straight out so we're too far for anyone to see us, then turn north and follow the coastline. Once we get a few leagues north of Drogave, anyone who sees us won't recognize us anyway."

Kel thought for a few more minutes before answering. "Okay, I'll go. But only if you promise we'll destroy the boat and walk home, like you said."

"Absolutely. That's the key to making the plan work. If anybody found the remains around here, it would raise too much suspicion."

"You know, if I die, I'll haunt you forever."

"Don't be so dramatic. You're not going to die. The worst thing that will happen is you'll get a little sunburned."

Kel smiled for the first time since leaving the general store. "I think the best part is that we'll be rid of the boat for good."

Flyn looked away to the west, toward the ocean. "For you, maybe."

For Flyn, destroying his boat was far from the best thing about the plan.

CHAPTER 2

The day of their departure came eight days later. They had nearly three full weeks until the late spring planting started. By Flyn's calculations, plenty of time to make the almost sixty-league journey to Osthorp by boat, then the thirty-league trek home on foot. He even planned a one-day stop for the spring festival, which would give them a bit of a rest between legs.

Kel met Flyn at the boat before dawn. Flyn had had trouble sleeping the night before and had arrived an hour earlier. His gear was already stored in the watertight lockbox and he had pulled the boat from its hiding place. While he waited, Flyn watched it float among the reeds of the small inlet that led to the open ocean, wondering if he would actually be able to destroy it when the time came.

"Are you ready?" Flyn asked Kel when he arrived.

"No, but I'm sure you're not going to let that stop me." Kel dropped his pack on the ground with a huff. His new hat sat cocked to one side on his head.

"Cheer up, Kel. This time tomorrow, we'll be leagues away from all our problems without a care in the world."

"We'll be in the middle of our biggest problem."

"Then think about the spring festival and all the food, and drink, and girls in their spring dresses dancing in the streets looking for a stranger from the West to dance with."

"Not if they see me with you." Kel finally smiled.

"We'll see about that, but if you don't get your gear stowed, we'll never know."

Kel threw his pack into the lockbox, which Flyn secured. Flyn's heart raced as they climbed into the boat. He breathed in the salty tang of the ocean carried by a slight breeze. With it came the sound of early morning breakers hitting the beach to the south. To the east, a deep red glow over the island marked the coming of the new day.

"Let's go," Flyn said, almost whispering in deference to the moment. He turned his back to the morning glow and faced the darkness to the west.

The boat slid almost silently away from the shore and through the reeds, the only sound coming from their paddles dipping into the water. They didn't speak, the path to the sea well ingrained in them both. In the front of the boat, Kel looked to shore every few seconds, but there was no one watching them. Just the empty grass field that sloped down to the water.

After a few minutes, the break in the seawall that protected the small lagoon from the surf came into view. The sound of the waves was louder now, the whitecaps of the breakers seeming to glow in the early morning twilight. As they approached the break, Flyn could feel the water surging in and out with the surf. The hardest part about launching the boat was timing their exit through the seawall to avoid a wave crashing down on them and throwing the boat into the rocks.

They maneuvered the boat to the side of the break where the current wasn't as strong.

"Hold it here," Flyn said, trying to stay quiet and still be loud enough for Kel to hear him over the surf.

He watched the water, looking for the natural lull between groups of waves. They used their paddles to keep the boat in place until the right moment.

"Now!"

A wave crashed down on the seawall, sending tons of water through the break. They paddled as hard as they could to the break and caught the outflow. The current spat the little boat through the narrow gap in the wall and into the open water. They kept paddling until they were beyond the surf zone and could rest.

Flyn turned to look back. The horizon was getting brighter, the orange glow silhouetting the island. If not for the whitecaps from the breaking waves, he wouldn't have been able to tell where the water stopped and the land began.

"We need to go," Kel said. "Somebody could be watching us and we would never see them."

"It's too dark for anybody to see us on the water." But he stuck his paddle in the water and helped Kel paddle the boat farther away from the shore.

When the sun finally broke over the horizon, the boat was at least half a league from shore, far enough away to avoid anyone seeing them from land. At this distance, the twenty-foot boat would be little more than a speck on the water.

"Told you we could do it," Flyn said.

"I'll be happier when we're farther north and we don't have to be so far out." Leave it to Kel to find the downside.

"We should keep our distance today. Tomorrow will be safe enough to stay closer to shore."

Kel just grunted in response.

They turned the boat north, setting an easy pace to avoid wearing themselves out. They didn't talk much for the first hour or so. They had never been so far from shore and even Flyn was a little nervous. Knowing how to swim was one thing. Swimming for an hour back to shore was something else.

And what about Kel? If the boat sank, how would he save Kel?

Not that he was really concerned about the boat sinking. The seams were freshly tarred and the sea was calm. There was no point in worrying about things that weren't going to happen. So Flyn forgot about sinking boats and settled in to enjoy the trip.

Eventually, even Kel started to relax a little bit. They mostly talked about what Osthorp would be like. They had both been to a lot of places on the island, but neither one had ever been to Osthorp. They had heard the stories about the saloons that had music and dancing all day long and theaters where the performers were suspended from the ceiling with wires and flew around the stage. And apparently, Osthorp had festivals and parades to celebrate just about anything, though the spring festival was the most well-known.

"I've heard their Matching Day lasts all week," Flyn said. Matching Day was the traditional day that young men and women of Trygsted would meet and marry. The fall before their twentieth birthday, young men were expected to travel to another town for Matching Day to find a wife. It was usually an all-day party that ended with a dance. The young men and women would spend the day trying to find a spouse.

At the end of the dance, all the young women would line up to be chosen. When chosen, the she could accept or reject her suitor. If she rejected him, he could try to choose another.

At least that was the tradition. The whole thing was becoming more of a formality, with couples having met and chosen each other before Matching Day. There were still a few remote towns that held to the old ways, though those were growing rare.

By law, a man could only marry before he turned twenty, so if none of the women would have him, he would spend the rest of his life without a wife. But even that tradition was under pressure as more women were being choosier about their husbands.

Flyn and Kel had both dated girls as teenagers, but neither had yet found a wife. With their Matching Day only a few months away, the thought of going to Osthorp to celebrate for a week seemed like a good idea. Flyn pointed out that their excursion could be like a scouting trip so when they came back in the fall, they would already be familiar with the town.

Their talk faded as the morning wore on, the heat from the sun in the cloudless sky sapping their energy. They paddled through the morning, taking breaks every hour or so. During their breaks, they splashed themselves with cool water from the sea and ate small snacks. Flyn even jumped into the water for a swim on occasion. Kel, of course, stayed in the boat.

Around noon, they took a longer break for lunch, eating fruit and dried meat, and drinking berry wine from one of Flyn's waterskins. After eating, Kel pulled his hat over his eyes and fell asleep. Flyn tried to do the same, but without a hat, the sun was too bright, so he tried fishing instead.

The boat bobbed and bounced in the gentle swells, moving slowly north with the current. This far from shore, Flyn could no longer see the ocean floor, just deep-blue water. His fishing line disappeared into the depths, swallowed by a dark realm somewhere below the boat. He stared into the abyss with butterflies in his stomach, wondering what creatures may be lurking beyond his sight.

He moved back from the side and pulled in his fishing line. Maybe he shouldn't swim or fish anymore until he could see the bottom again. Just to be on the safe side.

Flyn stretched, surveying the horizon. Big, puffy clouds were beginning to fill the sky, moving slowly south. A haze had settled in, causing the shoreline to the east to appear fuzzy. To the northeast, the haze seemed to make the sky and ocean appear darker.

A cool breeze picked up, carrying the smell of the ocean. And maybe something else—a sharp, almost tangy smell underneath. Or maybe he was just smelling the sweat from his sleeping friend.

He yawned and stretched again. The lack of sleep was catching up with him. Maybe a small nap. He pulled off his tunic and lay back, using it to cover his face. The gentle rocking of the boat, water lightly splashing against its sides, the far-off call of seagulls: within minutes, Flyn was fast asleep.

A loud crash jolted Flyn from his slumber.

The sun and blue sky were gone, replaced by dark clouds. The gentle breeze had turned into a fierce wind that turned the once calm, blue sea into a dark, turbulent cauldron. Flyn sat up, the thunderclap still rumbling across the open water. In front of him, Kel gripped the sides of the boat so tight, the tendons stood out on his arms.

"Flyn?" Kel didn't try to turn around.

The boat rocked and bounced in the rough water. The wind turned the tops of the waves into whitecaps, whipping across the peaks and sending salt spray through the air, pelting Flyn's face and bare chest.

"Quick, grab a paddle," Flyn yelled over the mounting storm. "We have to get to shore!"

Flyn found his tunic lying in the bottom of the boat, which was already starting to fill up with water. He pulled on the wet garment to protect himself from the stinging spray, then grabbed his paddle and started propelling the boat toward the distant shore. Kel didn't move.

"Kel! I can't do it by myself."

Still Kel didn't move. While Flyn could paddle the boat by himself under normal circumstances, loaded down with two people and all their gear, he would have a hard time in ideal conditions. There was no way he could get them out of the storm by himself.

"Kel," he tried again, "you have to help or we'll never make it. It's either paddle or swim."

Kel finally let go of one side and reached for his paddle, but a wave struck the front of the boat, pitching them up and down. Kel latched on to the side again.

"Come on, Kel!"

Again, Kel reached down and groped for his paddle. This time he was able to grab it.

"Good, now paddle! As hard as you can!"

Slowly, Kel started paddling, flinching and grabbing the side of the boat with each wave.

"Keep paddling, don't stop!"

"That's easy for you to say. I can't swim!"

Flyn turned the boat toward the shore, but that put them sideways to the waves coming from the north. Each one rolled the boat to the right, threatening to toss the hapless pair into the ocean. Every time the boat somehow managed to right itself.

Still, they paddled on.

Flyn had never been on the ocean during a storm before. The monstrous waves were larger than any breakers he had seen pounding the beach. When they were in the troughs, some of the waves towered twenty feet over their heads. They could only see the shore for the brief moments they were on top of a wave. Then he would clench his jaw as the boat ran down the back side of the wave, sometimes dipping under the water before riding up the face of the next wave.

Whenever they reached the peak of a swell, the wind, whipping across the tops of the waves, would send more spray into their eyes. To their left, the sky grew even darker, punctuated by flashes of lighting. The low growl of thunder mixed with the high-pitched scream of the wind and the constant slap of water against the side of the boat.

More and more water filled the boat, making it harder to paddle. Each wave threatened to topple the tiny craft. For the first time since he had built the boat, Flyn wished he was on land. If the people who had tried to reach Vahul had run into a storm like this one, he understood now why they were never heard from again.

He wondered if anyone would ever hear from *him* again.

"Faster, Kel!" Flyn dug the paddle into the water as hard as he could, struggling toward the shore that didn't seem to be getting any closer. Kel, too, paddled harder. Their only hope was to reach land before the storm flipped the boat.

Another bolt of lightning flashed over their heads, the crack of the thunder piercing Flyn's ears almost immediately. Then the wind slowed to a slight breeze. Even the waves relaxed to a comparatively small five or six feet.

"Is it over?" Kel asked, laying his paddle across his lap and looking around.

"I don't know," Flyn replied, "but keep paddling. If it's not over, I want to get out of it as quick as we can."

Kel resumed his paddling. Without the strong wind, the going was easier, but the boat was still half full of water, hampering their progress.

Ahead of them, the sky grew fuzzy as the rain washed over the island and into the sea toward them.

"We're going to get wet," Flyn said.

"We're already wet," Kel replied.

Flyn grinned. He could handle wet. Just so long as the storm didn't pick up again.

In less than a minute, the downpour was on them, instantly drenching any part of them that was still dry. The rain reduced their visibility to only a few yards, completely obscuring their view of the shore. Flyn tried to use the waves as a guide to keep the boat pointed in the right direction.

Worse than the rain, the wind resumed its assault, and with it, the waves grew larger, each one seemingly bigger than the last. The boat managed to climb the first few, but soon the waves were too high. They found themselves stuck in a trough, green walls of water rising far above their heads.

Then the wave broke.

The white, foamy crest roared down from above, a great beast determined to destroy them in one massive strike.

"Hang on!" Flyn dropped his paddle and grabbed the sides of the boat. Kel wasn't so quick.

There was nothing they could do. The wave washed over the boat, tipping it on its side. Flyn managed to hold on, but Kel was washed overboard and beneath the water.

As the wave passed, the boat, now completely swamped, struggled to stay upright. Flyn wiped the water from his eyes and searched the surface for his friend.

Kel's pale face emerged from the water, his arms flailing over his head.

"Flyn! Help!" Kel's voice was small and faint against the roar of the wind and waves.

"Hold on, Kel! I'm coming!" Flyn gritted his teeth and inched forward, trying to reach the rope that was tied off in the front of the boat. A gust of wind whipped his tunic up into his face and threw more salt spray into his eyes. Flyn forced his way forward, in spite of the burning in his eyes, and found the rope, more by feel than sight. The salt water had almost completely blinded him. Holding on to the rope with one hand, he used the other to wipe his eyes.

Too late, he saw the next wave bearing down on him. It hit the small craft broadside, crashing over the top, rolling the boat over, and throwing Flyn into the sea.

He managed to hold his breath before hitting the water, but the wave pushed him under. Rolling and twisting in the current, he lost track of which way was up. Light and dark green flashed before him, then the green was replaced by black.

The boat tumbled in the wave, striking Flyn on the head. He saw a bright flash, then nothing.

———

Flyn tried to open his eyes.

Too bright.

He squinted against the glare.

Water. Sunlight.

He was cold in spite of the hot sun beating down on him. His shoulders hurt. He couldn't move.

Slowly, his eyes adjusted to the light.

He was alive.

He was lying on a floating log, blue sky above and blue water below.

At the other end of the log was a body. It was Kel. He still had his stupid hat.

"Kel," Flyn tried to say. His throat was dry and all he could manage was a hoarse whisper. He tried to pull himself along the log and found he was stuck. More precisely, he was tied to the log with a rope running under his arms. Most of his body was in the water, though he couldn't feel it.

He pulled himself onto the log, which loosened the rope that had been holding him above the water. Sharp tingling filled his arms as the blood flow returned.

He rested, that small effort exhausting him.

How was he alive?

At the other end of the log, Kel looked up.

"Flyn?"

Flyn nodded.

"I wasn't sure if you were dead or alive."

"What happened?" Flyn said, his voice still a whisper.

"A wave hit the boat and flipped it over and you fell in. I thought you were gone. I was able to grab the rope and pull myself back to the boat and then you popped up next to me, so I grabbed you and tied the rope around you so you wouldn't sink again."

Flyn looked closer at the log: it wasn't a log—it was the bottom of his boat.

"How long?"

"A few hours, I guess. The sun's going down, so it must be past dinnertime."

They were well off shore, but Flyn could see a small strip of land in the distance. He pointed. Kel turned to follow the gesture.

"Guess we better start kicking if we want to get back to shore before dark," Kel said.

Flyn looked at the water lapping at the sides of the capsized boat. Feeling was just starting to return to his legs. Getting back in the water wasn't high on his list of things he wanted to do, but spending the night on the water wasn't either, so he held his breath and slid back into the icy sea.

At the other end, Kel climbed into the water and they started kicking, using the remains of the boat to hold them up. The shore was a long way off.

They kicked without talking for a long time, the only sound coming from the water sloshing around the overturned boat.

"If the sun's going down, why's it in front of us?" Kel said after a while.

Flyn stopped kicking and stared at the shore. Their village was on the west side of the island, which meant the sun should be behind them. It wasn't. It was right in front of them.

"Maybe you were wrong," Flyn said. "Maybe we were out all night and it's morning now instead of evening."

"No. I never slept. I tried, but I couldn't. I couldn't find any more rope to tie myself off. I was afraid I would roll into the water if I fell asleep."

"Did the storm carry us to the other side of the island?" Flyn asked after a minute.

"That must be it." Kel started kicking again. "Guess we made it quicker than we thought we would." He laughed.

Flyn grinned, but he didn't feel like laughing. He was cold and sore. He just wanted to curl up in his bed and sleep for about two days. His grand plan wasn't working out like he'd hoped.

They kicked for what felt like hours before the shore seemed to get any closer. By then, the sun was falling behind a thick veil of clouds. Without the sun, the water chilled them even more.

Ahead of them lay a wide swath of beach, beyond which stood a forest of dark trees. As they got closer, the faint roar of waves crashing on the beach reached Flyn's ears. Even so, it was almost fully dark before he finally felt the tug of the tide start to pull them into shore.

Unable to kick anymore, they rested and let the waves carry them toward the beach. Flyn almost cheered when he felt his feet touch the sand.

There was no time to celebrate, though. They still had at least thirty yards to go to what looked like a rock-lined shore. The next wave confirmed Flyn's fears as it crashed into the rocks and sent a spray of water into the air.

"Look out!" Kel called out, but it was too late. The surf picked them up and hurled them toward the rocks.

Flyn pulled his head down and braced himself behind the boat just as it crashed into the rocks. Water surged up around him, tumbling him over the remains of the boat and into the sand on the other side of the rocks. The impact knocked the air out of him. Seawater rushed to fill his empty lungs.

The wave retreated, pulling Flyn with it and smashing his body against the rocks again before flowing back out to sea. For a brief moment, Flyn lay in the wet sand, coughing up the salty seawater. Then the next wave came crashing down, sending him tumbling again.

This time, Flyn was able to dig his fingers into the sand to keep from being pulled back into the rocks. He lay still for a moment, then pulled himself up to his hands and knees before the next wave surged in. Still coughing and spitting, he crawled out of the surf and collapsed on the beach.

After catching his breath, he looked around for Kel. His friend was lying in the sand a few yards away, not moving.

"Kel?" Flyn's voice was hoarse, barely audible above the sound of the surf.

"Yeah?" Kel's voice wasn't much better.

"Let's not do that again," Flyn said, then rolled onto his back.

They didn't move for a while, recovering from their ordeal. Flyn felt he could have slept right where he fell.

"Well, look on the bright side. We don't have to take the boat apart now," Flyn said after a few minutes. "I think the surf took care of it for us."

"I would have rather done it myself," Kel replied. "I don't think I'm ever going to get in a boat again as long as I live."

After hours in the icy water, the cool evening air, and their wet clothes, they were both shivering.

"We need to build a fire," Flyn said through chattering teeth.

"I'm sure we'll find plenty of wood in the trees, but how are we going to light it?"

"I had flint and steel in my pack. I don't suppose it survived. It was in the storage box."

"I doubt anything survived that," Kel said.

Without much hope, Flyn struggled to his feet. Kel followed him back down to the water where the boat had been demolished. A few pieces of wood floated in the eddies of the surf.

"Not much left," Flyn said.

Kel didn't reply. He was looking around the rocks in between waves.

"Hey," he called out. "I found it!"

Flyn rushed over, dodging an incoming wave. Wedged between the rocks was the metal strongbox that had been bolted into the bottom of the boat.

"Help me lift it," Flyn said.

They had to wait for the next wave to pass, but between the two of them, they wrestled it free and carried it onto the beach.

It was dented and scraped, but still closed. Flyn's heart quickened as his numb fingers fumbled with the latch. Finally unlocking it, he opened the cover and reached into the dark compartment. He let out a small whoop of excitement when his hand closed around one of the packs.

"It's still here!"

"This must be our lucky day," Kel said, leaning over the side of the box trying to see.

"I don't even think it's wet." He had sealed the strongbox to keep supplies dry, but after everything it had gone through that day, he was surprised to find it had worked. The packs themselves were made from oiled cloth to make them waterproof, though that would be of little help if they were submerged. There was no way to keep water from getting in through the opening.

"Does that mean the food is still good?" Kel asked.

Flyn's numb hands struggled to undo the straps that held the pack closed, but he finally unbuckled them. As he opened the pack, the smell of oranges and ham and wheat cakes filled his nostrils and made his stomach growl. He hadn't realized how hungry he was.

"Tonight, we eat like kings," Flyn said, grinning in the dark. "But let's get that fire going first."

He closed the pack and slung it onto his back. Kel pulled his own pack out of the box. His spirits lifted, Flyn led the way back to the tree line to find a spot to spend the night. Beside him, Kel hummed to himself as they walked, no longer complaining about their situation.

Closer to the woods, the ground transitioned from sand to hard-packed dirt. They selected a level spot close to the first trees and cleared a space to build a fire.

Flyn looked into the trees. In the dim light, he could only see a few feet into the forest. But it wasn't what he couldn't see that bothered him. It was what he couldn't hear. No birds, no bugs. Not even a frog. From the look on his face, Flyn guessed Kel was sensing it too.

"What kind of trees are these?" Kel asked, apparently not wanting to talk about the eerie quiet.

"I don't know. They're not like any trees I've ever seen."

The trees grew almost perfectly straight. Even though he couldn't see the tops in the dark, they seemed to be incredibly tall. But the strangest thing about them was their leaves. They were unlike any leaves Flyn had ever seen or heard about. They were thin, only a fraction of an inch at their widest, and only an inch or two long. The ground was covered in them, making a soft blanket over the hard dirt. The air was filled with a thick, almost minty scent.

"The wood is sticky, too."

Flyn picked up a fallen branch. Kel was right. It was sticky.

"I hope it burns," Kel said.

They spent the next half hour stumbling around in the dark, gathering enough wood to last through the night. The exercise took off some of the chill, but Flyn was glad once the fire was going.

The sticky wood burned bright and hot. They stripped out of their wet clothes and hung them on sticks near the fire to dry, then sat down to their late-night picnic.

They each had two cakes, a small slab of ham, and an orange. They finished off the berry wine Flyn had brought. Not a feast, by normal standards, but under the circumstances, the meal rivaled the best Harvest Day dinner.

"How did that storm sneak up on us?" Kel asked between bites.

Flyn shook his head. "I've never seen anything like it. The sun was shining when I laid down to take a nap."

"I know. It was a perfect day. Then I woke up to thunder. And when it was over, it just seemed to evaporate."

"I must have missed that part," Flyn said.

"Just like you to sleep through the whole thing."

Flyn grunted. He wouldn't call almost drowning, then spending the next several hours unconscious, sleeping, but Kel was trying to lighten the mood, so he kept the thought to himself.

"It's just a good thing I built the boat so strong or we'd be dead right now."

"Lucky, like I said." Kel stuffed the last of a wheat cake into his mouth and washed it down with a swig of berry wine.

"Yeah, lucky." Flyn wasn't feeling very lucky, though he supposed it could be worse. At least they were back on land.

"Now will you listen to sense and not play with boats?"

"Four years and we never flipped it once. Whenever a storm came along, we always had plenty of time to get back to shore. I don't think that storm was natural."

"A demon storm?" Kel laughed. Neither of them believed the old tales about demons and magic.

"You know what I mean. It wasn't normal."

Kel took another swig of wine and passed it to Flyn.

"Maybe it just seemed that way because we were so far out from shore," Kel said. "We must've been at least half a league out."

"Maybe."

"And being out that far was pretty stupid."

Flyn chewed on a piece of ham, but didn't respond. Kel was just making excuses. He knew as well as Flyn why they had been that far out.

"No," Flyn replied after a bit. "What was stupid was both of us falling asleep while we were that far out."

Kel shrugged and shifted his focus back to peeling his orange. They ate in silence for a while, staring at the fire.

"Too bad about the boat, though," Flyn said after a while.

"Really? After everything we've been through today? You still want to go back out on the water?"

"Sure." Now that he was warm and had food in his belly, he wasn't as shaken up as he had been earlier. "We were just careless, that's all."

"What about all the rumors? About people finding out about the boat? And what about all that talk of getting married and raising a family?"

"I know. We can't build another one, but I can dream."

"Not me. My only dream is of a hot meal and a soft bed."

"Well, you at least have to admit that it's been an adventure."

"I, for one, have had enough adventure to last me a lifetime. I'll just be glad to be home."

"It'll be a story we'll tell our grandkids." Flyn laughed, but he too was thinking of home.

Kel changed the subject and they talked a while longer about which girls they were going to try to ask out when they got home and who would win the annual fall tournament. When their clothes were dry, they got dressed and spread out their bedrolls on opposite sides of the fire.

As they lay down, Flyn wondered if he would be able to sleep after spending most of the day unconscious, but he was asleep within minutes, Kel still talking about his plans for the summer.

CHAPTER 3

Flyn and Kel woke before dawn. The fire had died and an early morning fog had rolled in, leaving them cold and damp. Flyn cleaned up in the surf before breakfast, though washing off the dried salt with salt water didn't really help much. Kel opted to stay dry until they could find some fresh water.

Breakfast consisted of a wheat cake each, more dried meat, and another orange.

"When we get to some fresh water, we'll need to fill up the skins too," Flyn said. They had emptied two of their four waterskins already.

"So which way do we go?"

They looked up and down the beach, then into the forest.

"We have three options," Flyn said, stating the obvious. "Around to the north, around to the south, or straight through to the west."

"I vote south, to Osthorp."

"We may already be south of Osthorp," Flyn reminded him. "We don't know how far the storm blew us."

"Worst case, we get to Karnot, then we can take the road back to Drogave. Maybe we'll come across another village before we get to Karnot."

Karnot was at the southernmost tip of the island. Except for Osthorp, neither of them knew any of the villages along the western or northern coasts, so Karnot might be the first one they'd reach if they went south.

"That might take six or seven days. We'll need food and water before then and we might not find anything on the coast. I lost my fishing pole, so we won't have the fish we were counting on. I think we should cut straight across. Eventually we'll hit a road and we're more likely to find fresh water in the woods than on the beach."

"But all the rivers eventually flow to the ocean," Kel argued.

They debated for several minutes. The fog prevented them from seeing very far along the beach, which didn't help their decision process. Eventually, though, it came down to food.

"Going inland we'll have a better chance of finding fruits or nuts to eat," Flyn said. "I still have my knife, so we could even make a spear to kill a squirrel or maybe even a wild pig."

Kel grumbled some more, but finally agreed with Flyn that their chances for food were better going inland.

They kicked out the remains of their fire and covered it with sand, then shouldered their nearly empty packs and set off into the woods.

The fog wasn't limited to the coast. It drifted through the trees, dampening what little sound there was. Even as the morning grew brighter, they still didn't hear any birds or animals. Just an occasional drip of water as the fog condensed on the trees.

The strange trees grew bigger as they went deeper into the forest, some as big as twenty-five feet across. The tops were lost in the mist, though Flyn suspected that he had underestimated their height the previous night.

"They look even stranger in the daylight," Kel remarked at one point. "Look at the bark." The reddish, stringy bark was intermingled with moss, making it look almost like hair, though not like the hair of any creature Flyn had ever seen.

The other thing they noticed was the change in the ground. It grew rockier as they went and seemed to be sloping upward, though they couldn't be certain. Rocks began to appear scattered around the ground. Soon the rocks became boulders, forcing them to detour off their track. By the time they stopped for a break, they weren't even sure they were headed in the right direction anymore.

"We should have gone around," Kel said, taking off his boots to rub his feet.

"Then you'd just be griping about sand in your boots," Flyn said, but he was wondering the same thing himself. "Besides, we're committed now. No point in complaining about it."

While they rested, Flyn tried to listen for running water. The fog was thinning, but he still didn't hear anything. Even wildlife.

"Have you noticed that there's no birds?" Kel asked as if reading his mind.

"Yeah. I haven't heard any animals." Flyn looked around, not sure what he was looking for. "There's something else not right, but I can't put my finger on it."

"Not right how?"

"I don't know. It's just a feeling." He looked up at the giant tree they were sitting next to. It looked to be as old as the rocks and boulders strewn about the area. "Come on. Put your boots back on. I want to keep moving."

Flyn tried to work out their direction while Kel laced up his boots.

"I think that's the way we need to go," he said, pointing toward a slight rise littered with loose rock and small boulders.

"That way's much easier." Kel pointed in another direction.

"If we pick the easiest path all the time, we'll never get anywhere. I'm pretty sure we've been going uphill for the last hour, so we should keep going that way. Without the sun, that's our only clue about what direction to go."

"We could always go back," Kel said, almost to himself.

"You can go back if you want," Flyn said. "I'm going that way." He started walking toward the top of the rise.

"Hey, wait for me!" Kel jumped up and hurried after Flyn.

At the top of the rise, the ground leveled off, making their trek easier for a while and allowing them to stretch their sore legs. As the morning drew on, the fog burned off and they were able to catch glimpses of blue sky between the branches of the massive trees. And yet the tops were still out of their sight, towering higher than Flyn could have guessed.

Shortly before noon, by Flyn's estimate, they came to a stream running fast and clear. Rejoicing, they clambered down the bank and into the cool water.

"That's just what I needed," Kel said, rinsing the crusty salt from his skin and hair.

"Refreshing," Flyn agreed, splashing the cool water on his chapped face. "And it tastes better than the water from the well at home."

They drank and bathed for several minutes before refilling their waterskins and continuing on their journey.

"The air is warming. We have water. Now if we could find a bite to eat, this might turn out to be a decent day after all."

Finding water had greatly improved Kel's mood.

"I'm just hoping we come to a road soon," Flyn said. He was relieved they had water now, but he would feel much better once they had a bearing on where they were going. He was about to say as much when he heard voices in the distance.

"Road or no, we need to find—"

"Shh!" Flyn held up a hand in front of Kel. He listened for a moment. He couldn't make out distinct words, but there were definitely people talking somewhere up ahead.

"Someone's up there," Kel said, jumping to his feet.

"Hold on," Flyn whispered. He put a hand on Kel's shoulder to stop him from rushing toward the voices.

They listened some more, but Flyn still couldn't make out words.

"What?" Kel whispered.

"I don't like the sound of those voices."

"We're lost in the woods and there's people up ahead somewhere. What's not to like?"

"I just think we should try to keep quiet and get closer to see who it is before we start yelling for help. Just in case."

"What are you talking about? Just in case of what?"

"I've had a bad feeling all day. I don't know why, but I just think we need to be careful."

"Fine, but I think the knock on the head you took is messing with your thinking."

Flyn started toward the voices, staying close to the stream, hoping the sound of the water would help mask his footsteps. It also made the voices harder to hear, so as he moved forward, he was careful to stay behind trees to avoid being spotted. Kel may have been unconvinced by Flyn's bad feeling, but he kept close and hid behind the trees as well.

They reached a point where the creek veered away from the voices. Flyn stopped.

"Stay here and hide," Flyn whispered. "I'll sneak up to get a closer look. If they're friendly, I'll call back for you."

Kel nodded and squatted behind a tree with a massive twenty-foot-wide trunk. From the look on his face, he wasn't as sure about the strangers ahead of them as he had been a few minutes before.

Flyn snuck forward, tree to tree. Like most of the Andor clan, Flyn was very agile and could move almost silently when he wanted to. And right now, he wanted to.

The voices grew louder as he approached and what he heard made him more nervous than before. The voices were deep and gravelly, at times sounding more like growls than words.

Up ahead, the ground sloped down into a shallow bowl, clear of trees. Flyn pressed close to a tree on the edge of the clearing and peeked around the side.

A narrow path led into the clearing on the opposite side from Flyn, and out again to his right. That way, he thought was the shore where he and Kel had washed up the previous evening. He inched around the tree a little more to see the source of the voices.

In the center of the clearing, four large men sat in a circle, eating and talking.

He pulled back behind the tree, hoping they hadn't seen him.

"So I grab her hair and pull her off her horse and say: 'I don't care if you're Queen of the Trolls, you belong to Lord Jarot, now!'"

The four men laughed, snorting and grunting like pigs rooting for their dinner.

"What she say then?" another of the men said.

"She didn't say nothing 'cause I popped her in the mouth!"

Another round of laughter.

"That's not what I hear," a third one said. "I hear she stab you in the leg with her pig knife."

More laughing.

"She tried."

Flyn peeked his head around the tree again to try to get a better look.

They were larger than any men Flyn had ever seen and their skin had an odd blue-green tinge. Coarse, dark hair, matted with dirt and sweat, covered their heads. Thick, bumpy brows stuck out over their large, deep-set eyes. Their mouths and noses protruded from their faces like short snouts. With shoulders twice as wide as Flyn's and arms bigger than his legs, he guessed they would be able to snap him in half like a twig.

And the smell. Even from where Flyn hid behind the tree, a good fifteen feet from the closest of them, the sour odor was enough to choke on. Far worse than any barnyard stench.

"Where you take her?" The second one again.

"Ugglar sent her to the Master's palace to be one of his personal servants. She won't last. Too much fight in her. The Master will probably feed her to the wolves like he did with the last one Ugglar sent."

"All right," the fourth one said. "Break time's over, you lazy louts. We have trespassers to catch."

"What make Ugglar think there's humans out here?" the second one asked.

"Some pixies saw two of them last night down by the beach, but you don't need to worry why. Ugglar says go, we go. Now move!"

Flyn's blood ran cold. Two humans down by the beach last night? They could be talking about him and Kel. And they didn't sound like a rescue party.

The large men grumbled as they packed up their sacks. When they stood, Flyn could see they were even bigger than they had looked sitting down. The tallest, the one who seemed to be in charge, stood at least eight feet. Even the smallest was a full head taller than Flyn. The third one had a belly the size of a barrel.

"Maybe it's elves," the second one said. "I hopes it elves. I hates them long-eared tree rats."

"Better hope it's not a dwarf," the first one said. "He'll chop your toes off with his ax!"

The others laughed at the second one who spat out a curse Flyn didn't recognize.

"I don't care what it is. Let's just catch it so we can go back home."

"What's the matter, Graglak?" the one in charge said. "You miss your soft bed?"

"I miss good food," the third one, Graglak, replied. "We've already been on patrol for two weeks. Let the younger louts do the long patrols. I'm too old for this."

"If you don't quit your griping, this'll be your last patrol. Now get moving!"

They continued their bickering as they left the clearing along the path toward the shore.

Flyn stayed hidden behind the tree until their voices faded down the hill, then carefully picked his way back up to the creek where Kel was still hiding.

"What did you see?" Kel asked.

"I think they were orcs."

"Very funny."

Flyn understood Kel's skepticism. Orcs were creatures from campfire stories told to scare children. They were no more real than dragons or werewolves.

"I'm serious. They're looking for two people they heard were camping by the beach last night."

Kel looked at Flyn sidewise. "You want me to believe that a pack of fairytale monsters is roaming the woods looking for us. Ha, ha."

"I know how it sounds, but it's true. They're huge and they have green skin and everything. I heard one of them say he hoped they found elves and another say it might be dwarves."

"Oh, and now you want me to believe in dwarves and elves too? You almost had me with the orcs, but you went too far with the elves and dwarves. Really, who is it?"

Flyn sighed. "Come on. I'll show you where they were."

"What, they're gone? You let them go without getting help?"

Flyn ignored the protest and led Kel to the clearing. The orcs had left bones and trash from their meal laying around, along with deep imprints from their boots in the mud.

"Look," Flyn said, pointing to one of the footprints. It was twice as wide as his or Kel's foot and almost twice as long. Other prints covered the area, finally leading out along the path to the east.

Kel knelt down to get a closer look at the footprint. He ran his finger along the edge, then compared the inch-deep print to his own footprint, which barely made an impression in the ground. He looked up at Flyn.

"Orcs? For real?"

Flyn just nodded.

"On Trygsted?"

"That's the other thing," Flyn said. "I don't think we're on Trygsted. I think instead of blowing us around the island, the storm blew us to a completely different island."

Kel stood up and stared at Flyn.

"But there aren't any other islands," he said.

"That's what we were always taught," Flyn said. "But orcs and elves aren't supposed to exist either. And that's not all. Look."

Flyn pointed up above the treetops to the west. Kel turned and looked to where Flyn was pointing.

"Is that..." Kel's voice trailed off.

"A mountain," Flyn finished for him. "Those are only supposed to exist in fairytales too, but there it is."

Kel slumped to the ground and held his head in his hands, mumbling to himself.

"Come on, Kel. We need to start moving. I don't think we want to be here if those guys come back."

He helped Kel to his feet and led him up the path, away from the orcs.

"If there are orcs and elves and other islands, what else is true? Dragons? Wizards?"

Flyn just shook his head. He was having almost as much trouble accepting it as Kel. He was just better at dealing with it. Which was probably a good thing, because those orcs hadn't looked like they would care that Flyn and Kel were lost and just trying to get back home. Not that he knew how they were going to do that.

"Flyn? How are we going to get home?" Kel asked, apparently thinking the same thing.

"This path has to lead somewhere. If we can find a village, we can try to get help."

"What if it leads to an orc village?"

"Hopefully it leads to a human village. All paths have to lead somewhere, right? We'll just have to be careful. Besides, we can travel faster on the path. Unless you have a better idea."

"Fine," Kel grumbled. "But don't blame me when we stumble into a village full of monsters."

They spent most of the afternoon walking in silence, both lost in their thoughts, trying to come to grips with their current situation. Flyn listened intently for anyone who might be in front of them, or, for that matter, behind them. In spite of their size, the orcs he had seen had moved faster than he would have guessed. He was concerned that they could easily overtake him and Kel.

But he heard no sound of pursuers, only the birds that had begun to sing after they had passed the orcs. Just a few at first, but soon the trees were alive with their chirps and whistles. Whether the orcs had caused them to go quiet or something else, Flyn didn't know.

After they had put a couple of hours between them and the clearing where the orcs had stopped, they took a short break to look for some food. Besides the birds, they had started to see squirrels and other small game, so Flyn used his knife to fashion a spear out of a fallen tree branch. He unwound the strands from a piece of rope to tie his knife to one end. After some trial and error, he got the feel for the makeshift weapon and soon they had a pair of squirrels to eat.

"Fish of the forest," Flyn said, holding the pair in front of him by the tails.

"How're we going to cook them?" Kel asked. "We don't have any pots or pans and I'm not eating raw squirrel."

"There's plenty of stones around. We can use them to rest a spit over a fire. But let's get away from the path first. Just in case those orcs come back."

They found a spot well off the path near a small stream and while Kel skinned and cleaned the squirrels, Flyn gathered wood and built the fire. Before long the two animals were roasting over the flames.

"Let's make another spear," Flyn said once their meal was cooking. "If we both have spears, we'll have a better chance of catching some more food." *And defending ourselves from orcs,* he didn't add.

Kel wasn't very good at woodworking, so while he tended to the cooking, Flyn found a tree branch and made another spear. The strange, sticky wood was somewhat flexible and easy to carve. Given how soft the wood was, he decided to make a couple more as spares, in case one broke.

With only one knife, Flyn decided to carve the end of each staff into a sharp point instead of using the knife as a spearhead. He used the cooking fire to harden the points. By the time their lunch was ready, they had two spears each, sturdy enough to double as walking sticks.

"I've been thinking," Kel said while they waited for their meal to cook. "If we're on a different island, shouldn't we head back to the coast?"

"I've been thinking about that too, but I think we need to keep as far away from those orcs as possible. Once we find a village, we can ask for the best way to get to a village on the coast where we can stay while we build a new boat. Maybe we'll even find that on this island they aren't afraid of the water we won't have to build our own."

"I hope so. I don't want to build another one."

Flyn grinned. "We built the last one when we were just kids. This time we can build a better one. And one that's more stable."

"And bigger."

"Yeah, that would probably be a good idea."

Kel poked at the fire with a stick. Flyn finished the last spear and set down his knife.

"Cheer up, Kel. We'll find a way home." Flyn was trying to stay positive, but Kel's mood was starting to drag him down too. What was really nagging at him, though, wasn't how they would get a boat. The wood in this forest looked like it would make a great boat. They just needed to find some tools. With just a single knife, it would take months to build one. But he was sure they would overcome that problem.

No, what really troubled him was that they had no way of knowing which way to go once they had a boat. The storm and the currents could have taken them anywhere. The storm had come from the northeast, so he assumed that's the way they would have to travel to get home. But how far was Trygsted from here? And what if the ocean currents had sent them in a different direction?

He didn't know if Kel had thought of that particular problem yet, and he wasn't going to bring it up.

"Good thing the squirrels are so big here," Flyn said to change the subject. They were starting to smell pretty good too.

"We should've killed a couple more. I'm starving."

"We can get some more while we walk. Then we can have a big dinner. Maybe we'll even find a rabbit or a pig."

Kel perked up. "You think they have rabbits here?"

"They have squirrels, so why not rabbits?"

"Let's skip the pig, though. They're a lot of work."

As they talked and ate, Flyn almost forgot about the orcs and that they were marooned a long way from home. Kel seemed to feel better after the meal too. When they finished, they used water from the creek to put out the cooking fire and top off the waterskins. Then they made their way back to the trail and continued their journey into the unknown.

The afternoon passed by without running into more orcs. Or anyone else, for that matter. They didn't find any rabbits or pigs, but they soon had their packs stuffed with squirrels. They wouldn't go to bed hungry.

By early evening, the forest had begun to thin out somewhat and they could see that the path ran along the foothills of a whole mountain range, not just a solitary mountain like Flyn had thought earlier. The path was getting closer to the steep slopes, too. By what should have been dinner time, they were close enough that the mountains hid the sun, putting the castaways in shadow. The temperature had dropped as well, causing Kel to start grumbling about not having a cloak to wrap up in. Flyn too wished he had brought one, but when they had left home the previous morning, they couldn't have known they would need them.

The previous morning. Flyn had trouble accepting that they had been away from home for less than two days. After everything they had been through, home almost felt like a distant memory. He wondered what his parents and brother were doing. He imagined they were sitting around the dinner table, talking and laughing, no idea that he and Kel were so far from home. He wondered if they were thinking of him.

"I don't think we're going to find a village today," Kel said, breaking Flyn out of his thoughts.

"Probably not."

Evening twilight had come earlier than they expected. Flyn shivered, wishing again for a warm cloak.

"There's a stream up ahead," he said, pointing. "Let's follow it off the trail for a bit and find a place to camp for the night. I could use a fire to warm up by."

"Me too," Kel said.

The pair set off through the trees. Flyn suggested they follow the stream for at least ten minutes to get far enough off the path that any travelers wouldn't see their fire. As an extra precaution, they built it on the other side of the largest tree they could find, putting the trunk between them and the trail that was at least four furlongs back.

With running water, a fire, and a half-dozen squirrels, their campsite was almost comfortable. They each ate one of the squirrels and some more fruit, but with no idea how long before they reached civilization, they decided to save the rest of their provisions. They might not be able to catch squirrels every day.

Their bellies full, they laid out their bedrolls and sat staring at the fire, listening to the pops and crackles and enjoying its warmth.

"Flyn?" Kel asked after a while. "What do we do if we can't get home?"

Flyn continued to stare into the fire and didn't answer right away.

"We keep trying, I guess," he said after a long pause.

"Forever?"

He paused again before answering. "I suppose if we're still here when winter comes, we'll have to find a place to stay until spring, but even if that happens, we'll keep trying."

"You promise? You won't leave me here?"

"Yeah, I promise."

"Good."

"But we can't stay here that long. We have to be home before our Matching Day."

"For all the good it'll do you. The only way you're going to get a wife is if mine has a desperate friend."

Flyn smiled at Kel but didn't reply. The truth was Kel was nervous about finding a wife. He had never actually said it, but Flyn could tell. Kel could never muster up the courage to ask a girl out. Flyn had introduced him to every girl he had ever dated. But now wasn't the time to tease him about it.

They talked into the evening about girls, and where they were going to live after getting married, and what they were going to do for a living. After overhearing the orcs talk about the pixies that had seen them sleeping the night before, Flyn was in no hurry to go to bed. Even though Kel didn't say anything, Flyn suspected he felt the same.

After a while, the conversation slowed and their eyes started to droop. Unable to stay awake any longer, they lay down next to the fire.

"Don't forget your promise, Flyn," Kel said, his tired voice barely louder than a whisper.

They were both asleep in minutes.

They woke early the next morning with the same cool, damp fog as the morning before filling the forest. Flyn stoked the fire to dry out their blankets and take the chill off while they ate a cold breakfast of fruit and leftover squirrel. While it wasn't bacon and eggs, they both agreed that it was far better than the alternative: creek moss or grubs from rotting logs. They ate quickly, both wanting to get on their way. Neither wanted to spend another night in the woods.

Once back at the forest trail, Flyn stopped and examined the ground for footprints. He wasn't an expert tracker by anyone's measure, but what he was looking for didn't require much skill and he found it almost right away.

Big, heavy bootprints crossing the creek. The orcs had passed back this way sometime during the night.

Flyn shivered and not from the chilly morning air.

"Look," he said to Kel, pointing at the prints.

Kel gasped and clamped his hand tightly over his mouth, like he was holding in a scream.

"They're going the same way we are. What do we do?" Kel's voice was barely louder than a whisper behind his hand.

"I think they're just going back to where they came from. They're moving a lot faster than us, so I don't think we have to worry about them, but we should be extra careful."

They set off at a slower pace than Flyn would have liked, just to make sure they didn't accidentally run into the orcs. As the morning drew on, the trail continued to climb higher and closer to the mountain slopes until it emerged from the forest completely. Walking between the massive trees on the right and the steep stone walls on the left, Flyn felt like they were traveling through a deep gulley. The trail twisted and turned along the cliffs and slopes, preventing them from seeing more than twenty or thirty yards ahead. Which of course meant nothing could see them beyond that distance either, but it slowed their pace as they had to stop and peer around every corner before moving on.

Around midday, the path turned toward the mountains and into a crevice in the cliff towering over them.

"Now what?" Kel asked. "We can't follow the path into the mountains."

"We don't really have a choice. We know there's no villages back the way we came."

"We don't know if there's anything that way either," Kel said, waving toward the mountains. "Besides, the path may lead to a village the other way, past where we found it."

"Those orcs went into the mountains," Flyn said, pointing to the large footprints leading into the fissure in the cliff. "And they were talking about humans, so there must be humans that way somewhere. We have no idea what's in the other direction."

"Okay," Kel said, finally giving in. "But let's at least eat first."

"We better cook everything. We don't know if we'll be able to find wood once we get into the mountains."

As before, they moved off the path to build their fire. The slower pace throughout the morning had given them a good chance to look for more squirrels. They had even caught a rabbit, much to Kel's delight, and found some blackberries.

They ate the rabbit and cut the meat off the squirrel. While they were eating, they dried out some of the pelts over the fire and used them to wrap up the cooked squirrel meat. With their food packed and waterskins filled, they returned to the cleft in the cliff.

The crevice was narrow, only about two to three feet wide in most places. The cliffs on either side were too tall to see the tops. The ground, although relatively flat, was littered with pebbles and small stones that they would occasionally kick. The sound of the skittering rocks bounced off rock walls, echoing away into the distance. Every time, Flyn would freeze, listening for some reaction. Surely the orcs must hear them coming.

But no reaction ever came and they would move on. At least the flat ground made walking easier than it had been in the forest.

Ahead of them, the path was mostly straight, with only a few small turns.

While the traveling was easier, Flyn was more nervous than ever. If the orcs showed up in front of them, they had no place to hide, and he was sure the orcs could outrun them. To be on the safe side, Flyn kept their pace slow and his eyes focused on the gloom ahead, looking for any movement. He strained his ears for any small sound of the orcs.

The orcs weren't the only thing bothering Flyn. The closeness in the crevice made him uncomfortable. The immense walls rose on either side until they seemed to almost meet high above their heads. Only a small slit of blue told him they weren't in a cave. But even that didn't help. The narrowness of the opening gave the feeling that the walls were closing in on them, ready to tumble down at any moment.

"It's just in your head," Flyn whispered to himself.

"Flyn?" Kel sounded as uncomfortable as Flyn.

"Nothing. Everything's fine," Flyn whispered back. He didn't dare turn to look at his friend, to let Kel see the fear in his own face. He had to stay strong for both of them, even though he didn't feel it.

The floor of the crevice rose slightly as they moved deeper into the mountains, but not enough to overcome the cliffs. After about an hour or so—it was hard to tell with no reference to the sun—the path came to an end, surrounded on three sides by the cliff walls.

"Now what?" Kel asked.

Flyn looked around for an opening in the cliffs, but couldn't find anything.

"Where did the orcs go?" Kel's voice edged on panic.

"I don't know, but be quiet," Flyn whispered.

"Did they climb the cliffs?" Kel asked, quieter this time.

Flyn just shook his head. He had no idea. They stood quietly for several minutes, listening and scanning the cliffs.

Then he heard the clicking of a falling pebble.

"Flyn? Where—"

"Sh!" Flyn whispered, putting his hand up. He turned his head to one side, trying to listen for the faintest sound.

"There," he whispered. "Did you hear it?"

"Hear what?"

"Voices. Up above us somewhere."

The echo chamber created by the sheer rock walls carried the sound of deep voices from somewhere way above them. Although he couldn't make out the words, he was sure they were voices of the orcs.

Flyn looked up, trying to find the source.

"How did they get up there?" Kel was looking up too.

"There." Flyn pointed to what looked like a crack in the right cliff face. They hurried over and discovered it was actually a rough staircase cut into the rock. In the dim light, they had almost overlooked it.

Flyn followed the steps with his eyes, looking for the orcs. Far above them, near the top of the cliff, he saw them: four tiny figures, almost like bugs from this distance.

"How could they not have seen us?" Kel asked, his voice barely above a whisper.

"More of that luck we've been having, I guess. Come on."

Flyn pulled Kel back farther into the crevice where they would be at the orcs' backs, and against the cliff wall so they couldn't see the orcs anymore.

"We can wait here for a while before we climb up." He pulled off his pack and sat down.

"And then what?" Kel stayed standing, glancing between Flyn and the top of the cliff.

"And then we keep going. What choice do we have?"

"Why did I agree to go with you on that stupid boat in the first place?"

Kel sat down in a huff and refused to say anymore. Flyn shrugged and pulled an orange out of his pack. He only had a few more left, but they wouldn't last as long as some of the other food. Kel eventually decided to eat too.

Flyn listened to the distant voices of the orcs. He supposed it was a good thing they were so loud. Otherwise they might have heard him and Kel earlier. But he was still surprised the orcs hadn't seen them walking through the narrow ravine. After all, other than being narrow, the path was completely open with nothing to hide anyone walking through.

Not having an answer to that, he turned his thoughts to the bigger problem. They had no idea how long they would have to follow the road before finding a village. They had brought enough food for a week, assuming that they would catch fish for lunch and dinner. At the rate they were eating, the meat they had in their packs would only last them a few more days. Unless they found another food source in the mountains, they would need to cut back on how much they ate. Which would mean they probably wouldn't have enough energy to maintain a very fast pace. Still, if they were careful, they might stretch their supplies to five or six days. After that, they would be in trouble.

He decided to wait to discuss it with Kel. He was frazzled enough. Better to let him relax before throwing another problem on him.

The orcs' voices faded away as Flyn and Kel ate their short meal.

When they were finished, Flyn crept to the stairs to look, but as far as he could tell, they were gone. He beckoned to Kel to follow him.

"Maybe we should wait a little longer," Kel said. "So we don't run into those orcs at the top."

"It'll take us over an hour to climb to up there. They'll be long gone by the time we get there. Let's go."

Flyn started climbing. He didn't bother to look back. He wanted to focus on the steps. They were uneven, many of them broken and crumbling away. The stairs were wide enough, almost four feet, but he didn't want to take any chances on falling. Kel would follow him, even if he didn't want to.

The climb took longer than Flyn had guessed, nearly an hour and a half. They both stumbled several times, but managed to catch themselves before they could fall. The steps were in worse condition the higher they got. In many places, the steps had eroded away completely, leaving a steep, gravel slope. In other places, small pieces of rock broke off as they stepped on them.

The steps must be ancient, Flyn thought, carved hundreds of years ago. He wondered who had built them and why. Certainly, to put so much work into it, the path must lead somewhere, though he had to admit to himself, as old as these stairs were, that wherever they led could have been destroyed or abandoned long ago.

As they climbed, they discovered why the orcs hadn't seen them far below in the crevice. With the bright sun above, the bottom was shrouded in complete darkness. If not for the noise, an entire army could march up the crevice path, and someone near the top of the stairs would never know. While that was a comforting thought regarding their trek through the mountain fissure, knowing that there could be someone down there looking up at them and they would never see them was quite the opposite.

They hurried as fast as they dared up the final couple hundred feet, staying as close to the wall and as far from the drop-off as they could. By the time they reached the end of the stairs, they were both sweating and panting. Flyn staggered a few feet from the cliff and sat down, his back to a large boulder. Kel struggled over and collapsed next to him.

They examined their surroundings as they rested and caught their breath. The stairs had emerged only a few dozen feet from the top of the cliff. Looking down, Flyn saw where they had been standing hours earlier looking up. At the top of the stairs, the path continued, turning back along the top of the ravine and heading farther into the mountains. It appeared to be climbing to a low point between two peaks many leagues away.

The outcropping they were sitting on was only about twenty feet wide and maybe fifty feet long. The east and south sides dropped off into cliffs, the north side rose up in a steep slope that climbed up and away to the peaks farther north. The path, leading west, was the only way to go.

To the east lay the forest they had been traveling through. It ran north and south as far as they could see. Beyond the forest, the ocean with its deep blue water stretched to the hazy horizon. Flyn thought he could almost see the whitecaps on the waves.

Somewhere across that vast, blue expanse was home.

CHAPTER 4

Seeing the ocean, and having thoughts of home, made Flyn more anxious than ever to find help. Kel, already uneasy with their predicament, became more dejected with the news about their limited rations. Flyn tried to reassure him that they would find a village or town long before they ran out of food, but Kel knew better.

Homesick and despondent, they set off again, following the path up into the mountains. It wandered left and right as it climbed the slopes, avoiding the steeper, less passable areas. Even so, the trek was not an easy one. Some areas had been washed out from decades, if not centuries of weathering, leaving only a slight rut, overgrown with scrub grasses and weeds, to indicate its presence. In other places, the path ran along the top of steep cliffs or large fissures so deep that falling pebbles never seemed to hit the bottom. In spite of the rough going, Flyn was sure that following the ancient path was their best chance of finding help.

Flyn led the way, setting a quick but steady pace. He wanted to make it through the mountain pass before their food supply was exhausted. They found very little vegetation along their path, and nothing that looked edible. The only animal life seemed to be birds, soaring high above them on the mountain winds—larger than any they yet had seen since arriving on the strange island. If there was anything they could hunt to eat, it was well hidden.

The first part of the trek was warm and bright. With thoughts of running out of food motivating them, they made good time over the rough terrain. The end of the first day found them camping at the entrance to the mountain pass, tired and discouraged.

The next morning, they awoke to low-lying clouds that shrouded the mountain peaks above them. The chill, damp air cut through their warm-weather clothing, leaving them cold and miserable. With no wood to build a fire, they had no choice but to move on, hoping the hike through the mountains would warm them. By midday, the clouds opened and dumped a steady, drenching rain on them that lasted for the rest of the day and into the night.

The mountain pass provided no shelter to escape the constant downpour, so they decided to keep walking through the night. At least the path was much easier going than the climb up to the pass. There were no cliffs to fall off, just large boulders to navigate around and loose rock under their feet that made their footing unsteady.

But the rain brought a new hazard. Water running off the slopes on either side gathered in the ravine and flowed down along their path. What started as a simple annoyance, soaking their shoes and making their footing less sure, soon became a hazard. Small debris rushed down the growing stream, banging into their ankles and threatening to knock them off their feet. Throughout the night, the stream grew deeper and stronger, driving them up the steep slopes to avoid being washed away. By the dawn of their third day in the mountains, they were exhausted to the point of collapse.

They sat down to rest and eat the last of their fruit and a few bites of meat, too tired to be very hungry, and too wet to want to eat. Neither spoke as they ate. Even Flyn was beginning to feel they had made the wrong choice in coming into the mountains. In hindsight, if they had known the reality of their situation on that first morning on the beach, he would have suggested following the coast instead. Flyn was thankful that Kel wasn't pointing that out to him, though from the look on his friend's face, Kel must have been thinking it.

As the morning light grew from dark gray to light gray, they were able see their surroundings for the first time since nightfall. The valley was wider now. The slopes weren't as steep, and the flat bottom, though still flooded with runoff, was much broader than what they had traveled through the previous day. Although they couldn't see very far with the rain and fog, it seemed to open even more to the west. Maybe that meant the pass was coming to an end and they would be out of the mountains soon.

"Look," Kel said.

Wiping the rain from his eyes, Flyn looked to where Kel was pointing.

Across the narrow valley, twenty or thirty feet up from the flooded bottom, was the dark opening of a cave.

Flyn smiled and clapped Kel on the back. A cave would make a fine place to get out of the deluge and catch a few hours of sleep.

With great effort, they helped each other to their feet and worked their way across the rushing flood waters. They found the water wasn't very deep, only a few inches, and so using their spears as walking sticks to steady themselves, they managed to negotiate their way across and scramble up to the cave.

Once inside, both men collapsed on the floor, relieved to be out of the rain. For several minutes they just sat, looking out from the opening of their refuge at the dreary storm.

"It would be nice if we had some wood to start a fire," Kel said after a bit. They were both chilled to the bone. Flyn too would have welcomed a fire to warm up by.

With no chance for a fire, and having been awake for a whole day struggling through the mountains, they resigned to sleep. They stripped off their wet clothes and hung them from small outcroppings on the cave wall, not really expecting them to dry. Their bedrolls, fortunately, were still somewhat dry, though everything in their packs was a little damp from the moist air.

Even lying on the rock floor of the cave, both weary travelers were asleep within minutes.

It was dusk when Flyn awoke. Outside, the rain had stopped, though he could still hear water running down the slopes and into the stream in the ravine. The fog had thickened as well. He could only see a few feet beyond the mouth of the cave. Next to him, Kel was still asleep, snoring softly.

As much as he didn't want to, Flyn stood up and stretched. He was sore from his neck to his toes, whether from hiking through the mountains or sleeping on the floor of the cave, he didn't know. He supposed it was a combination of both, not that it much mattered. He stood in the mouth of the cave and watched the fog drift by while stretching and massaging his muscles.

Even though the rain had stopped, the air was still moist and cool. As he suspected, the clothes hanging on the wall were still wet, so he dug through his pack to find his spare clothes, thankfully dry. After dressing, he woke up Kel, who was not happy at all about it. Grumbling, he dressed in his spare clothes as well.

Dinner was light, a wheat cake each and squirrel meat. They sat on a large rock near the mouth of the cave, using their rolled-up bedrolls as cushions. Though they both liked wild game cooked over an open fire, cold squirrel was getting a little old.

"When we get home," Kel said, picking at his meal, "I'm never eating squirrel again."

"Well, it's almost gone, then we can eat the ham." They still had cured ham in their packs, but it would last longer than the squirrel meat, so they were saving it.

"And then we'll have to eat our clothes. We better find some more food soon."

"Did you notice the valley this morning? It looked like it was widening. Maybe we're coming to the end."

"None too soon."

"Let's pack up and get moving," Flyn said, finishing his meager meal.

Kel groaned. "Why don't we stay here for the night. It'll be completely dark soon and I don't want to spend another night stumbling through the mountains."

"It'll be easier tonight without the rain. Besides, unless you want to start eating your clothes, we shouldn't waste any time. If we can get another league or two before we go to sleep again, we'll be that much closer to more food. And maybe better food."

"Fine." Kel sighed. "Let's get this over with."

They packed up their bedrolls and tied their wet clothes to the outside of their packs to keep from getting the rest of their gear wet. Shouldering their packs, they were about to set off when they heard a rumbling noise from farther in the cave.

"What was that?" Kel asked, peering into the blackness.

"I think someone's coming," Flyn whispered. "Find a place to hide in case it's more orcs."

They scrambled out of the cave and onto the mountainside, looking for someplace to hide. A large boulder sat on the other side of the gulley. They hurried down the slope, half running, half sliding, then across to the boulder. The water running through the mountain pass had shrunk to a small stream, allowing them to cross it in a single step. Reaching the boulder, they spun around and looked back at the cave, a mere fifty feet from their hiding spot.

At first, they saw nothing but the dark opening in the side of the mountain. Flyn was about to say that maybe they had been imagining things, but then a faint flickering light appeared. As they watched, the light grew brighter, reflecting off the ceiling of the cave, and they could hear voices. Faint at first, they grew louder as the light grew brighter, echoing out of the cave opening. The voices were loud and deep. With the echo, Flyn couldn't make out the words.

Then they saw them. Two large men emerged from the cave. They were even bigger than the orcs, maybe ten or twelve feet tall, with shoulders almost as wide as Flyn and Kel were tall. Their heads looked to be about three feet wide, big even for their huge bodies. They each carried a torch the size of a small tree.

Flyn and Kel ducked behind the rock before they were spotted.

"Me hungry," one of the men said.

"You always hungry," the other one replied.

"That because you eat too much. Don't leave me my share."

"Not my fault you eat slow."

The first one growled, a low rumbling noise that sounded like thunder.

"Come on, slowpoke," the second one said. "We find you food."

The second one laughed, a sound that was more like a howl than a laugh.

Flyn heard rocks and pebbles skittering down the opposite slope as the two men made their way to the bottom of the ravine.

"Me want good food tonight. No more goat."

"Goat all there is in mountains. Have to go to valley for deer or cow."

"Then we go to valley."

"Valley long way away. And humans in valley."

"Then I eat humans too. No more goat!"

The voices faded as they moved away.

Flyn and Kel looked at each other, eyes wide.

"Was that the orcs you saw?" Kel asked.

"No. Those were way bigger. I think they were ogres."

"Ogres?" Kel muttered, shaking his head and staring after the ogres. "Orcs and elves and dwarves, now ogres?"

"Worry about it later. We have to follow them."

"What?" Kel spun around and stared at Flyn. "First you want to follow orcs, now you want to follow ogres? The boat must have hit you on the head harder than I thought. You've lost your mind!"

"Quiet down. I haven't lost my mind. Did you hear what they said? They're going to a valley where humans live. That's where we need to go. And if we hurry, we might be able to warn the people in the valley that the ogres are coming."

"But the ogres..." Kel's voice trailed off. He turned to look toward the ogres, their torches fading in the distance.

"We'll just have to stay back far enough so they don't see us. Come on, before we lose them."

Flyn ran around the rock they were hiding behind and after the lumbering ogres. Kel started to say something else, but Flyn didn't wait around to argue with him.

"Wait for me," Kel said, running after Flyn.

The pair hurried after the ogres, catching up with them after a few minutes. They got close enough to hear them talking, though not close enough to make out what they were saying. Staying back wasn't hard. The problem was keeping up. The ogres moved through the rocks and boulders strewn about the ravine with relative ease, and with their long legs, their pace was almost a jog for the smaller humans.

After an hour, they had to slow down and let the ogres move on. They couldn't continue the quick pace in the best of conditions. With the poor footing, and already being sore and tired, it was hopeless.

Finally, Flyn stopped. They found a rock to sit on and catch their breath.

"We'll never keep up with them," Flyn said.

Kel nodded, still too out of breath to talk.

"Let's just take a break. Then we'll keep going at a slower pace and get a few more leagues behind us before we stop for the night. In the morning, we can look for their tracks. They shouldn't be too hard to find." The ravine had gotten wider, more of a valley now, but there still seemed to be only one way to go.

They rested for a bit, then resumed their trek, this time at a more maintainable pace. There was no sign of the ogres or their torches. The widening valley allowed them to avoid the remnants of the flood waters still running away to the east. Even so, the path was not easy. They had to dodge boulders, some as big as houses, that were scattered throughout the valley, and the ground was uneven and broken. But the fog had lifted a little and moonlight filtered through the drifting mist, somewhat lighting their way. In any case, it was better than the soaking rain of the previous night.

At last, Flyn called a halt for the evening. Exhausted, they searched for a place to sleep, before finally settling on a small flat spot a few yards up the northern slope. Several large boulders hid their campsite from the valley, though neither of them would have dared to light a fire with the ogres around, even if they had been able to find wood.

After a short meal, they crawled into their bedrolls, both too exhausted to speak much.

Flyn drifted off to sleep with thoughts of trees and grass and warm sunshine.

Morning didn't bring trees and grass, but it did bring the sun. By the time they awoke, the sun was riding high in the bright blue sky, the only clouds small, white puffy cotton balls drifting lazily above them.

"I almost think I'm getting used to sleeping on hard ground," Flyn said as he stretched.

"That's all well and good for you. I'm just trying to remember what it used to feel like to not have sore muscles."

Flyn laughed, his mood improved with the weather.

They ate the last of their squirrel meat for breakfast. Even though their food supply was running dangerously low, neither was sad the squirrel meat was gone. Still, they would have to conserve their supplies. Flyn figured if they were careful, they had maybe two days of food. Three if they really stretched it.

Flyn examined the valley to the west while they ate. What had started as a narrow ravine, maybe twenty or thirty feet across, was now a wide canyon, a hundred yards or more across from slope to slope. He hadn't noticed through the night that the waters had receded, leaving scattered pools across the valley floor, along with boulders and the remains of old landslides. The path they had been following was now paved with flagstones, running straight through the middle of the valley. To the west, the southern slope appeared to veer off, hinting they may be nearing the end of the mountain pass.

They finished their breakfast, packed their gear, and set out as quickly as they could. They talked freely as they walked, enjoying the sunshine that truly warmed them for the first time since before the rain. The paved road made the journey almost pleasant. Only occasionally did they need to move off the path to avoid a boulder that had found its way onto the ancient roadway. The road stayed close to the northern mountain, and after a couple of hours, they couldn't even see the bottom of the slope of the southern mountain. Though some of the paving stones that made up the road were cracked, and some missing altogether, the road ran perfectly straight as far as they could see in either direction.

It was nearly lunchtime when they came to an intersection with another road. The intersection was a large circle around the remains of a broken statue. The road they had been following continued on the far side of the circle, while the second road led off to the south. Unsure of which way to go, they decided to stop for lunch while they contemplated their options.

Flyn had hoped to find tracks from the ogres leading down one of the roads, but apparently the rain had washed any dirt from the stones, leaving nothing to record the passage of any travelers before them. There were no signs or other indicators pointing to the valley the ogres had mentioned. They debated the choices while they ate, neither of them having a good argument for one choice over the other. Flyn wanted to continue to the west, the way they were already headed, guessing that the southern road led back into the mountains. Kel wanted to take the southern road because it led away from the northern peaks, which seemed to continue on forever.

They were still debating when Flyn saw someone coming up the road from the west. Two large someones.

"The ogres!" Flyn said in a loud whisper.

The only place they could find to hide was behind a large boulder several yards away from the path. Flyn scurried around the boulder, with Kel close behind, and crouched down, hoping the approaching ogres hadn't seen them. Flyn peeked his head around the side to watch.

The ogres were running when they reached the intersection. They were carrying large sacks over their shoulders that seemed heavy, even for the massive beasts.

"See, nothing here," the first one said, putting down his load.

"I know I see something." The second put down his sack as well.

"You not see nothing."

"Maybe it was humans Kargguk looking for."

"Maybe old stone man here get up and run around."

"We should look 'round. Maybe Kargguk reward us for catching his escaped slaves."

"Why give them to Kargguk? Just put them in sack and take them home to eat."

"Kargguk get mad if we eat his slaves."

"How he know what we eat?"

"He have magic. He know."

While the ogres argued, Flyn looked for a way to escape. There were plenty of boulders to hide behind. If they could make it to one a little farther away, they might have a chance.

They needed a distraction. Flyn picked up a small rock. Maybe if he could throw it the other way, the sound would distract the ogres and he and Kel could sneak away. The two seemed dumb enough to fall for it. He looked at Kel and pointed to the rock in his hand, then to the next boulder. Kel nodded.

Flyn heaved the rock as hard as he could toward the southern road.

"What that?" one of the ogres said.

The ogres ran toward the sound.

Flyn and Kel hurried to the next boulder, crouching down to try to stay out of the sight of the ogres. It didn't work.

"There they are!" yelled one of the ogres.

"Run, Kel!" Flyn dropped his spears and ran, no idea where he was running to, just running and dodging boulders. Behind him, he could hear Kel stumbling and slipping on the loose rock, trying to keep up. Farther behind, the ogres. They might have been faster on open ground, but the boulders and other landslide debris gave the advantage to the smaller humans.

The ground rose sharply as they started up the northern slope, still sliding in the loose rock and ducking around boulders. Flyn glanced over his shoulder, but could not see their pursuers, though he could still hear them yelling and cursing somewhere behind.

He and Kel may have been defter in negotiating the fallen rocks, but the ogres had more endurance. The humans were already slowing down and the ogres were closing the distance.

"Hurry, Kel. Or we'll end up their dinner!"

They pushed harder, running along the slope now instead of up. Flyn searched ahead and to their left and right for a boulder or outcropping they could duck behind and outmaneuver their pursuers. Their only chance was to change directions without the ogres knowing.

Then Flyn slipped. The rock gave way under his feet, sending him sliding down the slope on his back. He grabbed at the ground, looking for anything to catch himself. Below him, the slope ended in a narrow fissure that he was headed straight for. He stuck his heels into the ground, trying to slow his fall, to no avail. The crack in the earth loomed ahead. Pebbles and stones pelted his head. Kel was sliding down the slope above him.

In a last desperate attempt to save himself, Flyn grabbed at the top of the cliff as he slipped over the brink. He stopped with a jerk, hanging on to the edge. Then Kel came down on top of him and the pair tumbled into the crack.

Flyn hit the ground hard and fell back as Kel landed on his chest, knocking the wind out of him. Rock and dirt fell behind them, showering down on the hapless pair lying at the bottom. The yells from the ogres came closer, and more gravel poured into the crevice and on top of them, burying them in loose rock. Unable to move, Flyn resigned himself to his fate.

The rain of rock slowed and eventually stopped as the sound of their pursuers faded.

"Flyn? Are you okay?" Kel was still lying next to him, where he had stopped after bouncing off Flyn's chest.

"I think so," Flyn replied, his voice hitching as he tried to catch his breath.

They were lying in a narrow crevice, only two or three feet wide. Fortunately, it wasn't very deep, only seven or eight feet.

"I can't believe we're still alive." Kel was extracting himself from the rock and debris that almost completely covered them.

"I think all this gravel is what saved us," Flyn said, sitting up and brushing the dirt off his face. "It sounded like they went right over the top of us. They must not have seen us."

They finished digging themselves out of the rockslide, but didn't try to climb out of the crevice yet. They decided to wait a while to make sure the ogres were long gone.

Flyn's chest hurt when he breathed and he suspected he might have a cracked rib from Kel landing on him. Both were scraped and bruised, but otherwise not seriously injured.

"If we ever get home," Kel said, "don't ever ask me to go on one of your adventures again."

For a long time, Flyn and Kel sat in the bottom of the small fissure, not daring to climb out. At one point, they thought they heard the ogres shouting in the distance, though with the wind whistling over the top of the crevice, they couldn't be sure. Eventually, Flyn's sore ribs forced him to move.

"Do you think they're gone?" Kel asked.

"I don't know. We're going to have to climb up and take a look. I'll give you a boost and you can look around."

Flyn boosted Kel enough for him to grab the edge and pull himself up.

"I don't see anything," Kel said.

"Climb out," Flyn gasped. The strain of boosting Kel sent fresh waves of pain through his chest.

With Flyn's help, Kel scrambled out of the crevice. Flyn fell back to the ground. He sat holding his side and gritting his teeth through the pain. Kel looked down at him from the top.

"Are you okay?"

"I'll be okay," Flyn said. "Just need to rest a minute. Go look around."

Kel disappeared, leaving Flyn to recover as best he could. After a few minutes, Kel's head popped over the top.

"All clear. No sign of the ogres. They must have given up. Even the big sacks they were carrying are gone."

Flyn nodded and climbed to his feet, steadying himself on the wall of the crevice. After a bit of a struggle, Kel was able to pull him out of the hole. They both collapsed, one panting from pain, the other from exhaustion.

"Let's see if we can find our spears and get out of here," Flyn said after he recovered somewhat.

After a short search, they located two of the spears.

"Forget the other two," Flyn said. "We have to get moving in case the ogres come back. Besides, once we reach the valley, we should be able to get help, so we won't need to hunt for food."

"I hope you're right," Kel said.

At least the choice of direction was clear now. The ogres had been to the valley, and they had come back on the western path.

"We better stay off the path in case the ogres come back," Kel said.

"They would see us anyway, unless we climb up the hillside and dodge around the boulders." To the south, there was no cover at all.

Kel stared at the mountainside to the north for a minute, then sighed.

"Okay," he said. "I suppose we should be more concerned about our food than the ogres anyway."

Though the afternoon was just as bright and sunny as the morning, their cheer and easygoingness was not.

They traveled without talking, carefully watching ahead and frequently checking behind them for any sign of the ogres. Flyn had no desire to test his wits against them again. They hurried along the path as fast as Flyn could walk without causing himself to breathe heavily. Their goal was to make the valley by nightfall.

Humans lived in the valley, or so the ogres had said. When they had started their journey along the path, they had just hoped to find people, always assuming that if they found them, they would be friendly. As they came closer to their destination, Flyn began to wonder if that would be true. Everyone else they had encountered so far had been anything but friendly. His hope was that since the orcs and ogres (and apparently pixies, whatever those were) seemed to dislike humans (or like them as food), then perhaps the humans would be friendly to other humans.

The possibility that such an environment might make the people of the valley be distrustful of any strangers, human or no, was beginning to creep into Flyn's thoughts. If Kel felt the same, he didn't say. But they didn't have much choice. They knew how the orcs and ogres felt. At least with the humans, there was a chance for help.

Before they had traveled more than a couple of hours, the path began to slope down and they could see trees far off in the distance. The sight of the trees encouraged them to pick up their pace, as much as Flyn's injury would allow, anyway. They were determined not to stop until they reached the forest ahead, forgoing a dinner break and instead snacking on some of their remaining food as they walked.

The sun was already sinking toward the horizon and the trees were still at least a league away.

It was dusk before they reached the first sign of greenery, and fully dark before they reached the trees. The stone road had begun to disappear as the land transitioned from rock to dirt. At first, dust and silt had just covered it in a few places, but as they had traveled farther, the stones became more broken and uneven until the road turned into just a dirt track with only an occasional broken flagstone to show that it had once been paved.

At the edge of the forest, the road split, one branch turning to the south, the other continuing straight to the west. Tired from their long day, and unsure of which path to take, they decided to camp for the night. Flyn pointed out that in the morning, they might be able to find tracks on the road, especially after the rain from the previous few days. If they could find human-sized footprints, they might have a better idea of which way to go.

They agreed that camping on the road was a bad idea, so they moved into the woods to find a place to sleep. After the sun had gone down, the air had quickly changed from cool to cold. The trees sheltered them from the wind, but it would be a chilly night. Kel wanted to build a fire, but after the encounter with the ogres, Flyn felt a fire would be too risky. Eventually, Kel relented. They settled for a cold dinner, then climbed into the bedrolls, hunkering down in the blankets to ward off the cold.

Kel was asleep in minutes, but Flyn's injury kept him awake. Every breath was agony. He tried lying on the opposite side and taking shallow breaths, but every time he started to drift off, another wave of pain would hit. Although he didn't normally drink whiskey, he was wishing for some now. Just a little to dull the pain so he could sleep. Even the disgusting pain medicine his mother used to give him when he was younger would be better than lying on the ground in misery.

After a while, he couldn't take the pain anymore. He rose from his blankets and stretched to relieve the ache in his side. Nothing seemed to help, though. That the rest of him was sore too didn't help matters. He decided to go for a short walk to stretch his legs.

Since they hadn't built a fire, they had chosen a spot not too far from the path. Flyn was back to the fork in the road in a couple of minutes. The moon was still climbing in the cloudless sky and once he left the trees, he could easily make out his surroundings. The wind had died down, leaving everything still and quiet. Just the chirps and calls of the bugs and birds of the night. Somewhere in the distance, a wolf howled.

Standing in the middle of the intersection, Flyn took a slow, deep breath to stretch his sore ribs. The air still smelled of damp earth from the rain, mixing with the other smells of spring. If he closed his eyes, he could almost imagine he was standing in the Brekkness Forest. Which was where he and Kel were supposed to be right now, instead of wherever they were. He didn't even know the name of the island they were on. Not even the fairytales they had heard as children had names for the lands where the stories took place. The only land beyond Trygsted that he had ever heard of was Vahul. And this place didn't look much like the afterlife described in the tales.

A noise from the southern road interrupted his thoughts. Someone was coming, though he couldn't see anything yet. A furlong or so to the south, the road went over a hill, blocking it from view. A faint glow reflected off the trees on the other side of the hill.

Flyn scrambled back into the woods to hide and crouched down behind a large trunk to watch the road. He considered going back to wake Kel, but there wasn't time. Whoever was coming was moving fast, not bothering to conceal themselves.

He watched as four men on horseback rode over the top of the hill, torches in their hands. They rode up and stopped short of the crossroad, their horses snorting and grunting, ears twitching.

The men were all dressed in dark armor. The vests were made of overlapping plates of leather, covering the torso, shoulders, and upper arms. The pants were similar, with leather plates covering their boots. Leather helmets protected their heads. Each had a sword hanging from his saddle.

The man in the lead got off his horse and walked to the crossroad, holding his torch down to examine the ground. After a few seconds, he turned back to the others.

"They were here," he said. "There's a lot of prints, but they definitely came through here."

"Which way?" one of the other men said.

"Hard to tell. There's prints going all over. It looks like they might have gone back into the pass, but then came back and headed toward Gurnborg."

"Gurnborg? Why would they go there? I've never heard of ogres working for Jarot. If that's changed, then war may be closer than we feared."

"There're more prints here too," the first man said. "Human size."

"Did somebody get away?"

"Can't tell that, but there's two sets of human footprints heading into the woods." The man pointed toward the trees. The other men turned to look where he was pointing. They looked right at Flyn.

"You there," the second man said, drawing his sword. "Come out here."

Flyn hesitated. Were they rescued or captured? After everything they had been through since being swept to this land by the storm, he found he wasn't sure. The men before him could be friendly and helpful, or they could just as easily be hostile. The man with the sword certainly wasn't acting particularly friendly. But then, Flyn was the one hiding in the trees.

He stood up, checking that his hunting knife was in its place on his belt. It was a small comfort. A knife wouldn't be of much use against a man armed with a sword. And certainly not four of them.

"Easy now," the man said. "We'll not harm you if you mean no harm to us."

Flyn eased out from behind the tree. The other two men still on their horses had drawn their swords as well. Flyn put his hands out in front of him and walked slowly toward the road.

"Who are you and what are you doing hiding in the woods?" The man handed his torch to one of the others and climbed off his horse. He waited for Flyn, his sword in front of him.

"My name is Flyn. Flynygyn Geirrsen."

"That answers who you are but not what you are doing here."

"My friend and I are lost. We're looking for help to get back home."

"Well, Flynygyn Geirrsen, my name is Gudbrant, son of Adalwolf." The man lowered his sword, but kept it in front of him. "Where is this friend you speak of?"

"He's sleeping. Back there." Flyn pointed into the woods.

Gudbrant studied him for a minute then lowered his sword completely.

"You certainly look lost, boy. Where is home?"

"We're from—"

A loud shout interrupted him.

"Get 'em lads!"

Flyn turned in time to see three orcs jump out of the trees from behind him. He recognized one as the large orc he had seen the first day.

He tried to run, but one of the orcs knocked him aside. His head hit a tree. His vision blurred and faded. As he lost consciousness, he heard a familiar voice.

"There's the other one! See, Kargguk! We tell you they here!"

CHAPTER 5

Flyn paced around the small room, occasionally stopping to look through the bars in the only window. The street outside was dark and quiet. He had no idea how long he had been there, only that the moon had set and dawn had not yet come.

The only furniture in the small room was a chair and a cot. A lantern hung in the corner and an earthen pitcher of water, now empty, sat on the floor next to the cot. Even though he was exhausted, he was too frustrated to sleep. He had given up banging on the door and yelling to be let out several hours ago.

He was standing at the window again, looking out at the empty street, when the lock clicked and the door opened. Gudbrant, now without his armor, entered the room.

"Why am I locked in here?" Flyn asked. His face flushed with anger and frustration.

"Just relax." Gudbrant closed the door and motioned toward the cot, indicating he wanted Flyn to sit. "Let's discuss what you were doing wandering around in the woods last night."

Flyn stayed standing.

Gudbrant was taller than Flyn, over six feet. Flyn had trouble estimating his age. From deep lines around his eyes and mouth and across his brow, he seemed to be much older than Flyn, though he carried himself as a younger man. His clothing was simple, a dark green tunic with brown pants and heavy leather boots, but clean and well-tailored. On the left side of his chest, the tunic bore an insignia of a bird with spread wings, its talons extended below it as if it was about to grasp its prey. The neck of the tunic was trimmed with two gold braids.

Gudbrant shrugged and sat in the chair. Crossing his arms, he looked up at Flyn with raised eyebrows and waited. After a long awkward moment of silence, Flyn sat down on the cot.

"You haven't answered why I'm locked up," Flyn said, calmer this time.

"I apologize, but these are dangerous times. You may be exactly who you say you are, a lost traveler. But then you may not. We can't afford to take that chance. I'm sure you understand."

"No, I don't understand. I don't understand any of this. I don't even know where I am. And where's Kel? Do you have him locked up too?"

"Kel? Is that the name of your companion?"

"Yes. Where is he?"

Gudbrant hesitated and looked away before answering.

"You're in the town of Garthset. As for your friend…" Gudbrant paused again. "We were able to drive off the orcs. Fortunately, the ogres didn't get involved. But the orcs took a captive with them when they left. It must have been your friend."

Flyn jumped up, ignoring the pain that flared in his side. "Are you sure? He was sleeping in the woods off the path. Did you check for him?"

Gudbrant nodded. "We found your campsite and gathered your belongings. Your friend was not there. We found this on the ground."

Gudbrant pulled something out of his pocket and tossed it to Flyn.

It was Kel's stupid hat.

"We have to go after them! I have to save Kel!"

"I'm sorry for your friend, but there's no rescuing him." Gudbrant looked at Flyn, pity in his eyes.

"What do you mean? We have to save him."

"Once Jarot's slavers capture a man…" He paused for a moment. "Or a woman, there's no rescue. His forces are too great. Even if we knew where your friend was being taken, which could be almost anywhere, we would need an army to free him."

Gudbrant looked away again.

"But there must be something we can do?"

Flyn could not accept that his friend was gone. He had talked Kel into coming on his grand trip around Trygsted, and that made Kel his responsibility. Even if Flyn could find a way home, he would never go back without Kel. How could he? Kel's family would never forgive him, even if he somehow found a way to forgive himself. The pair had rarely been apart for more than a few days at a time. Kel was his brother, in some ways even more than Ty.

No, more than just a brother. Kel was Flyn's anchor. He kept Flyn out of trouble. At least most of the time. It was Flyn who always came up with the wild schemes and plans. Kel was the voice of caution. He usually talked Flyn out of his more dangerous ideas. And even when he couldn't, Kel still managed to keep Flyn from getting into too much trouble. If not for Kel, Flyn would probably be sitting in the Drogave jail. Or worse.

Like the one he was in now.

He looked up at Gudbrant. "Why would they take Kel?"

Gudbrant raised his eyebrow. "To be a slave for Jarot, of course."

"Who's Jarot?"

Gudbrant stared at him before answering. "He's the last of the Yonarr."

"The Yonarr? What's that?"

"Where is it that you come from?" Gudbrant asked after a long pause.

"We live on another island called Trygsted."

"Trygsted?" Gudbrant stood up. "I have no time for liars. I'll have someone bring you some food when the kitchens open, then you can be on your way. Until then, you'll stay here. With the door locked."

Gudbrant turned to leave.

"Wait!" Flyn jumped up and grabbed Gudbrant's arm. "I'm not lying. I'm Flynygyn Geirrsen of the Andor clan. I live just outside

Drogave, on the west coast of Trygsted. Kel and I were trying to travel around the island in our boat when we got caught in a storm that blew us to your island. You have to believe me."

Gudbrant looked down at Flyn's hand then up at Flyn. Flyn let go of his arm and stood, waiting.

"You're of the Andor clan," he said.

Flyn nodded.

"And you live on Trygsted."

Flyn nodded again.

"This isn't Trygsted. This is Tirmar, and it isn't an island." Gudbrant walked out, closing the door behind him. Flyn heard the lock click.

The sun was up before the door opened again. A young girl brought in a tray filled with breakfast foods. She didn't speak, just smiled shyly at Flyn, then set the tray down and left.

A guard stood outside the door, sword drawn, waiting for her to deliver the food. He was dressed in the same brown pants and green tunic as Gudbrant, though without the gold braid around the neck. He was even bigger than Gudbrant, almost seven feet tall. He could almost pass for a small orc. Apparently to keep him from trying to overpower the delivery girl and escaping. Not that the guard was necessary. Flyn wasn't in any condition to overpower anyone. Even without the injury to his ribs, several days of climbing and hiking with limited food left him far from his peak form.

The meal the girl left was more than he had eaten since leaving home. Flyn hadn't realized quite how hungry he was until he smelled the bacon, eggs, and toasted wheat cakes. Within minutes he had devoured the entire meal and washed it down with a large mug of a fruit juice he didn't recognize. If nothing else, at least they had good food.

After he ate, Flyn spent the next hour staring through the bars in the window at the morning outside.

From what he could see, he was in a large village or small town.

The window overlooked the street in front of the building. Other buildings he could see looked to be shops for food, clothing, and tools. They all appeared to be made from stone, with wood doors and shutters. Even the roofs seemed to be made from thin, overlapping slabs of rock. The street was paved with flagstones, similar to the mountain pass, though not with the same level of craftsmanship.

People moved quickly along the street, not stopping to socialize. Everyone seemed to be focused on their tasks, whatever they happened to be. Occasionally, pairs of men on horseback rode by, wearing the same kind of leather armor worn by the men the previous evening. For all the people, the street seemed oddly quiet. The only sounds were from the horses' hooves on the flagstones and the clanging of a blacksmith hammer from somewhere nearby.

Flyn sighed and turned away from the window. He was still trying to understand what Gudbrant had said. The orcs had kidnapped Kel to be a slave for someone named Jarot. But why Kel? He remembered the ogres saying something about escaped slaves, but he and Kel weren't slaves.

And why would Gudbrant think he was lying about coming from Trygsted? He had clearly heard of Trygsted, which was more than Flyn could say about Tirmar. And he had said Tirmar wasn't an island. What did that mean?

Flyn had more questions now than he had before he had met Gudbrant and his people. Why were they holding him captive? He hadn't done anything to them. Although, he supposed none of that mattered now. All that really mattered was getting out and finding Kel.

Flyn looked up as the door opened again. Gudbrant came in, the guard standing behind him, sword still drawn.

"Well, Flynygyn of the Andors, the Thane wants to speak with you."

"Why?" Flyn wasn't feeling very cooperative after being locked up for hours.

"I guess he found your story more intriguing than I did, although I think it's a waste of time. You're obviously lying, and it's not even a very good lie. Do you really expect people to believe that you're from Trygsted or part of the Lost Clan?"

"Lost Clan? What does that mean?"

Gudbrant grunted. "Let's go. The Thane is a very busy man, especially now. You'll not keep him waiting."

Flyn followed Gudbrant from the room. The guard fell in behind him.

Gudbrant stopped at the door to the street and turned to Flyn. "Don't try running. Harvig here is faster than he looks. I suspect the Thane will allow you to leave after he's spoken with you. Unless you prove to be something more than a liar."

Flyn just nodded, then followed Gudbrant out the door.

The air still had a cool bite, like a crisp winter morning in spite of the season, though the sun was just cresting over the mountain peaks to the east, promising a warmer afternoon. Only a few wispy clouds floating overhead interrupted the expanse of rich blue sky. The light spring breeze carried the same flowery spring scent Flyn had noticed before. Suddenly, he was very homesick.

The road in front of the building only went a few hundred yards to the east before ending at a gate in a large stone wall. Several guards stood on top of the wall, looking out beyond it. A small building that Flyn suspected housed more guards stood next to the closed gate.

Gudbrant led him away from the gate, the sun at their backs. The town was bigger than Flyn had first guessed. The buildings continued beyond his sight, all of them made of stone, but of varying designs. Most of them low, squat buildings housing various shops. Aside from signs identifying them, the fronts of the shops were mostly unadorned. A few of the buildings appeared to be residences, some single-story structures like the shops, others two stories. Many of the residences were distinguished from the shops by low hedgerows or flower gardens in the front. Flyn noticed that very few of the windows were open. On most, the shutters were closed tight.

Side streets intersected the main road at regular intervals. Most of the streets were dirt, though a few were paved with the same flagstones as the main road. The buildings on the paved side streets were predominantly shops and saloons, while those on the dirt streets seemed to be mainly houses, though not as nice as the ones on the main road.

People traveling the other way passed them without stopping. Some glanced suspiciously at Flyn, though none spoke. They all hurried along, going about whatever business they were attending to. Most had swords or daggers attached to their belts. Flyn sensed a tension in the air of the street, a foreboding even in the bright morning sunshine.

After several blocks, they arrived at a large building with three stories, the only one he had seen with more than two. A tower built into the middle of the building climbed another thirty feet above the roof. At the top was a large bell and several guards watching the streets in all directions. Unlike the gray stone the other buildings were made from, the stone of this building was almost pure white. The entrance to the building was a pair of massive wooden doors, reinforced with metal bracing. Guards stood on either side of the doors, swords drawn. Above the doors, carved in a stone lintel: "To Serve the People of Garthset."

The guards saluted Gudbrant with their swords as the trio approached. Gudbrant returned the salute, then the closest guard pulled open one of the doors. Flyn followed Gudbrant into the building.

The floor and walls of the main hall were made of the same white stone as the exterior. They almost seemed to glow in the light of the lanterns that were mounted on the walls. The ceiling was made of wood, polished to an almost mirror finish. Several doors, every bit as magnificent as the main doors, lined both sides of the hallway, three on either side. Each had a plaque mounted on it, denoting its purpose: Treasury, Defense, Agriculture, and others. Apparently offices for the town administrators.

At the far end of the hall, a stone staircase led up to the second floor. Another pair of guards at the bottom of the staircase saluted Gudbrant as the group passed.

On the second floor, another hallway led to a pair of closed doors, again flanked by a pair of guards. The walls were still stone, only here the floor was the same highly polished wood as the ceiling. Instead of doors, the walls of the second-floor hallway were adorned with paintings of serious-looking men dressed in fancy clothes, most appearing quite old. The oldest portraits were the ones at the very end of the hall, by the double doors.

Once again, the guards saluted Gudbrant, who returned the salute, then stepped up and knocked on the door. The door was immediately opened by another guard stationed inside the room. The neck of this guard's tunic was trimmed in a single gold braid, similar to Gudbrant's double braid.

The guard saluted, then greeted Gudbrant.

"Captain Gudbrant. The Thane is waiting for you."

"Thank you, Lieutenant."

Gudbrant led Flyn into the room. Harvig stayed at the door with the Lieutenant.

The room spanned the width of the house, with windows on either side as well as the front. The walls were the familiar white stone as the rest of the building, though they were mostly covered with paintings and tapestries.

Opposite the door was a large desk with two chairs in front of it. Behind it sat an elderly man, shuffling papers. He stood as they entered and came around the desk to greet his visitors.

"Health and happiness, friend!" the man said, grasping Flyn's forearm in greeting. Flyn reciprocated, eyeing the man. He smiled at Flyn, but the smile showed no happiness.

He was almost as large as Gudbrant, though not as lean. A nasty-looking scar ran down one cheek from his eye to his square jaw. His deeply lined face was framed by long, gray hair, tied back. His clothing appeared to be made from silk, with a dark red tunic and dark blue pants. A leather belt with a large, gold buckle was wrapped around his waist. His feet were covered in brown leather shoes, buffed to a shine that rivaled the finely polished floors and ceilings.

The man held Flyn's arm for a moment, his eyes, pale blue and deep-set, staring straight into Flyn's.

"Come, have a seat so we can talk," he said, finally releasing Flyn's arm. He sat in one of the chairs in front of his desk and motioned for Flyn to sit in the other. Gudbrant stood still between the chairs, his hands clasped behind his back.

"My name is Meinrad," he said after Flyn sat. "I'm the Thane of Garthset. And your name is Flynygyn?"

"Most people call me Flyn."

"Flyn. Very good, then. I trust you had a good rest in the barracks? I know they aren't the most comfortable accommodations."

"It was fine," Flyn said, more to be polite than because it was true.

"Good, good. Gudbrant tells me that you claim to be part of the Andor clan?"

Flyn nodded.

"And that you are from Trygsted?"

"Yes, but he thinks I'm lying."

"And why shouldn't he?"

"I don't understand. You've heard of Trygsted?"

"Of course."

"Well, I've never heard of… Tirmar is what you called it?"

Meinrad nodded.

"On Trygsted, we're taught that there are no other islands or other people."

"Do you know anything of the Yonarr or the Revolution?"

Flyn shook his head.

"I don't think he's lying," Meinrad said to Gudbrant, who just grunted in response.

"Why don't you tell us how you ended up here," the Thane said, turning back to Flyn.

"I suppose it all started when I built a boat a few years ago." Flyn recounted the story of his boat, of how people in Drogave were becoming suspicious of him and Kel, and their plan to take the boat to the other side of Trygsted to destroy it. He told them of the storm, and everything that had happened since, including their encounters with the orcs and the ogres.

When he was finished, Meinrad sat back, watching Flyn and stroking his chin.

"That's quite a tale, young man," he said after a long moment. "And why should we believe you?"

"I don't know," Flyn said, shaking his head. "But I don't really care. I just need to find Kel."

"Well, that's quite impossible."

"That's what Gudbrant said, but I don't really understand why," Flyn said. "Anyway, I have to try. It's my fault he's caught up in this mess. Why won't you just let me go? I don't even know why am I being held here. I didn't ask for help. I can find Kel on my own."

"Gudbrant here is the Captain of the Garthset Militia. It's his job to protect this town and its citizens. We don't get many visitors these days. It's not safe to travel, with the orcs constantly patrolling the valley. So those few we do get, we have to question their loyalties. Jarot has tried to send spies into Garthset before."

"Who's Jarot? I heard the orcs mention that name, then Gudbrant mentioned him this morning."

"Well, Gudbrant?" Meinrad said, turning to the impassive soldier. "Do you still think he's lying?"

"Perhaps he's just mad."

Meinrad grinned. "Perhaps. Or perhaps he truly is from the Lost Clan."

"What's this Lost Clan? Why is it so hard to believe I'm from Trygsted?"

Meinrad glanced at Gudbrant before responding. Gudbrant just stared straight ahead at the shield hanging on the wall behind the Thane's desk.

"Because, young man, Trygsted is a myth."

Meinrad stood and walked to one of the windows.

"Long ago the Yonarr ruled over Tirmar," Meinrad said, staring out the window. "There were great cities and machines. The world was full of magic. I suppose, for the Yonarr, life was good."

He turned back and looked at Flyn.

"For humans, life was not. You see, the Yonarr were very powerful, but there were too few of them to maintain their cities. They had to rely on slaves. Human slaves."

He walked back to his desk and sat in his chair.

"Almost all the humans in Tirmar were slaves to the Yonarr. The elves and dwarves too, for that matter. They had many other slaves as well. Orcs and trolls were chief among them, but unlike the humans, elves, and dwarves, the orcs and trolls didn't care about being subjugated. In fact, they thrived on it, so the Yonarr used them as slave masters to keep the others in line."

"And the ogres too?" Flyn interrupted.

"No, the ogres weren't slaves. The legend is that they are descended from the Yonarr, but if they are, they're very different beings. The Yonarr are powerful and intelligent, maybe more than even the wisest of humans. Ogres are dull brutes, but they tend to keep to themselves unless they want something.

"In any case, that was how it was for hundreds of years. Perhaps thousands. No one knows for sure. Over time, the Yonarr grew lazy and the slaves began to rebel. How it began, I do not know. But however it began, the humans and elves and dwarves were able to overthrow their Yonarr masters and thus began the Tirmar Revolution.

"The war lasted decades, and in the process, all the Yonarr cities were destroyed, and most of the Yonarr were killed or driven from Tirmar. Eventually, Mijon, the ruler of the Yonarr, was defeated. The remaining Yonarr fled, along with the orcs and trolls and others who were loyal to them.

"The humans were led by four leaders: Ilfin, Ranjer, Mundar, and Andor."

"Andor?" Flyn interrupted again.

"Yes. They each had a different philosophy about the world, and so after the war, they went their separate ways. But the people were lost without them, so the humans divided into the four clans, each following the leader whose philosophy they identified with. Andor felt the Yonarr would one day return, so he left Tirmar with his followers. He built great ships to find the mythical land of Trygsted where legend had it the Yonarr could never go.

"The problem was that it was just a legend. Most people thought it was just a story mothers told their young children before the war to give them hope that one day they would be free from the Yonarr. There were some who believed it was real, but no man could get there, that it was an enchanted realm that required great magic to enter. Very few believed Andor would find Trygsted, so only a handful followed him when he left. Some say as few as fifty, others as many as five hundred, though there were no records to be sure. They sailed from Egrathwaite and were never heard from again.

"So, Flynygyn of the Andors, you see why your story sounds like a tall tale."

Flyn sat back, trying to absorb what the Thane had told him.

"I've always wondered why there was only one clan on Trygsted," he said finally. "Our priests teach that our clan was chosen by Andor the Great to live on Trygsted and that he brought us there from Vahul, where we return when we die."

Meinrad laughed. "You're not from Vahul. But perhaps you were chosen by the gods to live in Trygsted. No others who have ever looked for it since have found it."

"But what about this Jarot? Gudbrant said he was the last of the Yonarr, but you said they were all dead."

"No, I said they fled Tirmar. A few decades ago, orcs began appearing in remote parts of Northeastern Tirmar. At first it was just rumors about orcs capturing unsuspecting travelers. After a while, orc raiding parties began attacking smaller towns and villages, taking prisoners back into the Nidfel Mountains. Over time, they began to travel in the open, their war cries calling Jarot's name.

"The Ilfin clan was a peaceful people. After the war, the other clans argued that we should prepare for the return of the Yonarr. The Ilfins, however, believed that if we just left them alone, they would leave us alone. After all, there were only a handful of them left, and though they are immortal, they can't procreate. So the Ilfins argued that they would never again be a threat.

"A miscalculation, I suppose. Our ancestors never thought the orcs and trolls would follow a single Yonarr. I suspect that's why Jarot chose this part of Tirmar. Our clan was easily splintered, many of our people taken as slaves. Those remaining retreated to the larger towns, such as Garthset. For a time, there was still trade between the towns, but of late, Jarot's forces have grown too powerful. Rare is news from others of the Ilfin clan. Rarer still is news from the other clans. Those who are caught by Jarot's minions are never seen again. My own daughter was taken not even two weeks ago."

Meinrad bowed his head and didn't speak for a long time.

Flyn broke the silence. "Did you send anyone to try to find her?"

Meinrad looked up, his eyes filled with tears.

"No," he said, shaking his head. "As I said, there's no rescuing someone taken by Jarot."

"But she's your daughter," Flyn insisted.

"Don't you think I want to rescue her?" Meinrad yelled, jumping to his feet and leaning over the desk toward Flyn. "I would give anything to have her back, but there's nothing I can do. Gudbrant wanted to go after her single-handedly. Stopping him was the hardest thing I have ever had to do in my life."

Meinrad sat back down. "Brenna, my dear, sweet Brenna. I miss you so."

He turned away to hide his sobs from his visitors.

"My Lord," Gudbrant said. "We'll take our leave of you."

Meinrad didn't respond.

"Let's go," Gudbrant said to Flyn.

The two men left the way they came, only this time Flyn walked next to Gudbrant instead of behind. Harvig had hurried out ahead of them and was out of sight before they reached the street.

Gudbrant was quiet as they walked.

"You know," Gudbrant said after a few minutes, "I almost disobeyed the Thane's order and went after Brenna."

"Why? If it's so impossible to rescue people who have been taken, why would you risk it?"

Gudbrant sighed and was quiet again. As they reached the barracks, he stopped and turned to Flyn.

"Because she was to be my wife."

"I'm sorry," Flyn mumbled. He didn't know how else to respond.

"If you go after your friend, you'll likely be killed."

Flyn nodded. "I understand, but I have to try."

Gudbrant studied him. "I can see that no one will talk you out of it."

"No. I would never be able to live with myself if I didn't at least try."

Gudbrant nodded slowly before responding.

"You won't go alone. I'm coming with you."

Flyn was anxious to set out to look for Kel, but Gudbrant insisted that he complete his recovery before leaving. He told Flyn the ride would be hard, and if they were forced into a fight, Flyn would be worthless if his ribs hadn't healed yet. The town doctor told him he should wait a month before getting involved in any strenuous activity. Flyn refused to wait longer than two weeks.

During his recovery, Flyn and Gudbrant met with Meinrad to discuss their plans to search for Kel and Brenna. As Gudbrant predicted, the Thane was less than accommodating.

"No," Meinrad said when Gudbrant told him of their plan. "Absolutely not. I forbid it."

"My Lord," Gudbrant said, "I know in the past we have never been successful in rescuing those taken, but that is not a reason not to try."

"Don't you think I want her rescued, Gudbrant? She is all I have left. Without her, my only purpose in life is to be Thane, until such time the people feel another should sit in my stead. It is a hollow existence. I weep for my little girl every night, and wake every morning hoping her loss was just a terrible nightmare. I grieve for her absence, but mostly I grieve for what she must be enduring, wherever the foul Jarot has taken her. And yet, I am powerless to change this. I'm just an old man, and what is an old man without a wife or children?"

Meinrad paused, his eyes full of tears.

"If her rescue were possible, I would go myself to bring her home from whatever damnation she is suffering. What I will not do is send more of my people to their deaths or worse to try and save her. As much as I grieve for her, her life can be no more important than any other."

He turned to Gudbrant.

"I know you grieve for her as well, my friend. Do not let your grief become your doom. I will not have your death on my conscience."

"Let your conscience be clear, My Lord. You are not ordering or even asking me to go. I go of my own free will. And if I may beg your pardon, I will go without your consent if necessary."

The old man sighed and put his arm around Gudbrant's shoulders.

He led Gudbrant to the window where they could see the town laid out around them. Flyn stood alone, for the moment, ignored by the two men.

"What do you see when you look upon Garthset?"

"I see my home."

"Do you know what I see? I see my family. Now more so than ever. A Thane is not their ruler. He is their leader. They have put their trust in me to guide them, to keep them safe. With the threat of war on our doorstep, my best tool, my only tool, to keep them safe is the Militia. And you, my old friend, are the handle. Without you, that tool is useless."

"Haller can lead in my place while I am gone. He's a very capable soldier."

"But he lacks experience. No, you cannot abandon your family in its greatest time of need. You and I suffer the same fate. We are not granted the privilege of having our own lives, of making choices for ourselves. We must put Garthset, indeed the entire valley of Asgerdale, ahead of our own desires."

"I understand, My Lord. And yet, I still must go. I will see her safely returned home or die in the trying. I have no choice. I have tried to accept her fate as the will of the gods, but alas, I am haunted by Brenna in my dreams. I cannot lead the Militia while my heart holds out hope that she yet lives. If I must resign my position, so be it."

"Would you sacrifice all of Garthset for one woman? Surely, you see the folly in that?"

"I do, My Lord. And still I must follow my heart."

Meinrad sighed again and walked back to his desk. On top of the desk was a map. He looked at it for several minutes before speaking again.

"Very well, Gudbrant," the Thane said. "It seems I cannot stop you from going. I shall at least provide you with the best chance for success. But tell me, where will you look for her?"

"I'll start at Gurnborg," Gudbrant said, pointing to a town on the map. "Surely they would have taken her there first. If she's not there, we'll find someone who has seen her and knows where they've taken her."

"I think I know," Flyn said, speaking for the first time since they had arrived in the Thane's audience chamber. A thought had come to him.

Both men looked up at Flyn, their eyebrows raised.

"And how would you, stranger to our land, know where our enemy has taken my daughter?"

"Our first day in Tirmar, when we came across the orc patrol. I didn't know who they were, so I hid and listened to their conversation. One of them was talking about a woman he had recently captured. She was on horseback and they talked about how she fought back. She even stabbed one of the orcs with a knife. Apparently, she told one of them that she was someone important."

Gudbrant and Meinrad exchanged a glance, then turned back to Flyn.

"Did they say anything about what she looked like?" Gudbrant asked.

"No. But she had long hair. One of the orcs said he pulled her off her horse by her hair."

Meinrad gasped, but Gudbrant just scowled.

"Sorry, that's just what he said." Flyn realized he probably should have left out that detail.

"That could be her," Gudbrant said to Meinrad. "She was on horseback when she left that morning and she certainly would have fought back."

"Even if it was her, how does that help?" Meinrad said. "Already knew she was captured by those filthy animals."

"That was the thing," Flyn said. "They were talking about how she was being sent to the master's palace."

Meinrad sat down in his chair, as if his legs had collapsed. Gudbrant hung his head.

"Why?" Flyn said. "What's so special about the master's palace?"

"It's Jarot's personal residence," Gudbrant said. "That's the one place we cannot go." He sat down in one of the chairs in front of Meinrad's desk and put his head in his hands.

The color had drained from Meinrad's face. He sat staring at nothing, his jaw hanging loose.

"Why can't we go there?" Flyn asked.

"Because, my young friend, that is the most well protected place in all of Tirmar. Not even a ghost could slip in there without Jarot knowing about it."

"I'm still going," Flyn told Gudbrant.

After leaving the Thane's Manor, he and Gudbrant had returned to the barracks. Gudbrant was even quieter than usual on the walk back. Now they were sitting in the mess hall, their lunch plates nearly untouched.

"I suspected you would say as much." Gudbrant stared at his now-cold soup as he slowly stirred it. "The Thane has forbidden me to go, but he has no authority over you. You may do as you please. Take fair warning, though. Your quest is destined to fail."

"Maybe so, but I have to go." Flyn had explained himself to Gudbrant several times in the days prior. He didn't see a point in discussing it again.

He and Gudbrant had grown close during Flyn's recovery. Flyn had been encouraged about his chances by having Gudbrant at his side. They had spent much time planning their journey to Gurnborg, the logical first destination. Now, knowing he would be on his own, the hopelessness he had felt his first day in Garthset returned.

"You won't go alone, Andor." Gudbrant was looking at him now, apparently guessing his thoughts.

"But what about the Thane's orders?"

"He forbade me to go," Gudbrant said, a small smile on his face. "He never said no one else could go with you."

"Who?"

"I'm going to send Randell with you. He's my best tracker. You met him the night we found you in the woods."

Flyn was surprised by the offer.

"Gudbrant," Flyn said after a long silence. "I am grateful for the help, so don't take my question the wrong way, but why? After all you've said about how we'll likely die trying to find Kel and Brenna, and how you wouldn't allow anyone else to risk his life on a fool's errand. Why have you changed your mind?"

"A fool's errand, yes, with little chance for survival. But alone, you stand none. Randell has already volunteered to help. I told him no, but now... Perhaps the two of you will at least discover the fate of your friend. Maybe you will find him serving meals to the orcs in Gurnborg. Or working in the mine."

Gudbrant fell silent again and returned to stirring his soup. Flyn, too upset to eat before, now found himself too excited to eat.

"I would prefer you should get some rest," Gudbrant said. "You'll leave this evening, just before the gates are closed for the night, and we have much to accomplish before then. Our first task will be to make sure you're better equipped."

Gudbrant rose without finishing his meal. Flyn hurried after him.

"Our first stop will be the armory. We should be able to find something to fit you. And you'll need a better weapon than that knife."

Gudbrant led him through the barracks to the rear of the building, an area Flyn had not been to before. Soldiers guarding the entrance to the armory saluted Gudbrant and let them pass without comment. Once inside, Gudbrant introduced Flyn to the duty guard, a stout man named Agilric. He instructed Agilric to outfit Flyn with anything he needed, then left before either could say anything.

Agilric brought him a leather harness, similar to the one Flyn had seen Gudbrant wearing the night they met, and a pair of leather leg plates. He even found a pair of old leather armguards that fit Flyn. Flyn came across a leather helmet that would protect most of his face as well as his head.

Flyn had never worn armor or used a sword, so he had to rely completely on Agilric's help to make sure everything fit properly. Agilric gave him a belt that had holes for attaching weapons and pouches. To these, he attached a short sword, a large pouch, and a waterskin. Wearing all the gear, Flyn could barely move. He also felt a little foolish, like he was a child dressing up for the harvest festival. Still, the armor and weapons gave him some comfort that he would be better protected should he find himself in a fight with an orc.

He was still trying on boots when Gudbrant returned. Randell, the tracker, was with him. Gudbrant introduced Randell to Flyn, and then turned his attention to Flyn's gear.

"Not the best-fitting armor I've seen, but it'll do," Gudbrant said, inspecting and tightening Flyn's harness and armguards. "You're a little smaller than most of my militiamen."

Flyn had noticed that too. He was smaller than just about everybody in Garthset, even the women.

Gudbrant made a few more adjustments, then stood back to look at him.

"You look like you're ready to take on Ugglar himself."

"Ugglar?" Flyn remembered hearing the orcs mention the name.

"He's one of Jarot's Lieutenants. He's in charge of the garrison at Gurnborg."

"Where we're going?"

Gudbrant nodded.

"Does he even know how to use that sword?" Agilric asked.

Everyone turned to Flyn. His cheeks flushed with embarrassment. He looked to the floor and shook his head.

"Don't worry about it," Gudbrant said, clapping him on the shoulder. "Randell can teach you a few things this afternoon. At least enough to keep you from cutting your own leg off."

The three militiamen laughed. Flyn wanted to sink into the floor and crawl away.

"Do you know how to use a bow?" Gudbrant asked.

"I'm great with a bow," Flyn said, perking up. "I can hit a running deer at fifty yards."

The men laughed again.

"Well, then let us hope the orcs run no faster than a deer!"

Agilric led Flyn to a long rack full of bows. He tried several before settling on one. Agilric attached a quiver to Flyn's belt, then showed him to the barrels full of arrows. Flyn filled his quiver, inspecting each arrow before storing it.

"I think I'm ready," Flyn said when he was done.

Gudbrant smiled and nodded. "Very good, don't you think, Randell?" Gudbrant said, turning to the tracker.

"I'd feel better with you at my side, Captain," Randell said, frowning at Flyn. "But let us see what the young one can do with that sword before we judge one way or another."

Gudbrant thanked Agilric for his service, then led Flyn and Randell to the courtyard where Flyn would spend the next few hours with Randell learning how to fight.

CHAPTER 6

F lyn was sore from his afternoon sword training with Randell, and his ribs still ached from his injury, which didn't help. He had never realized how hard sword fighting was. Randell had been patient with him, teaching him a basic fighting stance and how to slice and parry. He didn't know how much it would help, but at least by the end of the training session, he wasn't dropping the sword as much. Randell promised to teach him more during their travels. Flyn hoped that he would be able to defend himself by the time he needed to use his new skill.

As planned, Flyn was waiting for Randell near the main gate just before sunset. He was wearing his new leather armor, his sword and quiver of arrows attached to the belt, as well as his new waterskin and a belt pouch full of what Gudbrant called "high energy snacks." He had attached his old hunting knife to the belt using waxed twine.

Gudbrant had provided him with a new pack, larger than his old one, filled with provisions for the journey, mostly cured meats, dried fruits, and hard loaves. The pack had a belt that, when used properly, took the weight off the shoulders, making it easier to carry for long treks. Flyn was grateful for that, as his new pack was significantly heavier than the one he had carried from home. It even had pockets on the outside for tools like his flint and steel, and eating utensils. In the top of the pack, another gift from Gudbrant, was a new bedroll made with a fur lining that made it warmer than his own simple blanket.

Other items Flyn had tied to his pack included a coil of rope and a new cloak, one better suited for their journey through the mountains. Made from oiled leather and lined with fur, like the bedroll, it provided protection from cold, wind, and rain. It even had a hood to keep his head warm and dry. He had gloves made from similar material in the cloak's pockets.

Across everything he carried his new longbow.

Randell told him their path may take them higher into the mountains, and this time of year, storms were common. They might even see snow, though most likely they would be dealing with cold rain and bitter winds. Without the right clothing and equipment, they would die from the elements without any help from the enemy.

Flyn had been anxious to start on their journey all afternoon. Now, waiting at the gate with all his gear, he was more nervous than eager. Mentally reviewing everything he had packed, and the challenges ahead, he began to wonder if he was doing the right thing.

The task before them was daunting. First, they had to travel through the mountains, a potentially treacherous journey even without the weather or orcs to deal with. They would then have to infiltrate an orc garrison and find Kel, or if he wasn't there, find someone who could tell them what had happened to Kel. If that was the case, they might have to travel even more dangerous routes. Assuming they even found his friend, the hardest part would be rescuing him from his captors without being captured or killed themselves.

Each step seemed to be a near impossible task. And yet, even if they located Kel and found a way to rescue him, their biggest challenge remained. They would have to elude orc patrols, and most likely pursuers, all the way back to Garthset. Orcs who were stronger and faster, and were more familiar with the land than Randell.

Surely their chance of ever seeing Garthset again was small.

And yet, in his heart, he knew he still must try. He couldn't live knowing Kel's fate was in his hands.

"Are you ready?"

Flyn started. Randell had walked up behind him while he was lost in thought. He was dressed similarly to Flyn, with leather armor and a large pack. He carried a bundle of short, metal poles.

"As ready as I can be, I think. What are those?" Flyn asked, pointing at the bundle.

"These are for our tent. I'm carrying the canvas. You get to carry the poles. Turn around."

Randell secured the poles to Flyn's pack. When he was finished, he turned Flyn around and stepped back, inspecting him.

"Looks like you have everything in place. Let's get moving before they close the gates for the night."

Flyn nodded and followed Randell through the main gate. His guide waved to the guards keeping watch on top of the wall. Flyn's heart raced and his stomach fluttered as they passed under the archway. Then they were through, the city behind them, the valley forest in front. Flyn stopped and looked back through the gates.

"You aren't changing your mind, are you?" Randell asked with a grin.

"No. I was just expecting Gudbrant to come see us off."

Randell grunted and turned back to the path. "So did I. In fact, I haven't seen him since your training session this afternoon. Something important must have come up. Let's get moving. I want to get at least three leagues before morning."

Flyn turned his back to the town and jogged to catch up with Randell.

Their plan was to travel at night. They would be less likely to run into patrols that way and they could hide their camp in the woods during the day. They would also have better luck sneaking into Gurnborg in the dark, so Gudbrant had suggested they should acclimate themselves to working at night. With everything that was against them, they should avail themselves of even the smallest advantage.

Gurnborg was almost a week's journey by foot. Randell had wanted to take horses. They could have made the trip in two or three nights on horseback, but Gudbrant had pointed out that stealth was more important than speed, and there was no way to hide two horses. They had even discussed taking a third person who could return with the horses when they got close to their destination. Gudbrant had rejected that idea as well, with no explanation. Flyn suspected that he didn't want to ask anyone else to risk his life on a journey that was all but doomed to fail.

"So why did you agree to come with me?" Flyn asked after they had been walking for a while.

Randell didn't answer immediately. When he finally spoke, his voice was quiet and far away.

"I owe Gudbrant my life."

Again, Randell was quiet for a while. For a minute, Flyn thought he wasn't going to say any more than that. Finally, he continued.

"When I was a boy, Asgerdale was peaceful. There were no walls around Garthset, and many people had farms in the valley. We knew of Jarot, of course, but his fortress is far to the north and his minions never traveled this far south. There were rumors from farther north of orcs raiding outlying farms and small villages and taking prisoners back to Jarot's palace to be his slaves.

"In those days, most thought Jarot was just an orc warlord, if he existed at all. Gurnborg hadn't even been built yet. The Yonarr were gone, so no one even considered that Jarot might be a Yonarr. Stories of people disappearing were discounted as being victims of the harsh conditions in the north."

They walked in silence for a while before Randell continued.

"One night, an orc raiding party came into Asgerdale and attacked some of the outlying farms. I heard them smashing down the door to our house."

Flyn looked over at Randell, but the militiaman's eyes were lost in the past.

"I was only six years old at the time. I cracked my bedroom door to see what was happening. My father ran down the hall, yelling at the orcs, telling them to get out. The orcs just laughed at him, then one of them hit him with a club. My mother screamed and another one smacked her and knocked her to the ground. I didn't know what else to do, so I hid under my bed. When they started searching the house, I was terrified that they would find me, so I crawled out from under the bed and climbed out the window. I ran as fast as I could to the woods and when I looked back, I saw the orcs carrying off my mother and sister. They bound them by their hands and feet and threw them onto a cart. I never saw my father. Before they left, they set fire to our house, our barn, and our fields.

"I hid in the woods until morning. By then, the only thing left of my home was a pile of smoldering ash. I knew my father was dead and his body was somewhere in the midst of the remains of our house. I like to think the orcs killed him before they set fire to the house. The alternative is too hard to bear."

Again, Randell stopped speaking for a while.

"Anyway, sometime later that morning or early afternoon, a militia patrol from Garthset came to investigate. They had seen the smoke. I hid when I heard the horses coming. I watched as they sifted through the debris, looking for survivors, I suppose. Eventually, one of the men saw me looking out from a tree. It took him a while, but he finally convinced me to come out. He asked me what happened, and I told him. In the end, I cried and he held me until I stopped. Then he gave me some food and water. When they left, he put me on his horse in front of him and brought me back to Garthset.

"I've never forgotten what Gudbrant did for me that day. If he hadn't seen me, or convinced me to come out, I would have died out there. For a long time, I wished I had. The Thane found a family to take me in and raise me, and Gudbrant checked in on me almost every day. As I grew older, he taught me how to hunt and fish and ride a horse. Eventually he gave me my first sword and taught me how to fight. When I was old enough, I joined the militia. That was before it was mandatory for men to join when they came of age. I did it more than to just avenge my family. I did it because I wanted to be like Gudbrant.

"You asked me why I agreed to come with you. I would do anything Gudbrant asked of me. There is no doubt of that. But I hate the orcs with all my being. I have no illusions that I'll ever see my mother or my sister again, but if there's a chance of rescuing Brenna…"

Randell was quiet for a moment, then turned to Flyn. "If I can help you rescue your friend, then perhaps I may gain some peace. But I suggest you prepare yourself for failure. I have never heard of anyone being rescued from Jarot or any of his garrisons. His orcs seem just as content to kill humans as they do capturing them in the first place. Of course, the Ilfin clan is not really known for their fighting skill. Most would prefer to negotiate a peaceful solution than fight, but Jarot isn't interested in negotiating. Trying to convince them is like trying to get a horse to fly."

Flyn just nodded. Randell's story made him feel foolish about his own quest. Kel was like his brother, but Randell had lost his whole family. What right did Flyn have to ask his aid? He couldn't imagine going through what Randell had lived through.

"Thank you," Flyn said after a while. It was all he could think to say.

"I didn't mean to bring you down," Randell said, smiling. "But you asked. I haven't spoken of it in a long time, though I think about my family nearly every night before I fall asleep. I think maybe telling you helps me see my purpose in this quest a little clearer as well."

"So, tell me about Gudbrant," Flyn said.

Randell laughed. "Gudbrant. Now that's a subject that will take the entire journey to discuss. What would you have me tell you?"

"Why don't you tell me about—"

Randell stopped, putting his arm across Flyn's chest to stop him as well. He crouched down and eased off the road to the wood line, pulling Flyn with him.

"What is it?" Flyn whispered.

"I thought I saw movement on the road up ahead."

The moon was bright in the sky, allowing them to see the road and the tree line fairly well, albeit in shades of gray. Flyn looked, straining his eyes, but he didn't see anything out of the ordinary, moving or still.

"There!" Randell whispered and pointed to a spot a hundred yards away where the road curved to the left.

Flyn looked, but saw nothing but road and dark forest. Beside him, Randell was on his knees, sword in hand. Flyn hadn't even seen him draw it. His heart racing, he drew his own. The only sound he could hear was his pulse pounding in his ears.

Then, after several long minutes, Flyn finally saw something. A shadow slowly detached from the wood line and began moving toward them. Then another followed.

Flyn's mouth went dry, his chest and stomach tightened. In front of him, the end of his sword was shaking. He tried to stop it, but the shaking only got worse.

"Deep breath," Randell whispered next to him. "Breathe slow."

Flyn did as Randell instructed, trying to calm himself as the shadows crept closer. He tried to remember what Randell had taught him earlier that afternoon, but his mind was blank. He couldn't even remember which foot was supposed to be forward.

As the shadows came closer, their shapes clarified into the form of humanoids, though with the moon behind them, Flyn couldn't see their faces or make out any details. He couldn't even judge their sizes or how far away they were. They could be orcs or humans or maybe some other creature he knew nothing about.

The shadows were almost upon them when they stopped. Flyn clenched his jaw as his stomach threatened to relieve him of its contents.

"You there!" one of the shadows yelled. "Stop hiding like a pair of scared rabbits and come out."

"Gudbrant!" Randell yelled.

Flyn, still frozen with fear, watched as Randell jumped to his feet and ran out to meet the pair of figures in the road. Upon reaching the lead figure, Randell embraced him. They exchanged a few words, then Randell turned and called to Flyn.

"It's all right. It's Gudbrant and Harvig."

Flyn sighed in relief. He stood up, using his sword for support. His knees felt weak. Slowly, he walked out to the small group, his wobbly legs threatening to collapse.

The figures were indeed Gudbrant and Harvig.

"What are you doing here?" Flyn asked.

"I must apologize for the deception. I could not let it be known that I was joining you. Not after the Thane forbade it. I sent Randell with you because I knew he would keep you safe until I could rejoin you. My plan was to sneak out with no one knowing, but Harvig here already suspected my plans. He refused to allow me to leave unless I let him come with me. He really left me no choice." Gudbrant glanced back at the large militiaman standing silently behind him.

"But surely the Thane will suspect?" Randell said.

"Suspect perhaps, but he won't know. That was why I could not be seen leaving with Flyn. I spread rumors of an orc raiding party to the west and sent a patrol to investigate. Harvig and I left with the patrol. Once we were far enough from Garthset, I told the platoon leader I was feeling ill and sent them on without me. Harvig would escort me back to Garthset. Only instead of returning, we came here to wait for you."

"So everyone in Garthset will think you are with the patrol until they return," Randell said.

"Exactly. And they may even think that we were ambushed on the way back, so even then, the Thane won't know of my insubordination, though he may suspect."

"When we return, you will be lucky if all he does is remove you as Captain of the Militia."

"If we are successful in rescuing Brenna, he may do with me as he wills and I will happily accept his punishment."

"So you mean to go all the way to Uskleig?"

"What's Uskleig?" Flyn asked.

"It's the city Jarot built around his citadel," Gudbrant replied. "It's located far to the north, where the Estlaeg Mountains meet the Nidfel Mountains."

"And what if we aren't successful?" Randell asked.

"I will see Brenna freed or die trying."

"But everything you said about obeying the Thane?" Flyn interrupted.

"I was truthful when I spoke those words to you, Flyn. My decision was made after. But that is enough talk. We have a long road ahead of us."

Gudbrant and Harvig turned and walked off to where they had been waiting.

"This is unexpected," Randell said to Flyn. "But I feel our chance for success has just improved."

Gudbrant and Harvig gathered their gear and the small band of men set off again. Gudbrant approved of Randell's plan to try to put at least three leagues between them and Garthset before stopping.

The company made its first camp of the journey not far from the crossroads where Flyn had first met Gudbrant and Randell. Approaching the crossroads again in the dark gave Flyn a strange sense of familiarity. The last time he had seen the crossroads was on a night not much different from the one he was in now, the early glow of the coming sunrise reminding him of the fading glow of a sunset many weeks before. Even the earthy smell of a recent rain was the same.

The sight brought back memories of that night, the last time he had seen Kel. The orcs rushing from the trees, the ogres yelling from behind, the flash of steel as the militiamen fought to defend themselves from the onslaught.

A new thought occurred to him. The orcs had already found Kel when they attacked.

"I could have saved him," Flyn said, not realizing he had spoken out loud.

"Saved him?" Randell asked. "Kel?"

"Yes. I couldn't sleep that night, so I went for a walk. The orcs found him while I was at the crossroads. If I had just stayed with him, I could have woken him up and we could have escaped."

"If you had done that, you would have been captured as well. And without you to persuade Gudbrant to try to rescue Brenna, no one would be coming to save you."

"He's right," Gudbrant said. "Do not dwell on what brought you to a place. The past can serve to warn and to teach, but it makes a poor place to live. Know that because of your actions, your friend has a chance to yet see freedom. And your courage has reminded me that sometimes our own safety is secondary to those we love."

Flyn didn't respond. He didn't feel courageous or selfless. He felt guilty. He wasn't some hero from a fairytale, off to rescue the princess from the evil giant. He was just a man trying to fix his mistake so his friend didn't suffer for it. He didn't understand how that could motivate anyone. At least he wasn't on his own. The task seemed much too big for him alone.

Rather than debate his purpose in their quest, Flyn focused on helping Randell set up their tent. They had found a small clearing off the road to make camp that was surrounded by brush on three sides, hiding them from the road. Gudbrant and Harvig set up their own tent opposite Flyn and Randell.

They built a small fire to take the edge off the early morning chill. As they got closer to Gurnborg, they would have to go without as the chance of being noticed would be too great. This close to Garthset, they were unlikely to encounter a patrol.

"But what of the orcs that captured Kel?" Flyn asked. "They were right here."

"We haven't seen them that close to Garthset in many years. I think they were only here because they were looking for you and your friend."

"But why would they be looking for us?"

"That I cannot answer, but clearly they wanted to capture you as well as Kel. You said they were looking for you shortly after you arrived in Tirmar?"

"It was dark when we came ashore. They were looking for us the next morning. I heard them say something about pixies seeing us on the beach."

"There are pixies that live in the forest on the other side of the Estlaeg Mountains. They are timid, and won't fight unless cornered, but they are no less dangerous. They frequently act as spies for Jarot. But even for an orc, the coast of the Mithar Ocean is a many-day journey from Gurnborg. They must have been there already. But that still doesn't explain why Jarot would be so interested in you."

Flyn didn't know the answer to that question any more than Gudbrant.

The company ate a small meal, then crawled into their tents for some much-needed sleep.

The next three nights passed slowly, though they made good time, traveling over twenty leagues. Most of the time Randell traveled in front, searching the road for signs of other travelers, especially orcs.

Harvig was tasked with traveling fifty or sixty yards back to watch for anyone trying to sneak up from behind. He mostly traveled off the road, just inside the tree line, to stay hidden from sight. Flyn rarely saw him, except when they stopped to rest.

He and Gudbrant traveled together in the middle, talking quietly to pass the time. Gudbrant wanted to know about Trygsted. He seemed fascinated with their culture and customs, asking questions about everything. In turn, Flyn asked about Garthset and the Ilfin, although Gudbrant didn't tell him much more than he had already learned from Meinrad. Mostly Gudbrant confirmed that the Ilfin were loath to take up arms, except in the most dire circumstances. In Garthset, outside those in the militia, very few knew how to wield a sword.

Their travel was mostly uneventful, until the third day when they were awakened by the noise of an orc patrol on the road. Fortunately, they were well hidden and the patrol passed by without stopping. Later that afternoon, the patrol passed by again, presumably returning to Gurnborg. That night they traveled with little talking, listening and looking for any sign of the patrol. Other than footprints along the dirt road, they saw and heard nothing.

Each morning the mountain peaks at the western end of the valley were closer than the morning before and by the end of the fourth night, they found themselves at the edge of the valley and the end of the forest. Ahead of them lay only rock and occasional trees and scrub bushes. Gudbrant called for a halt and they spent their last day in the cover of trees.

Flyn looked at the imposing peaks in front of them, thinking they seemed taller than those on the east side of Asgerdale. The road they had been following led to a mountain pass, but unlike at the other end, the pass wasn't a wide valley between the peaks. Here it was a twisting trail that climbed up into the mountains, disappearing quickly in the lower peaks.

"It's not an easy path," Gudbrant said. "Even without the orc patrols, Ingekirk Pass is dangerous. In many ways, more dangerous than the orcs. There are places where the path runs along narrow ledges with high, unclimbable cliffs to one side and deep ravines on the other. Treacherous enough in the light of day, but we must travel at night. That will slow us down considerably, adding at least a day to our journey."

"Should we travel the pass in the daylight then?" Flyn shivered at the thought of traveling along a narrow ledge in the dark.

"I only wish that were possible. By daylight we will assuredly be seen by the patrols."

Flyn grumbled to himself, not happy with either prospect, but nothing more was to be gained by debating the point. He instead focused on helping Randell set up their tent and preparing the campsite.

The weather had turned cooler overnight and the morning brought a stiff, cold breeze down from the mountains in front of them. None of them wanted to chance a fire that could give away their location this close to the enemy patrol routes, especially after the patrol the previous day, so they ate a cold meal, then went to bed. They hunkered down in their bedrolls to keep warm. The tents protected them from the wind, but not the cold.

In addition to no fire, Gudbrant decided seeing a patrol meant it was time to start setting a watch. Tired from travel, but not yet ready for sleep, Flyn volunteered to stand the first watch.

Gudbrant had positioned him within sight of the road so he could watch for enemy patrols. He sat with his back to a tree and his sword across his lap. Randell had continued his sword training during their voyage, but Flyn still wasn't very confident with it. He knew a few days of training wouldn't mean much against an experienced soldier, especially one twice his size. Still, having the sword gave him some comfort. From time to time while watching the road, he ran his finger along the blade, feeling the cold steel through his leather glove.

Although he knew they were only halfway to their goal, entering the mountains made it seem more real. Perhaps because the mountains were orc territory, or perhaps because his last trip through the mountains had almost ended with him as the main course at an ogre dinner. Traveling through the lush, green lands of Asgerdale, he had almost been able to forget where they were headed. The harsh reality of the mountains shattered that illusion. Each step brought them closer to their destiny, success or failure.

But success might be farther away than he hoped. Gudbrant had reminded him that there was the possibility that Kel wasn't in Gurnborg. Most of Jarot's slaves were used for farming, and there were no farms near Gurnborg. Which meant that, like Brenna, he may have been taken elsewhere. Most of the farm land was west of the mountains. Still, Flyn clung to the hope of finding Kel in Gurnborg. Even though they would have to travel beyond the mountains before they turned north to search for Brenna, finding Kel in plains that covered thousands of leagues would be an insurmountable task.

Flyn pulled Kel's hat out of his belt pouch. It seemed like a silly thing to carry with him, but he felt that he owed it to Kel to return the stupid hat. Stained with sweat and salt water and covered in mud, it barely resembled the one he'd bought from Mr. Famsen so many weeks ago. Still, he vowed to carry it with him until he could return it to his friend, whether that was in Gurnborg or beyond.

Wherever Kel was, Flyn hoped he was okay. If they had him doing farm work, at least that was something he was used to. Not so much different from being home, right? Kel could survive a little longer plowing fields and planting crops until they found him. Then he and Kel could find a way home.

Home. By now their parents must think they were dead. They had been gone for almost a month. He wondered what his mother was doing. Probably fixing breakfast while his father and Ty took care of the early morning chores. He wondered if he would ever see them again.

By mid-morning, as the sun began to peek over the mountains, he crept back to camp to arouse Gudbrant for the next watch. He had not seen or heard any patrols, which seemed to make Gudbrant nervous. Too tired to be concerned, Flyn crawled into his bedroll and was asleep before he could spend any more time thinking about orcs or what fate the mountains might hold for them.

Flyn awoke to hushed voices outside the tent. He was alone, as

Randell had the last watch of the day. Flyn dressed quickly and went out to see what was going on.

The temperature had dropped even more since the morning and the afternoon sun was hidden behind a thick cloud layer. Randell and Gudbrant were huddled together in discussion. They looked up when Flyn exited the tent. Gudbrant waved him over.

"Randell and Harvig have seen several orc patrols leaving the mountains today, none have returned. We have to decide if we are going to wait for them to return or continue at dusk as we planned and risk a returning patrol overtaking us in the mountains. Randell thinks we should wait. I feel we should go. I'm concerned that staying here we risk more chance of being discovered than if we keep on the move. What do you think, Flyn?"

"I thought you were in charge," Flyn replied, not sure what else to say. What did he know of orcs or avoiding enemy patrols?

"Not here," Gudbrant said. "On this journey, we're all in it together, and we all have a say. Besides, I think my days of giving orders are over."

Flyn nodded, trying to evaluate what he had heard and come up with an opinion.

"Is there any place to hide once we get into the mountains?" he asked.

"That depends on where we are," Gudbrant said. "In some places there are crevices and caves, but in others…"

"In other places our choices are to run through the dark on a narrow ledge to avoid a patrol, or try to fight the patrol on the ledge," Randell finished for Gudbrant.

Flyn thought about it for a little while before answering.

"I think I agree with Gudbrant. There's a chance a returning orc patrol will overtake us, but we haven't seen them at night, so maybe they won't travel through mountains in the dark. On the other hand, staying in one place too long seems to be a sure way to get caught."

"Well thought out, Flyn," Gudbrant said, smiling. "Randell, wake Harvig. Let's see what he has to say about it."

While waiting for Harvig, the others prepared another cold meal. As they ate, Gudbrant explained the situation to Harvig.

"Captain, I'm here to keep you safe," Harvig said when Gudbrant had reviewed the choices. "Whether you choose to stay or go, I will be by your side."

"You're not being very helpful," Randell said.

"I'm not much of a strategist," Harvig replied. "I'm better at executing plans than coming up with them. But if I had to choose, I would choose to go. I always prefer doing something to sitting around waiting."

Gudbrant turn to Randell and shrugged. "Sorry, old friend, you're outvoted."

Randell grunted. "You know I'll do whatever you ask of me, but I think this is the wrong choice."

Nothing more was said about it. The company finished their meal and packed their gear, but remained hidden in the trees until dusk. With the cloudy sky, dark was upon them sooner than they expected.

Randell led the way as before, with Gudbrant and Flyn following behind single file. Harvig stayed even farther back so he could better distinguish between sounds coming from behind from those ahead of him. As the light faded, Flyn quickly lost sight of the large militiaman. Even Randell, only a few paces in front of him, became just a moving shadow among shadows.

As Gudbrant had warned, the mountain pass was not an easy trek. The path twisted and turned as it climbed the lower slopes of the Estlaeg Mountains. In some places, the original path had been blocked by fallen boulders with a new path around the blockage that was even rougher than the main trail. In other places, the path clung to narrow ledges that fell away into seemingly bottomless abysses. Everywhere the path was covered in loose rock and gravel, making for unsure footing.

The overcast sky served as a blessing and a curse. On the one hand, the party was almost invisible, even to each other. There was very little chance anyone would see them unless they happened to stumble into the middle of a patrol. But the lack of moonlight made the treacherous path even more dangerous. Fissures and drop offs appeared out of the gloom almost under their feet. To keep from stumbling off a cliff or losing their footing, their pace was even slower. With no visual reference, Flyn felt as if they were making no progress at all. Just an endless climb to nowhere.

They climbed the narrow mountain pass through the night with no sign of orc patrols, from ahead or behind. Flyn wondered if perhaps even orcs weren't stupid enough to try to negotiate the hazardous mountain pass in the dark.

The air grew colder as they climbed and the wind grew stronger. At times, Flyn feared it would pull him from the cliffs and toss him into the deep mountain ravines. The wind's icy fingers wormed through his clothing to nip at his skin. He pulled his cloak tightly around his body in a futile attempt to ward off the bite of the wind. By morning, they were hunched over against the wind, faces hidden in their hoods.

There was no distinguishable daybreak, just a gradual lightening from near complete darkness to a dull gray morning. The clouds had grown darker overnight, threatening a storm to come. Before full light, Randell found a crevice away from the path that sheltered them from sight as well as the wind. They set up camp with very little talk, hurrying into their tents and bedrolls to try to warm their numb bodies.

Again, Flyn stood the first watch. He alternated between huddling between the rocks to shelter himself from the wind and walking back and forth in their crevice to try to keep warm. His fingers and toes were numb long before his watch was over.

Throughout the day, several more orc patrols passed them. Each sentry saw at least one patrol headed east toward Asgerdale. None returned.

"I am concerned that we have seen at least half a dozen patrols leaving the mountains for the valley," Gudbrant said as they discussed the news. "Either they are looking for something"—he glanced at Flyn—"or these patrols are more than just patrols. They may be planning on raiding some of the few remaining farmsteads outside the city walls."

"But the only farms left are even farther south than Garthset itself," Randell said. "They've never gone that far south before."

"No, they haven't. Which is why I'm concerned. If only we had a way of warning the militia."

"There is no way one of us could reach them before the orcs," Harvig said. "Not on foot, and we don't have horses."

"I know. Perhaps the Thane was more prophetic than I realized when he said Garthset needed me. It was selfish and foolish of me to come."

"You are being too hard on yourself, Captain," Harvig said. "Even if you were there, you could do nothing. You wouldn't know of the raid until it was over."

Randell nodded in agreement.

"You may be right," Gudbrant said, "but that doesn't change that I came on this journey for selfish reasons."

"You came on this journey to help me and save the Thane's daughter," Flyn said.

Gudbrant smiled at him. "You seem to always find the bright side of the coin, Flyn. I hope this journey doesn't change that about you."

They finished their evening meal and packed their gear. By the time they were back on the trail, snow had begun to fall.

CHAPTER 7

The snow fell steadily throughout the next several nights and days. At first, Gudbrant expressed concern that they were leaving tracks in the snow, but that concern was short-lived as the snowfall quickly covered them. At times the wind whipped the snow around to the point that they had to stop for fear of falling off an unseen cliff. At other times the wind died completely, leaving just a gentle snowfall. During those calms, they were able to move quicker than before. The white of the snow made the ground easier to see, reflecting what little light there was, as well as providing a stark contrast between the ledges and the ravines beyond.

The days blurred together until Flyn could not distinguish one day from the next. The pass through the mountains never changed, each peak looking like the next, each valley like the last. When the snow finally stopped falling, they barely noticed. Every breath of wind blew the snow from the ground back into the air to fall and drift anew. Flyn began to wonder if the mountains would ever end. Even the normally stoic Harvig showed signs of weariness.

On what Flyn guessed was their fifth morning in the mountains, tempers that had been burning slowly under the surface finally boiled over.

"We must be lost," Harvig said when Gudbrant called them to halt for the day. "We haven't even seen an orc patrol in days. We're likely to die without ever meeting the enemy."

"If you feel you are better at finding a path almost destroyed by time, then covered in snow, then you have my blessing to take the lead," Randell replied, glaring at Harvig.

"Maybe I should. I have been through this pass before and I don't remember any of this." Harvig waved his arms at the cliffs and peaks around them.

"How can you tell? They all look the same. Have you ever been through the pass when it's covered in snow?"

"And how many times have you been through these passes? Never, I would guess."

"I don't need to have been on a trail before to follow it. Perhaps if you spent less time in the dining hall and more time in the forest, you might be able to do it yourself."

"Enough!" Gudbrant intervened. "We are neither lost nor will we die before we have a chance to fight the enemy unless we continue this fighting amongst ourselves. I do not know how far we have gone, but our destination cannot be but two or three more nights' travel. Randell has done well in spite of the conditions, Harvig. And Randell, you would do well to remember that Harvig has prevented your loss of limb more than once."

Harvig grumbled in response to Gudbrant's scolding. Randell continued to glare at Harvig but said nothing more.

"We are all fatigued, both in body and spirit, and though we are close to the garrison, it will do us no good to arrive having lost our fingers and toes to the cold or to each other. I spotted a small patch of trees a short distance back. I suggest we try to gather as much wood as we may and risk a small fire. We should be able to find deadfall to burn which will produce little smoke and allow us to keep warm during our watches."

The rest of the company immediately agreed, the argument between Randell and Harvig forgotten. They backtracked down the trail and found the trees Gudbrant had spotted. Within half an hour, they had settled into a sheltered hollow, a small fire warming their frozen hands and feet. They had each made an extra trip to the trees to gather enough wood to last them throughout the day.

For the first time in over a week, they had a warm meal before bed. Even standing watch was less of a chore, as they could periodically warm their hands and feet by the coals. When they packed up to continue their journey at dusk, their spirits were restored. Harvig and Randell apologized to each other for their earlier outbursts, though to Flyn it seemed that there was still some friction between them.

Before setting out, they dumped armfuls of snow on the remains of their fire to extinguish it. A large cloud of steam rose from the hissing coals that at first melted the snow before it finally cooled off enough to be covered.

A loud yell echoed from the cliff walls.

Gudbrant cursed under his breath.

"A patrol," he whispered to the others. "They must have seen the steam as we put out the fire. Quick, draw your swords and find cover! With luck, we can surprise them. Flyn, your bow!"

Flyn grabbed his bow and followed Gudbrant to a cluster of boulders a few yards from the crevice where they had sheltered for the day. Harvig took up position on the other side and Randell found cover near the path.

Flyn knelt down, laying his sword on the ground in front of him. He steadied himself against the rock and pulled three arrows from his quiver. Two he set on the ground in front of him, the third he nocked in his bowstring. Sighting down the arrow, he aimed at the spot where the path bent around the cliff, ready to draw back as soon as the patrol stepped into view.

Gudbrant was at Flyn's side, his sword ready. To their right, Harvig was crouched with his sword drawn, as still as the boulder he was hiding behind. Randell was out of sight on the other side of the clearing. They waited, quietly watching the path, barely breathing for fear that any sound may give away their presence to the enemy. The pounding of his heart was so loud in Flyn's ears he was afraid the sound would carry across the clearing.

Then the voices of the orcs came from around the cliff face, soon followed by the scrape and shuffle of boots on loose rock.

Flyn's bow shook in his hands.

"Steady now," Gudbrant whispered to him.

Flyn took a deep breath to settle his shaking hands, his eyes never leaving the bend in the path.

The first orc stepped around the corner.

Flyn pulled back on the bowstring and let the arrow fly.

He completely missed his target. The arrow struck the cliff next to the lead orc and shattered. As the orc turned to see what had hit the cliff, Flyn nocked the next arrow and drew back.

This time he was on the mark, his arrow piercing the orc's throat.

The orc grabbed his neck and tried to yell. Only a gurgling gasp escaped his lips. He fell to his knees, still holding his throat, as the next two orcs turned the corner. The second one earned an arrow to the heart for his trouble.

The third orc paused for only a second to see what had happened to the first two before he rushed toward the source of the arrows. With no time to pull more arrows, Flyn dropped his bow and picked up his sword. He jumped up, preparing to meet the onrushing orc, but before the orc could reach him, Gudbrant leapt from behind the rocks, sword raised. With a wild yell, he swung at the surprised orc with both hands on the hilt of his sword. In less than a second, the orc's head was separated from his body and both fell to the ground, lifeless.

Flyn stopped, staring at the dead orc. The blood that flowed from the wounds was blue.

Two more orcs ran around the corner toward Gudbrant and Flyn, bringing Flyn back to the battle. At the same moment Randell and Harvig jumped out and rushed toward the attackers.

The first of the two orcs reached Gudbrant, swinging a large ax at the militiaman's head. Gudbrant dove to the side, avoiding the swing, and rolled into a kneeling position. A quick thrust of his sword pierced the orc's leg.

More blue blood.

As Harvig and Randell converged on the last orc, a loud roar erupted from around the cliff. For a second, the stunned humans stood still. From around the corner came a beast larger than anything Flyn had ever seen.

It dwarfed the humans, and even the orcs. Twice as big as the ogres Flyn had encountered on the other side of the valley, the creature stood nearly twenty feet tall with feet large enough to crush a man. Its fingers, three on each hand, ended in long, sharp claws, nearly a foot long. Wiry, black hair, patchy in places, covered its bumpy, dark green skin.

The creature's enormous head was shaped like a dog's, with ears that pointed straight back. Large tusks stuck out from its jaw and fangs longer than its claws protruded from its mouth.

Flyn shrank back in fear.

"Mountain troll!" Gudbrant yelled as he jumped to his feet.

The orcs took advantage of the distraction. The one engaged with Gudbrant rushed forward, slamming into him. The last orc swung his club into Randell, knocking him to the ground.

Still off balance, Gudbrant swung his sword at the orc, striking him in the arm. Meanwhile, Harvig had reached Randell and defended him from a follow-up blow from the orc.

The orc fighting Gudbrant had his back to Flyn. Mustering all of his courage, Flyn threw himself at the orc. Its foul stench filled his nostrils, making him want to turn away. The brute's blue-green skin glistened with sweat in spite of the temperature.

The orc had raised his ax to smash down on Gudbrant. Flyn lunged forward, stabbing at the orc's exposed side and sinking his sword to the hilt in the orc's ribs. The orc let out a blood-curdling yell, dropping his ax. Flyn's sword was ripped from his hand as the orc turned toward him. Gudbrant attacked with a quick slash to the orc's throat. Before the orc had even hit the ground, Gudbrant raced off to help Randell.

Flyn scurried back to avoid the falling orc. Blue blood bubbled from the gash in the orc's throat as he took his final breaths. The orc looked up at Flyn, reaching out with one hand. Flyn couldn't move. His feet seemed to be stuck to the ground as he watched the orc's chest rise one last time, then fall with a final gasp whistling from his wounded neck.

"Look out!" Gudbrant yelled at Randell, bringing Flyn back to his senses.

The mountain troll was slow, but with its long legs, it was soon on top of the melee. Randell rolled out of the way just before the troll could smash him with a large foot. Gudbrant swung his sword at the troll's leg, but the blade just bounced off its thick hide. From where he was still lying on the ground, Randell managed to stab the troll's foot, but the beast didn't seem to notice. It swung at Gudbrant with its claws, catching him in the chest as he tried to dodge the blow.

While Gudbrant and Randell were busy with the troll, Harvig battled the last orc. The orc blocked most of Harvig's blows with his club while Harvig dodged the slower moving orc's attacks. They circled each other, trying to find an opening, but neither could gain an advantage over the other.

Flyn, still in shock, watched the battle, torn between the two sets of combatants. As Gudbrant dove away from another swipe from the troll, Flyn broke his paralysis and picked up his bow again. He nocked an arrow and pulled back on the string. Aiming for the troll's head, he released the arrow. The arrow bounced harmlessly off the side of the troll's skull.

Randell had regained his feet. He and Gudbrant stood on opposite sides of the troll, one distracting it while the other attacked, then switching roles as the troll turned. Their strikes did very little to hurt the monster, either glancing off its hide or just causing minor wounds to its arms and legs. Gudbrant tried to duck under its swinging arms to attack its body, but each attempt had to be abandoned to avoid being crushed.

Flyn loaded another arrow and pulled back on the bow. He followed the troll's head as it swung from one side to the other with a brief pause as it switched directions. He focused on his target, shutting out everything around him. As the troll's head moved to the left, Flyn took a deep breath, following just ahead of it. Just before its head stopped moving, Flyn began to slowly exhale and loosen his grip on the bowstring.

The arrow struck the troll in the eye. The troll howled as it threw its head back in pain, reaching up to grab the arrow.

Gudbrant and Randell both attacked the now-defenseless troll, stabbing into its belly and up into its chest as high as they could reach.

The troll howled even louder. Flyn dropped his bow to cover his ears from the terrible sound. Blood—red, Flyn noticed—poured from its wounds as it staggered back. The two militiamen pressed the attack, tearing into the troll's body with vicious stabs. It staggered backward to try to escape, but it was too late. When it finally fell, Gudbrant jumped up on its chest and delivered the killing blow.

On seeing the mountain troll fall, the last orc turned and fled, running back the way the patrol had come.

"Get him!" Gudbrant yelled. "He'll warn others that we're here."

Harvig and Randell sprinted after the escaping orc. Flyn followed, but it wasn't until he was already around the corner that he realized that he didn't even have a weapon with him, having dropped his bow. His sword was still in the body of the orc he had killed. Ahead of him, the orc had dropped his club and was running faster than the humans could manage. Even Harvig, with his long strides, couldn't keep up.

On the left side of the path, the cliff rose hundreds of feet. Flyn couldn't see the top. On the right side was a steep drop-off into a dark abyss. The path was so narrow that Flyn wondered how the troll had managed to traverse it. He slowed, realizing there was no point in risking a fall off the ledge when he didn't even have a weapon.

Up ahead, the cliff cut back to the left and the ledge followed. Slipping in the loose rock as he tried to make the turn, the orc lost his balance and fell, almost skidding over the edge. Harvig ran full speed at the orc, dropping to the ground at the last second and sliding into the prone orc. His foot slammed into the orc's face, sending the brute toward the abyss. The orc scrambled to grab on to anything he could to keep from falling. Harvig's leg was all he could grasp.

The orc slid over the cliff, pulling Harvig after him. Randell reached Harvig just in time to grab his arm before he followed the orc. Bracing his feet, Randell tried to pull Harvig back, but the ground provided little traction. The weight of the orc hanging from Harvig's leg was pulling both militiamen over the side. Flyn ran as fast as he could to reach them before it was too late.

Skidding to a stop next to Randell, Flyn grabbed Harvig's other arm and pulled with all his strength. Slowly, he and Randell pulled Harvig back to the path, but the orc was still holding on to his leg.

"Let go of me, you ugly beast!" Harvig kicked the orc in the face with his free foot. Once. Twice. The third time, the orc lost his grip. Flyn and Randell fell back, pulling Harvig with them.

The orc's screams echoed through the ravine as he fell.

"Any trouble?" Gudbrant asked as they walked back into the clearing where the battle had taken place.

"Nothing we couldn't handle," Randell said.

"The orc almost pulled Harvig off the cliff," Flyn said.

"Like I said," Randell replied with a grin. "Nothing we couldn't handle."

"You can tell me about it later," Gudbrant said. "Right now, we need to get rid of these bodies. If another patrol comes along, we don't want them to raise an alarm. Help me with the orcs."

The orcs were too heavy for one man to move, but together Harvig and Gudbrant were able to pull the bodies to the edge of the ravine and roll them in. Randell gathered their fallen weapons and the severed orc head, which he sent over the side with the bodies. Meanwhile, Flyn retrieved his sword, still buried in the side of the orc he had stabbed, and recovered his arrows. He found four, salvaging three of them. The shaft on the fourth arrow was cracked. Though he remembered shooting five, he couldn't find the fifth one.

"The Andor outdid all of you," Gudbrant said as they worked. "Three kills, by my count. And a timely shot to the troll."

"He got a head start on us with that bow," Harvig said.

"And it looked like he saved your skin from that other one, Captain," Randell said.

"That he did," Gudbrant said, laughing. "Get back to work."

After a few minutes, they had finished with the orcs. Flyn stood at the edge of the ravine, looking down at the bodies lying on the rocks below.

"It doesn't seem right to just throw them over the cliff like that," Flyn said.

"We don't have time to bury them," Gudbrant said, putting his hand on Flyn's shoulder. "And a funeral pyre would draw too much attention. Besides, it's a lot better than what they would have done to our bodies had the battle gone the other way."

"What—" Flyn started to ask.

"You really don't want to know." Gudbrant turned back to the clearing. "Let's try to cover up the blood with fresh snow."

The bright blue blood stood out on the white ground. Even without the bodies, there had clearly been a battle.

"I didn't know orcs had blue blood," Flyn said.

"The small ones do," Randell said.

"Those are the small ones?"

Randell grinned. "Come on. Help us cover it up."

Using their feet, they scraped clean snow over the blood, covering up as much as they could see in the fading daylight. That task complete, all that was left was the troll.

The massive beast was too heavy to drag, but working together, they were able to roll the body over the side. The ravine was too dark to see where it landed, though the sound of breaking tree limbs and a loud thud as it hit the bottom left no doubt that it had. The crashing echoed up and down the ravine. Using more snow, they covered up its blood like they had the orcs'.

"Let's get moving before someone comes to investigate that," Gudbrant said.

The group grabbed their gear from the ditch where they had spent the day and hurried back down the path. As they passed the spot where Harvig had almost been pulled to his death, Flyn looked over the side for any sign of the orc, but it was too dark to see. Harvig stayed as far from the edge as he could.

"The fire may have been a mistake," Gudbrant said after a while.

"Why?" Flyn asked. He was hoping for another fire at the end of the night's trek.

"You think that patrol was sent to investigate it?" Randell said from in front. Harvig was too far behind them to join the conversation.

"Possibly. They certainly saw it when we put it out. If they were just a random patrol, then we may be okay. But they weren't equipped for an overnight journey, which means they'll be missed sooner rather than later. It's possible their disappearance may be blamed on the weather. Another patrol will be sent out tomorrow to find out what happened to them."

"But if they were sent to investigate smoke and they don't return, it won't be just one patrol we have to avoid," Randell finished.

"If that's the case, very likely we will find the whole pass flooded with patrols tomorrow. We won't be able to avoid them for long."

The group continued on in silence. Flyn had just started to feel good about the battle with the orc patrol. Gudbrant's prediction that they may be in even bigger trouble tomorrow quenched his excitement, replacing it with dread.

Their path lay relatively clear, the snow having been packed down by passing patrols. Any evidence of the small party was lost among the numerous tracks left by the orcs. Most of the drifts had been pushed aside by the giant mountain troll, its tracks clearly visible among the others.

Flyn shuddered, thinking of the huge beast that only a few hours earlier had been walking the same path. Now it was dead, lying at the bottom of a ravine somewhere behind them, with only footprints to show it had ever existed. And lying with it, the bodies of five orcs, three of which Flyn himself had killed. The first two hadn't felt much different from shooting a deer or a pig. At least, he kept telling himself that. But the third one had been up close. Its stench still seemed to linger in Flyn's nostrils.

He had never killed a person before, had never even considered it until recently. While Randell had been teaching him to fight with a sword, he had known in the back of his mind that one day he might have to kill. He understood that the ultimate outcome of a sword fight was to kill or be killed. But to actually do it was a very different thing.

Even though the orcs had been trying to kill them, and Gudbrant might have died if Flyn hadn't stepped in, had they deserved to die? He was directly responsible for the death of three people. They might not have been human, but they were people nonetheless. What gave him the right to decide their fate? He was no god.

He wiped away a tear from his cheek and looked at Gudbrant. The militiaman's stern features were clear even in the dim evening light. The eyes that peered out from that face were as cold as the snow on the ground. Flyn knew that Gudbrant held no remorse for the deaths they had caused. Flyn wondered how a man could get that way.

"Are you okay?" Gudbrant asked, turning toward Flyn with a raised eyebrow.

"I'm fine." Flyn looked away, embarrassed for being caught staring.

"Was that your first time?"

Flyn avoided Gudbrant's gaze and didn't respond.

"It's not easy taking a life. Even when your own life is in danger. It's okay to feel bad about it."

Flyn nodded, finally looking at Gudbrant.

"If you weren't upset, I might be a little worried about you." Gudbrant grinned. "You should have seen Harvig after his first kill."

"Harvig?" The big militiaman seemed devoid of emotion. Flyn couldn't imagine him feeling bad about killing an enemy.

"He may look tough, but after his first melee, he wandered off into the woods and retched. But don't let him know that I told you that. He might just pound me into the ground for saying anything."

"What about you?"

"Well, I wasn't as bad off as Harvig, but it took me a while to get over. You never feel good about it, but after a while, you come to accept that you must value you own life over those who would take it from you."

Flyn nodded again, thinking about Gudbrant's words.

"What about Randell?" he asked after a few minutes.

Gudbrant sighed and didn't answer right away.

"Randell is a different story. I suppose deep down he feels bad about taking another life, but after what the orcs did to his family, I've never seen a shred of remorse from him. Then, when they took Brenna, it was too much for him. I don't think he would have gone on his own, but I couldn't have kept him from coming with me. The two of them have a special bond."

Flyn looked at Gudbrant, confused. "I thought Brenna was going to be your wife?"

"She is," Gudbrant said. "But she and Randell grew up together.

She's like a sister to him. In some ways, I think maybe losing her to the orcs was harder on him than it was on me or Meinrad. He lost another sister. That's one of the reasons I wanted him to come with us. I knew he wouldn't hesitate if we had to fight. I can't say that for all of my men."

"Why not?"

Gudbrant smiled at Flyn. "The Ilfin clan doesn't raise warriors. Not like the Mundars."

"Mundars? Didn't the Thane say Mundar was one of the leaders in the Revolution?"

"He was. He was a fierce warrior. The stories say that he preached 'Peace through power.' After the war, those who agreed with him followed him and became the Mundar clan. They focused their energies on training soldiers to defend themselves from the Yonarr, should they ever return. Of course, the other clans thought they were out of their minds. The Yonarr had been defeated." Gudbrant paused. "I guess they were right after all."

"Where are they now?"

"I wish I knew. To my knowledge there hasn't been any contact with the other clans in over a hundred years. And since the coming of Jarot, we haven't even had much contact with the rest of the Ilfin clan."

Flyn nodded, not really knowing what that meant. Everything was so different from Trygsted. Having no contact with another part of the clan was unheard of. Except those who were banished.

They fell back into silence. A few weeks ago, Flyn hadn't even known there were other clans. He had thought the entire world was an island barely thirty-five leagues across. Now he was trekking through the mountains of another land, with men from another clan, fighting creatures he had only thought existed in children's stories. It all seemed to be too much to take in.

Later in the evening, as they trudged along the icy path, snow began to fall again, but by that point, Flyn barely noticed.

The path began descending after a while, the rocky surroundings giving way to trees similar to those Flyn and Kel had found along the coast, only smaller. Gudbrant informed him they were called "pine trees." Very little snow covered the ground, as the trees formed a tight roof over the forest floor. Only the path they were walking on was exposed to the sky. In the moonlight, it looked like a glowing, white ribbon meandering through the dark trees.

As they descended, the snowfall turned into a misty rain. The wet air cut through their clothing like knives, in spite of the warmer temperature. Flyn's cloak, pulled tight around him, provided little warmth. Shivering in the dampness, he forced himself to think of Kel and how what he must be going through was far worse than being cold and wet. Those thoughts didn't do much to raise his spirits.

They traveled for several hours with no sign of another patrol. Flyn was just beginning to think they would make it to Gurnborg without any more trouble when Randell came running back down from a crest in the path ahead of them.

"Patrol!" he said in a harsh whisper when he reached them.

"Up into the trees," Gudbrant said, pointing up the hillside to their left.

Randell scurried up the slope, Flyn close behind. Gudbrant stayed at the edge of the path until Harvig caught up, then followed the other two. The trees were smaller than those along the coast, but they grew close together, providing plenty of cover for the group. They stopped thirty or forty yards from the path and ducked behind a clump of trees.

"What did you see?" Gudbrant asked.

"A large patrol coming up the path. I couldn't see how many, but there were a lot of torches."

"Damn," Gudbrant said. "Okay, everyone stay quiet. If we're lucky, they won't spot us."

They waited, huddled in their hiding spot, the path invisible in the dark. The muffled sound of voices drifted over the top of the hill, rising and falling in a rhythmic beat. Then a flickering light began to illuminate the trees below them. The voices broke over the crest in the path, a marching cadence in a language Flyn didn't understand. The orcs' chanting and the pounding of their marching feet echoed through the woods and hillsides. Flyn felt the ground tremor as the patrol passed through the trees.

And they kept coming, group after group. Each group, with a torch bearer at the front, was armed with large axes, or spears, or massive two-handed swords with blades at least six feet long and nearly a foot across. Some carried shields, and all wore helmets and chain hauberks. Some of the orcs with shields banged their weapons on their shields in time with the marching beat. Others thumped their fists against their chests. Between some of the groups were mountain trolls, their large bodies breaking tree limbs as they passed through the forest.

Flyn shrank down behind his tree, peering around the trunk at the column of soldiers. Their torches lit up the forest as bright as daylight. He was sure the orcs would spot them hiding in the trees if one of the patrol just looked up.

But none did. They just kept marching and chanting and pounding.

Following the soldiers were humans leading pack mules that were loaded with chests and sacks. They were accompanied by smaller orcs with prods and whips that they would occasionally crack. The humans' legs were shackled together, causing them to shuffle instead of walk. Chains around their waist were attached to the mules they led.

One of the humans fell, tripping on his shackles.

"Get up, you lazy dog," one of the orcs yelled, cracking the whip across the man's back.

The man struggled to his feet and hurried to get back into his place in the line. The orc smacked him with the whip again and laughed. Flyn gritted his teeth and clenched his fists. The thought of shooting the orc crossed his mind. He held fast, knowing that if he did, it would just draw the orcs' attention. Then he and his small band would be quickly overwhelmed and captured. Or killed.

A final group of armed orcs brought up the rear.

"That was no patrol or raiding party," Gudbrant said after the last torch was out of sight and the marching chant fading into the night.

"That was a full-sized company," Harvig added.

"Is all of that to look for us?" Flyn asked. Surely they wouldn't send out scores of soldiers to look for one missing patrol.

"That's hard to say," Gudbrant said. "Perhaps, but they had supplies for an extended journey. I think they're off to war."

"To Garthset?"

"Most probably."

Even in the dark, Flyn could tell Gudbrant was again questioning his choice to come on their journey.

"Let's get moving," Gudbrant said. "At least with that many orcs on the move, there will be fewer in Gurnborg."

The group picked their way back down to the path, watching the direction the orcs had come from for any stragglers.

The path, wet from the rain and snow, had been reduced to nothing more than a rutted, muddy slash through the forest. The vegetation along both sides of the path had been beaten down. Even small trees had been smashed by the passing trolls. All the remaining snow was gone.

They resumed their positions, Randell scouting ahead and Harvig watching behind.

"What are we going to do when we get to Gurnborg?" Flyn asked Gudbrant after a while.

"We'll have to figure that out when we get there. First we have to get there, then we'll have to find a way in without getting caught. After that, I don't know. I've never been inside the garrison."

"But you think Kel is there?"

"I'm sure that's where they took him. Whether he's there now or not remains to be seen."

Flyn nodded, not wanting to think about what they would do if Kel wasn't there.

They hadn't traveled far when they came to the edge of the forest and the path turned down the hill into a wide, shallow valley. Randell was waiting for them, crouched just inside the tree line.

"Look," he said, pointing.

On the other side, pinpoints of light dotted the hillside.

"Gurnborg," Gudbrant said.

CHAPTER 8

The path to the valley floor, or what remained of it, switched back and forth along the mountainside, the slope too steep to go straight down. The two-furlong distance from top to bottom took nearly half an hour of slipping and sliding to cover. The group gathered together at the bottom of the slope for a few moments of rest.

The valley floor seemed to be relatively flat, at least compared to what they had been traveling through for the last several days. The path turned into a full-sized road at this point, leading straight across the valley toward Gurnborg. The tall grass that lined the road was mostly trampled into the ground for several yards on both sides from the company of orcs that had passed through.

Though the valley contained little natural cover, with only scattered clumps of trees and small bushes, the misty rain and low-lying clouds limited the visibility enough to keep them hidden from any lookouts at the garrison.

"That's enough rest," Gudbrant said after a few minutes. "Sunrise is only a couple of hours away and I want to be inside before daybreak."

With no sudden drop-offs or steep climbs, they traveled much faster than they had in the mountains. Before long they came to a fork in the road. What appeared to be the main road continued to the west. It was rutted and overgrown with weeds, apparently not often used. Splitting off to the north, the road again turned into not much more than a muddy path that led toward the orc stronghold. Gudbrant gathered them together.

"From this point on, we have to be even more careful. They'll have roving sentries, especially along the road. And once we get close, we'll need to stay out of sight of the guard towers as well."

Gudbrant took the lead, with Randell directly behind, then Flyn, and finally Harvig in his usual spot in the rear. Gudbrant led them off the path, along the right side of the road. They moved at a much slower pace now, crouching down among the tall grass. Between the main road and the northern slope, there were no trees or bushes, just a wide-open field. Flyn recognized the grass as wheat, not much different from what he had planted at home in the fall and harvested in the early summer.

They hadn't traveled far when Gudbrant signaled for them to stop and crouch down. Flyn couldn't see anything but the grass around him and a vague outline of Gudbrant a few feet ahead. Then he heard voices coming from the road. The voices were too far away and too quiet to understand, but he recognized them immediately as orcs. One of the patrols Gudbrant had warned about.

They stayed crouched down in the grass until the voices disappeared. Gudbrant peeked out to make sure all was clear. Then he signaled for the others to follow and they resumed their crouching walk.

Twice more they had to stop and hide from passing patrols before they reached the foot of the slope. Each time, Flyn strained to hear the sentries over his own beating heart, sure that one of them would see the disturbance in the wheat and come to investigate. But none of them did. The sentries walked past the hidden group, oblivious to their presence. Even when they reached the edge of the field, Flyn was still convinced one of the orcs would see the path of crushed grass through the field and raise an alarm.

"I suspect they're not very concerned about intruders," Gudbrant said, seemingly sensing Flyn's apprehension. "They're mainly concerned about large groups of soldiers that might try to attack. No one would be stupid enough to try to break into the garrison."

Ahead of them was a tree-lined slope leading to the orc garrison. Watchtowers loomed above the forest, their ramparts a darker shadow against the night sky. The lower walls were hidden behind the trees, though they could see torches flickering through the leafless tree limbs. Torches burned on either side of the road where it entered the trees. Two more sentries stood alongside the torches. More torches spread out on the hillside marked the road's winding path to the gates.

The sentries on the road were no more than two hundred yards from the band of would-be infiltrators. Nearly fifty yards of scrub grass and low-lying bushes separated the wheat field from the wood line.

"How are we going to get past those guards?" Flyn asked.

Gudbrant grinned. "Easier than you may think. Standing next to those torches, they won't be able to see much farther than the light of the torches. If we stay quiet and move slowly, they'll never see us."

Flyn was skeptical, but said nothing. After all, Gudbrant had far more experience at this kind of thing.

"We'll cross one at a time. I'll go first. Randell next, then Flyn, and Harvig, you cover the rear. Wait until the person ahead of you is across before you start."

Randell and Harvig nodded. Gudbrant looked at Flyn.

He was still unsure, but nodded anyway.

"Okay," Gudbrant said. He took one more look at the sentries, then started across. He moved slowly, crouching and watching the orcs as he went. It took him over a minute to cover the open ground and disappear into the trees on the other side. Randell followed as soon as they lost sight of Gudbrant.

Finally, it was Flyn's turn. The guards hadn't moved. Harvig gave him a pat on the back. He took a deep breath and stepped out of the wheat.

A shiver passed down his spine, though he wasn't sure if it was the cool night air on his face or fear of being out in the open. He glanced back at Harvig, who urged him on with a wave of his hand.

Another step. Now he was completely exposed. If the orcs looked his way, they would surely see him.

There was no way he would make it across. This was madness. This whole plan was absurd. What had he been thinking? There was no way they would make it into the garrison, much less be able to find and rescue Kel. He should have just stayed in Garthset. He couldn't go home without Kel, but if he didn't go home at all, at least he wouldn't have to face Kel's family and explain to them how his stupid plan of paddling his boat around Trygsted led to Kel's capture, and maybe death. He could never face that. If he stayed in Garthset, he could at least be alone in his shame.

"Go on!" Harvig hissed from behind him, making him flinch.

Flyn took another deep breath and started across the open field, crouching as he had seen Gudbrant and Randell do. He forced himself to go slow. Every fiber of his being wanted him to run, run as fast as his legs would carry him. Each painfully slow step took him farther from the safety of the wheat field, but seemed to bring him no closer to the trees ahead. One step at a time, he inched his way toward the spot where Gudbrant and Randell had disappeared, his eyes moving between the woods and the orcs.

Halfway across one of the orcs turned toward him. Flyn froze, not daring to move a muscle. The guard looked straight at him. Flyn braced himself to run. His best plan would be to turn around and run back into the wheat field where he could hide, maybe evade the orcs long enough to escape back to the other side of the valley and, if he was lucky, back into the mountains. From there he could make his way back to Garthset. Sweat dripped into his eyes, blurring his vision.

How had he ever thought he would be able to sneak into an orc fortress to save Kel?

The orc turned away, leaning on his halberd.

Flyn breathed a sigh of relief. He wiped the sweat from his eyes and continued on wobbly legs. When he reached the trees, he collapsed to his knees.

"As I said," Gudbrant whispered, "they can't see beyond the torchlight."

Flyn was still on the ground when Harvig arrived.

"No time to rest, Andor," Gudbrant said. "We have a long climb ahead of us."

The steep slope was covered in boulders, trees, and briars. Fallen logs and tree branches added to the mix of obstacles. Their view of the fortress was completely blocked. Even the torches on the fortress walls were hidden from view. The climb ahead of them seemed impossible.

"It's a very effective natural barrier," Gudbrant said. "Probably why they chose this spot for their garrison."

"Can we make it to the top?" Flyn asked. He certainly didn't think so looking at it.

"That, my friend, is what we are about to find out."

Gudbrant picked a spot between a tree and a small boulder and started to climb. The others followed, working their way up over the smaller rocks and around the larger ones. Gudbrant seemed to know exactly where to go, finding a path up the mountainside where none could be seen. Flyn struggled to keep up with Gudbrant's pace, but the militiaman never outdistanced the others, sometimes slowing or even stopping to allow them to catch up.

Each time Flyn climbed over another boulder he paused, knowing that somewhere above them in the dark, sentries in the guard towers were looking for them. If the guards saw them scrambling among the rocks and trees, the group wouldn't know until they reached the top where the orcs would be waiting. If they were lucky, they would be captured and used as slaves.

That wasn't the way Flyn wanted to find Kel.

Flyn's arms and legs ached from the endless climb. He was bruised from slips and falls, though thankfully his armor had protected him from serious injury. Still, Gudbrant kept climbing. At one point Flyn turned to look back at Harvig, whose labored breathing he could hear over his own. Looking down, his head grew light, and dizziness overtook him. If not for the tree limb he was holding, he would have toppled right over Harvig to a certain painful death. He didn't look back again.

When they were nearly to the top, Gudbrant called a halt. The others climbed up next to him, gasping and panting to catch their breath. The misty rain had become an early morning fog, hiding much of the fortress ahead of them. To their left, the main gate was lit up by giant lanterns hanging above it. Unlike the simple torches used to light the road up the mountain, the lanterns used hoods to direct the light toward the ground. Here, anyone approaching the gate would be illuminated by the lanterns, yet unable to see any guards stationed on top of the wall.

The wall of the fortress, at least thirty feet high, disappeared into the fog beyond the main gate. To their right, it continued for several hundred feet where it ended in one of the massive guard towers they had seen from the valley. The tower's top was hidden in the mist. Which also meant they were hidden from the guards in those towers, much to Flyn's relief.

"The weather seems to be on our side this morning," Gudbrant said. "Even so, our path becomes tricky from here. We have no chance to make it in through the main gate. There is, however, another way. I've heard there is a smaller, back gate that's used to bring in ore from the mine. I don't know how hard it will be to reach, nor do I know how well guarded it is, but perhaps they aren't expecting anyone to try to sneak in. Their main concern seems to be defending against a large, frontal assault."

"And what if it is guarded as well as the front gate?" Flyn asked. He was amazed they had gotten as far as they had, but he was sure their luck would run out soon.

"Let's just scout it out," Randell said. "Then we can come up with a plan."

"Agreed," Gudbrant said. "If anyone has any questions, now is the time to ask."

He looked at Randell and Harvig. Both shook their heads. Flyn had a thousand questions, but decided that knowing the answers would probably make him feel worse. When Gudbrant turned to him, he shook his as well.

"Good. When we get to the top, we will work our way around to the east. We'll stay in the cover of the trees as long as we can."

He turned and began climbing again, the rest of the company close behind.

The last part of their climb was easier. In a few minutes, they were looking at the bottom of the wall, no more than a hundred yards from the tree line. The fortress was built on a large mesa, though Flyn couldn't tell whether the plateau was natural or man-made—orc-made, he corrected himself. The ground between the walls and the trees was all mud and rock. The mud was filled with thousands of footprints, still fresh. Flyn suspected that the large group that had passed them earlier that night had started here.

Gudbrant led them along the edge of the trees around the fortress, moving slowly to avoid making any noise that might alert the guards that were sure to be on the wall. Flyn hoped fog would help conceal them from searching eyes, just four insignificant shadows among the trees.

As the group rounded the corner of the fortress, the trees came to an end. Ahead of them lay open ground, bounded by the fortress wall on the left and a sheer cliff climbing into the fog on the right.

The fog was growing thicker. Now the top of the wall was completely hidden.

"We are fortunate," Gudbrant whispered to the group. Any other time, there would have been no way for them to move past the wall surrounding the garrison without being spotted. Gudbrant hurried to the cliff wall, to stay as far from the fortress as they could.

The walk along the plateau was quick and easy compared to the climb up the mountainside. Even so, the fortress was massive. Flyn estimated about two furlongs from the front corner with the guard tower to the back corner. They continued along the cliff until they were well past the corner and the back wall of the fortress was lost in the mist. Ahead of them, the cliff turned to the west and became a steep slope. A path ran from the back of the garrison to the slope and up into the mountains. Except for a few weeds, the ground between the cliff and the fortress wall was completely bare. If not for the fog, the party would be completely exposed.

"Not much cover to sneak in," Harvig said.

"No, there's not," Gudbrant said, staring into the mist. "Randell, do you think you can scout out the gate without being seen?"

Randell thought for a moment. "I suppose I could try to get to the wall, then crawl along it. The fog should keep the guards on the wall from seeing me."

"Exactly what I was thinking. Let's do it. Even with the weather, it will be getting light soon. I would like to be inside the garrison by then."

Randell dropped his pack and sword, taking only a dagger with him, then turned toward the gate.

"Don't take any unnecessary chances." Gudbrant put a hand on Randell's shoulder.

"Don't leave without me."

Randell started toward the gate in a crouched walk. The fog closed in around him and before he had walked more than a few dozen yards, he was gone.

How long Randell was gone, Flyn couldn't guess. With no reference to the sky, he lost track of time. He and Harvig sat with their backs against the cliff wall, snacking on dried meat sticks, waiting for Randell to return. Gudbrant paced back and forth, occasionally stopping to stare into the gloom. As they waited, the fog grew thicker. Eventually they couldn't even see the path into the mountains anymore, even though it was less than fifty feet from them.

"What's taking him so long?" Gudbrant muttered. "I should have found a better way."

Harvig seemed unconcerned with the fate of the other militiaman.

At last Randell appeared out of the gloom, seeming to materialize before their eyes. Gudbrant ran to him.

"What did you see?" he asked before Randell had even made it all the way back to the group.

"I managed to get very close to the gate. The fog is quite thick near the wall." Randell sat down and reached for his pack. "Two orcs guard the back gate, same as the front, though I heard more on top of the wall."

"Just the two?"

"That's all I saw."

"What about torches and lanterns?"

Randell shook his head, taking a long drink from his flask. "None. I guess they aren't concerned about the back door."

"I've been working on a plan while you were gone."

The plan seemed simple enough: distract the guards and run through the gate.

The first step of their plan was to try to look like the human slaves they had seen earlier. Sneaking around inside the garrison would be hard enough, but dressed for battle, they would be spotted immediately.

They hid their packs, weapons, and armor among the rocks and covered them as best they could with smaller rocks. Gudbrant found two branches and erected them in a cross several yards to one side of the spot with their gear.

Flyn had his hunting knife tucked into his belt, hidden under his tunic. The others did the same with their daggers. All of the slaves they had seen had been wearing worn clothes, so they tore holes in their pants and tunics. For a final touch, they used mud from the field to dirty their clothes and faces.

When they were finished, Gudbrant stood back to examine them.

"It's not perfect, but it will do," he said. "We don't want to get up close and friendly with the orcs anyway."

To Flyn, the others looked as ragged as the slaves, though perhaps better fed. Their journey from Garthset, especially the trek through the mountains, and their encounter with the orc patrol had already done most of the work. Even so, the reality of their situation was beginning to set in. While he had always known their goal was to infiltrate the garrison at Gurnborg, seeing the fortress and preparing to actually sneak in gave it a whole new perspective.

"All right," Gudbrant said after making a few final adjustments. "We go now, or not at all."

With a final nod, Gudbrant turned and disappeared into the fog. Randell looked at Flyn and Harvig, then, without a word, led them in the direction of the fortress.

The thick fog surrounded them, a cold, wet blanket, deadening sound as well as sight. The air hung heavy and silent. They had lost sight of the mountain slope behind them, and the fortress wall in front of them was well shrouded. Flyn had no idea how Randell knew which way to go. He just followed the militiaman, hoping he knew the way.

The fog ahead began to grow darker until, finally, the fortress wall materialized in the gloom. Randell paused when they reached it, signaling Flyn and Harvig to remain quiet. After listening for a moment, he motioned for them to follow and hurried along the wall toward the rear gate. They followed him as quickly as they dared, keeping close to each other to avoid getting lost in the fog. After a couple of minutes, Randell stopped. Even though they couldn't see the guards yet, they must be close to the gate.

They crouched down and waited.

The sun must have risen because the mist was a lighter gray now than before. Still, they could see no more than a few yards in any direction. Thankfully, the top of the wall was still obscured from view, hiding them from the orc sentries stationed there. Even so, Flyn hardly dared to breathe for fear of alerting the guards to their presence.

After a few minutes, the sound of a bird whistle came out of the fog. Randell nodded to Flyn and Harvig. It was Gudbrant's signal. He was in position. Randell pursed his lips and replied with a similar call.

They started toward the gate, staying crouched down and moving slow. Before long, two vague, dark shapes appeared in the gloom. The guards. They stopped and waited.

The bird call came out of the mist again. Ahead of them, one of the guards said something to the other, but they were still too far away to hear the words. Then something clacked in front of them. The guard turned to look at the wall. Then a dull thud.

"Hey!" the guard yelled.

"What?" the other guard replied.

"Something hit me head."

Another dull thud.

"Ow!" the second guard said. "Somebody throwing rocks."

Thud. The first guard reached up and rubbed his mouth.

"Go see what's out there," the second guard said to the first.

The guard trudged off into the mist.

Thud.

"Stop that!" the remaining guard yelled.

A clatter of rocks, then another thud.

"Now you making me mad!" The second guard tromped off into the mist after the first.

Randell motioned for Flyn and Harvig to follow him, then ran for the gate, watching for the guards in the fog. When they reached the gateway, Randell stopped and pressed his back against the wall. He peered around the corner, then slipped through the opening. Flyn followed with Harvig close behind.

The wall was thick, at least twenty feet. The gateway was like a tunnel through the wall. A raised portcullis hung over their heads, its spiked bars pointing down at them. Large, wooden doors stood open at the far end of the gateway.

Past the gateway, the road continued, disappearing into the garrison, flanked by low buildings on both sides. On the other side of the gate, stairs led to the top of the wall. There was commotion up there now. Orcs shouting down at the gate guards.

"Come on," Randell said in a loud whisper. "They might send reinforcements."

The trio ran along the inside of the wall until the gate was out of sight, then ducked into an alley. Gudbrant had told them to wait no more than five minutes for him. If he couldn't make it, they were to go on without him and he would meet with them when they exited the garrison.

The orcs on the wall continued to yell. Flyn could only assume they were running down the steps and out the gate to join the hunt for the intruder. There seemed to be little chance for Gudbrant to escape, much less sneak into the garrison. Yet they still waited, as planned.

Five minutes passed. Then ten. And still they waited. The yelling from the guards had stopped and all else was quiet.

"We have to go," Randell whispered after fifteen minutes had passed.

"You go if you want," Harvig replied. "I'm waiting for Gudbrant."

"If we split up, we'll probably all get caught," Randell argued. "Besides, Gudbrant told us not to wait for him. He's probably hiding in the mountains somewhere."

"I have a bad feeling that something has happened to him. I want to stay until I know for sure he's all right." Harvig peeked around the corner toward the gate.

"If he's been captured or killed, we won't find out about it by waiting here. Our best option is to stick to the plan."

"Whatever we do," Flyn said, "let's do it quick. You two arguing is just going to attract attention."

"He's right," Randell said, lowering his voice. "We can't stay here. We're too close to the guards."

"I'm holding you accountable for whatever happens to Gudbrant." Harvig scowled as he stood up. "So what do we do now?"

"We stick to the plan," Randell said. "We search for Flyn's friend. The garrison isn't that big."

They decided to start along the wall, searching for buildings that looked like they might house prisoners or slaves. They started with the one they were hiding behind. There were no bars on the windows, so they suspected it was a troop barracks. Flyn volunteered to look through the window.

The building was one long room, with a low ceiling, and bare, wood walls and floor. Lanterns hanging at regular intervals provided light. Low-lying cots lined both sides of the room and a heating stove sat at each end. Several orcs milled about, some of them kicking those still in their cots. Flyn wondered how bad the prisoner accommodations must be if this was how the soldiers lived.

He ducked down before he was noticed and shook his head at the others. Harvig returned from checking the building on the other side of the alley.

"Empty," he whispered.

Randell nodded, then led the way out of the alley and back to the wall.

The fog wasn't as thick inside the fortress walls, though they still couldn't see very far in spite of the brightening sky. Flyn supposed that the fog hid them from the orcs just as much as the other way around. Still, they had several close calls, with orcs appearing out of the mist in front of them without warning. Each time, they managed to duck into an alley or hide behind a small building before they were seen.

They snuck along the north wall, checking every building along the way. Most were storehouses or weapons lockers. One appeared to be a dining hall, though it was dark and empty. Not until they were working their way toward the middle of the garrison along the eastern fortress wall did they find any sign of prisoners.

About halfway along the east wall, they found a building with no windows and a large wooden bar across the door.

"That has to be a stockade," Harvig said. "Why else would there be a bar on the outside of the door?"

"And if it's barred on the outside, there's probably no guards inside," Randell added.

The building was smaller than most of the others they had investigated, only about twenty feet long and ten wide. And unlike the others that were wooden, this one was built from stone block. It sat in the middle of an open courtyard with several stocks lined up in front of it and what appeared to be a gallows.

No one was around.

"If they have prisoners in there, shouldn't there be guards posted outside?" Flyn asked.

"I doubt they're worried about anyone escaping," Harvig said. "That bar looks pretty solid."

"Do you think Kel might in there?"

"I don't know, but we should check," Randell replied.

Randell peered around the corner, then ran across the open courtyard to the small building. Once there, he knelt down and looked around again for guards, then waved at Flyn and Harvig. Harvig raced across the open courtyard and crouched down next to Randell.

Flyn took another look around, then followed the other two.

The sound of voices and clanging metal drifted out of the fog. Though they still couldn't see more than fifty feet in any direction, the fog was beginning to lift. Without the fog, they would soon be exposed to the waking garrison. If Kel wasn't in this stockade, Flyn was afraid they would have to give up their search.

"Help me with this," Harvig said, trying to lift the massive wooden beam securing the door. It took all three of them to lift it from the brackets holding it in place. Once the bar was free, they let it fall to the side, where it landed on the ground with a loud thud.

Randell quickly pulled the door open and they peered in.

The inside of the building was completely dark except for the light coming through the open door. It was nearly empty, with plain wood walls and a dirt floor. Shackles hung from the walls at regular intervals. In the shackles straight across the room from the door was a person.

The figure appeared to be a woman, only about four-foot tall, with broad shoulders and muscular arms and legs. Her flaming red hair fell to her waist. She was dressed in torn rags, not much different from those they had seen on the slaves with the orc raiding party. Her feet, twice as wide as Flyn's, were bare.

As she lifted her head to look at them, Flyn realized that some of her hair was actually a beard as long as the rest of her hair.

"Who are you?" she asked, blinking in the light.

Randell rushed over to her.

"My name is Randell," he said, trying to undo her shackles.

"Well, don't get me wrong, I'm glad to see you, but you should have run when you had the chance. If they catch you, you'll be hanging right here beside me."

"We're not trying to escape," Randell replied. "We're here looking for someone."

"You mean you broke *in* to this place?" She shook her head. "By the way, you'll have an easier time with those shackles if you use the keys hanging by the door."

Randell looked up and blushed. On a hook next to the door hung a ring of keys. He grabbed the keys, then went back to free the woman chained to the wall.

"Thank you, lad," she said once her hands were free. "Now who are your silent friends?"

"Harvig is my name."

"And what's the matter with you?" she asked, looking at Flyn. "Ain't you ever seen a dwarf before?"

"I'm sorry," Flyn stammered. "I didn't mean to stare, but no, I've never met a dwarf."

"Heh," she grunted. "You look like you ain't seen much of nothing. What's your name, Skinny Boy?"

"Flyn."

"Well, thank you all for freeing me. My name is Sigrid Kirr."

"Pleased to meet you, Sigrid," Randell said. "How did you come to be a prisoner of the orcs in Gurnborg? I didn't think there were any dwarves this far east anymore."

"Aye, there aren't. Me brother and me were looking for an old mine in the southern Estlaeg Mountains. Rumored to still be full of gold, but it was abandoned during the Tirmar Revolution. Didn't know about Jarot and all these damn orcs. We didn't even see them coming. They grabbed us up and hauled us up here. The bastards killed Osgar when we were trying to escape. I've tried to escape a few times since, but I never make it past the gates. They lock me up in here for few days, then send me back to the mine to dig out iron for their blacksmiths."

"How long have you been a prisoner?" Flyn asked.

"Hard to say. Days blend together when you're stuck inside a wooden box. A month or more, at least."

"We're looking for two people we think the orcs brought here a few weeks ago," Randell said. "One was a woman, tall, long black hair. The other was a man, probably about his size." He pointed at Flyn.

"I remember a woman like that being brought in several weeks ago. Fiery lass. She wasn't here long. Don't know what happened to her. As for the other one, there's a lot of Ilfin men here, and you all look alike to me."

"This one wasn't an Ilfin. He was an Andor."

"An Andor! Well, why didn't you say so?" Sigrid laughed.

No one laughed with her.

"You're serious," she said after a studying them for a moment. "Well, there was a young lad that came in claiming to be an Andor. The pig-faces had him locked up in here, trying to break him. I was in here at the time, caught after another escape attempt." She snickered. "Anyway, they didn't believe him. Kept trying to get him to admit he wasn't an Andor. Claimed he was from Trygsted and everything." Sigrid chuckled again.

"He is from Trygsted," Flyn said.

Sigrid cocked her head and looked at Flyn with a raised eyebrow.

"Flyn is an Andor as well," Randell said. "He's trying to find his friend."

"Well, you're out of luck, lad. The bastards hauled him off to Uskleig."

"Isn't that where Brenna is?" Flyn asked.

"If what you heard is true," Randell said, "then it would seem both of them are personal guests of Jarot."

"But why would they take him there?" If what Gudbrant had told him was true, he might never see Kel again.

"When Ugly-lar found out your friend claimed to be an Andor, he came down here to interrogate him himself. The poor lad was in tears, completely broken. There was no way he was lying. I figured him for mad. But I guess big boss pig-face believed him. A couple of hours later, a pair of uglies hauled him off. Said Jarot himself wanted to talk to the boy."

"What does that mean?"

"It means," Randell said, "that your friend is most likely already dead. I'm sorry, Flyn."

Flyn's knees went weak and he slumped down against the wall. Kel dead? He didn't want to believe it.

"But why would they care about Kel?" Flyn asked. "He wouldn't hurt anybody."

"Because of what he represents," Harvig said. "During the Revolution, Andor was the one who led the rebellion. According to legend, he was a wizard. Some say he was more powerful than even the wizards of the Ranjer clan. According to some myths, if the Andors ever return, they'll bring magic with them more powerful than anything used in the Revolution."

"But Kel isn't a wizard and neither is anyone else on Trygsted. The only wizards I've ever heard of were in fairytales."

"I never said I believed the myths," Harvig said. "I'm just telling you why Jarot might want to talk to your friend. He's probably afraid that if an Andor has returned to Tirmar, his days may be numbered."

"I wonder..." Randell said to himself.

"Wonder what?" Harvig asked.

"Just thinking out loud, but I'm wondering if those troops we saw weren't an invasion party, but a search party. I'm sure Jarot has learned by now that Kel didn't travel to Tirmar alone. Suppose he sent those troops to find Flyn?"

"All that just to find me?"

"Well, even if Kel isn't a wizard, Jarot may still think you are."

"I hate to interrupt," Sigrid said, "but we best be going. They'll be bringing me my breakfast soon and I for one don't want to be locked up again."

"The dwarf is right," Harvig said, not noticing the scowl Sigrid gave him.

"But where do we go?" Flyn asked.

"We need to find a way out, then we head north to Uskleig," Randell said.

"We aren't going anywhere without Gudbrant," Harvig replied.

"I would do anything for Gudbrant, you know that. But he asked me to go to Uskleig and try to rescue Brenna. And that's exactly what I plan to do. He can take care of himself. There's no point in us getting captured lurking around the garrison trying to find him when he's probably outside hiding in the mountains."

"We don't know that. He may have been captured. We have to search for him."

"You two can argue all you like, but I'm leaving," Sigrid said. "I suggest you come with me and argue about it later."

Sigrid walked over to Flyn, still slumped against the wall.

"Come on, lad. I'm sorry about your friend, but you won't do him no good by getting yourself captured too."

She reached out to help Flyn to his feet.

"I'm not leaving the garrison until I know Gudbrant isn't a prisoner," Harvig was saying. "They know who he is. They'll torture him for information as long as they can keep him alive. I'm not going to let that happen."

"He said he would wait for us outside the fortress if he couldn't find a way in after us," Randell argued. "The orcs sent reinforcements, so he had to hide. While you stand here and argue about it, he's waiting for us outside."

"Do those two always bicker like that?" Sigrid asked Flyn.

Flyn just shrugged his shoulders.

"All right!" Sigrid said. "That's enough. I'm leaving with the Andor. If you two want to stay here and argue like a couple of wash-women, you can do it without me." She turned to Flyn. "Come on, laddie."

Flyn and Sigrid started toward the door when the light was suddenly blocked out.

"Ho, ho! What do we have here?" The loud deep voice came from the dark shape at the door. An orc.

"Damn!" Sigrid spat.

The orc moved into the room.

"Trying to escape again, you hairy rat?" the orc growled at Sigrid.

"Aye, you ugly beast," Sigrid replied. "I'll not be your monkey girl."

The orc scowled, then turned to the humans. "And more workers for the fields. I don't know how you got here, but you belong to the master now."

Harvig pulled his dagger out of his belt and leapt toward the orc. But the orc was ready for him. Before Harvig could strike, the orc smashed him in the face with a large fist. Flyn cringed at the sound of bones crunching. He watched helplessly as Harvig fell back against the wall and slumped to the floor. The orc laughed and turned to the others.

"Anybody else want to play?" the orc snarled.

The rest stood still.

The orc turned his head and yelled out the door. "Bring him in."

Two more orcs came through the door, dragging an unconscious man between them.

It was Gudbrant.

The orcs carried Gudbrant to the wall and secured him in a pair of shackles, leaving his limp body to hang by his wrists. Then they joined the other orc blocking the door.

"Chain 'em up," the lead orc said.

The other two closed on the humans and the dwarf.

CHAPTER 9

"Why you here, pink-skin?"

Flyn winced as the orc hit him with the whip again.

The orcs had chained them up and left them for several hours before returning to take Randell for questioning. When they brought him back, he was bruised and bleeding, barely conscious. Flyn was next.

"I said why you here?" Another whack with the whip.

They had taken him into the courtyard, ripped off his tunic, and put him in one of the stocks. The orc with the whip cracked it on his back every time the other orc asked a question. The pain was unlike anything he had ever felt before. Streaks of fire crisscrossed his back.

"You here to rescue the mole-girl?" *Crack.*

While they had been questioning Randell, Sigrid had told him what to expect. She said they would beat him until he gave them answers or passed out. They would show no mercy. Knowing that hadn't made it any easier.

"Why you want her? She even uglier than you."

He didn't want to tell them anything, but the pain was becoming unbearable. He just wanted it to stop.

"You puny even for a pink-skin. That why you want mole-girl? She more your size?"

The next strike of the whip caused Flyn to cry out. He couldn't help himself. The pain was too much. He let his head drop.

"Stop. Please." He had lost his will to fight. "I'll tell you what you want."

The orcs laughed. The one with the whip gave him another crack.

"I'm looking for my friend," Flyn cried out. "No more, please."

"What your friend's name? Maybe I see him." The orcs howled with laughter. "Your friend belong to Lord Jarot and now you do too."

The orc grabbed Flyn's hair and pulled his head up.

"Now, puny maggot, how many more pink-skins running around Gurnborg?"

"None," Flyn said, trying to shake his head. "It was just four of us."

"You lie to me, you get the poker." The orc pointed to a metal rod sticking out of a nearby furnace. The coals inside the furnace were glowing red. "How many pink-skins hiding outside the gates?"

Flyn shook his head again. "No more. Just us."

Another orc walked into the courtyard. This one wore a black sash with a red skull insignia across his chest. The orc questioning Flyn turned to the newcomer and saluted.

"Have you learned anything from the new prisoners, Garguk?" the new orc said.

"He said he here looking for his friend," Garguk snarled. "He claim just four of them here. Other ones not talk yet."

"Good. Ugglar wants to see that one," the new orc said, pointing at Flyn.

"Yes, Captain." He turned to the orc with the whip. "You heard Captain, get him out."

After releasing Flyn from the stocks, the orcs shackled his wrists to a chain and led him away from the courtyard.

The fog had lifted, allowing Flyn to get his first good look at the garrison. Most of the buildings were long wooden structures, similar to the buildings they had investigated earlier. In the middle, however, a larger building looked over the entire complex. A single tower rose from the middle of the keep. Unlike the other buildings, this one was built from stone blocks, like the fortress walls. The keep seemed to be where they were leading him.

They passed other prisoners, busy fixing equipment or hauling supplies, their feet chained together, and in some cases chained to nearby posts. Flyn noticed most of them were men, though a few were women. He saw people of all ages, some only children, all captured by the orcs and forced into slavery. Some stopped to stare at Flyn as he passed, only to receive a reprimand from an orc overseer. He noticed that none of the slaves were dwarves.

The orc Captain led the way, followed by the one who had been questioning Flyn. The pace set by the orcs was more of a jog for Flyn. Whenever he started to fall behind, the orc would yank the chain attached to his wrists, jerking him forward and causing him to stumble. He tried not to fall, remembering what he had seen on the trail. As they walked, the orc with the chain continued to taunt Flyn.

"If you think my questions hard, wait 'til you meet Ugglar. He not as nice as me. After you meet Ugglar, you won't be able to work in fields."

Flyn barely heard him. His back throbbed with pain, alternating between a fiery burning and a dull ache. It was all he could do to focus on not tripping.

Near the center of the garrison, they came to a main road, at either end of which Flyn could see the front and back gates. The orcs paused for a group of prisoners being led toward the back gate. The captives were chained together in a line and carried picks, shovels, and other mining equipment. Some pulled carts shaped like rectangular buckets. Slaves headed to work in the mine, no doubt.

The orcs led Flyn across the main road and up a walkway to the main keep. The orc captain stopped when they reached the entrance.

"I'll take him from here," the captain said.

Garguk handed the chain to his captain, then turned to Flyn.

"If you still alive when Ugglar done with you, we gonna play some more." The orc laughed, then walked off toward the stockade.

Two orcs, with the same sash as the captain, guarded the entrance to the building. They saluted, then opened the doors as the captain approached. Flyn stumbled along behind.

Inside, the building was lit with torches mounted in brackets on the stone walls. The ceiling was stained with black soot, and the air was filled with a sharp, acrid smell coming from the torches. Other than the torches and a few doors, the walls were plain, bare stone, rough cut like the outer walls.

More orc guards were stationed in the corridor. They stood at attention and saluted as the captain passed. The captain ignored them.

At the end of the hall another pair of doors was guarded by two more orcs, who saluted and opened the doors like the ones outside. The captain dragged Flyn inside the room and flung him to the floor. The doors closed behind them with a loud thud.

Another orc, bigger than any Flyn had seen yet, was sitting in a chair on the other side of the room.

"So this is the Andor?" the big orc said.

"Yes, sir," the captain said, saluting.

"Good. Unchain him, Rakug. He's no threat here."

The captain pulled Flyn up by the chain and snarled at him as he removed the shackles. He dropped them to the floor in front of Flyn with a loud clang.

"Kneel before Commander Ugglar, maggot." Rakug pushed Flyn back to the floor.

The commander got up from his chair and stood over Flyn.

Ugglar was different from the other orcs Flyn had seen, not just by his size. His skin was dark red and he had tusks projecting up from his lower jaw.

"He looks just like the other Andor, don't you think, Rakug?"

"Yes sir. Just as puny and just as weak."

"The other one said your name was Flyn," Ugglar said. "Is that your name?"

Flyn nodded. There was no point in lying. Kel must have told them everything. Not that he blamed Kel. Flyn had always seen himself as the stronger of the two, and if they could break him, Kel would have been easy.

Poor Kel. He had always followed Flyn, no matter how stupid the idea, no matter how bad the plan. And now his loyalty to Flyn had probably cost him his life.

Kneeling on the cold, stone floor in front of the most powerful being he had ever known, Flyn clenched his jaw and swore to himself that he would avenge Kel's sacrifice. Someday, somehow, he would find a way.

"Lord Jarot will want to see you, too," Ugglar was saying. "He says your friend is a good talker. Told him everything there is to know about Trygsted and the Lost Clan of the Andors. Not so lost anymore, are you?"

"We don't mean anyone any harm," Flyn said. He knew the plea was useless, but if he was ever to see his day of retribution, he would have to continue to play role of the beaten prisoner. "We just got lost. All we want to do is go home."

The orcs laughed.

"You'll go home very soon," Ugglar said, still laughing. "You'll join your friend in Uskleig as Lord Jarot's personal guest."

Join his friend? Did that mean Kel was still alive?

"I just had to make sure you were the one we've been looking for before I contact the Master with the good news."

Ugglar grabbed Flyn's arms and yanked him off the ground. Flyn struggled to pull away. The foul stench of the orc's hot breath overwhelmed him, making him want to retch. His skin crawled as Ugglar sneered at him.

"But first," Ugglar said, "I need to know a few things."

Ugglar stared into Flyn's eyes, his massive hands squeezing Flyn's arms.

"Your friend didn't seem to know anything about the Ilfins at Garthset, but you're traveling with the captain of their guard. Surely, you know more than your friend."

He dropped Flyn to the floor and walked over to the wall where various weapons hung.

"I don't know anything about them," Flyn pleaded. "I just met them."

"And they just decided to help you sneak into my fortress to look for your friend because they're helpful? I think not."

Ugglar selected a short rod that looked like a small pitchfork, but with only two prongs. He held it up in the air in front of him so Flyn could see it. Suddenly, a flash of light, like a bolt of lightning, arced between the prongs.

"But if you're telling the truth, we'll find that out too."

Flyn closed his eyes and thought of the ocean. Warm breezes across icy-blue water. Floating in his boat. The sound of seagulls in the air.

"Flyn? Wake up, Flyn."

Flyn opened his eyes, but saw only fuzzy shapes.

"He's awake," another voice said.

He rubbed his eyes. A face moved into his blurred vision.

"Are you okay?"

"Give the lad some room. He's had a rough day."

He blinked and rubbed his eyes again. Gudbrant's face came into focus.

"Can you hear me?" Gudbrant asked.

Flyn tried to speak, but nothing came out, so he nodded. Everything was sore. His back burned where they had whipped him, his chest was covered in burns from Ugglar's lightning stick.

He tried to sit up, but didn't have the strength.

"Easy now." Gudbrant helped him into a sitting position.

He was back in the stockade. The others were gathered around him, anxious looks on their faces. Beyond them, two orcs stood guard by the door.

"Here you go, lad. Take a few sips." Sigrid held a metal cup to his lips and tipped it up. The water was warm and had a foul taste to it, but he drank it anyway. He hadn't had anything to drink for hours.

"Easy, lad. Not too much." Sigrid took the cup away. "Better?"

Flyn nodded.

Randell and Harvig were watching him from a few feet away. Both were covered in welts from the orc's whip. Harvig's face and nose were swollen and bruised.

"You should see yourself," Harvig said, noticing Flyn staring at him.

Flyn looked away, embarrassed, though he didn't know why.

"Don't listen to him," Randell said. "He's just mad because that orc got in a sucker punch that knocked him out."

"I'd like to see you do better," Harvig replied.

"Are you sure you two aren't married?" Sigrid said, chuckling.

"That's enough," Gudbrant said. Then he turned back to Flyn. "What did they want from you?"

Flyn took the water from Sigrid and had another swallow before answering.

"Ugglar wanted everything I know about you and Garthset and your people. He wanted to know how many people lived there, how many soldiers, how it's being guarded, what kind of scouts you have. Fortunately, I don't really know any of that. But you do. He said he was going to torture you next to get the answers."

"I expected as much," Gudbrant said. "What else?"

"He wanted to know everything about Trygsted and the Andor clan. I don't understand. Why would he care about a bunch of people who don't even know he exists? We're just a bunch of farmers and shopkeepers. We're no threat to the orcs or this Jarot. The people on Trygsted don't even know Tirmar exists. And even if they did, they certainly wouldn't climb into boats to go fight a bunch of orcs. The Andors hate boats."

"That's a topic for another time," Gudbrant said. "For now, you need to eat. They'll chain us up again soon, and you'll need your strength." He glanced back at the guards, then back to Flyn.

The "meal" was a plate of some kind of meat, burnt to the point of being unrecognizable and tasting like charcoal. The plates were made of lightweight metal and there were no forks or knifes. Basically, no chance of turning anything into a weapon. Not even a bone in the meat. Flyn ate what he could, and washed it down with more of the repulsive water. He had barely finished when the door opened and Garguk came in.

"Break time's over, maggots. Back to the chains."

The two guards took each of them in turn and shackled them to the wall while Garguk blocked the door, should any of them try to make an escape attempt. There was little need. As bad off as Flyn was, the others were little better. They were all bloody and bruised from being interrogated by the orcs. Even Sigrid, who had nothing to do with them, had been beaten to find out if she knew anything about the men from Garthset. Flyn felt bad for her, having to endure the orcs' brutality because of him and his friends, but Sigrid seemed to be handling the pain better than the humans.

"Rest up, maggots," Garguk said. "Tomorrow we'll have more fun."

When the orcs left, they took the torches, leaving the prisoners in the dark. The only light came from a thin crack under the door. After a while, Flyn noticed it was just enough light that he could make out the shapes of Gudbrant and Randell, who were chained up on either side of him.

"Is everybody ready?" Gudbrant said, his voice barely audible.

"Ready for what?" Flyn whispered back.

"Just stay quiet and follow our lead," Gudbrant replied.

From his left, Flyn heard chains rattling. A moment later, Sigrid appeared out of the gloom. She hurried across the room and he heard the clinking of the key ring being lifted off its hook. She unlocked Gudbrant's shackles, then moved on to Harvig. Gudbrant pulled the chain through the loop holding it to the wall. He told Flyn to leave his chain attached to the wall. A few minutes later, all five prisoners crouched around in a circle across from the door. All but Flyn had a four-foot length of chain with a shackle on each end.

"How did you do that?" Flyn whispered, astounded at how fast Sigrid had escaped the shackles.

"Dwarves are good at that sort of thing." She chuckled.

"But, if you could do that, why didn't you escape a long time ago?"

"Aye, the metal shackles are easy, lad. What's not so easy is a door barred on the outside by a hundred-pound wooden beam. But do you really think I spent all night hanging from the wall like some hunting trophy?"

Flyn nodded in amazement, forgetting that no one could see him.

"We don't know how many of them there are," Gudbrant said. "I suspect there will be two. If there's only one, even better. If there's more than two…"

"Since their war party set off last night, they've been short-handed," Sigrid said. "There may be no guards at all."

"In which case, we have a different problem," Gudbrant said. "All we can do is try. Harvig, you take the left side, I'll take the right. Flyn, stand up and hold on to the ends of your chain so you look like you're still shackled to the wall. Randell and Sigrid, hide in the shadows on either side until you see an opening. When I give the word, Flyn, you need to make a lot of racket. Make the guards think we're trying to escape. Everybody ready?"

Everyone replied that they were. Harvig and Gudbrant took up positions on either side of the door. Randell helped position the shackles on Flyn's wrists so he still appeared to be locked up, then disappeared into the darkness. Sigrid was already hiding on the other side.

"Now, Flyn."

Flyn took a deep breath, then began shouting.

"Hey, don't leave me! Take me with you!"

Sigrid and Randell rattled their chains and banged them against the wall.

"Hey! What going on in there?" a voice said from outside the door.

"Quiet, Flyn!" Randell yelled. "Do you want the guards to hear us?"

There was a scraping and a thump as the crossbar was removed and dropped to the ground. The door opened and a large orc stepped through.

"Quiet down," the orc said to Flyn.

Gudbrant and Harvig swung their chains at the orc's head. The shackles hit his skull with a dull crack and the orc collapsed, falling face first in front of Flyn.

Behind the orc, a second guard was already coming through the doorway. When he saw the first guard drop, he tried to step back, but it was too late. Gudbrant's chain whistled through the air, hitting the orc in the face. The end of the chain whipped around his head and the shackle smacked him in the cheek.

The second orc stumbled back, the chain still wrapped around his head. Sigrid raced forward to help Gudbrant pull the orc into the building. Harvig swung his chain down on the orc's head. The guard's knees buckled and he collapsed in the doorway. Harvig pulled his chain back and readied himself for the next guard.

Meanwhile, Randell had jumped on the first orc. He pulled a dagger from the orc's belt and used it to dispatch the fallen guard before he could recover.

No third guard came through the door. All was quiet outside the stockade.

Sigrid and Gudbrant pulled the other guard next to the first and Randell took care of him as well.

The whole exchange lasted less than fifteen seconds. Flyn was still standing against the wall holding on to his chain.

"That was a well-executed plan," Sigrid said. "You lads are all right." She turned and looked at Flyn. "You can put your arms down now, laddie. The fight's over." She chuckled and turned her attention back to the orcs.

They searched the orcs for weapons, or anything else that might be useful, and came up with just another dagger. Gudbrant took this and Randell kept the other. Harvig opted to keep his chain. As did Sigrid.

"It's no ax," she said, "but it beats a little knife."

"What do we do next?" Flyn asked.

"We hadn't gotten that far in our plan," Randell said. "We're open for suggestions if you have any ideas."

Flyn thought for a minute.

"Actually, I do have an idea."

Exiting the stockade, they found the sun had already set and the light was fading. They had used the chains and shackles to tether their feet together, and then some of the other chains to link themselves together like Flyn had seen the miners earlier in the day. Sigrid hid the keys on a string around her neck. Her beard completely covered any sign of them under her shirt.

"This will never work," Randell said.

"Sure it will," Flyn replied. "I know I haven't met a lot of orcs, but the one thing I've noticed is the smarter ones are in charge and the ones in charge don't do guard duty. As long as we look the part, and don't run into any of the smart ones, we should be fine."

"Aye, I think the lad is on to something," Sigrid said. "These lumbering oafs aren't exactly the sharpest picks in the mine, if you know what I mean."

"Agreed," Gudbrant said. "The time for discussion is past. We need to move quickly. Someone will eventually find the bodies of the orcs we killed and we must be out of the garrison before that happens. Otherwise, we'll never escape."

"If it doesn't work, we won't stand a chance," Harvig said. "Chained up like this, we'll never be able to outrun them."

"Chained or not, if it doesn't work, we'll never have a chance to try," Gudbrant said. "Now let's get the door closed and barred so no one passing by thinks anything unusual is going on."

"Won't they notice there are no guards?" Randell asked.

"There weren't any guards this morning when we got here either," Flyn said. "They only put guards out front after we broke in. How likely is it that a random passerby knows the change in procedure for the stockade?"

No one else had any more objections, or better ideas, so after Gudbrant checked to see if anyone was around, the group exited the building and barred the door behind them. They quickly moved away from the lockup area and onto a back street.

With their earlier attempts at disguise, along with the torture they had endured, they looked like any other group of slaves Flyn had seen. Sigrid led, followed by Flyn, Gudbrant, Randell, and Harvig at the end of the line to protect their backs.

"Which way?" Flyn asked Sigrid. She knew where the mining supplies were stored.

"This way." Sigrid headed toward an alley.

She led them through a maze of alleys and back streets, which kept them mostly out of sight, but the chains forced them to move slower than Flyn would have liked to avoid making a lot of noise. They passed very few people, humans or orcs. Only once did they have to stop and hide from passing orcs, a pair meandering to or from some guard post.

Most of the buildings they passed were dark and empty. Barracks for the troops sent out the previous night, Flyn suspected. Through the few lighted windows they did come across, they could see other prisoners sitting down for their evening meals, the same sort of charred meat Flyn had eaten earlier. Guards stood around watching the prisoners eat. The escapees ducked under the windows as they passed, although chances of those inside seeing them were slim.

Sigrid led them along a route that put the doors to the dining halls on the other side of the buildings.

Night had settled over the garrison by the time they reached their destination. Lanterns had been lit along the main streets, but the side streets were left in darkness. The door of the toolshed Sigrid had brought them to was well hidden from the closest main street. Outside the shed, carts like the ones Flyn had seen earlier were lined up along the wall. Sigrid opened the door and peered inside.

"Picks and shovels for everybody," she said as she started handing out the tools.

The pickaxes had wooden handles and metal heads with a pointed end on one side and a flattened, chiseled end on the other. Sigrid gave hers a few test swings, easily controlling the heavy tool with one hand.

"I'd still prefer an ax," she said. "This will do, though."

Flyn hoped he wouldn't have to try to fight with the pickax. It was heavy and awkward for him, even with both hands. The others seemed to manage, though being chained together gave them little room to maneuver. Should they have to fight, only Sigrid and Harvig would have much chance of hitting their target.

"Harvig gets to pull the cart," the dwarf said. "Works best if you put your shovel and pick in it so you have both hands to pull."

Harvig nodded, but the scowl on his face said he wasn't happy about it.

They set out, pickaxes over one shoulder, and shovels over the other. With their disguise complete, the need for stealth had diminished, allowing them to move quicker. Even so, Sigrid kept them off the main streets to minimize their chances of running into guards.

"Keep your heads down and shuffle your feet," Flyn told the others. The prisoners he had seen earlier had all been dejected and beaten. To pull off his plan, they had to appear just as sullen as the rest of the prisoners, though for Flyn, it wasn't much of an act.

Even though the back gate was less than two furlongs away, they took nearly ten minutes to reach it. Sigrid chose the darkest, most unused alleys, of which there were many. Most of the buildings seemed to be empty barracks and galleys. Although the journey took longer than a more direct route, they encountered no orcs on the way, much to Flyn's relief.

The group found themselves hiding behind the same building they had hidden behind that morning while they had waited for Gudbrant. The gate was less than one hundred yards away, far closer than they had realized that morning. There was no one between them and the gate.

"Now comes the hard part," Sigrid said, almost to herself. She turned back to the rest of the group. "Remember, keep yer head down. Don't look up at them or they'll know something's up. No slave would ever look an orc in the eye unless he wants a beating. We don't want that kind of attention."

The others nodded.

Flyn's heart was already racing. Though freedom was only a short walk away, it looked to be leagues.

Back in the relatively safe confines of the stockade, his plan had seemed so simple, so brilliant. He had been absolutely sure of it. Now, standing in the open, chained to his companions, the idea of trying to fool the guards seemed ludicrous. They were sure to be caught. Then the orcs would haul them back to the stockade and discover the dead guards. They would most likely kill the humans and dwarf on the spot.

"Let me do the talking," Sigrid was saying. "Don't say nothing unless one of them asks you a question. Then keep your answer short. They may be stupid oafs, but they aren't complete fools."

She stuck her head around the corner, then signaled for them to follow her.

Once around the corner, they were completely exposed. Flyn felt as if a thousand eyes were watching him. His heart pounded even harder in his ears, his breathing quickened. He glanced up to the top of the wall, unable to keep his head down.

An orc was watching them as they made their way to the back gate.

Flyn forced himself to look down at his feet. Sweat poured down his body, burning the wounds on his back left by the whip. His legs felt like he was walking through thick mud, the gate seemingly growing farther away with each step rather than closer.

Sigrid stopped suddenly, causing Flyn to almost run into her. He looked up at the gate.

An orc patrol was coming through the gate, only a few yards in front of them.

The lead orc glanced over at the escapees, chained together and loaded down with tools. Flyn looked away, sure the orc would stop and question them. He swallowed against the queasy feeling in his stomach.

The orc turned away from them, continuing on his way without pausing.

The other orcs ignored the group completely.

Flyn exhaled, not realizing he had been holding his breath. His stomach was still twisted in a knot and his knees felt weak. He had to put a hand on Sigrid's shoulder to keep himself steady.

"Let's go," Sigrid whispered.

Flyn looked back at the others. Gudbrant wiped sweat from his brow and Randell had lost all the color in his face. Harvig, as stoic as ever, seemed completely unfazed.

"This is it," Sigrid muttered.

They turned the corner and entered the gateway.

As when they entered the fortress, the portcullis was open. Just beyond it, a guard stood on each side of the opening. One of the orcs turned toward them as they entered the gateway, the sound of their rattling chains echoing through the tunnel.

"Steady now," Sigrid whispered back to them.

The guards moved to block the gateway as they approached. Sigrid walked right up to them. Flyn looked at his feet.

"Where you think you going?" one of the guards said.

"To the mine," Sigrid replied.

"It's night. There's no work in the mine at night."

"It's always dark in the mine," Sigrid said. "I just go where I'm told. The Master wants to increase production to arm more troops for the war."

"Nobody tell me about it," the first orc said.

"Nobody ever tell us nothing," the second orc said.

"Where your taskmaster?" the first orc said, stepping closer to the group.

Flyn's heartbeat was so loud in his ears, he was surprised the guards didn't hear it. He clenched his jaw and kept looking at his feet.

"Rounding up the other crews," Sigrid said. "I guess he got a late start and sent us ahead."

"He going to be in trouble," the second orc said.

"Who's your taskmaster?" the first one said.

"Garguk."

"Not like Garguk to be late."

"I heard he was busy interrogating some new prisoners for Master Ugglar."

"You can't go to mine without taskmaster."

"I just go where they tell me," Sigrid said. "I don't care if we wait here for Garguk. It's all the same to me."

Sigrid sat down in front of the orc. Flyn hesitated, then did the same.

"Of course," Sigrid continued, "I wouldn't want to be you when he shows up and asks why we aren't in the mine working."

The guards looked at each other.

"Me don't want to make Garguk mad," the second orc said.

The first one growled and cursed under his breath, then stepped back.

"Go on, get to work you lazy maggots," the orc said. "You rest when work is done."

The group stood up and Sigrid led them out of the fortress and into the fresh mountain air.

Once the wall and the guards disappeared in the darkness behind them, they stopped and looked at each other.

"I can't believe that worked!" Randell said.

"Aye," Sigrid said. "Truth be told, I wasn't so sure myself."

"But you said it would work," Flyn said.

"Well, that might have been a little fib. I figured, what did we have to lose?"

"Well done, Flyn," Gudbrant said.

"A bold plan," Harvig added. "The Andor is more courageous than he looks."

"Enough talk," Gudbrant said. "Sigrid, get us out of these chains."

The dwarf pulled out the key and unlocked the shackles on her ankles and waist, then started to unlock the others. She was interrupted by the sound of a loud bell coming from the garrison.

"What's that?" Flyn said.

"That's the alarm," Sigrid replied.

"I guess they found the bodies of the guards we killed," Gudbrant said. "Give me the keys."

Sigrid handed the keys to Gudbrant.

"Flyn, you and Sigrid get to the gear. We'll be right behind you."

Flyn turned and ran, not waiting to see if Sigrid was following him. He slipped and skidded as he ran up the crushed rock path toward the cliffs towering up in front of him somewhere in the dark. The bell continued to ring behind him.

He stopped when he reached edge of the slope that led up to the mine and turned to look for Sigrid. To his surprise, she was right next to him, the pickax still over her shoulder.

"Dwarves are faster than we look," she said in response to his unasked question. "Which way?"

"This way," Flyn said, pointing. Even though he wanted to stop to catch his breath, under the circumstances that didn't seem like a good idea. He set off along the base of the slope at a slower pace, looking for the marker Gudbrant had made. The darkness hampered their search. The sun had completely set and the moon was not yet visible above the mountain peaks to the east.

Gudbrant and the others caught up to them before he had found the marker.

"They haven't sent out a search party yet, but you can be sure they will. Gear up quick."

Sigrid watched for pursuers while the humans pulled on their armor and packs. Flyn was happy to have his sword and bow again, though he was disappointed by the loss of his hunting knife.

"Now where do we go?" Flyn asked as they gathered their gear.

"Hemdown," Gudbrant replied. "It's a town in the Blaslet Plains, a few days' travel from Gurnborg, but it's closer than any place in Asgerdale. And easier to reach, given our circumstances."

"Will they help us?" Flyn remembered his reception at Garthset.

"I think so. They're Ilfin, at least, so they won't turn us away."

"You, maybe," Sigrid said. "But what do they think of dwarves? The Ilfin clan isn't known for welcoming outsiders."

"As long as you're with us, they'll accept you as a friend."

Sigrid grunted in response, but said nothing.

"I suggest we leave tracks heading away from our path," Harvig said.

"Good idea," Gudbrant said. "Can you and Randell handle it?"

"Perhaps I should go with him," Sigrid said. "After all, they're expecting to see my footprints as well as yours."

"Even better. Get going so you can make it back before the orcs catch up to us."

Harvig left his pack, taking only his sword, followed by Sigrid with her pickax. They slipped quietly into the darkness, heading east, back the way the group had come from.

Gudbrant found a place for the rest of the group to wait. He sent Randell back toward the path from the fortress to watch for search parties. From their vantage point, they could see torches lit up outside the back gate and along the top of the fortress wall. The alarm bell had stopped ringing, replaced by yelling, though it was too far away to understand.

"How do we get to Hemdown?" Flyn asked, more to pass the time than anything.

"Normally we would take the road we followed through Ingekirk Pass. It continues on down into the plains, all the way to the west coast of Tirmar. Hemdown was originally just a small outpost used by trappers and prospectors who used to work in these mountains. Over time, it grew to be a major trading town. Before Jarot, merchants from Garthset regularly traveled to Hemdown to sell their goods and to buy goods from other lands. Meinrad was one of the traveling merchants before he became Thane. A quite successful one."

"Really?" Flyn said. "I had assumed he had been a soldier."

Gudbrant laughed. "Meinrad? I don't think he's been in a sword fight in his life. He's a good leader, but he's no soldier."

"What about that scar on his face?"

"He doesn't talk about that," Gudbrant said, grinning at Flyn. "He likes people to come up with stories about how he single-handedly fought off a band of marauders who ambushed him, or some other wild tale. The truth is much more mundane. He was harnessing his horse to a wagon when the horse spooked and kicked him in the face. But don't tell anyone. The only reason I know is because Brenna told me."

Gudbrant looked away, toward the fortress, and was quiet.

"Anyway, we can't take the main road with the orcs looking for us," he said after a long pause. "We'll have to climb down the mountain slopes and through the forests until we reach the Blaslet Plains. Once there, we'll need to consider our options."

Flyn nodded, not that the information meant much to him. At least climbing down the mountain slope should be easier than climbing up.

A loud noise from the garrison broke into his thoughts.

"Here they come," Gudbrant said.

A group of orcs marched out of the gate, each carrying a torch and a mace. As they made their way from the fortress, they used their torches to search the ground on both sides of the path.

Just then, Randell slipped in behind the boulder they were using for cover.

"The first search party is on the way," he said.

Gudbrant nodded and pointed. "We noticed. And they don't look like they're interested in capturing us." He paused and watched the orcs make their way across the plateau. "Nothing else?"

"No, all's quiet between here and the path to the mine. At least for now. Harvig and the dwarf better get back soon, because it won't stay that way for long."

As he spoke, there was a clattering of stones to their left. The three men drew their swords and waited. A moment later, Sigrid appeared out of the darkness.

"Best be on our way," she said as she reached them. "The big guy's right behind me."

"Okay. Load up."

Flyn sheathed his sword and shouldered his pack. He was about to sling his bow across his back, then decided better of it. Instead, he nocked an arrow.

Harvig arrived, out of breath, just as they were ready to go.

"Can you keep going?" Gudbrant asked as he threw Harvig his pack.

Harvig nodded and waved for them to get moving.

Randell led the way, picking the easiest path he could find across the face of the mountainside and keeping them far enough up the slope that any searchers looking up wouldn't see them in the dark.

Down on the plateau, the orcs reached the abandoned cart. They stopped and searched the area before moving on. Two of the searchers moved ahead of the rest, making their way to the mountainside where Flyn and his companions were. Gudbrant signaled a stop at a small gulley where they all crouched down. Peering off the lip of the gulley, they watched as the orcs got closer.

"Ready that bow," Gudbrant whispered to Flyn.

Flyn held the bow out in front of him, ready to bring it up and take aim at one of the orcs. He was shaking all over. The arrow clicked quietly against the arrow rest.

"Easy, lad," Sigrid said. "Wait to see if they take the bait."

The orcs stopped at the bottom of the slope.

"Look!" one of the orcs said. "Footprints."

"We get them now!" the other one said.

They turned off the path and ran along the bottom of the slope, following the tracks left by Harvig and Sigrid.

Flyn lowered his bow and breathed a sigh of relief.

"Let's move quickly, before the rest of the group gets here," Gudbrant said.

They snuck out of the gulley and, moving as fast as they dared in the dark, hurried along the slope until the torches of Gurnborg were lost in the night.

CHAPTER 10

The odd group spent the night climbing down the side of the mountain. All were tired and sore from their captivity and interrogations, especially Flyn, but none wanted to spend the night in the open with the orcs chasing after them. They moved as quickly as the darkness allowed and even though they saw no sign of pursuit, they didn't pause until they reached the forest that covered the mountain's lower slopes. Even then, after a short break, they continued on for another hour before stopping for the remainder of the night.

Their camp was spartan, even by the standards Flyn had come to accept since his fateful boat trip so many weeks before. They decided to not set up their tents, instead opting to just sleep sitting up against trees still wearing their armor, their swords lying on the ground next to them. A fire, of course, was out of the question. All were asleep within minutes, except Harvig, who took the first watch.

It seemed to Flyn that he had just closed his eyes when he found himself being shaken.

"Wake up, lad." Sigrid's hand was on his shoulder.

"Is it morning already?"

Sigrid chuckled. "I should think that if we weren't in the trees, we would see the sky lightening with the coming of dawn, but there's still enough of the night left for the others to sleep awhile longer. For you, on the other hand, sleep time is over. It's your turn to take the watch."

Flyn yawned and tried to stretch. Every muscle in his body ached, though he couldn't tell if it was from the torture he had endured, the days climbing through the rugged terrain, or sleeping against a tree. He supposed it was all three. Adding to his discomfort, his back itched and burned. With his leather vest, he couldn't even scratch his back on the tree.

He stood up and took off the vest. Sigrid, sitting against a nearby tree, watched, an amused grin on her face.

"My back itches," Flyn said.

"I imagine it does," she replied. "If we were in Kridheben, I know a healer who'd have you fixed up in a jiffy. Alas, we're a long way from the halls of home."

"Is that where you're from?" Flyn rubbed his back on the tree while he talked.

"Aye. Most beautiful place in the world. You should come visit someday."

"I'll do that. Right after I rescue Kel..." Flyn trailed off. *If I rescue Kel.*

"I'll show you the Shrine of Brontee and the Kaygen Cathedral. And the Crystal Hall of Drysten. Now there's a sight worth the travel to see. It was carved out of the living crystal back in the days of Kirr himself. Special braziers were built to send light through the crystals. The caretakers can make it look like the sun is setting inside the mountain or turn the whole hall into fire. Elves may have their rockets and sparklers, but nothing they have compares to the light shows in the Crystal Hall."

"Rockets and sparklers?" Flyn sat down across from Sigrid.

Sigrid cocked her head and stared at Flyn before responding. "Rockets are small tubes that fly up into the air and explode into thousands of sparks of colored light. Sparklers are kind of the same, but they don't go into the air. You've never seen them?"

"We don't have anything like that back on Trygsted," Flyn said. For all the wonder people had shown about his home, it seemed pretty boring compared to what they had in Tirmar. "But we don't have elves or dwarves either."

"Ah, you don't know what you're missing," Sigrid said, shaking her head. "I'll have a lot to show you after this is over."

Flyn nodded, but didn't reply. He didn't have much confidence that there would be an *after*.

Sigrid broke the silence after a few minutes. "Tell me something, Andor. How is it you're so far from home? And how did your friend get himself captured by the pig-noses?"

Flyn sighed. "It's my fault. Me and my stupid boat. Kel didn't even want to come."

He recounted everything he and Kel had been through since they left Drogave.

"That's about the craziest thing I've ever heard," she said when he finished. She had an odd look in her eye. "A whole clan living on an island that doesn't like boats?"

"That's a whole different story." Flyn frowned. She thought the strangest part was that the Andors didn't like boats?

Sigrid shook her head. "Well, I suppose it's not much stranger than the Redmarr clan."

"Who are the Redmarr clan?"

"The Redmarrs are dwarves who don't like being underground. They live in towns and cities just like humans. And some of them even shave their beards. Especially the women." Sigrid spat. "Trying to look more human or something." She looked up at Flyn. "No offense."

"So all dwarf women in your clan have beards?"

"Aye, why wouldn't we?"

"I'm sorry. I don't mean to be rude, but I've never seen a woman with a beard."

"You humans are a strange lot." Sigrid chuckled.

Flyn yawned.

"Why don't you go back to sleep?" Sigrid said. "I won't be going back to sleep, so you may as well rest. Besides, you need it more than I do."

"No," Flyn said. "It's my turn. I'll do it."

"If you say so, Andor."

Flyn leaned back against the tree and yawned again.

Flyn and Sigrid woke the others while the forest floor was still covered in shadow. After a hasty breakfast, the group set out again, climbing down the side of the mountain.

The trees and undergrowth hampered their travel, pushing them along the slopes one way or the other, sometimes many furlongs before finding a clear path to the west again. At times, cliffs and ravines blocked their way forward. Small gullies would merge with larger gullies to form ravines. They followed these when they could, climbing out if they turned too far to the south and toward Ingekirk Pass, where their pursuers were no doubt searching for them.

Several times they heard patrols, usually far in the distance, though once they thought they glimpsed a group of orcs moving through the trees on a ridge across a narrow valley from them. Each time they stopped and found cover, but no one came across them.

After a day and a half of trudging through the foothills of the Estlaeg Mountains, they reached more level ground and soon the last of the trees.

"Best if we rest here for a while," Gudbrant said. "The trees will shelter us from spying eyes. We can begin our journey across the open plains under the cover of night."

The tired group settled down to rest for a few hours. Flyn dropped to the ground where he stood and fell asleep without eating or even removing his pack. The sun was below the horizon in front of them when Gudbrant woke him. Flyn could barely move his aching muscles. He sat by himself, not talking to the others, nibbling on jerky.

The rest of the party wasn't in much better shape than Flyn. Even the resilient Sigrid grumbled to herself as she ate. Harvig, his nose and face still swollen and purple, hadn't spoken much at all since they had escaped. Like Flyn, he ate alone and didn't speak.

Randell and Gudbrant discussed the path ahead of them. Neither could remember exactly how far Hemdown was from the mountains, though both agreed it was at least two days along the road. Gudbrant felt it was one day by horse, so two days on foot. Randell argued that to make the distance in one day, the horse would have to be carrying only a passenger, and therefore it was probably more like three days on foot.

Regardless of how far it was, they would be spending at least one, possibly two days in the open. Which meant they would have to stay well north of the road to avoid being seen by orcs that might still be looking for them. And traveling by night would be harder without the sun to help guide their direction.

"What does it matter?" Flyn said after the two had been going back and forth for a while.

"It matters because we don't want to wander too close to the road," Gudbrant said.

"Or too far away from the road and miss Hemdown entirely," Randell added.

"Yes, I know, but we don't even know how far from the road we are now."

"Well, we can't go looking for it just so we can follow it," Randell said.

"No, but we can follow a star."

"A star?" Randell said.

"Yes. Back home, I had been thinking about taking my boat out at night. I never did get the nerve to do it, but my main concern was how to keep a straight course. I spent every night for a month watching the stars. They move through the sky, like the sun, but there's one star that stands still."

"Skadyarna," Gudbrant said. "In the northern sky."

"Exactly. If we keep it directly to our right, we'll always be traveling west."

Sigrid chuckled. "The lad is smarter then he lets on."

"And you've done this before?" Gudbrant asked.

"Well, for short distances. But it always works."

"I think we should give it a try," Randell said.

Gudbrant and Sigrid accepted Flyn's plan. Harvig said nothing, seemingly unconcerned with how they proceeded.

The orange glow of sunset had faded to the purple of twilight by the time they were ready to move again. Once they left the trees, Flyn found Skadyarna. Squaring his shoulders and holding his arm out, he turned until the star was straight above his outstretched fingers.

"That way," he said, pointing in front of him.

They set out across the open plain under the cover of complete darkness. They would have a couple of hours before the moon rose behind them, and they hoped to be far enough from the mountains by then that none on the open peaks would see their passage. Gudbrant and Randell led the party, followed closely by Flyn and Sigrid. Harvig trailed behind as usual, to watch for pursuers.

Shortly after leaving the forest, they crossed a road going north and south.

"That way lies Uskleig," Gudbrant said, pointing north.

The road disappeared into the darkness, no sign of the evil it led to. The way they must travel to save Kel and Brenna. Flyn shivered in spite of the warm evening air.

They traveled without speaking for a while, the only sound the soft swishing made by the tall grass brushing against their legs. Far to their left, they caught an occasional glimpse of light.

"Orcs with torches on the road," Gudbrant said.

No one else spoke.

Flyn found himself thinking about what Ugglar had said about Kel. If Jarot wanted him, perhaps Kel was still alive. But maybe that wasn't such a good thing. From the brief torture he experienced, Flyn couldn't imagine having to endure it for days or weeks. Whether Kel was alive or dead, Flyn couldn't abandon his friend, even though it meant almost certain death for himself.

He still remembered Kel's words from weeks ago: *If I die, I'll haunt you forever.*

"I suppose you will," he whispered to himself.

"What was that, lad?" Sigrid said from next to him.

"Nothing. I was just thinking about Kel. Wondering if he was still alive."

"Have faith," she said, putting a hand on his shoulder. "If he's anything like you, he'll survive."

"If he does, it'll just be to tell me 'I told you so.'"

Sigrid laughed. "Then here's to 'I told you so!'"

They walked in silence for a few minutes, then Sigrid started to sing.

> *On the ancient plains of Harbregard*
> *through bleak and barren dusty haze*
> *the dawn light gleamed on steel afar*
> *a mighty army on the plains ablaze.*
>
> *The false gods sent their armies forth*
> *thrice the sword and ten-fold horse.*
> *Still Andor rode to meet their force,*
> *and rallied human, elf, and dwarf.*
>
> *Yonarr magic and ancient charms*
> *proved no match for the warriors bold.*
> *With freedom's cry the slaves took arms*
> *to storm the gates of Mijon's hold.*
>
> *Swords of free and swords of thrall*
> *rang out across the plains at dawn.*
> *An angry swirl of dust and pall*
> *that fates of all would hinge upon.*

Her voice faded into the night.

"What's that song about?" Flyn asked.

"It's called 'The Last Ride.' It's about the last battle of the Tirmar Revolution when Andor brought together Kirr, Redmarr, and the others to lead the last assault on the Yonarr. It goes on to tell about how they breached the gates of the city and how Mijon used the last of his magic to destroy the Yonarr and their civilization."

"Meinrad mentioned Mijon. Wasn't he leader of the Yonarr?"

"He was their leader for hundreds of years. Maybe thousands. Nobody knows. When he saw the war was lost, he summoned all his power to destroy all the Yonarr cities and all their magic."

"Why would he do that?"

"The stories say it was to keep their magic from the rebels. Whatever his reason, after that, the Yonarr forces scattered. Everyone believed Mijon's magic had destroyed all the Yonarr as well, since they all disappeared afterward. I guess some of the old songs will have to be changed."

The party marched on, and by the time the moon rose, they were far from the foothills of the Estlaeg Mountains and the eyes of searchers there. Even lights on the road to the south had disappeared. Still, they pressed on with only occasional short breaks. None of them wanted to chance a rogue patrol stumbling on them in the dark.

The rolling hills and flat prairies of the Blaslet Plains stretched as far as Flyn could see in the light of the half moon. He suspected that even in daylight he wouldn't see anything but grass in front of them. Behind them, the mountains still loomed, their snow-covered peaks glowing pale blue in the moonlight.

"These fields remind me of home," Flyn said after a while. "My father and brother will have all the crops planted by now. I should have been there to help."

"Once we find your friend, we'll figure out a way to get you back," Gudbrant said. "You know, these fields used to be farms, before Jarot came."

"They don't look like they've been harvested or plowed in a long time," Flyn said.

"No, not for many years," Gudbrant said. "Most of the Blaslet Plains between Hemdown and the Estlaegs used to be farmland. This was the primary source of food for the Ilfin clan, from Garthset to Haugerholm. They even traded crops with the Mundar and Ranjer clans when we still had contact with them."

"What happened to all the farms?"

"Jarot's forces destroyed most of them. Those closer to Uskleig are now run by the orcs with the people they've enslaved."

Flyn nodded. All those people, driven from their homes or captured by the orcs to be slaves.

Not for the first time since leaving home, Flyn wished he had never tried to take his boat around Trygsted. He wondered what his family was doing, whether they had given up hope of ever seeing him again. He wished he could talk to them, to let them know he was alive and trying to get home. To his surprise, he even wanted to know if his father and Ty ever got their milking machine working.

The fields of grasses gave way to other fields. Corn, beans, and other vegetables, all growing wild. Next to one field, they found an old burned-down house. The remains were overgrown with weeds and brush. An old well next to the house turned out to have clean water that they used to refill their waterskins.

As they sat and rested, Flyn looked up at the moon. Wiping a tear from his eye, he wondered if his family was looking up at that same moon, somewhere hundreds of leagues away.

After walking through the night, the party camped the next day in a hollow surrounded by tall brush to hide them from prying eyes on the road. They still did not take a chance on a cooking fire, knowing the smoke would be easily spotted by any traveling along the road they suspected was less than half a league away. They slept on the open ground, in case they needed to make a quick escape should an orc patrol stumble upon them.

The following night was much the same. Rolling hills, grasslands, wild fields, and the occasional ruins of a house, most burned down, the rest collapsing on their own from disuse. They saw no more lights from the road or any other sign they were still being followed. Even so, they grew anxious to reach Hemdown and its relative security from the orcs of Gurnborg.

As the sky began to lighten in the east, Gudbrant stopped.

"There," he said, pointing to his left.

The others followed his finger. To their south and a little east, lights twinkled in the distance.

"Is that Hemdown?" Flyn asked.

"It is," Gudbrant replied. "Unless I'm very much mistaken. It's less than a league away. We can reach it before sunrise."

The party turned south, heading straight for the lights. The distance proved to be farther than it appeared. They walked for over an hour before they reached the town. The lights were coming from large braziers, burning bright atop a great stone wall, even larger than the one surrounding Gurnborg.

"I haven't been to Hemdown in many years," Gudbrant said. "Much has changed since my last visit. Let us hope there are still friendly faces behind these walls. Friendly or no, best we keep our business to ourselves as much as possible."

Guards patrolling the top of the walls watched them as they made their way around the city to the main gate. Hemdown was larger than any town Flyn had ever been to. On Trygsted, only Osthorp and Andorkirk, the capital of Trygsted, were bigger, and he had never been to either. They walked for the better part of an hour before they reached the gate. By then, the sun was rising about the mountains in the east.

The gate was open, guarded by men in leather armor, metal helmets, and armed with swords. As the travelers approached, the guards stepped forward to block the way, watching them carefully. On the wall above the gate, two archers stood with arrows nocked, ready to draw.

Without hesitation, Gudbrant stepped up to the closest guard, who put his hand on the hilt of his sword.

"I am Gudbrant, Captain of the Garthset Militia. I would speak with your captain."

The guard eyed Gudbrant suspiciously for a moment before answering.

"No one has passed this way from Garthset in years. Why should I believe you are who you say you are? You look more like the captain of a troop of vagabonds than the captain of a militia."

"We have had a difficult journey and spent some time as guests of the orcs at Gurnborg. But perhaps we should let your captain judge the merits of my claim."

The guard looked at him for a moment more, then turned to a message runner sitting by a guard house.

"Summon Captain Adalbern. Tell him that someone claiming to be from Garthset wishes to speak with him."

The messenger jumped up and ran off down the street.

"Adalbern?" Gudbrant asked. "What came of Captain Wynnstan?"

"You can wait over there," the guard said, ignoring Gudbrant's question and pointing to the guard house. "Remove your weapons and leave them with the guards inside."

Gudbrant tried to get more from the guard, but he refused to answer any questions. Resigned to wait for Captain Adalbern, the party filed into the guard house. Inside, two guards sat at a table. One of them pointed to a row of shelves, all empty. The guards watched as the party unstrapped their weapon belts.

"I don't like this," Sigrid said, putting her pickax on one of the shelves.

"Patience, my friend," Gudbrant said. "These are dangerous times and we are strangers here. Trust is hard to come by, when every day brings the possibility of war."

"I, for one, would rather sit here unarmed than sit in an open field hoping an orc patrol doesn't find us," Flyn said.

Sigrid grumbled but said no more.

A quarter hour passed before the guard they first met came in. He was joined by another man pulling a small cart with food and a jug.

"The Captain is attending to other matters and will be here when he can. In the meantime, he has sent some refreshments for you."

The second man passed around plates and mugs, then filled the mugs with wine and set trays of fruits, breads, and cheese on the table. When he finished, he left without saying a word.

"Thank you," Gudbrant said.

The guard nodded, then turned and followed the other man out the door. Flyn and his companions stood around the table, staring at the food.

"Well, I'm not shy," Harvig said finally. He sat down, filled his plate, and started eating. The others joined him, and soon they were talking, laughing, and filling their bellies with the first fresh food they had eaten in almost two weeks. In Sigrid's case, months.

When the food was gone, they sat back and drained their mugs. Flyn was surprised by how much he had eaten. He hadn't realized just how hungry he had been. He yawned and stretched. With his belly full, he was ready to go to sleep. He was beginning to wonder just how long they would have to wait when the door opened again.

The man who walked through the door was dressed in a uniform similar to the one worn by the militiamen in Garthset. Two gold braids trimmed the neck of his tunic, like those on Gudbrant's.

"You must be Captain Adalbern," Gudbrant said, standing to greet the man.

"And you must be the one who claims to be the Captain of the Garthset Militia," the captain replied.

"Gudbrant, at your service. I knew Captain Wynnstan. What became of him?"

"You have not been to Hemdown in a long while then. Captain Wynnstan was killed in a battle with the orcs many years ago."

"I'm sorry to hear. He was a good man."

"He was," Adalbern said. "Now, what brings you all the way from Garthset with this...lot." He eyed Sigrid suspiciously.

"The reason behind our journey is a long tale and not for idle conversation. Perhaps we can go somewhere to talk in confidence?" Gudbrant glanced at the two guards.

Adalbern paused before answering, his eyebrows raised.

"I can send the guards outside, but I must insist you send the rest of your party out as well," he said.

"We can agree to that," Gudbrant said. "But Flyn should stay. He's at the heart of the matter."

Gudbrant signaled Randell and Harvig to leave the guardhouse. Sigrid followed. Once they were gone, Adalbern sent the two guards out as well, then sat at the table. Flyn noticed he sat on the side closest to their weapons. Gudbrant took a seat opposite Adalbern. Flyn, not sure where he was supposed to sit, sat next to him.

"Now, Captain, perhaps you can give me some answers?"

"You are familiar with the tale of Andor and the Lost Clan, are you not?"

"Of course," Adalbern said. He leaned back and folded his arms.

"Well, I present to you Flynygyn Geirrsen of the Andor Clan."

"I'm a very busy man. Please don't waste my time with fairytales," Adalbern scoffed. He moved to stand.

"No, it's true," Flyn said. "I'm from Trygsted, and until a few weeks ago, I didn't know anything about Tirmar or that there were any other clans in the world."

"Trygsted. And where is Trygsted?"

"It's an island not too far off the east coast of Tirmar. I don't know exactly how far. I got lost and found myself here."

Flyn told Adalbern about everything that had happened to him until he'd met Gudbrant outside of Garthset.

"We were searching for a pair of ogres that raided a nearby farmstead when we found Flyn," Gudbrant said. "While we were trying to figure out who he was and why he was there, an orc raiding party attacked us, aided by the very ogres we were looking for. We drove them off, but they had Flyn's friend. After Flyn healed, and much discussion, I decided to help him find his friend and try to rescue him." He left out the part about disobeying the Thane's orders.

"The orcs grab people all the time," Adalbern said. "Rescue from Gurnborg is impossible. Surely you aren't that foolish."

"It is true that I had another motive. The orcs took the Thane's daughter and my wife-to-be."

"You expected to break into Gurnborg and rescue *two* prisoners?" Adalbern sat back again, shaking his head.

"It's more complicated than that, but we did sneak into Gurnborg."

"Now I know you're lying to me." Adalbern stood up. "As I said, I have no time for fairytales."

"Talk to Sigrid, our dwarf friend outside. She was a prisoner there."

"What of your friend and the Thane's daughter? You just left them?"

"We discovered they were moved to Uskleig."

Adalbern laughed. "I don't know whether to be amazed by your story, or just throw you out. I'm far too busy. We have real problems. Orc raiding parties from Gurnborg are becoming more numerous, and coming closer to Hemdown every day. In the last two days alone my scouts have reported dozens of them between here and the mountains. Good day, Captain Gudbrant. You may lodge in

Hemdown as any other traveler. Your weapons will remain here until you depart."

Adalbern turned to leave.

"You're seeing more orcs because they're looking for us."

Adalbern turned back and stared at Gudbrant, apparently trying to decide if Gudbrant was telling the truth.

"So you riled up the orcs and led them here?"

"Not intentionally. The majority of the orc force left for Asgerdale the night we snuck in. If not for that, we would never have escaped. Even so, they still have enough to send out patrols to search for us. And they're very determined. You see, Ugglar discovered Flyn is an Andor and intended on sending him to Uskleig to be interrogated by Jarot himself. We believe that's why his friend, Kel, was taken there."

"Perhaps it would be best if you didn't stay here," Adalbern said, his voice quieter. "If they are after this one, as you say, they may try to attack Hemdown searching for him."

"Please. We are tired and wounded. We have very little of our supplies left. Turning us away would most likely mean our deaths. Perhaps I could speak to your Thane," Gudbrant said.

"No, that is out of the question." Adalbern paced back and forth, his jaw clenched and his face drawn.

"If the orcs are going to attack, they'll attack whether we're here or not," Gudbrant pointed out. "But as I said, most of their force went to Asgerdale, so they don't have enough troops to mount an assault on Hemdown."

"Regardless, why should we aid you when you are the cause of our turmoil?"

"Blaming us for the orcs' actions is foolish and naive, and to turn us away because they have stepped up their patrols is cowardice. I have never known the militia of Hemdown to be cowards."

Adalbern scowled at Gudbrant, who returned the captain's gaze without blinking. Finally, Adalbern looked away and sighed. "Very well. You can stay until tomorrow. After that… We shall see."

"Thank you. Perhaps you'll join us for dinner this evening and we can discuss matters further."

"Perhaps."

Adalbern left quickly, leaving Flyn and Gudbrant alone.

"Well, at least we can sleep in a bed for one night." Gudbrant smiled at Flyn. "Come on. Let's find the inn and get settled."

Noon had come before they left the guardhouse. The gate guard directed them to an inn called The Blue Dragon, a short walk from the gate.

The sun beat down on the dusty street that was already thick with people. On either side of the main road, merchants shouted out to the crowd, offering everything from exotic fruits to "magic" trinkets. Butchers peddled fresh beef, pork, chicken, and other meat Flyn didn't recognize. Other merchants offered live versions of the same.

"Is it always like this?" Flyn said, staring in wonder. He imagined that this was what Osthorp must be like during one of its festivals.

"No," Gudbrant said. "It used to be busier. Or course, even Garthset used to be busier, though never like this."

Flyn nodded, overwhelmed by the sights and sounds. He had never seen so many people in one place before. He felt dizzy from the din of the crowd and the braying of the livestock. Somewhere a blacksmith hammer clanged. Merchants reached out and grabbed passersby, trying to pull them into their makeshift shops. Shoppers pushed and shoved their way past the travelers.

The group pressed through the throng of people, choking on the sour, sweaty stench of the people, the spicy and pungent scents from the food carts, and the musky aroma of the livestock. Sigrid scowled as people hit her in the face with hands, elbows, or packages, seemingly oblivious to the dwarf.

Gudbrant stopped at several merchants so they could purchase new clothes, which he also paid for. None of the merchants had anything to fit a dwarf, so Sigrid had to make do. She ended up with a tunic that came to her knees and pants she would have to cut off.

At the inn, the common room was already filled with lunch patrons. Gudbrant flagged down the innkeeper, who provided them with room keys and told them where they could find the well. Then he pardoned himself for not having more time to help them and rushed off to return to his lunch crowd. The travelers, too tired to concern themselves over his abruptness, retired to their rooms.

Later that afternoon they met back in the common room, now mostly empty. Clean and rested with their new clothes, they all felt refreshed. Sigrid, truly free from her captivity, didn't even mind that her new clothes didn't fit right.

"A far sight better than what I had before," she said.

The innkeeper approached as they were talking.

"Good afternoon," he said. "I apologize again for earlier. The noontime crowd is very demanding. I trust your rest was satisfactory?"

"Yes, thank you," Gudbrant replied.

"Good, good. Captain Adalbern has left a message for you. He said the Thane requests your presence at the Thane's Hall at the dinner bell. If you leave now, you should just make it," the innkeeper said, and proceeded to give them directions to the Thane's Hall.

Gudbrant thanked him and the innkeeper returned to the kitchen.

"Well, let's not keep the Thane waiting," Gudbrant said.

The party left the inn and followed the innkeeper's directions. The shops and homes were similar to those in Garthset, most built with stone, although some were constructed of wood. As they made their way deeper into the town, the structures grew older, with cracks in the stones, or corners crumbling away. Moss and ivy covered many of the walls. Some buildings showed signs of repair work, though even that appeared to have been done long ago. The streets too grew older with more cracks and missing flagstones, especially after they had left the main road.

Finally, the street they were on ended in a large circular courtyard with a fountain in the middle. On one side was a temple with a bell tower and on the other a large stone building, bigger and better maintained than the others. Two sentries flanked the large double doors into the building.

"This must be the Thane's Hall," Gudbrant said.

The guards stepped in front of the doors as they approached.

"Halt," one of the guards said. "State your name and business."

"I am Captain Gudbrant of Garthset. The Thane invited us to join him for dinner."

"You will wait here," the guard said. He opened the door and spoke to someone inside, then turned back to continue blocking the way.

After a few minutes, the door opened again and Captain Adalbern came out.

"Captain Gudbrant," he said. "Good of you to come. I recounted your tale to the Thane and he wishes to discuss it with you. Please, follow me."

The guards held open the doors and the travelers followed Adalbern into the building. The interior was much like that of the Thane's Hall in Garthset, with polished wood floors and ceilings and lanterns hung on the walls to provide light. Adalbern led them through several hallways until they reached a large dining room.

A table that Flyn guessed could seat thirty people filled most of the room. The walls were covered by tapestries, many depicting farmers harvesting crops and horses pulling carts full of produce. Guards were positioned along the walls around the room. Chandeliers hung from the vaulted ceiling, providing light from hundreds of candles.

Adalbern led them to the table where an old man with gray hair about his shoulders sat. He was wearing a long, flowing robe and around his neck he wore a gold pendant of a circle and cross. He rose to meet the travelers.

"My Lord," Adalbern said. "May I present Gudbrant, Captain of the Garthset Militia."

"Health and happiness to you, My Lord," Gudbrant said, holding out his hand.

"Health and happiness, Captain," the Thane said, clasping Gudbrant's arm. "I am Theodard, Thane of Hemdown."

Gudbrant introduced the rest of the party to the Thane. "These are my closest friends, Randell and Harvig. Sigrid is a dwarf from the Kirr Clan. And this is Flynygyn of the Andors."

Theodard stepped forward to look at Flyn, eyeing him up and down.

"Well, he doesn't look like an Ilfin, but an Andor?" The Thane shook his head. "I cannot believe that. The Andors were lost at sea, if they ever existed at all."

"Please, I don't mean any disrespect," Flyn said. "Wherever I go, people seem to have a hard time believing that I'm from Trygsted. I don't understand why and I'm not even sure why it matters. Everyone seems to think there's something special about the Andors, but we're just people. In fact, back on Trygsted, no one would believe me if I told them about you."

"Well, Andor or not, Adalbern told me your story, but I want to hear it from you. Sit and we'll talk while we wait for dinner to be served."

Theodard returned to the seat at the head of the table. He directed Flyn to sit next to him on one side, and Gudbrant on the other. The rest filled in seats on either side, with Adalbern at the end. Once they were settled and drinks poured, the Thane urged Flyn to recount his travels.

For the second time that day, he described what had happened to him since he and Kel had set out on their trip. Theodard interrupted him periodically, asking for clarification and additional details as he went. Dinner was served while they were talking. When Flyn was finished, the Thane sat thinking.

"Well, Adalbern," he said after several minutes. "What do you think of our guests?"

"My Lord, I can't believe that this man is of the Lost Clan, but at least part of their story appears to have some truth to it. The orcs of Gurnborg have been very active in the Blaslet Plains for the last few days, which corresponds to when they claim to have escaped. And their armor is clearly from Garthset."

"Then you think they are lying about this man being from Trygsted."

"I do, but I do not know for what purpose."

"My Lord," Gudbrant interrupted. "Whether you believe Flyn is an Andor or not should not matter. We ask nothing more of you than to let us rest and recover in Hemdown. We shall pay for our lodging and supplies, and when we are sufficiently rested, we will be on our way."

"Then why the insistence to meet with me this morning?" Adalbern said.

"I felt it would be a courtesy to inform you that I was here and to warn you of the orcs that are searching for us. However, you seem to have knowledge of the orcs' movements already, so my counsel would seem to be unneeded."

Theodard chuckled and Adalbern frowned. Gudbrant turned his attention back to the Thane.

"My Lord, I believe Flyn is an Andor, and so does Ugglar. We mean to rescue his friend from Uskleig and by the grace of the gods, perhaps my Brenna as well. None of that need be your concern, but we require rest and supplies before we set out on our task."

"Very well," Theodard said. "You may stay in Hemdown as you like, but should the orcs attack, looking for the Andor, why should I not give them what they want?"

"Surely you wouldn't do such a thing," Gudbrant said.

"I didn't say I would. I merely asked why I should place the life of one stranger over the lives of my people. After all, the orcs don't seem to be intent on killing him."

"They want to send him to Uskleig and hand him over to Jarot, a fate worse than death itself."

"And yet that's exactly where you want to go. Wouldn't giving him to the orcs accomplish what you wish anyway?"

"Our hope is to not end up Jarot's prisoners."

The Thane laughed. "You must be a fool. If you attempt to break into Uskleig, Jarot's prisoners is exactly what you'll become. That is if you aren't killed in the process."

Gudbrant clenched his jaw, but said nothing.

"And truthfully, Captain, I don't know why you would believe this boy's story anyway. He hardly looks like an Andor. At least according to the stories."

"Stories handed down for over a thousand years. Certainly a few details may be distorted."

"Regardless, he doesn't look like a legend."

"Please, My Lord," Flyn said. "I don't know anything about

legends or your stories about my ancestors. I just want to save my friend."

Theodard looked at him for a few moments before answering.

"Well, you may claim to be whomever you wish. I shall not let it bother me anymore." He turned back to Gudbrant. "So, Captain, it has been some time since we have had a visitor from Garthset. Perhaps you can enlighten us with news from Asgerdale?"

They rested for two weeks, recovering from their ordeal at Gurnborg. Adalbern brought a healer to attend to Flyn's injuries. By the time they were ready to start out again, the pain was gone, though the healer told him the scars would never go away. All things considered, he supposed it could have been worse.

The healer was able to help Harvig as well, though he had to re-break Harvig's nose to fix it. He spent several days with his nose bandaged.

By mutual agreement, the party's identity wasn't revealed to the citizens of Hemdown. Captain Adalbern and Thane Theodard were concerned that if news of their presence leaked out to the orcs, the city may face an attack. Gudbrant's concern was of the enemy discovering their plans to travel to Uskleig.

The orcs never attacked Hemdown, though reports of increased orc patrols continued to come in. Gudbrant had requested to be kept informed about the orcs' movements, and Adalbern had agreed, grudgingly. Each evening, a messenger brought the day's reports to the group during their evening meal. They hoped to stay in Hemdown until the activity subsided.

Gudbrant spent the days looking for information regarding the land between Hemdown and Uskleig with little success. He found a few people who used to live on farms, but none who had been east of Hemdown in the last ten years. Even the traders avoided the land between Hemdown and Uskleig.

Two weeks after Flyn and his companions arrived in Hemdown, a grizzled trapper named Byorn checked into the inn. That evening, after many rounds of ale, Byorn spoke of strange creatures he had encountered in the Nidfel Mountains to the north. Flyn and Gudbrant gathered around with the other inn guests to listen to his tall tales.

"So there I was," Byorn was saying. "Just me and the beast, a wall of rock to my left, a thousand-foot ravine to my right. I had nowhere to run. We stared at each other, each waiting for the other to make the first move. Its eyes glowed red as coals, its fangs like daggers, its foul stench filling the air. Every time it stepped toward me, I waved my torch in front of me, forcing it back.

"I don't know how long we stood there, staring each other down, but I knew my torch wouldn't last much longer. If I didn't make a move soon, the beast would get the best of me."

Byorn paused to take a drink of his ale and look around at his audience, who leaned closer.

"Then I saw my chance. It threw its head back and howled into the night, whether in frustration or to intimidate me, I don't know, but I used its distraction to my advantage. I leapt forward, swinging my torch at its head with all my might. It tried to move away, but too late. The torch struck it in the head, knocking it back, the flame singeing its fur. Before it recovered, I struck again, this time hitting it square.

"The beast stumbled back and I swung again, driving it to the ledge. Just before it went over, it grabbed my arm, its claws digging into my flesh."

Byorn pulled up the sleeve on his left arm, revealing a nasty-looking red scar.

"It almost pulled me over the cliff with it, but I managed to catch hold of a tree. It glared at me with those red eyes and I swear by the gods it spoke as it fell. 'Your soul will burn!' it said. Then it fell and I heard its screams echo from the ravine."

A murmur rolled through the crowd. A few left, commenting that the old man was a liar or senile. The rest ignored the skeptics.

"What was it?" one of the inn's guests asked.

"That I don't know," Byorn said. "Half man, half beast. A face like a wolf, arms and legs like a bear. Whatever it was, I never saw nothing like it in all my days."

"It was a vargolf," another man said.

"There's no such thing," someone else said. "Vargolfs only exist in children's tales."

"They do exist," said yet another man. "I saw one once when I was a boy."

The room erupted in argument. Byorn sat back, drinking his ale and watching the fray with a grin.

"Come on," Gudbrant said to Flyn. "I want to talk to this man."

Flyn followed Gudbrant to the table where Byorn was seated.

"Excuse me," Gudbrant said. "You seem to be a man of the world. Would you mind if I asked you more of you travels?"

"Not at all, my good man. Please, join me." Byorn motioned to the chairs at the table.

"My name is Gudbrant and this is Flyn." The pair sat down across from Byorn.

"If you liked that tale, let me tell you of a time I was hunting boars in the Fuldarl Forest."

"Actually, I'm more interested in your adventures in the Nidfel Mountains," Gudbrant said.

"Ah, well, the Nidfels are a cold, dangerous place, as I've told. The wolf creature I battled wasn't even the most terrifying beast I've encountered there."

"But why the Nidfels? Aren't you worried Jarot's orcs will catch you?"

Byorn laughed, his eyes sparkling. "There are far worse things than orcs in those mountains." He drained his ale and shouted for another before continuing. "No, even the orcs are afraid to travel in the Nidfel Mountains."

"But what of Uskleig?" Gudbrant said. "Surely they aren't afraid to travel there?"

"Uskleig is at the eastern end of the Nidfels," Byorn said with an air of smugness. "Where they meet the Estlaegs. The orcs patrol the Estlaegs, but they let the creatures of the Nidfels protect that approach to the city. Not until you get within sight of the citadel itself will you find hide or hair of an orc."

"That is truly amazing," Gudbrant said, eyes wide in mock astonishment. "The orcs are so powerful. Why should they be afraid?"

"You have much to learn of orcs, my friend." Byorn laughed again. "They're big, and they're strong, even brave, when up against a weaker foe. But orcs are a superstitious lot. Stories of demons and other powerful monsters keep them out of the Nidfels."

The innkeeper brought Byorn's ale to the table.

"Let me buy your drink for you." Gudbrant turned to the innkeeper. "Please put this on my bill."

The innkeeper nodded and left.

"Thank you, friend. I can always tell a man of good upbringing, and you, sir, are one."

"It's the least I could do for your time. You certainly have had some interesting adventures," Gudbrant said. "And you surely must be the bravest man I've ever met."

"Between you and me," Byorn said, lowering his voice, "this town is full of cowards." He sat back, nodding his head.

"Well, we don't want to take up any more of your time," Gudbrant said as he stood up. "Thank you for indulging us."

"Anytime, my friend. Perhaps tomorrow night I can tell you of the time I battled a nykkyn."

"You are indeed a man of wonder," Gudbrant said. "Perhaps we will join you tomorrow evening."

Flyn followed Gudbrant back to the table where the rest of the party was waiting.

"You don't believe those stories he was telling, do you?" Flyn asked after they sat down.

"I believed your tale. Why shouldn't I believe his?" Gudbrant said.

"But that's different."

Gudbrant grinned. "No, I don't believe his stories of fighting off a vargolf or a nykkyn. But I learned some valuable information from him."

"What could you possibly have learned from him that was of any value?"

"I learned that the orcs don't patrol the Nidfel Mountains. And that means we can approach Uskleig undiscovered."

"But what of all the demons and monsters that keep the orcs away?"

"Surely, Flynygyn of the Andors, you do not believe the ramblings of an old wanderer?"

"But if there aren't any monsters, what keeps the orcs away?"

"Fear. Fear that there may be monsters in those mountains. And perhaps there really are some powerful creatures living there. But if our friend Byorn can survive there, then I have no doubt we can as well."

"If he was actually there." Flyn was dubious.

"I believe he was. One thing about tellers of tall tales. There is usually a nugget of truth to their stories. I would suspect he was in the Nidfels and actually saw a wolf creature, but I don't believe he fought it."

"So when do we leave?" Sigrid said.

"Are you still sure you want to join us?" Gudbrant said.

"Aye. You lads saved me life. For that, I shall give you what aid I may."

"Very well. We welcome your help. As to when, I think we should leave soon. Flyn is healed and we are all rested. We'll spend tomorrow gathering what supplies we may need for the journey and set out the following day."

"Good," Harvig said. "The sooner we rescue Brenna and the Andor's friend, the sooner we can return home."

Randell nodded in agreement.

CHAPTER 11

Flyn and his companions left Hemdown fully rested and recovered. Flyn was glad to be on their way again. During their stay, he learned more of the horrors of Jarot and his minions. Their treatment of cooperative prisoners sounded miserable. What they would do to the uncooperative ones was too terrible to mention. The more he learned, the more anxious he grew about Kel. He was afraid if they took too long, they would find his friend already dead, either from torture or outright execution.

Gudbrant and the others tried to convince Flyn that Kel's capture wasn't his fault, that it was just bad luck. Flyn pointed out that whether it was his fault or bad luck, he couldn't just leave his friend in the hands of Jarot. He would go by himself, if necessary, to try to rescue Kel.

But all vowed to join Flyn on the journey to Uskleig. Gudbrant was willing to sacrifice everything, even his life, if necessary, to save Brenna. And while he had suggested Harvig and Randell return to Garthset, neither would return. Remembering what Gudbrant had told him about Randell and Brenna, Flyn understood why Randell wanted to go. But Harvig was a mystery to Flyn. He wondered what would compel him to join such a desperate cause. He obviously admired Gudbrant, and had sworn to protect his captain, but he never spoke of why. When Flyn had asked, Harvig had merely said he owed Gudbrant, and would not elaborate.

Of all the party, Sigrid was the oddest. She had no allegiance to Flyn or Gudbrant, other than the rescue from Gurnborg. Gudbrant and Flyn both tried to convince her that she owed them nothing and did not need to come on a quest that would very likely end in all of their deaths. But she would not be dissuaded. Flyn felt there was another reason. Perhaps she was still looking to avenge her brother's death. Or maybe it was something deeper. Whatever the reason, Flyn was glad for her help.

They had resupplied in Hemdown, purchasing extra provisions and a mule to carry them. Like the clothing, Sigrid wasn't able to find armor in her size, though she did find a helmet and had settled for a leather hauberk that came to her knees. A local cobbler made her a pair of custom-fit boots. She had even found a proper battle ax to replace the orc mining pick.

After their shopping and paying for their stay at the inn, Gudbrant's coin pouch was significantly lighter. As none of them wanted to stay in Hemdown any longer than necessary, the end of Gudbrant's coin was of little concern, though Flyn promised to pay him back, somehow.

Gudbrant had learned of a path that spanned the length of the Nidfel Mountains. The Yord Trail ran from the Estlaegs in the east, all the way to the Adimark Tundra where the Nidfels ended in the west. Though there were no maps of it in Hemdown, from what he had learned, the trail most likely passed very near Uskleig. Gudbrant suggested they travel to Kaldersten, a small trading outpost in the foothills of the Nidfel Mountains, to learn more about it, maybe even find a map.

With plans made, on the morning of their fifteenth day in Hemdown, the small party left by way of the west gate. No orc patrols had been spotted west of Hemdown, so they felt safe traveling by road, which would ease their journey in both time and comfort, as there were several small villages along the road to Kaldersten.

Their first day ended in the village of Inefel, where the northbound road to Kaldersten met the westbound road. The village consisted of nothing more than a tavern, a general store, and a few homes. Gudbrant was still concerned about Jarot's minions discovering their plans, but west of Hemdown, travelers were more common than to the east, so the group drew no undue attention.

The next morning, they started north. The spring rains had mostly ended and summer was in full bloom, making their travel mostly pleasant, in spite of the heat.

With no sign of pursuit, they relaxed, enjoying the summer air, and purposely not discussing their destination.

The lights of Kaldersten appeared in the distance the evening of the twentieth day from Hemdown. For two days, the road had climbed steadily through hilly terrain. Topping the largest hill they had climbed thus far, they discovered a large valley before them. In the center of the valley lay Kaldersten, glittering like a gem in the dirt. While the travel had been easy, the group was determined not to spend another evening sleeping on the ground. With their destination in sight, they pushed on into the evening.

According to Gudbrant's source in Hemdown, Kaldersten was a trading town, much like Hemdown in its early days. As Kaldersten was more of a frontier town than Garthset or Hemdown, Gudbrant warned that they should not expect much help there, though they would also not arouse much interest. People in frontier towns stuck to their own business, as long as you stuck to your own. Gudbrant was told that travelers in Kaldersten were known to forage the Nidfel Mountains for gems and precious metals. Nowhere else in all of Tirmar could they expect to learn more about the Nidfels—both its wildlife and passages through the mountains.

The town was in the middle of Kalderdale, a long, narrow valley in the foothills of the Nidfels. Roughly half of the population of Kalderdale lived in small farms that dotted the valley. The rest lived in Kaldersten itself, providing services in old, rundown buildings. The faded signs advertised general goods, blacksmithing and tailoring services, mining supplies, and other needs. The local inn, its sign showing an ice-covered beer stein and proclaiming the name as The Frozen Mug, dominated the main street through town. Kaldersten had no defensive walls, not even a town guard patrolling the streets. In fact, the streets were mostly deserted.

Gudbrant pulled open the door to the inn, spilling bright light into the street. Most of the tables were empty, with only half a dozen or so patrons who looked up from their meals as the travelers entered. Stairs on the right wall led to the second floor, and on the left, a large fireplace with a stone hearth provided warmth against the chilly northern evening. Along the back wall was a bar and a pair of swinging doors, presumably leading to the kitchen. The rest of the room was filled with long tables and benches. Lanterns hanging from brackets on the walls provided the room with warm, cheery light.

"Health and happiness, travelers," a man called out from behind the bar. "Welcome to The Mug. Will you be staying with us this evening or just stopping in for a hot meal?"

"We'd like rooms, if you please," Gudbrant replied. "For two nights. And boarding for our mule, if you can manage."

"That we can, sir."

The innkeeper came from behind the bar and shook hands with the travelers.

"My name is Svendar," he said. "Anything you need, just ask."

Svendar was taller than all the travelers but Harvig, with thinning gray hair and an unshaven face. His eyes gleamed over his round, red cheeks. His clothing, though clean, was old and grease stained. An equally old and stained apron was tied around his prominent waist.

"Fortunate for you, we're not very busy yet," he said as he led them upstairs to show them to their rooms. "Another few weeks and we'll be full for the summer, though I'm sure we would manage something."

"Our fortune would seem to be yours as well," Gudbrant said, smiling at the old man.

"It would indeed, my friend. I'll have washing water brought up to your rooms. You may join us in the common room when you are ready for your evening meal."

With that, Svendar disappeared back down the stairs, leaving the travelers to settle in.

After cleaning up and changing clothes, the group gathered together again in the inn's common room. The innkeeper brought them roast beef, potatoes, beans, and warm bread with butter. Cold ale filled their mugs, which were frozen as the name of the inn promised.

By the time their food was served, they were almost alone in the common room. A scruffy-looking man sitting by himself in the corner, drinking ale from a no-longer-frozen mug, was the only other guest. He watched the group intently as they ate, rubbing the stubble on his chin.

"What do we do now?" Flyn asked Gudbrant, trying to ignore the man.

"First, we must resupply and rest," he replied. "Though I do not wish to stay long. Every day we delay, our chances of rescuing Brenna and Kel alive diminish."

"How far is it to Uskleig?"

"Be careful about stating our destination out loud," Gudbrant said, lowering his voice. "In a remote town such as this, the enemy may have spies."

"Why would anyone help those monsters?" Flyn said.

"Money is the usual reason. Power is another." Gudbrant glanced at the man in the corner. "To answer your question, however, four or five days. Perhaps six if we can't find the Yord Trail or some other good path through the mountains."

"Why can't we just travel through the foothills?" Randell asked. "Surely that would be easier than trudging through the mountains."

"It would, but we would likely encounter orc patrols. We would like to avoid them as long as possible."

Randell nodded.

The man in the corner was still watching the group over his mug.

"Why's that man watching us?" Flyn whispered to Gudbrant.

"I have no idea," Gudbrant said. "But I think we should find out."

Gudbrant turned to the man. "Is there something we can help you with?"

The man grinned, showing gaping holes where most of his teeth should have been. "I think it's me who can help you."

"How can you help us?" Flyn said. "You don't even know us."

"I know more than you think, boy." The man chuckled, then drained his ale and slammed the mug on the table. He stood up, using the table and chair to steady himself, then stumbled over to the table where Flyn and his companions were seated.

Harvig started to get up, but Gudbrant put a hand on his arm and he sat down again.

"Three Ilfins, a dwarf, and a boy," the man said, still grinning. He sat down next to Flyn.

"Our business is our own, old man," Sigrid said from across the table.

"That's good sense, these days," the man replied. "But I can guess at your business. There aren't too many that come from the south without goods to trade."

Flyn glanced at Gudbrant, but no one replied.

"That can only mean one thing," the man continued. "You're prospectors." He grinned his toothless grin again and sat back in his chair, arms crossed.

"You seem to presume a lot, but you don't even tell us your name," Gudbrant said.

"The name's Gunnulf and I've been prospecting in the Nidfels since before any of you was born. Excepting maybe you." He looked at Sigrid.

"Why should you think we are prospectors?" Gudbrant asked.

"If you're not here to trade, there's only one other reason for a man to come to Kaldersten from the south. To try his luck with the Nidfels."

"Very astute," Gudbrant said, playing along with Gunnulf's assumptions. "So what help might you be able to offer?"

"As I said, I've been prospecting here for a long time. The Nidfels are a dangerous place. I've seen a lot of men come from the south, men with years of experience at prospecting in the Estlaegs. But the Nidfels ain't the Estlaegs."

Gunnulf stared menacingly at each of them.

"But I'm thirsty," he said, leaning back in his chair and grinning again. "Perhaps you could offer me an ale in exchange for a little bit of my knowledge?"

Gudbrant flagged down the innkeeper and ordered another round of ale.

"I am much obliged," Gunnulf said. "Now, where was I? Oh yes. The dangers of the Nidfels. In the Estlaegs, your biggest threat is the weather, or maybe a perky ogre. Well, at least if you stay away from the orc strongholds. But the Nidfels are another beast."

"Why's that?" Flyn asked.

"The weather is a bigger problem for one. Storms come from nowhere, with blinding snow even this time of year. Winds stronger than any you've ever known can pick you off a mountain trail and throw you into a ravine before you know what's happening. And that's if you can find a trail. Not many exist because so few brave the Nidfels."

"If it's so dangerous, how is it you've survived all these years?" Randell asked.

"Because I'm smart," Gunnulf said with another big grin. "I'm smart and I'm experienced. That makes me good at what I do."

"What else can you tell us?" Flyn asked.

The innkeeper brought the round of ale and left without interrupting.

"I can tell you much." Gunnulf took a long drag of his ale. "The Nidfels are full of strange beasts. Some are just curiosities, but others... Well, I don't want to frighten the young one right before bedtime."

Flyn felt his face flush. "I'm not as young as you think. And I've been in more dangerous situations that anything you've told us about."

"All right, boy," Gunnulf said, leaning toward Flyn. "You want to know about the dangers? I could tell you stories that'd turn your hair white. There are beasts living in the Nidfels with claws as long and as sharp as daggers and teeth as big as spikes. I've seen grown men crying for their mommas just at the sight of some of them. I've seen battle-hardened warriors torn limb from limb. The likes of you wouldn't last long enough to piss your britches."

Flyn glared at the old man and was about to respond, but Gudbrant interrupted before he could speak.

"You're good at telling tales, but you haven't yet given us any useful information."

"As I have said, there aren't many paths through the Nidfels, but those that do exist are where they are for a reason. Leave the trail at your own doom. The trails will lead you around the worst of terrain and the areas where the most dangerous beasts live. Not that the paths are safe for the unwary."

"So how do we stay safe?" Flyn asked, trying to remain calm.

"Don't go into the mountains!" Gunnulf laughed. "There's nothing safe about prospecting, boy. You want safe, go back and hide in your mother's apron 'cause the mountains will kill you."

"I think we've heard enough of your prattle, old man," Gudbrant said. "We aren't interested in fairytales and ghost stories."

"Think of them as fairytales at your own risk. And don't say I didn't warn you when a vargolf sneaks into your camp or a deeser drains your soul from your body because you wandered into her domain."

"I'm sure we'll manage," Harvig said.

"I'm not sure why you are trying to frighten us off from the Nidfels, but our business is not concerned with monsters and demons," Gudbrant said. "Good evening."

"Wait a moment," Gunnulf said. "If my warnings seemed over-stated, it's only because I wanted you to understand the dangers for those who are new to the Nidfels. You need not think I'm trying to scare you away. On the contrary, I would like to offer my services as your guide."

"And what manner of payment do you seek for your services?" Gudbrant asked.

"I don't feel twenty-five silver fennings per day is too much to ask for expertise such as mine."

"We could hire a squad of soldiers for that," Harvig scoffed.

"But do the soldiers know the Nidfels?"

"We'll pay you one gold mark for five days," Gudbrant said.

"One mark for five days?" Gunnulf stood up. "I won't risk my life for ten fennings a day."

"That's what we're prepared to offer you."

Gunnulf looked hard at Gudbrant, apparently trying to decide if he could negotiate a higher rate.

"I want payment up front," he said. "And you provide my food."

"Done. We depart the morning after next."

"You drive a hard bargain, Southlander. One more thing. I always get the first watch. If I'm to lead you, I don't want my sleep interrupted."

"As you wish," Gudbrant agreed. "Just be ready to leave the morning after tomorrow."

"I'll be ready." Gunnulf finished his ale, then left the group with no further words.

"Are you sure we need him?" Randell said once they were alone again.

"He may have been dramatic about it," Gudbrant replied, "but he was right about the Nidfels being a dangerous place. Having a guide will be useful."

"But for a whole gold mark?" Randell shook his head. "That's nearly a month's pay. It seems like a lot for just a guide for a few days."

"Perhaps, but if it gets us safely to our destination, it's worth it." Gudbrant smiled at Randell. "Besides, I'm not asking you to pay for it."

"I don't trust him," Flyn said.

"He's a frontiersman," Gudbrant said. "They are an odd sort, and not wholly civilized, but that's no reason not to trust our new friend."

"Is there anything else I can get for you this evening?" the innkeeper asked as he approached the table.

"Do you know that man?" Flyn said. "Gunnulf?"

"He comes to Kaldersten once or twice a year," the innkeeper replied. "Always offers his services as a guide to anyone who might need it. From my understanding, he does the same at other towns along the Nidfels, west of here. But I can't say I really know him."

"Does he know what he talks about or is he just full of stories?"

"He is a bit of a storyteller," Svendar said. "Still, he's been around for nearly as long as I have, so I think he probably knows his way around the mountains pretty good."

"Good to know," Gudbrant said. He stood up. "I thank you for your hospitality and your insight, but I believe I've had enough for this evening. We've had a long journey and much to do tomorrow."

Everyone thanked the innkeeper and said good night.

Later that night, even though he was exhausted, Flyn couldn't sleep. He lay in his bed, going over their conversation with the frontiersman. In spite of Gudbrant's words, and those of the innkeeper, Flyn still didn't trust the man.

CHAPTER 12

With their fresh supplies packed on the mule, and one last meal in their bellies, the party departed Kaldersten. Their departure was sooner than they would have liked. Two nights of rest weren't enough to fully recover from their journey from Hemdown, but the fates of Brenna and Kel urged them on.

Uskleig was less than twenty leagues from Kaldersten, according to Gudbrant. Even though traveling through the mountains would slow their pace, he felt they would arrive before the end of their fifth day. They had brought enough supplies for two weeks, with extra to account for their guide for five days and two more people on the way back.

The sky was gray and a chill wind blew down from the mountains as they set out, cutting through their cloaks. With the smell of rain in the air, Gunnulf had tried, unsuccessfully, to talk them into waiting for better weather to leave. They were all anxious to complete their journey and rescue Kel and Brenna.

They still had no idea how they would accomplish that task. As none of them had ever been to Uskleig, they would have to wait until they got there to come up with a plan. Gudbrant warned that it wouldn't be as easy as getting into Gurnborg had been, and if they were captured, there would be little chance for escape. Their biggest, possibly only, advantage was that the orcs would never expect someone to try to rescue a prisoner. The thought was too inconceivable.

As they left town, Gunnulf pressed them about their intentions.

"Did you have a particular area in mind or do you need me to suggest some locations to prospect?" Gunnulf asked.

"For now, just get us to the Yord Trail," Gudbrant said. "Once there, we'll discuss our destination in more detail."

Gudbrant had advised them not to discuss their plans with anyone prior to leaving, even Gunnulf.

"Suit yourself." Gunnulf shrugged and kept walking. The others followed, with Flyn leading the mule at the rear of the party with Harvig.

The rain started a little more than an hour out of Kaldersten, a light mist that turned into a steady drizzle, leaving everything damp and cold. The road north from the town diminished to a narrow, muddy trail through the wooded foothills and lower slopes of the Nidfels. The air grew colder as they climbed, turning the rain into sleet, then finally snow. Flyn welcomed the snow over the rain, preferring cold over wet.

By midday, the trail had disappeared under a thin blanket of snow. Gunnulf trudged on, seemingly unconcerned about the lack of a visible path. He led them through winding ravines, along sheer cliffs, and over the smaller peaks, always moving deeper into the mountains. Flyn hoped Gunnulf really knew where he was going because Flyn was utterly lost.

Whether by luck, or by Gunnulf's skill, they encountered no beasts, whether normal or supernatural, save birds and a few squirrels. Flyn suspected the real reason was because the stories were just myths and legends rather than because of any skill of their guide. Whatever the reason, he was glad that they didn't have that extra complication.

The snow stopped falling at some point in the afternoon, though with the wind blowing the drifts around, Flyn wasn't really sure when it stopped. Still, Gunnulf kept up the pace, seemingly confident in his direction. There was nothing for Flyn to do but follow.

He tried several times to start up a conversation with Harvig. The big militiaman responded to his questions with short answers, never elaborating or engaging in conversation.

"Are you ever going to tell me why you followed Gudbrant on this quest?" Flyn asked after a while.

"As I've told you, I owe him."

"So you've said. But why?"

Harvig was quiet for a long time. Flyn had decided to give up on his attempt at a conversation, and was about to move off to join Randell when Harvig finally answered.

"I was a thief when I met Gudbrant. I grew up on a farm in Asgerdale. Like Randell, the orcs destroyed our home when I was boy, though older than Randell. They burned our fields and killed our live-stock. We were fortunate that we weren't captured, but they had taken everything from us. With no home, and the clothes on our backs all that we had left, we traveled to Garthset for help."

Harvig was quiet again for a while before continuing.

"The Thane had set up shelters for those like us who had lost our homes to the orc raiding parties, but there was no work for my father. We did what we could to help the others displaced by the raids, but eventually I grew restless. At first, I just stole food, as what was provided to the refugees wasn't enough. Eventually, I learned how to pick pockets and discovered stealing money to buy food was easier than stealing the food directly. And the money bought other things."

"I can't know what that must have been like," Flyn said. "Surely, though, you can be forgiven your crimes, considering your circum-stances."

Harvig grunted. "There is no excuse for what I did. Others were just as bad off as we were. I didn't have the right to take from them. But I did. I was eventually caught and spent several months in jail, but that didn't stop me. As I got older, I grew until eventually I didn't bother with pickpocketing. I just took what I wanted. But of course, my size had a distinct disadvantage."

"What was that?"

"I was easily identified." Harvig chuckled. "Not many in the Ilfin clan grow to my size. I sometimes wonder if there isn't Mundar in my bloodline."

"Gudbrant told me about them. He said they're warriors."

Harvig nodded. "They're big as well."

Flyn wondered how big they must be if they were even bigger than the Ilfins.

"You were caught again?"

"I was, and this time they sentenced me to five years imprisonment. I had only been in prison a few months when the orc raiding parties started attacking Garthset. The Thane ordered the wall built around the town. Everyone who wasn't building weapons or standing guard was put to work, including the refugees and prisoners. When the wall was finished, they needed more men to guard it. Gudbrant had the Thane offer to pardon any man who committed to serve in the militia for the remainder of his sentence."

"So you owe Gudbrant for getting you out of prison?"

"No," Harvig replied, shaking his head. "I enlisted because I hoped to get revenge on the orcs for what they did to my family. I was full of hate and anger. But I discovered that hate doesn't absolve a man of guilt for killing. I got my revenge, but instead of feeling justice, I felt shame. Even though it was an orc, and it would have killed me without hesitation had I not killed it first, I killed it out of hate. And for that, I was ashamed of myself."

"But after everything the orcs had done to you? And you were fighting to defend yourself, surely you were justified?"

"Whether I was justified or not did not come into my thinking, neither at the time nor after. I struggled for many days until one night I could no longer stand the guilt. I had watch duty on the wall. When it was my turn to man the watchtower, I climbed up with the intent to throw myself from the top. When I got there, Gudbrant was waiting for me. He knew what I was planning, even before I knew myself."

"I'm sorry," was all Flyn could manage to say. He hadn't expected that.

"Not to worry. I've never spoken of that night with anyone but Gudbrant until now. I've felt as much shame about it as I did killing that orc out of hatred, but perhaps speaking of it out loud is not such a bad thing."

"And now you feel like you owe Gudbrant?"

"I do owe him. If not for him, I would have died that night. Instead, I have learned to let go of my hatred. Now when I must fight, I don't kill for hate or anger or vengeance. I do what I must to defend myself and my home from our enemy."

Flyn nodded, remembering his own battle experience, killing three orcs as if they were nothing more than wild animals. He had managed to avoid thinking about it until now. Their capture and escape at Gurnborg had provided a distraction. After that, he had just kept his mind on the road ahead. Even during the rest they had taken in Hemdown, he had forced himself to focus on what still lay before them. After listening to Harvig's story, he remembered what Gudbrant had told him after the battle, about it being okay to feel bad.

Only he didn't feel bad.

In spite of how he had thought he felt at the time, now he felt nothing. No remorse, no joy. He felt no different about it than he did slaughtering a pig for food. It had simply been a task that he had needed to complete.

What did that say about him?

"Not to worry," Harvig said, seeming to sense his thoughts. "You will come to peace with yourself. You have an inner strength. I think Gudbrant sees it too, which is why he chose to help you find your friend."

Flyn nodded, but didn't reply. He sure didn't feel an inner strength. He mostly felt numb.

The light was beginning to fade when they came out of the trees and entered a wide valley between two mountain peaks. The valley was covered in snow, giving it the appearance of a large, ice-covered lake. On the far side of the valley, the ground sloped up again, disappearing into another grove of trees.

"The Yord Trail lies just ahead," Gunnulf said.

"How far?" Gudbrant asked.

"No more than ten or fifteen minutes."

"We'll make camp here, under the cover of the trees," Gudbrant said. "We can start our trek on the Yord Trail in the morning."

The next morning broke bright and cold. During the night, a strong, northerly wind had cleared out the clouds from the previous day. In spite of the clear sky, the day promised to be a cold one.

"I'm going no farther until you tell me where we're going," Gunnulf said as they ate breakfast. "You're obviously not prospectors, as you led me to believe."

The others all looked to Gudbrant.

"Very well," Gudbrant said. "No, we are not prospectors. We will be following the Yord Trail east."

"The only thing east of here is Uskleig," Gunnulf said. "You can't be going there."

Gudbrant looked at Gunnulf but didn't reply.

"Uskleig?" Gunnulf said. "You must be out of your minds. Why would you want to go there?"

"Our arrangement requires only that you show us safe passage through the Nidfels. Our business when we reach our destination need not concern you."

"Our arrangement was for me to show you safe passage through the Nidfels. There's nothing safe about Uskleig. I wouldn't go there for all the gold marks in Tirmar."

"You don't have to get us inside. Just lead us to it and, when we have completed our business, lead us back."

Gunnulf scowled at Gudbrant.

"Fine," he said. "I'll take you to within half a league of the city, but after that, you're on your own."

"That will suffice," Gudbrant replied.

Gunnulf muttered to himself as he returned to his meal. Flyn couldn't hear what he was saying, only that he didn't seem very happy about the situation.

The Yord Trail turned out to be nothing more than a narrow, unmarked path through the mountains. If not for Gunnulf, they would have never found it, especially with the ground covered by snow. Even following it would have been a challenge. Their guide seemed to know where the path was even without being able to see it. At times, the path seemed to disappear completely, leading Flyn to think Gunnulf was lost. Then, minutes later, the path would reappear.

The trail led them around the steeper peaks, sometimes turning completely around before continuing its trek to the east. Gunnulf said that although they were within twelve leagues of Uskleig, the journey would take three or four days, assuming no unexpected obstacles. What he meant by that, he wouldn't elaborate. Flyn suspected the old man was trying to scare them again with hints of monsters lurking in the mountains, perhaps to try to get more money from them later, though they still hadn't seen any sign of anything larger than a rabbit.

One thing he had been right about though was the treacherous conditions. In many places, the trail was covered in ice and the wind seemed to never stop. At several points along the way, Flyn found himself inching along a sheer drop with his back to a cliff wall. Looking down hundreds of feet into a rocky ravine made his head swim and his stomach churn. Even the mule seemed to be uncomfortable in some spots.

Near the end of the fourth day from Kaldersten, they found themselves on a small plateau overlooking the eastern foothills of the Nidfels. In the distance, the Estlaeg Mountains marched up from the south to join their northern cousins. Laid out below the plateau was a city with a colossal tower in the center.

The tower was larger than any building Flyn had ever seen, rising above the surrounding foothills. Its sides were perfectly straight and black as coal, with the sheen of polished metal that reflected the setting sun. Smaller towers rose from the corners of its flat top. At its base, a complex of buildings surrounded it. A wall separated the fortress from the rest of the city, which in turn had its own wall. The city wall seemed to be ordinary stone, but the wall around the citadel appeared to be made from the same black material as the tower.

"Jarot's citadel," Gunnulf said, his voice almost a whisper.

The group stared at the city and its citadel in awe. The buildings of the city appeared to be more traditionally built from stone and wood, but the buildings of the citadel were made of something else, though Flyn couldn't tell what. But the construction wasn't the only difference. The buildings of the citadel were laid out along straight roads, the entire complex forming a perfect square in the center of the city. The rest of the city seemed to be laid out almost in random fashion, with roads twisting and turning around hills and rocky outcroppings. Though they were too far away to see people, Flyn could imagine the streets bustling with activity as people moved about, visiting shops or traveling home at the end of the day. Smoke rose from many of the buildings, mostly the white and gray smoke of cooking and heating stoves. Some buildings, however, spilled a darker smoke into the air. The smoke of foundries and blacksmiths.

Mountains surrounded the city on all sides. To the north, a massive peak rose higher than any they had yet encountered. Its crest was white with snow, the very top hidden in clouds. At its base, the mountain formed the north wall of the city, with the city's east and west walls abutting its steep slope.

"We'll camp here tonight," Gudbrant said.

No one objected. A small grove of trees covered most of the plateau, providing shelter from the wind and wood for a small fire. They camped as far from the edge of the plateau as they could to hide the light of their fire from the city below.

That evening, Gunnulf tried again to find out why they wanted to go to Uskleig.

"Are you spies?" he asked. "Are you looking for weaknesses in their defenses so you can attack Jarot in his fortress?"

Gudbrant didn't reply.

"You know you could never get an army through the Nidfels. You would have to go through Felmote Pass. But if you tried that, your army would be decimated before you even reached the gates."

"We're not spies and we're not planning an attack on Uskleig," Gudbrant said.

"Then what possible reason could you have to go there?"

Gudbrant sighed.

"I suppose at this point it doesn't matter whether you know or not," he said. "We're on a rescue mission."

Gunnulf laughed. "That's even crazier than an attack! You can't really expect to break into the most heavily defended fortress in Tirmar and come out alive?"

"My best friend is there," Flyn said. "And it's my fault. I'll do whatever it takes to rescue him."

"Or die trying?" Gunnulf laughed again. "More than likely what will happen. If you're lucky that is. You'll probably end up as one of Jarot's slaves, working to feed and supply his armies."

"That may very well be our fate," Gudbrant said. "Nevertheless, we must try."

"Well, crazy or no, you're going to need help of the gods to rescue your friend and escape again. But I can help you get in."

"I thought you said you wouldn't go into Uskleig for all the gold in Tirmar," Flyn said.

Gunnulf laughed again. "I said I could help you get in, not that I would go in with you. I should charge you another gold mark for what I know, but I feel bad for you. You're all going to die."

"Very well," Gudbrant replied. "We would be most grateful for your help."

Gudbrant drew a gold coin from his coin pouch and tossed it to Gunnulf. The old man bit the coin, then squirreled it away in his tunic.

"I haven't been this far east in many years, so the information may turn out to be worthless anyway." Gunnulf took a swig of wine from his wineskin. "Most people think Jarot built Uskleig, but he didn't. At least not the citadel. He built up the city around it, sure, but the citadel itself is far older. Some people think it's been there since before the Revolution. Now, I don't know about all that, but I do know the citadel has a series of tunnels under it. I don't know what they were originally for, but now they are mostly used for storage. And Jarot's dungeon. For people he wants to keep alive, but doesn't want to use as slaves for whatever reason."

Flyn glanced at Gudbrant. Could Kel be one of those prisoners?

"How does that help us?" Harvig said.

"Patience. I'm getting to that. So there's a whole tunnel complex under the citadel, as I said. But the citadel isn't the only way into the tunnels. There's a secret entrance into the tunnels north of the city."

"A secret entrance?" Flyn asked. "How do we find it?"

"I'm trying to tell you, if you'll just let me talk. The entrance is, or was when I was there last, hidden on a small plateau on the north side of Mount Yemsok, that tall mountain on the north side of the city."

Gunnulf took another swig of wine and grinned at his audience. They were all staring at him, eyes wide.

"How do we reach this plateau?" Gudbrant asked.

"Calling it a secret entrance may not be quite accurate. Some think the tunnels were built to allow whoever built the citadel to escape from a siege. It's impossible to climb up to the plateau from below, though you can scale down from it if you have rope. The only way to reach it is from above. As luck would have it, the Yord Trail goes around the city to the north and passes right above the plateau."

"Why would Jarot keep the tunnel open?" Harvig asked. "Clearly it's a weakness in his defenses."

"He may have closed it off, but I doubt it. No one travels the Yord Trail this far east anymore and as hard as the entrance is to reach, no army could ever use it as a way to invade the city. Besides, the tunnels are a maze of narrow passageways, easily defended."

"And how do you know of this entrance?" Randell asked.

"I've been prospecting these mountains for decades. When I was younger, and more adventurous, and Jarot wasn't as bold, traveling near Uskleig wasn't as dangerous as it is today. I had heard stories about the tunnels and wanted to find out for myself."

"Did you go in?"

"Of course. I was hoping to find storehouses full of gold and silver, or at least something worth selling. All I found were cells full of dead and half-dead prisoners. Never went back."

"Can you take us to the entrance?" Flyn asked.

Gunnulf laughed. "I won't go that close to Uskleig. But it's not that difficult to find if you know where to look."

"It appears we have a plan for getting into the city," Gudbrant said. "We should turn in. Tomorrow will be a difficult day."

The group dispersed to their tents, Gunnulf taking the first watch as agreed.

Flyn crawled into his bedroll and tried to sleep. He was buzzing with excitement. News of the secret entrance was his first ray of hope since starting on the journey to rescue Kel. Maybe Kel was in a cell somewhere in the tunnels and they wouldn't even have to go into the city or even the citadel to find him.

Maybe he and Kel would see home again one day.

The gray light coming through the crack between the tent flaps signaled dawn was near. Flyn stretched and yawned. Randell was still asleep on the other side of the tent. Flyn listened to the birds chirping as they woke and thought about the previous night's discussions.

Gunnulf had been quite adamant that he wouldn't go with them into the tunnels, though he had agreed to show them the plateau where the tunnels exited the mountain. At least he had after Gudbrant had paid him an extra gold mark. Even so, Gunnulf was convinced they were all headed to their deaths at the hands of Jarot's elite troops that guarded the citadel.

The entrance wasn't far from where they were, only a couple of hours, according to Gunnulf. They would easily reach it before noon. That meant that with a little luck, before the day was out, Kel and Brenna would be free and they would all be on their way back to Garthset. Then he and Kel would be able to focus on finding a way home.

Flyn crawled out of his bedroll, no longer able to lie still. Today was the day he had been working toward for so many weeks. Even though he was sore and tired from the constant travel and sleeping on the ground, not to mention the ordeal at Gurnborg, he wanted to get moving as soon as possible. He decided to get an early start on breakfast. The rest of the party would be awake soon, and they would want to eat before setting out.

Outside his tent, the crisp morning air felt good on his face. He stretched again as he looked through the trees toward the eastern horizon. From their campsite, all he could see of Uskleig was the top of the citadel's main tower. Behind it, the orange glow of dawn silhouetted the mountain tops.

Flyn turned toward the fire, intending to add fuel and stoke it up to cook breakfast. He stopped as something occurred to him. No one had awoken him for his watch shift. He had been assigned the last shift. Randell had the shift before him, but Randell was sound asleep in the tent. No one else was awake.

He hurried to Gudbrant and Harvig's tent and peeked inside. Both were sleeping, lightly snoring. Sigrid was still in her tent on the other side. He turned to Gunnulf's tent.

It was gone.

Flyn stood staring at the spot where Gunnulf's tent had been the night before. All that remained was a depression in the snow. Flyn rushed toward the trail, searching through the trees. Maybe Gunnulf had moved his tent during the night.

After five minutes, Flyn had searched the entire plateau. There was no sign of their guide.

He hurried back to the campsite and woke Gudbrant.

"Gunnulf's gone," Flyn said.

"What? What are you talking about?" Gudbrant said. He didn't seem quite awake.

Flyn told him what he had found when he'd gotten up a few minutes earlier.

"Wake Randell and Sigrid," Gudbrant said. He turned to wake Harvig and Flyn went to wake the others.

A few minutes later the group was standing next to their tents as Flyn recounted what had happened. It was Sigrid that noticed the other problem.

"Where's the mule?" she said. "And our supplies?"

They all look around, dumbfounded.

The mule and all of their supplies were gone as well.

"That rotten toad!" Sigrid said. "I'll string him up by his toes if I catch him!"

"I knew we couldn't trust him." Flyn was trying hard to control his anger. "We have to go after him."

"I think it's safe to assume which way he went," Randell added.

"We'll not catch him."

The others turned to looked at Harvig.

"If we assume he left as soon as we were asleep, then he has at least six hours head start," Harvig continued. "What's more, he knows these mountains. We do not. He won't stay on the trail longer than he has to. And if we try to search for where he left the trail, we'll have to travel at a much slower pace, allowing him to get even farther ahead of us."

"Harvig is right," Gudbrant said. "We have no chance of catching him. The only food we have is what little we have in our own packs. We only have one choice."

"We have to continue on to Uskleig," Flyn said.

Gudbrant nodded and the others slowly agreed.

"But how?" Flyn asked. "What if he was lying about the tunnels and the secret entrance?"

"I don't think he was lying about that," Gudbrant said. "Gunnulf strikes me as one who likes to embellish his tales, but not one clever enough to make up something as involved as his story about the tunnels. No, I think the tunnels exist, and he may have even been inside them, though I doubt he spent much time exploring. That path remains our best hope."

"Even if he was telling the truth," Randell said, "how will we find it?"

"One problem at a time, my friend," Gudbrant replied.

They took a quick inventory of their supplies and determined they had enough food for two meals, if they rationed carefully. They ate a small breakfast and saved the rest for after they reached the tunnels. After that, they would have to steal food from Jarot's citadel.

The only good news was they had plenty of water. They had been able to regularly refill their waterskins while in the mountains. After eating and packing their gear, they used the snow to fill them again.

The sun was above the horizon by the time they were ready to set out. The party shouldered their packs, which were lighter than Flyn would have liked. Only Sigrid's seemed to be normal sized, though Flyn supposed it was just a matter of perspective, since she was so much shorter than the rest of them.

Gudbrant led the party from the campsite and back to the trail. Flyn looked down the trail to the right, back the way they had come, hoping that maybe Gunnulf had a change of heart and was coming back. The trail was empty. He sighed, then turned left and followed the others.

The enthusiasm he had felt when he had awoken had drained away, leaving only a feeling of dread for what lay ahead.

For a while, the trail was easy to follow, even without Gunnulf. Though it was narrow, requiring them to travel single file, the path was mostly clear. It had turned northward, first making its way along the cliffs above Uskleig, then winding down between the lower peaks, soon losing sight of the city. Mount Yemsok, north of the city, grew larger as they drew closer.

The passage became more difficult, especially below the snow line where the trail turned to mud. Only Sigrid seemed unhindered by the unstable footing, plodding along at the back of the line, still muttering to herself about their traitorous guide. Fallen rocks and scrub brush began to cover portions of the trail, sending them off the path to avoid the obstacles. Eventually, the path seemed to disappear altogether.

Gudbrant led them on as best he could, always working toward Mount Yemsok. With no trail to guide them, their path consisted mainly of climbing over smaller rock outcroppings and skirting the larger ones. After two hours of scrambling and climbing, they found themselves in a shallow ravine with a creek running through it. To the east loomed the tall slope of Mount Yemsok.

"We can't go straight up," Gudbrant said. "We'll need to find another way."

"Don't forget what Gunnulf told us," Flyn said. "We can't climb up to the plateau, so we have to find a way to climb above it."

"But which way?" Randell said.

"Let's split up," Gudbrant said. "Flyn, Sigrid, and I will search the ravine to the north for a path. Randell and Harvig search to the south. We'll meet back here in half an hour. With luck, one group or the other will find a way up the mountain."

The others nodded in agreement. Harvig and Randell turned and headed off to the south.

"Good luck," Flyn said to himself, watching the pair walk away. He turned and ran to catch up with Gudbrant and Sigrid.

"I think we got lucky with the weather," Gudbrant was saying as Flyn caught up with them.

"How so?" Sigrid said.

"This ravine looks to be a riverbed. In warmer weather, it probably collects the snowmelt from the surrounding hills and mountains and turns that creek into a raging river."

"Aye," Sigrid replied. "That would make our job a wee bit difficult."

"What's that?" Flyn said, pointing to a spot ahead of them.

A break in the trees revealed a narrow dirt path winding up the slope.

"Good eye," Gudbrant said. "Let's see where it goes before we go back to meet the others."

He led the way up the path, Flyn and Sigrid hurrying to catch up.

The path was even narrower than the trail they had been on before, though easier to follow. The ground was completely clear, like it was well traveled. Branches on trees and bushes on either side of the path were broken. Gudbrant slowed down, then stopped at a bend.

"Look at this," he said.

The path bent around a large tree. Several parallel gouges cut through the bark on the trunk.

"Those look like claw marks," Sigrid said.

Gudbrant nodded. "Keep a watch out. Those look fresh."

They continued climbing the path, though at a slower pace. They came upon more trees with the strange scratches. Gudbrant had loosened his sword in its scabbard. Sigrid had unslung her ax and was carrying it in front of her. Flyn followed their lead and drew his own sword.

Around the next bend, the path led into a small clearing. On the other side of the clearing was a cave.

"Is that the opening to the tunnels?" Flyn asked. He couldn't believe their luck.

"Not unless that weasel lied to us about how to get to it," Sigrid said.

"Then this would appear to be a dead end," Gudbrant said. There were no other paths out of the clearing.

"Shouldn't we at least check?" Flyn really wanted the cave to be the entrance to the tunnels.

"Sigrid's right," Gudbrant said. "This can't be the entrance. For one thing, this is a natural cave. The tunnels under Jarot's citadel were constructed. Let's go back and see if Harvig and Randell had better luck."

A low, rumbling growl came from the cave. Gudbrant turned just as something large and gray leapt from the opening. The beast hit Gudbrant square in the chest, sending him tumbling into Sigrid, knocking them both down. Flyn jumped back, stumbling and falling on the uneven ground.

Flyn stared at the beast standing before him. It was taller than both he and Sigrid, taller even than Harvig. It stood with one foot on Gudbrant's chest, staring back at Flyn with its dark, deep-set eyes.

The creature's head was that of a wolf, with a long snout and a mouth full of yellow teeth. The longest fangs were like spikes, dripping with saliva. A thick, gray-brown fur covered the creature's lean, muscular body. Its powerful arms and legs were long, even for its large size. The dagger-like claws at the end of its fingers gleamed in the sunlight.

It pulled back its lips in a snarl and growled again, a rumbling in its chest that reverberated in the air like thunder. Sitting on the ground and paralyzed with fear, Flyn felt as if ice were running through his veins. The creature stepped toward him, raising its arm over its head, preparing to attack.

A loud yell startled Flyn. The creature turned in time to see Sigrid leap up and run at it, ax swinging. It snarled and stepped back, avoiding the swing of Sigrid's ax by mere inches. It brought its arm down, raking its claws across Sigrid's back and sending her tumbling back down to the ground.

The creature turned back to Gudbrant, who was struggling to get to his feet.

"Look out!" Flyn yelled, but it was too late. The creature swung its clawed hand at the militiaman, striking him in the side of his head. Blood sprayed from Gudbrant's cheek and neck onto the trees and bushes at the edge of the clearing. He fell to the ground, landing on his side. The creature leapt to Gudbrant's limp body.

"No!" Flyn yelled.

He picked himself up off the ground and ran across the clearing toward the beast, his sword raised. Still standing over Gudbrant's body, the creature turned toward Flyn. As Flyn pulled back to strike, the creature swung its arm at him, swatting him away like an insect. Flyn landed on his back, the wind knocked out of him.

On the other side of the clearing, Sigrid had clamored to her feet.

"Over here, you ugly mutt," Sigrid yelled.

The creature turned to face the dwarf, snarling and gnashing its teeth. The pair stared at each other, neither moving closer to the other. Sigrid's eyes burned with a fire Flyn hadn't seen in her before. A low growl rumbled in the creature's chest.

The beast leapt forward and they raced toward each other, Sigrid with her ax raised over her head, the creature with one arm pulled back, ready to strike.

They met in a clash of steel and bone, Sigrid's ax severing one of the creature's claws. It howled in pain. Sigrid pulled back, preparing to swing her ax again, but the creature was too fast. It swung its other arm, smashing her side and knocking her to the ground again. Before she could move, the creature jumped on top of her and pinned her to the ground.

The creature lifted its head in the air, its ears pinned back, and howled, a chilling sound that Flyn felt in his bones.

Flyn struggled back to his feet. He had one chance to attack before the creature could kill the prone dwarf. He raced toward it, his sword ready. He yelled and swung his sword with all his strength. The creature turned to see Flyn's sword arc through the air and bury itself in the flesh of its arm. Flyn felt the blade hit bone before the creature pulled its arm back, nearly ripping the sword from Flyn's hands.

As it stepped back, Sigrid, still lying on her back, swung her ax, striking the creature in the leg. Another howl erupted from the creature. Flyn leapt forward, thrusting his sword into the creature's chest.

The beast stepped back again, snarling and growling. Sigrid rolled over and scrambled to her feet to stand next to Flyn.

"Smelly as it is ugly," Sigrid muttered.

Flyn nodded, though Sigrid wasn't looking at him to see. He raised his sword again.

The creature stood in front of them, just outside the reach of their weapons, its chest heaving from its hard breathing. Its right arm hung limp at its side, blood pouring from the gash left by Flyn's attack. More blood streamed from the gouge in its chest. It glared at its two prey, eyes shifting from one to the other. It let out a series of loud barks that echoed off the surrounding mountainsides. Flyn flinched at the sound, but held his ground.

"Give me an opening, you vile beast," Sigrid said. She held her ax up, ready to attack.

The creature threw its head back and howled in frustration.

"Now!" Flyn yelled.

He and Sigrid leapt forward, Flyn swinging his sword at the creature's good arm, Sigrid bringing her ax over her head and down on the creature's chest. The blows struck the creature before it had time to react. Trying to step away from the attack, it stumbled and fell back. The force of Sigrid's blow sent it to the ground. Flyn flipped his grip on his sword and grabbed the hilt with both hands. With a growl of his own, he plunged the blade into the creature's chest.

A last yelp escaped the creature's mouth as its body shuddered, and then lay still.

Flyn collapsed to his knees, still holding on to the hilt of his sword sticking out of the beast's chest. He knelt like that for several seconds, trying to catch his breath. Finally, he let go of the sword and sat back. Sigrid stood beside him, breathing hard and holding herself up with her ax. They looked at each other and smiled.

Suddenly Flyn remembered Gudbrant. He jumped up and scrambled to the fallen militiaman, half running, half sliding in his haste.

Gudbrant was lying on his side where the creature had left him. His sword still clutched in his hand. Flyn rolled him onto his back. Gudbrant's cheek and neck were shredded where the creature's claws had struck him. Blood oozed from the wounds. His eyes stared lifelessly at the sky.

"Gudbrant!" Flyn yelled, shaking the body that lay before him. "You can't die! Get up!"

Gudbrant didn't respond. His head rolled to the side, causing his eyes to stare at Flyn.

Sigrid placed a hand on Flyn's shoulder.

"He's gone, lad."

Flyn shrugged off her hand and shook Gudbrant's body again, yelling at his friend's limp body. Tears streamed down Flyn's cheeks.

Gudbrant didn't respond.

Flyn sat back, wiping the tears from his face. "No, no, no," he said. "You have to be alive. I can't do this without you."

The sound of running feet came from behind Flyn. He ignored it.

"What happened?" Randell said.

"We were attacked," Sigrid replied quietly.

"Gudbrant?" Harvig asked.

"Dead."

Flyn bowed his head, sobbing.

CHAPTER 13

"He should be buried in Garthset," Randell said.

Harvig nodded in agreement.

The remaining four stood in a circle around the makeshift grave they had made for Gudbrant. They had dragged the vargolf down the slope and into the ravine where other animals or a spring flood would dispose of the body. For their friend and companion, the best they could do was bury him under a cairn of stones gathered from the surrounding slopes.

They had buried Gudbrant where he died. Randell had arranged his body, placing his sword on his chest and crossing his hands over the hilt. He had cleaned the blood from Gudbrant's face and neck, and replaced his helmet on his head. Once prepared, they made a circle of stones around the body, saying a ritual blessing with each stone placed.

"Go now, Brother, join your fathers," Randell said, placing the first stone.

"Go now, Brother, join your mothers," Harvig said, adding a second stone.

"They wait for you, Brother." Flyn added a stone.

"In Vahul where you shall live forever." Sigrid added a stone.

Go now, Brother, join your fathers.
Go now, Brother, join your mothers.
They wait for you, Brother,
In Vahul where you shall live forever.

———

I shall mourn you, Brother,
And I shall praise you.
In time I shall join you
In Vahul where I shall live forever.

———

Tarry no longer in this world.
Your body returns to the earth.
Let your spirit ride the wind
To Vahul where we shall live forever.

———

The ritual prayer had been repeated until the circle was complete, then they filled the circle with more stones, covering Gudbrant's body until they could find no more stones nearby. The cairn complete, they repeated the burial prayer again in unison, then stood in silent reflection.

Flyn was still in shock. With Gudbrant's body no longer visible, he was having trouble accepting that his friend was dead. He kept looking over his shoulder, expecting Gudbrant to come walking out of the woods and chastise them for sitting around when they should be looking for Kel and Brenna. But the only voice to come from the forest was the wind whispering in the trees.

They sat quietly next to the cairn and ate the last bit of their food.

"So you have the same funeral rituals in Trygsted?" Randell asked Flyn as they ate.

"No," Flyn replied. "We send our dead out to sea on funeral rafts. But we recite the same rites of death."

"You come from a strange clan," Sigrid said, shaking her head. "You don't use boats, but you bury your dead at sea."

Flyn didn't reply. He didn't want to talk any more about death.

"What do we do now?" Harvig said after a while. "We need to find more food or we'll never make it back to Kaldersten."

"We could always butcher the vargolf," Sigrid said.

No one answered.

"I didn't say I wanted to, but a starving man isn't picky."

"There's only one choice to make," Flyn said. "We keep going. If we can find the trail, we shouldn't be more than an hour from the tunnel entrance."

"We think we found it," Randell said. "We were on our way back when we heard the first howl. When we heard it barking, we started running, only we got here too late." Randell looked down at his hands.

"It wouldn't have made any difference," Sigrid said. "The beast surprised us. Even if you had gotten back sooner, I doubt there would have been anything you could have done. What's important now is that you found the trail."

"Wait," Harvig said. "You can't really be thinking about going on. Gudbrant is dead. We have no food. We don't even know where we're going. We don't have a chance. We would be walking into our own deaths."

"Even so, I'm going," Flyn said. "I have to go. If you decide to turn around, I won't blame you and I'll have no ill will toward you."

"I'm going as well," Randell said. "I promised Gudbrant I would do whatever I could to save Brenna and I won't back down now. Especially now. If I quit, it will be like he died for nothing."

"I told you I'd follow you," Sigrid said. "Right up to Jarot himself, if I have to. Besides, I don't have anything better to do."

"You're all out of your minds," Harvig said. "It doesn't seem I really have a choice. I either follow you to certain death, or try to make it back to Kaldersten on my own, which is likely to lead to death."

"That's the spirit, laddie," Sigrid said.

"What do we do about food?" Harvig said. "I'm not eating that… that thing. That would be like eating an orc."

"What other choice do we have?" Sigrid asked.

"We'll find food in the citadel," Flyn said. "That's what Gudbrant's plan was, and I think it's a good one."

"I agree," Randell said.

"I hope Gudbrant was right," Harvig said, shaking his head.

"Well, lads, as me great grandpappy used to say, 'Less talking and more walking.'" Sigrid stood up and re-slung her pack and her ax on her back.

Flyn did the same with his pack and bow. Randell and Harvig followed.

"Lead the way," Sigrid said to Randell.

Randell left the clearing, following the dirt trail that led back to the ravine. Sigrid and Harvig were close behind.

Flyn started to follow the others, then stopped at the top of the trail. He turned back to look at the funeral cairn where Gudbrant lay and wondered again how they would succeed without him.

The afternoon sun shone through the trees, highlighting the burial mound in the otherwise shaded clearing. Almost as if it were a bridge of light descending from the sky to lead Gudbrant to Vahul. As he watched, the light grew stronger, reflecting off the rock. For a minute, the mound seemed to glow, then the light faded as a cloud covered the sun and the mound again looked like just a pile of gray rock.

It was up to him now. The others were following him. Even Randell, in spite of his loyalty to Gudbrant, wouldn't go on alone. Without Gudbrant, Kel and Brenna's fates were in Flyn's hands. He knew that somewhere, Gudbrant was watching him and counting on him to finish the quest they started.

"I will," Flyn whispered. He turned back to the trail, hurrying to catch up with the others.

Burying Gudbrant had taken them several hours. Noon had come and gone before they reached the trail that Randell and Harvig had found.

No one spoke of the possibility that it might not be the Yord Trail. Even Harvig kept quiet about the chance that they could be following a false lead.

As they climbed above the tree line on the western slope of Mount Yemsok, the tower of Jarot's citadel came back into view, its black sides gleaming in the afternoon sun. With no view of the city or even the rest of the citadel, the tower appeared out of place against the mountain backdrop, a single black finger bursting from the rock and pointing to the sky. Mount Yemsok was reflected in its north face, as it might upon the surface of a mountain lake. No crack or seam could be seen in the sides, just a smooth ebony surface. Even where the sides met those of the smaller towers atop the main tower, no joint or seam was visible. The smaller structures had openings around their summits, where Flyn suspected sentries watched for approaching enemies.

The party traveled in near silence, the only sound their labored breathing and their boots scraping the dirt. Flyn didn't feel like talking, and apparently no one else did either. Randell walked with his head bowed, Harvig with a clenched jaw. Sigrid, normally chatty while traveling, plodded along with only an occasional comment about some stone or rock formation. Flyn tried to think of Kel to avoid thinking of Gudbrant. When that didn't work, he tried imaging what Brenna would be like, should they find her, but that just led to how they would have to tell her about Gudbrant's death. Finally, all he could do was focus on their path and hope it would lead to the entrance to the tunnels.

The trail zigzagged up the side of the mountain, avoiding the steepest parts of the slope. Although he doubted anyone would be able to see them from this distance, Flyn still felt exposed. Almost as if the tower itself seemed to be watching them. The scattered boulders and rock outcroppings provided little cover for the travelers. The others seemed to feel it too, glancing at the tower every few minutes. Finally, as the trail bent around to the northern slope, and the black tower slid from view behind the peak of Mount Yemsok, they paused for a rest.

"Did you feel it?" Randell said. "Something was watching us. Something evil."

"I felt it," Flyn replied. "Let's just hope they didn't pay any attention to us. After all, we are traveling away from the city, not toward it."

"Unless they figure out we're looking for the entrance to the tunnels," Harvig said.

"If they're as well hidden as Gunnulf said, I don't think they would expect that." Flyn felt like he was trying to convince himself as much as the others.

"Even if we find the right place, how are we going to get to it?" Harvig said. "If Gudbrant had a plan for that, he failed to mention it."

"Leave that to me," Sigrid said. "I'm a dwarf, remember? Moving around in the mountains is what we do."

"Come on," Flyn said after a few minutes. "Let's get moving again."

They shouldered their packs and continued along the trail.

"Watch down the slope for a plateau," Flyn said.

"How will we know which one it is?" Harvig pointed out.

Flyn didn't know the answer to that. He held out hope that if Gunnulf could find it, then they could too.

A rumble in his stomach reminded him of their lack of food. If they didn't find the plateau soon, they would be forced to turn back. They might find some nuts or berries in the forest below. Or maybe a few squirrels. But they wouldn't find anything to sustain them above the tree line. From the trail to the peak, he could see nothing but rock and, higher up, snow.

The trail again became hard to follow, washed out in places and covered in rock from landslides in others. Fortunately, there was no other way to go, so each time they thought they had lost the path, they found it again a short time later. Still, the lack of a clear path made for awkward footing, slowing their progress considerably. The sun was already beginning to throw long shadows, and Flyn was wondering what they would do if they lost the light altogether, when the path turned sharply to the right and the ground straight ahead fell away.

Flyn stopped and peered over the edge.

Below him, perhaps forty or fifty feet, was a small plateau.

"I think we found it," he said, turning back to the others.

They all moved forward and looked down.

"I'm not sure I would call that a plateau," Harvig said. "More of a ledge."

The plateau wasn't very wide, about twenty feet at the widest. Trees covered most of it, obscuring their view of the cliff. They had no way to tell if there was an entrance to a tunnel there or not.

"It's the first place we've found that even remotely resembles what the old man described to us," Flyn said. "We have to try."

"And if it's not the right spot?" Harvig asked. "Then what do we do?"

"That's the easy part," Sigrid said. "I'll go down and look. Then you can pull me back up."

"You have rope?" Flyn asked. His own rope had been in one of the packs the mule had carried.

"Aye, I do. There are some things you should always keep in your personal pack, 'cause you never know what might happen."

Sigrid took off her pack and rummaged through it. After a moment, she pulled out a bundle of rope.

"I'm going to show you how to climb down a cliff with just a rope," she said, grinning at their stunned faces. "First thing we need is an anchor." She found an outcropping a few feet up the slope from the trail and wrapped the rope around it, then threw the ends of the rope over the cliff.

"Now the fun part." She picked up the rope ends and wrapped them around her back, then between her legs.

"Here's the important part," she said. "Make sure you keep both ends together and wrap them around your arm so you can control your speed. To go faster, just loosen up a bit. To slow down, just swing your arm forward and tighten your grip."

She stepped to the edge of the cliff and looked down.

"Watch for me. After I check out the ledge, I'll tie myself off and you can pull me up so I can tell you what I found."

Before anyone could object, she was over the side of the cliff. Flyn watched from the top as she descended. In less than a minute, she was at the ledge. She unwrapped the rope and waved to her companions at the top of the cliff, then disappeared into the trees.

"There's more to that dwarf than meets the eye," Harvig said. He sat down and leaned against a rock.

"I've never met a dwarf before," Flyn said. "I guess I don't know what to expect from her."

"I've met a few," Harvig said. "Most of them don't like heights. In fact, I don't think I've ever heard of one that did."

"Gudbrant once told me about a dwarf he knew who lived with the elves of the Losalf clan…" Randell trailed off.

No one spoke for a bit at the mention of their fallen friend.

"Is a dwarf living with elves unusual?" Flyn said finally.

"It's unusual, but not unheard of," Randell said. "But the Losalf clan builds their cities in the trees, which would make most dwarves uncomfortable."

Flyn wondered how they could build entire cities in trees, then remembered the large trees of the forest he and Kel had traveled through when they had first gotten to Tirmar. He wondered…

"Did the elves used to live along the coast?" he asked. "On the other side of the Estlaeg Mountains?"

"A long time ago," Harvig said. "After the Revolution, most of the Losalf clan settled in the Garlunder Forest, in southern Tirmar. But some settled along the coast. Supposedly, there was only one small forest of giant cedar trees that they settled in. The forest that's there today was planted by those settlers. Eventually, though, they joined the others in the south. No one really knows why."

Flyn nodded and wondered what their cities would be like. Maybe he would get a chance to visit one day.

"She's back," Randell said.

Flyn went to the cliff and looked down. Sigrid was tying the ends of the rope around herself. When she was done, she looked up and waved. Flyn and Randell grabbed the rope and started pulling her up. Sigrid was a lot heavier than she looked. Harvig joined in and between the three of them, they hauled the stout dwarf back up the cliff.

"What did you find?" Flyn asked as soon as they pulled her over the edge.

"I think this is the place," she said as she untied the ends of the rope. "I found a cave that looks like it hasn't been used by anything in a while. I didn't have a torch, so I couldn't go far, but the ground is definitely constructed."

"How can you tell?" Flyn asked.

"A dwarf knows stonework when she sees it, and that cave is definitely stonework. It looks like a natural cave, but that's no work of erosion. It was built. Probably by dwarves, if I had to guess."

"No guards?" Harvig asked.

"Not near the entrance."

"So how do the rest of us get down?" Randell asked. "We can't do that fancy rope thing you did."

"Sure you can, lad. There's nothing to it. I'll show you. Who wants to go first?"

Randell and Harvig didn't answer.

"I'll go," Flyn said. "It looked like fun."

Sigrid chuckled. "Just be careful. It's a long drop if you mess up. And be glad you're wearing leather armor and gloves. This really hurts without it."

She threw the ends of the rope over the cliff again, then showed Flyn how to wrap the rope around his back and legs to create a makeshift harness.

"Now hold the two ropes together and we'll wrap 'em around your arm." She wrapped them once around his forearm and put the ropes in his hand.

"Now just lean back to keep tension on the ropes."

Flyn did as she told him, surprised that he didn't fall back.

"Now just let the rope slide through your hand a little bit and start walking backward to the edge." She showed him how to move his arm to control how fast the rope slid through his hand.

At the edge of the cliff, Flyn leaned back on the ropes and looked down. His head swam and his stomach tingled. The ledge below looked to be thousands of feet away. Beyond the ledge, the cliff seemed to fall forever.

He looked back up at Sigrid. She must have figured out what he was feeling by the look on his face.

"You're doing just fine, laddie. Just take a few deep breaths and don't look down. The first few steps are the hardest."

Flyn closed his eyes. The wind blew across his face, cool from the sweat on his skin. Far below him a bird called out. He forced himself to relax. Slowly, he opened his eyes. Sigrid was still in front of him, holding the ropes to keep him steady. Behind her, Randell and Harvig watched with wide eyes.

"One step at a time, laddie. One foot, then the other foot, then let a little bit of rope slide through your hand. Make sure you're leaning back or your feet will slip and you'll be dangling by your armpits."

Flyn moved one foot from the top of the cliff to the side. Then the other. Slowly he relaxed his grip on the rope. He felt it slide through his fingers and around his arms and legs and chest. He clamped down on the rope and the sliding stopped.

"Just like that and you'll be at the bottom before you know it."

He took another step and let a little more rope slip through his fingers. He was now hanging completely over the side of the cliff. There was no going back. He closed his eyes and took another deep breath before continuing. Left foot. Right foot.

His foot slipped and he fell. A scream began to erupt from his mouth, but before it could escape, he slammed against the cliff, knocking the wind out of him. He instinctively tightened his grip on the rope. His heart raced and his breath came in ragged gasps. The rough rock of the cliff poked his face.

"Flyn!" Randell yelled from above him.

"Just relax a minute, lad," Sigrid said. "Then get your feet back on the cliff. You'll be fine."

Flyn did as she instructed. The rope bit into his arms in spite of the armor, so he didn't wait too long to work his feet back onto the cliff. Once his feet were back on the cliff and he was once again leaning back in his harness, he paused to catch his breath. To his amazement, he was only about a foot lower than he had been when he lost his footing.

"I told you you'd be all right," Sigrid grinned at him. "Just take your time."

He took another step, this time making sure he was secure before moving his other foot. Slowly he worked his way down the cliff. He slipped two more times, but both times he was able to catch himself before he fell.

Ten minutes or ten hours later, he wasn't sure, he reached the bottom. Sigrid waved to him from the top of the cliff. Exhausted, he unwrapped the ropes and collapsed on the ground.

Harvig came next, followed by Randell, who took ten minutes to just make his first step over the cliff. Both slipped several times, but eventually they were all together on the ledge. Sigrid came last, walking down the cliff like she was taking an afternoon stroll through the park.

"That wasn't so hard now, was it?" Sigrid said once she reached the ledge with the others.

No one answered. Flyn was just glad it was over.

"If we leave the rope here, we can use it to climb back up when we come out," Sigrid said.

"It would also tell anyone who came along where we went," Harvig said. "We'll have enough problems with what we find inside. I don't want any extra surprises sneaking up behind us."

"That means the only way off this ledge is down," Sigrid said. She walked over to the edge and looked over the cliff. "At least we have enough rope."

"Gunnulf said that was the only way to go," Randell said.

"That slimy snake doesn't know the first thing about mountaineering," Sigrid said.

"I think it would be a bad idea to leave the rope hanging," Flyn said.

"Suit yourself," Sigrid said. She grabbed one side of the rope. "Last chance."

"Do it," Flyn said.

Sigrid pulled the rope down.

"No choice now." Sigrid coiled up the rope and stowed it in her pack.

"Just show us this cave," Harvig said.

Sigrid walked past the group and into the trees. They followed her to the back of the ledge.

In the cliff wall was an opening, eight feet tall and four across. A few feet from the opening, the light faded into darkness.

"I don't suppose you have a lantern in that pack of yours," Harvig asked Sigrid.

"No." Sigrid sighed. "I had one in the gear that witless weasel took. But I do have the oil for it in my pack. Chop a couple of limbs off one of these trees and we can make torches. I'll need a couple of strips of cloth."

While Sigrid went to work cutting a branch off one of the trees, Flyn pulled a spare shirt from his pack and ripped off the sleeves. In a few minutes, they were standing in front of the cave again with two torches, Sigrid with one and Harvig with the other.

"I hope this it," Randell said. "We've put in a lot of effort if it's not."

"This has to be it," Flyn said.

"Only one way to find out," Sigrid said and stepped through the opening.

The walls and ceiling of the cave seemed like any other cave to Flyn. Not that he had been in many caves. In fact, he had only been in one cave in his life and that one had ogres living in it. But this cave seemed no different to him. The floor of the cave seemed normal too.

"How do you know this cave isn't natural?" Flyn asked Sigrid. His question echoed into the dark.

"Keep your voice down," Sigrid said in a loud whisper. "If there are guards down here, we don't want to let them know we're coming."

"Sorry," Flyn whispered back. "I'm new to this cave thing."

Sigrid chuckled softly. "As to your question, first look at the floor. See how smooth it is? In a natural cave, the floor is uneven and littered with rocks of all sizes. You may find areas that are flat and smooth, but they aren't very big. Maybe a few feet across. A dozen or so at the most. But even those aren't generally smooth from wall to wall."

Flyn looked at the floor. Now that she had mentioned, he could see it. The floor was completely smooth and seemingly level from side to side, though it was gently sloping down. A few cracks here and there were the only noticeable imperfections.

"Now look at how the floor meets the walls."

Flyn looked. The floor curved up into the walls where it transitioned from smooth to rocky. Water dripping from the roof ran off to the sides of the cave where it collected in almost imperceptible troughs that carried it down into the depths of the mountain. The more he looked, the less natural it seemed.

"And see where the water is dripping from the roof of the cave? Stalactites are starting to form, but the biggest ones are only a few inches long. That means they're only a thousand years old or so."

"So?" Harvig asked.

"Well, that means the cave itself is only that old. Geologically speaking, this cave is a newborn. But it's too smooth to be that young. It should have a lot of rough edges where different bits eroded at different rates."

Sigrid stopped to examine a section of the wall.

"Still, they did a pretty good job," she said as she continued down the tunnel. "You certainly wouldn't have noticed if I hadn't pointed it out to you."

Flyn nodded, wondering how much work it must have been to build the tunnel. He tried to imagine teams of dwarves, toiling day and night to dig through solid rock, then taking the time to carve the walls and ceiling to look like a natural cave to the untrained eye, even centuries later. He still couldn't fathom why someone would go to all that effort.

The one thing Flyn did notice without Sigrid's help was how straight the tunnel was. Although the walls weren't straight, giving the illusion of bends in the tunnel, they had been walking in a straight line since entering the cave.

The floor was mostly dry, in spite of the water dripping from the roof. A fine dust covered the dry spots, marking their passage and leaving no doubt that someone had been there. The sound of their feet scuffing along the floor created strange echoes that sounded like someone was following them in the dark, just outside the reach of their torchlight.

Behind them, the light from the opening to the cave had disappeared. Beyond the orange glow of their torches, only darkness. Shadows danced and jumped on the walls and roof of the cave, adding to their disorientation.

Flyn tried to keep track of how long they had been in the tunnel by counting their steps, but soon lost count. With no outside reference, he couldn't be sure if they had walked ten minutes or an hour and ten minutes. The descending tunnel seemed not to change, other than an occasional rock that had fallen from the roof.

The damp air grew colder as they went.

After a time, the tunnel leveled off. Sigrid stopped and whispered to the others.

"I would guess that this tunnel will meet up with the dungeons under the citadel before long. Stay as quiet as you can to avoid alerting any guards."

Sigrid turned and continued on without waiting for replies. She moved slower now, stepping more carefully to avoid scraping her feet or kicking loose stones. The rest of the party followed her lead.

The nature of the tunnel had changed. The walls and ceiling were smoother now, the passage more resembling a square hallway than a cave. The walls formed perfect right angles with the ceiling and floor. From time to time small holes at the base of the walls allowed the water to drain away. Even to a layman, this section of the tunnel left no doubt it wasn't a natural occurring cave.

After a few minutes, the end came into sight. A pair of large steel doors blocked their path.

"I hope there's nobody on the other side of these doors," Flyn said.

"There's no light coming from around the doors," Sigrid said. "So unless they're guarding the door in the dark…"

Sigrid handed her torch to Flyn and grabbed the door handle.

"Everybody ready?" she said, looking back at them. Randell and Harvig drew their swords. Flyn followed suit.

"Go," Flyn said.

Sigrid pulled on the handle.

The door wouldn't open.

"Locked," she said. "Should have figured it wouldn't be that easy."

"Now what do we do?" Randell asked.

"You didn't bring me along for my charming personality," Sigrid said with a grin. She took off her pack and rummaged through it.

"Can you open the lock?" Flyn asked.

"Aye, if it was made by orcs. If a dwarf made it… Well, let's just see what we have. Hold the torch down so I can see."

Sigrid peered into the lock, then inserted something she had pulled from her pack. She jiggled the tool in the lock, then inserted another one. She worked the two tools, then twisted them. The lock clicked.

"An orc lock," she said. "Let's try this again."

Sigrid stowed the tools back in her pack, then grabbed the handle again. The others raised their swords. Sigrid pulled on the handle and the door squealed open.

On the other side of the door was another hallway, continuing straight into the darkness.

"If they didn't know we were coming before, they do now," Sigrid said as the echoes of the screech disappeared into the distance. She picked up her ax and led the way through the doorway.

"Better let me go first," Harvig said. "Everybody be ready."

Harvig handed his torch to Randell and moved to the front of the group. He led the way down the hall, followed by Flyn and Sigrid, with Randell bringing up the rear. They moved as silently as they could, listening for any sign of guards coming to investigate the noise.

Ahead of them, the tunnel intersected another tunnel that led left and right.

"Which way?" Harvig said when they reached the junction.

The new tunnel went straight in both directions as far as their torches could illuminate. Flyn stared first in one direction, then the other. He was about to suggest the left tunnel, for no reason other than they had to pick one, when they heard clanking metal and running footsteps coming from the right.

"Quick," Sigrid said. "Put out the torches."

Flyn and Randell threw the torches on the floor and stepped on the burning ends, extinguishing them and plunging the group into total darkness. Flyn moved toward the wall, one hand in front of him until he felt the cold stone on his fingers. He pressed his back to the wall and waited.

The footsteps drew closer, accompanied by a dim glow that grew brighter.

"It came from the back door," a breathless voice said.

At that, two orcs appeared in the intersection carrying torches and large clubs.

One of them never saw the intruders. Harvig's sword sliced through the air, striking the orc in the neck. He staggered back and collapsed against the wall.

Surprised by the flash of steel, the other orc stepped back and raised his club. Sigrid leapt forward swinging her ax over her head.

"Hey!" the orc shouted, swinging his club at the dwarf. As the club struck Sigrid in the side, her ax embedded in the orc's forehead, cleaving his skull. His mouth opened and closed as if he were trying to say something else, but the only sound that escaped his throat was a weak groan. He collapsed on the floor where he stood.

The entire battle had lasted mere seconds. Flyn and Randell were still standing against the wall as Sigrid sank to one knee, her ax falling to the floor.

"Sigrid!" Flyn yelled, running to her side.

"I'll be fine, laddie. Just knocked the wind out of me is all." Sigrid tried to grin, though it looked more like a grimace.

"Let me help you," Flyn said.

"We need to hide the bodies," Sigrid said, waving Flyn off.

"Where?" Randell asked.

There were no doors in the tunnel they had used to enter, and there were none they could see in either direction in the crossing tunnel.

"We could drag them to the entrance tunnel," Flyn said after they had conducted a quick search. "It doesn't look like they use it, so if we close the door, no one will find them."

"That should be good for the moment," Harvig said. "Though I suspect someone may come looking for them when they don't return."

Harvig and Randell dragged the dead orcs back down the hallway. Pulling the heavy bodies across the stone floor was a difficult task, each one taking both men to move. Flyn brought the orcs' weapons and used one of their torches to light the way. One of the orcs had a large ring of keys on his belt that Flyn took. With her injury, Sigrid wasn't of much help with physical labor, so she ripped pieces of cloth from the orcs' clothing to wipe up most of the blood from the floor.

When they were finished, Harvig turned to Sigrid. She was gasping for air, wincing with each breath.

"Perhaps you should wait here," he said.

"I'm not going to let a little bruise stop me," she said.

"He's right," Flyn said. "You look like you're hurt pretty bad."

"We need to move fast," Harvig added. "Are you sure you'll be able to keep up?"

"I'll outlast the lot of you," she said. "Now let's get moving."

Flyn shrugged at Harvig, who just shook his head in disbelief.

"You heard her," Flyn said.

"Wait a minute." Sigrid took some of the remaining oil and dripped it on the hinges of the steel doors. "That should keep them from squeaking," she said.

Her solution worked. The doors closed without the loud screech that had brought the orcs.

"We should leave it locked," Harvig said. "Like we found it."

Flyn tried the keys he had taken from the orc until he found the right one.

"Don't forget which one that is, laddie," Sigrid said.

"That shouldn't be hard."

The key was larger than the others, with a strange rune design.

Flyn looked at his companions in the dim torchlight.

"Let's go find Kel," he said.

Flyn led the party back to the intersection where they had fought the orcs. He carried one of the orc's torches. Harvig carried the other. Flyn and the militiamen had their swords out and ready. Sigrid carried her ax over her shoulder.

"Which way?" Harvig asked.

"I think we should start to the right, where the orcs came from," Flyn said.

No one else had a better idea. Flyn held his torch to the ceiling for a few seconds, leaving a black soot mark.

"To mark which tunnel we came from," he said.

"Good thinking," Randell said.

Flyn continued in the lead, following the passageway the orcs had come from. After a while, the tunnel changed. Brackets for torches began to appear at regular intervals, though no torches were in them now. Across from each bracket was a door.

At first the doors were mostly rotted and falling off their hinges. The rooms behind them empty or containing just trash and broken crates. After they had passed a dozen or so doors, the passageway turned to the left and the doors looked newer. Some of the doors were locked.

Flyn used the keys he had found on the orc to open these locked doors, though none of the rooms contained anything of much use. Mostly the locked rooms were armories, with weapons and shields. In one room they found crates full of gold and silver coins. Some crates contained jewelry, though nothing extravagant. A series of shelves held trinkets of varying craftsmanship.

"Jarot's treasure room?" Flyn asked.

"I don't know," Randell said. "He doesn't need money."

"Most of the jewelry is junk," Sigrid said. "It's probably worth more melted down."

"Whatever it is, it's not what we're here for," Harvig said from the doorway. He was watching the passageway.

"Okay, let's go." Flyn pocketed a handful of coins before leaving.

They continued down the passageways, checking every door, but finding nothing else of interest. At each intersection, they paused to examine the floor, always choosing the passage with the least dust. Flyn marked their way with the torch as they went. They found no sign that Jarot used the tunnels as a dungeon like Gunnulf had claimed. Only more storerooms for weapons and furniture.

"Maybe the cells are down one of the other passageways," Sigrid suggested.

"Only if the prisoners in them are dead," Harvig said. "Otherwise there would be some sign that someone has been down them recently."

They continued on, still hoping to find cells with prisoners and finding none. The passageway turned again. The doors in this new section weren't locked. The first few led to rooms with nothing but empty shelves. The fourth door they checked, however, turned out to be a pantry.

The shelves were full of canned fruits, dried vegetables, and loaves of bread. From the ceiling hung cured meats, sausages, and salamis. Flyn's stomach growled as he looked at all the food.

"Laddies, I think we hit the mother lode," Sigrid said. She pushed her way past Flyn and grabbed a loaf from the nearest shelf. Randell quickly followed her lead.

"We can't stay here," Harvig said, still at the door. "These pantries are freshly stocked, which means they use them. If we linger too long, we are bound to be discovered."

"Harvig's right," Flyn said. "Grab what you want and we'll go back to one of the empty rooms to rest."

"Let's fill our packs too," Harvig said. "In case we have to leave in a hurry."

They filled their packs with breads and dried meats, then grabbed as much food as they could carry and hurried back the way they came. They chose the first empty room they had found in this section, the one farthest from the pantry. Once inside, they closed the door and barricaded it with one of the empty shelves before they sat down to eat.

"Back home, this would be a pretty poor meal," Flyn said. "But right now, this is a feast."

Randell nodded, his mouth too full of ham to reply.

"Feast or no, I'm not comfortable sitting in a room with only one exit," Harvig said. "If we're discovered, we'll be trapped."

"It doesn't look like they use this room very much," Flyn said. "We're probably safe for a while. Let's rest a bit. We haven't stopped since we found the entrance to the cave."

"Aye, rest would be good," Sigrid said.

"At least keep your voices down." Harvig glanced toward the door. "We don't want to attract attention to ourselves."

They ate the rest of their meal without talking, as much because they were too hungry to talk as they were concerned about being discovered. The bread was mostly stale, the meat was too salty, and the dried vegetables without flavor.

They ate every last bite.

When he had finished, Flyn leaned back against the wall and yawned. A few more minutes of rest was just what he needed.

CHAPTER 14

Flyn awoke to the sound of shouting.

He blinked and rubbed his eyes, trying to see where the noise was coming from. He was in total darkness. They must have fallen asleep and the torches had burned out. Now they were barricaded in a storeroom with no light.

No light wasn't exactly right. Across from him he noticed a dim sliver of light on the floor.

The shouts grew closer, accompanied by the sound of clanking metal. Flyn couldn't make out the words through the closed door, though the voices were clearly orc. He stood up, putting his back to the wall to keep himself oriented, and drew his sword. Elsewhere in the dark he heard two other swords being pulled from their scabbards. He slid one foot forward, preparing to attack.

The light under the door flickered and grew brighter as the voices reached the door. Flyn held his breath. The shelf they had used to barricade the door might hold for a minute or two. He wasn't sure. The orcs were probably strong enough to break the door into pieces, making the barricade useless. At least it would give him and his companions the chance to make the first attack. With one or two orcs, they might stand a chance. Any more and they would be in trouble.

The shouts continued past the door, the light again fading.

Flyn lowered his sword and breathed a sigh of relief.

"That was close," Randell said from somewhere else in the room.

A spark from across the room almost blinded Flyn. A click and another spark, then one of the torches burst into flame, illuminating Sigrid's face.

"How about a little light," she said, grinning at the others.

They blinked at each other in the torchlight.

"I didn't mean to fall asleep," Flyn said.

"None of us did," Harvig replied. "We were lucky not to be caught. Those orcs are probably searching for the ones we killed."

"How long were we sleeping?" Randell asked.

Flyn shook his head. No one else seemed to know either.

"It doesn't really matter now," Harvig said. "We should get moving before the orcs come back."

"Go where?" Randell said. "So far all we've found is storerooms."

"We need to find our way into the citadel," Flyn said. He reminded them of what he had heard from the orcs so many weeks before: Brenna had been taken to be one of Jarot's personal servants. "That means that she'll be in the citadel."

"If she's still alive," Harvig said.

"I think we have to assume she and Kel are both alive," Flyn replied. "Otherwise, why are we here?"

Harvig grunted in response, but didn't say anything else.

"Why don't we leave our gear here, though," Flyn said. "Just take a couple of torches and our weapons. If we don't find Kel and Brenna in a few hours, we can come back here to rest before trying again."

They all felt this was a good plan. They stacked their packs in a corner and used another old shelf to hide them. Flyn leaned his bow against the wall next to the packs, then found the other torch. He lit it using Sigrid's torch while Harvig and Randell removed the barricade from the door.

"Keep the torches away from the door while I make sure the way is clear," Harvig said.

Flyn and Sigrid moved to the corner of the room. Harvig cracked the door and peeked through, then opened it enough to stick his head out and look down the hallway. Apparently satisfied, he opened the door fully and beckoned to the others. Flyn stepped up next to him and looked out himself.

There was no sign of the orcs who had passed by minutes before. In the opposite direction lay only darkness.

Flyn used his torch to mark the wall above the door, then led the way into the hall, Harvig following close behind. Randell took the torch from Sigrid and, ushering her in front of him, brought up the rear.

They continued checking the doors, though not as thoroughly as before. Most were pantries like the one they raided. One contained large kegs—orc ale, Sigrid speculated. None contained prisoners or additional hallways.

After a few minutes, they came upon a set of double doors. Light spilled out from under them.

"Something different, for a change," Sigrid said.

They stood by the doors for a moment, no one daring to open them. Finally, Flyn handed his torch to Harvig and stepped up to the doors. He motioned for the others to stand behind it to hide the torches. Once they were in position, he lifted the latch and slowly pulled one of the doors open a crack. He pressed his face to the edge of the door and peeked through.

On the other side was a short hallway leading to an open room. A stand holding unlit torches and a bucket of water stood next to the doorway.

Flyn carefully opened the door and slipped through. He stopped at the entrance to the room. Before him was a great hall, hundreds of feet across. Rows of columns, spaced fifty feet apart, rose to meet the ceiling, which arched between them. The floor was covered with black marble tiles, each three feet wide. The pillars and ceiling were covered in smaller tiles made of the same black marble.

Torches were mounted in brackets on the innermost rows of columns in the half of the room closest to the doorway. The torchlight reflecting off the dark tile bathed the nearest half of the hall in an odd orange glow. In the center of the room, a wide spiral staircase ascended through an opening in the vaulted ceiling. Beyond the staircase, the hall disappeared into darkness.

"By my pappy's beard," Sigrid whispered next to him. Flyn hadn't heard her walk up.

"I've never seen anything like this," Randell said from behind her.

"I knew this was dwarven work," Sigrid said, the awe still in her voice.

"What do you think they use it for?" Flyn asked.

"Hard to say," Sigrid said. "Maybe a dining room or meeting room of some sort. Anywhere else, I might think it was a cathedral, but I don't think the orcs care much for the gods."

"We don't have time to admire it," Harvig said.

Flyn nodded. "That stairway must lead to the citadel."

"We don't need these anymore," Harvig said. He extinguished his torch in the bucket of water and set it in the stand with the other torches. Sigrid did the same with hers.

"I never even imagined a place like this," Flyn said.

"Wait until you see some of the halls in Kridheben," Sigrid said.

Flyn stepped out into the room, looking for guards as much as to take in the beauty. The flickering light of the torches cast dancing shadows on the black marble, giving the illusion that the columns were moving. The dark ceiling was mostly hidden in shadow, with only occasional flickers of light reflecting off the marble.

He tried to step softly. Every scuff of their feet echoed in the massive room. He dared not try to talk for fear his voice would carry throughout the hall, alerting anyone who may be hidden in its dark shadows at the far end.

They reached the central staircase without seeing any guards. With one last check, Flyn began to ascend the stairs, the others close behind.

The staircase was tiled in with the same black marble as the floor. Its handrail appeared to be made of gold. The posts placed every ten feet were topped with large red gems that Flyn didn't recognize. The massive structure was twenty-five feet across, with a five-foot, marble-tiled column in the center. The steps were not only wide and deep, ten feet across and three feet deep, but tall as well, at least twice as tall as a normal step. Sigrid especially struggled, from her injury as well as her height.

The climb took them several minutes to reach the opening in the ceiling, a hundred feet above the floor. Above them, the stairs continued to climb, the way lit by torches along the curved walls. They stopped to rest before continuing. Sigrid was breathing hard, in obvious pain.

"Are you going to be okay?" Flyn whispered.

She nodded, her jaw clenched, holding her side where the orc had struck her.

They sat on the stairs for a short rest, sipping water from their waterskins. Flyn was examining the ceiling, now only a few feet above their heads. It was covered in thousands of small black tiles. He marveled at the amount of work it would have taken just to place them all, wondering how they had done it, a hundred feet off the ground. Another question for the dwarf.

"Everybody ready?" Flyn asked after a few minutes.

They were stowing their waterskins when they heard a noise below them.

Two orcs walked out of the hallway they had come from. They were arguing with each other, their voices echoing throughout the chamber.

"I'm senior guard, you go," one said.

"That why you should tell the captain."

"Me in charge. You go. Now!"

"Don't yell at me when captain mad you not go to tell him about guards leaving their post."

The orcs put their torches in brackets next to the opening, then one started toward the stairs. The other stood by the opening to the hallway.

Flyn gestured to the others, pointing up the stairway. They started up the stairs again as quickly as they could, staying close to the central column to avoid being seen by the orcs below.

In a few steps they were above the ceiling, closed off and hidden from the guards. Flyn kept a quick pace, hoping to stay ahead of the orc coming up the stairs behind them. The others followed close behind, Harvig helping Sigrid. In spite of her obvious pain, she pushed on.

After a few minutes, Flyn was unsure how far, maybe forty or fifty steps, they reached a landing with a door. The stairway continued on the other side of the landing.

"Which way?" Flyn asked the others, keeping his voice low.

"We're probably on the main floor," Sigrid said. "I would guess that's where the pig-face behind us is headed. Besides, we're looking for one of Jarot's personal servants. I would guess they're upstairs."

Harvig nodded, Randell just shrugged.

"Okay, we'll try the next floor first."

They could hear the orc on the stairs behind them now. Flyn raced up the steps as fast as he could without making noise. The staircase made a full turn before coming to another landing, identical to the one below. They stopped and listened.

Below them, Flyn heard the door at the first landing open, then slam closed. Exhausted, he collapsed on the stairs.

"Let's keep moving," Sigrid said after they had rested a minute. "No telling when more of them pig-faces'll come along, and I don't want to be in here any longer than I have to."

"Sigrid's right," Harvig said. "The longer we're here, the more likely we are to be discovered."

"Why don't we split up," Flyn said, still trying to catch his breath. "We'll be able to cover more ground and we'll be less likely to be seen if we aren't running around in a big group."

"But you and Sigrid don't know what Brenna looks like, and you are the only one who knows what Kel looks like," Randell said.

"That's why I think we should go in two groups," Flyn replied. "Me and Randell in one group, Harvig and Sigrid in the other."

"And how will we know Kel?" Harvig asked.

"Based on what I've seen, you'll know him. He doesn't look anything like an Ilfin. He looks more like me." Flyn described Kel to Harvig and Sigrid. "Besides, I don't expect to find him here. He's probably locked up in a cell somewhere. I'm hoping we'll find Brenna and she'll be able to help us find Kel."

"A good plan, lad," Sigrid said.

Flyn cracked the door and peered out. A hallway, lit by torches, extended in both directions. The wall opposite the door was lined with windows looking out to the night sky. Other doors were spaced along the wall with the door to the stairs. No one was around.

"You two go left," Flyn said to Harvig and Sigrid. "Randell and I will go right. We'll meet back here."

Flyn and Randell drew their swords and slipped through the door and down the hallway.

The floor was tiled with the same black marble they had seen in the rest of the citadel. The walls were painted light gray, though Flyn couldn't tell what they were made of. He ran his hand along the wall as they walked. It felt like stone, only it didn't have the cool feel of stone. And it didn't seem as solid.

"What do you think these walls are made of?" he asked Randell.

Randell put his hand on the wall.

"I don't know. It's not stone and it doesn't feel like wood. It's like nothing I've ever seen."

"This whole place is like nothing I've ever seen," Flyn said.

Randell nodded.

They moved on down the hallway, stepping as quietly as they could. At the first door, they paused.

"Ready?" Flyn asked Randell.

Randell nodded.

Flyn lifted the latch and pushed the door open.

Behind the door was a large, dark chamber. The light from the hallway only lit up part of the room, though from what he could see, it appeared to be a study or library of some kind. One wall was filled with books and scroll cases. The opposite wall was covered with strange paintings that looked almost lifelike, though Flyn had no idea what they were paintings of. In the middle of the room was a large table with no chairs around it. The only chair seemed to be the one behind the desk at the other end, in front of a large window that filled the entire wall.

The table was taller than a normal table, its top five feet from the ground. The desk and chair were also oversized, too big for even an orc. Not that he imagined orcs used desks very much.

Flyn closed the door and they moved on to the next one.

Most of the rooms were studies or meeting rooms, all of them larger than Flyn's entire house, though none as large as the first room. No one was in any of them. Flyn was beginning to think that this was a working floor and, being night, no one was here.

The second to last room wasn't a study. As soon as Flyn opened the door he knew. First, the rumbling sound of heavy snoring, then the foul stench of orc hit him. He pulled the door closed as quickly as he could without slamming it.

"What is it?" Randell asked.

"Orcs. I don't know how many, but more than one. I don't think I woke any of them up." Flyn's heart was racing. "Give me a minute before we go to the next one."

The last door was different from the other doors. This one was barred on the outside.

Flyn looked at Randell. His heart raced again, though this time from excitement. Together, he and Randell lifted the bar and set it aside. There was no other lock. Flyn lifted the latch and pushed the door open.

The dark room was adorned with none of the finery of the libraries and meeting rooms they had thus far investigated. A row of beds ran the length of the room on each side. Flyn and Randell stepped inside to get a better look and found that on the wall above each bed was a metal ring with chains. The other ends of the chains were attached to the ankles of prisoners who lay sleeping in the beds.

They approached the first bed. The prisoner was a young woman, about the same age as Flyn. Her straight, dark hair, high cheek bones, and thin nose made her distinctively Ilfin. Not that he expected to find any Andor prisoners besides Kel. He looked up at Randell.

"Is that her?" he asked.

Randell shook his head.

"What do we do?" Flyn whispered. They had never discussed what they would do with any other prisoners they found.

"I don't know."

"We can't leave them here."

"We may have to." Randell moved to the next bed.

Flyn looked down at the sleeping girl in front of him. Leaving her would be as cruel as imprisoning her himself. There had to be some way he could help the others, but he didn't know what.

"Flyn," Randell said in a loud whisper.

Flyn looked up. Randell was already halfway down the room. He was beckoning to Flyn.

He felt another pang of guilt as he stepped away from the first bed. He wondered what would happen to her after they left. Nothing good, he was sure.

Randell was waking the woman on the bed in front of him. She rubbed her eyes and looked up at him in a sleep-induced stupor.

"Brenna," Randell said again. "Wake up."

She bolted up in her bed and stared at the two men.

Flyn was stunned. Her raven hair fell about her shoulders, framing her smooth, pale face in the dim light. Her eyes were blue as ice, yet burning with fire. She wore a sleeveless frock made of rough linen. Even in the unflattering garment, he could see she was tall and muscular.

"Randell?" she said. "Is that really you?"

"It is," he replied. "We're here to rescue you."

Brenna looked at Flyn.

"M-my name is Flyn," he stammered.

"Is Gudbrant with you?" She turned back to Randell.

Randell bowed his head and shook it.

"Where is he? What happened to Gudbrant?"

"Later," Randell said. "Right now, we need to get you out of here."

"They keep the key for the shackles on a hook by the door," she said.

"I'll get it," Flyn said, happy to have something to do.

He ran back to the door and found the key ring hanging next to the door where Brenna had said it would be. It held a single key. Flyn grabbed it and hurried back.

"I don't suppose you have a spare pair of boots?" Brenna was asking Randell. "They don't give us shoes. I guess they figure it's harder to run away barefoot."

"Here it is." Flyn held out the key.

"Thanks." Brenna grabbed the key and unlocked her shackles. "Ugh. I hate those things."

Freed from her shackles, she stood up and wrapped her arms around Randell.

"I can't believe you're here," she said.

Standing, Brenna was even taller than Flyn. Her long arms and legs were covered in bruises and red welts that appeared to be from a whip. He felt his heart ache to think of the orcs beating her as they had him, though she didn't seem to be letting her injuries bother her. She stood tall and determined in front of him.

"What's wrong with your friend?" she said to Randell.

Flyn realized he had been staring at her. He turned away, glad for the darkness that hid his blushing.

"I'm sorry," he said. "I didn't mean to stare. I was just noticing how much they've beat you. I've suffered orc beatings myself, so I know what you've been through."

"They keep trying to break me," she said. "I won't let them. I actually expected them to grow tired of it and kill me by now."

"I'm glad we got here first," Flyn said.

Brenna smiled at him. He felt himself blush again.

"This is Flyn," Randell said. "He's looking for a friend the orcs brought here a few weeks ago."

"Good to meet you, Flyn," Brenna said. "And thanks for helping me. How do you know your friend is here?"

"He was captured by orcs who took him to Gurnborg," Randell said. "We tried to rescue him there, but found out from another prisoner that he had been brought here."

"They usually only bring prisoners here if they think they are of special value," she said. "What's special about your friend?"

"He's an Andor," Randell said.

Brenna looked at Flyn, then back to Randell.

"He's an Andor too?" she asked, pointing at Flyn.

"He is," Randell replied.

"I'm sorry, Flyn," she said, shaking her head. "There was an Andor brought in a few weeks ago. Jarot took him somewhere and when he returned…"

"What?" Flyn said. "What happened to Kel?"

"He was changed," she replied. "Jarot did something to his mind. Now he's one of Jarot's advisors."

Kel? Helping someone as evil as Jarot?

"No," Flyn said. "That can't be true. Not Kel. He's one of the kindest people I know. He would never help someone as evil as Jarot."

Brenna put a hand on his shoulder.

"Jarot has the ability to manipulate people's minds. Especially if they're already worn down. I saw your friend when they brought him in. He was scared. The orcs had tortured him. He kept pleading with Jarot to let him go. He just wanted to go home. The poor kid didn't stand a chance."

"Come on," Brenna said. "Help me free the others."

"We can't," Randell said. "We'll never be able to sneak out with that many people. They'll catch us for sure."

Brenna looked around at her fellow prisoners, still sleeping in their beds, then back to Randell.

"We have to help them. I'm not going to just leave them here. You don't know what it's like."

"Please, Brenna. We have to go."

"We can at least get them out of their shackles," she said. "They're smart girls. They can sneak out in small groups after we're gone."

Randell opened his mouth to respond, but closed it again when he saw Brenna's glare.

"Okay," he said, bowing his head. "But we have to be quick about it."

He and Brenna set about freeing the other women, fourteen more in all. Flyn sat on an empty bed lost in his thoughts.

For weeks he had struggled and fought to rescue Kel from Jarot. He had tracked him to Gurnborg, then Uskleig. Somewhere within the walls of this citadel, perhaps only a few dozen feet away, was his best friend, his brother, now a tool of the enemy. An enemy neither of them had known about three months ago back on Trygsted. An evil they would still know nothing about if Flyn hadn't talked Kel into his grand adventure.

And now Kel was gone. Or at least the Kel that Flyn knew. And the suffering Kel must have endured, the hopelessness he must have felt. All because Flyn had been bored living the life of a farmer. Kel had tried to talk him out of it, but Flyn hadn't listened. He had never stopped to consider Kel's opinions. Everything always had to be Flyn's way. *Come along, it'll be fun.* What Flyn had always seen as adventures, Kel struggled through just for a little bit of Flyn's admiration.

Why?

Why did Kel look up to him? He certainly hadn't earned it. He didn't deserve a friend like Kel. Or Gudbrant, or the others who had risked their lives to help him along the way.

Why had he built that damned boat? His mother had told him no good would come of it, and she had been right.

"Flyn." Randell was standing in front of him. "Time to go."

Flyn picked up his sword from the bed and followed Randell to the door where Brenna was explaining the situation to the other women.

"Go in small groups," she was saying. "Two or three at a time. Once you're in the tunnels, look for scorch marks on the ceiling at every intersection and take the tunnel with the mark. We'll wait for you outside until morning. After that, you're on your own."

A shout and a loud crash from the hallway interrupted Brenna. She and Randell hurried through the door. Flyn followed them.

At the other end of the hallway two orcs were attacking Harvig and Sigrid.

"Damn," Randell said. "Brenna, stay here."

Randell drew his sword and ran toward the battle. Brenna, unarmed and barefoot, ignored Randell's request and ran after him. Flyn didn't move.

The scene at the other end of the hallway seemed to be a dream. Just another piece of the horrible nightmare that had already seen the loss of two friends and would likely see the loss of more. Flyn wondered what would happen if he died in his dream. Would he die in real life? And then what? Would he go to Vahul? Or would he be doomed to wander for eternity, a lost soul. Certainly that was what he deserved.

Two more orcs had joined the battle. They had turned to face Randell and Brenna. Brenna had grabbed a torch from a bracket on the wall.

Harvig and Sigrid attacked the orcs while ducking and dodging their larger foes' clumsy swings of their clubs. As they pressed forward, the orcs stepped back until they were back-to-back with the other orcs.

Randell attacked with his sword, his strikes deflected by the orc's club. The other orc attacked Brenna. She ducked under the orc's club and stabbed at his chest with the torch. Sparks flew, and flame erupted. The orc dropped his club and tried to beat the flames from his chest.

Flyn was still frozen, watching the battle, when the door next to the prisoners' room opened. A large orc stepped out and looked toward the melee.

"Hey!" the orc shouted. "What going on here?"

The orc reached into the room and grabbed a club from next to the door.

"Intruders!" he yelled into the room, then ran to join the battle. A few seconds later, three more orcs burst from the room and ran after the other one.

His friends were outnumbered. Four more people were about to die.

Unless he did something.

"No more," Flyn said under his breath. No more of his friends were going to die on his account. He was going to save them or die trying.

Flyn raised his sword and ran after the orcs. The first one had reached the battle and engaged Brenna, who was dancing around swings of his club. The one she had hit with the torch was screaming, running around, engulfed in flames.

Flyn raced as fast as he could. The last orc was almost within reach. He pulled his sword back with both hands and swung with all his might as he caught up with the orc. The blade slipped under the orc's arm and into his side. The orc stumbled and fell to the ground, yelling in pain.

Flyn didn't stop.

The next orc turned at the sound of his companion's yell. What he saw was Flyn's sword swinging down on his head.

The sword smashed into the orc's face, cleaving his skull. The orc fell without uttering a word.

Ahead of him, the next orc had stopped and turned to face Flyn. The orc grinned and raised his club. Flyn kept running at full speed, determined not to stop until his sword was embedded in the orc's chest. He might not be able to save Kel, but the orcs would pay for what they had done.

Flyn yelled and held his sword out ready to strike.

The orc's grin faded as the point of a sword exited his chest. Flyn skidded to a stop. The orc dropped to his knees, eyes still on Flyn, then fell forward landing at Flyn's feet. Behind the orc, Randell pulled his sword from the orc's back.

The other orcs all lay dead, one still burning. The humans and dwarf looked around at each other and the bodies on the floor.

"Now that was a fight," Sigrid said, leaning on her ax. She grimaced in pain.

"Harvig?" Brenna said. She ran up to the big man and gave him a hug. "I should have known you'd be here."

"You don't think Randell could make it here all by himself, do you?" Harvig said with a grin. Flyn couldn't remember ever seeing the man smile before.

"And where did you find a dwarf?" she asked, smiling at Sigrid.

"The dwarf's name is Sigrid, lass," Sigrid said. "And you must be the Brenna I've been hearing about for the last few weeks."

"Pleased to meet you Sigrid. And thank you for your help. Now would someone please tell me where Gudbrant is?"

Harvig and Randell looked at their feet. Flyn wasn't sure what to say to her. He started to tell her, then stopped.

How did he tell her the person she loved was dead?

"Gudbrant loved you," Sigrid said, her voice softer than Flyn had ever heard it before. "He died to save you from this place."

Brenna didn't say anything. Her jaw clenched and a tear rolled down her cheek. She closed her eyes and stood silently for a moment. Then she took a deep breath and opened her eyes.

"When we get out of here, I want to know exactly what happened to him," she said quietly. "But right now, we need to go. All that noise was bound to attract someone."

"What about Kel?" Flyn said. "I can't leave without him."

"He belongs to Jarot now," Brenna said.

"Can't we do something to break Jarot's spell?" Flyn asked. "I have to save him. If it weren't for me, he wouldn't even be here."

"Once someone is under the control of a Yonarr, there is no saving them." She looked at Flyn, her eyes full of sorrow and compassion.

Flyn was taken aback. In spite of her own loss, she was concerned about him. He vowed that one day he would make up for his actions and earn that kindness.

"I refuse to believe he's gone," Flyn said, determined to save his friend. "You leave if you must, but I'm not leaving until I rescue Kel. There has to be a way."

"Aye, there's a way, lad," Sigrid said. "Kill Jarot."

"Fine," Flyn said. He turned to Brenna. "Where is he?"

"It's not that simple," Harvig said. "You can't just kill a Yonarr. Not like a man or an orc. Swords and arrows can't harm them."

"They can't be invincible," Flyn insisted. "They aren't gods, are they?"

"No," Randell said. "But they might as well be."

"Even during the Revolution, the only thing that could kill a Yonarr was their own magic," Harvig said. "And that was lost at the end of the war."

"Flyn," Brenna said. "You helped rescue me. I'll never forget that. I'll do everything I can to help you save your friend, but now is not the time. The best way to help your friend now is to live to fight another day."

Flyn looked into Brenna's eyes. He knew she was right. He couldn't help Kel if he was captured too. Or worse, killed.

He sighed and nodded his head.

Brenna smiled at him, then turned to the others.

"Come on," Brenna said. "We have to hurry. I just got out of those shackles and I don't want to be put back in them."

The party hurried back to the stairwell, with swords drawn. They waited as Harvig opened the door and listened.

All was quiet.

Harvig led the way and had just started down the steps when the door below them opened and someone came through.

Harvig turned from the steps leading down and ran up instead. The others followed him up to the next landing where they stopped and listened.

Two orcs were talking, coming up the stairs. Flyn peeked around the corner.

"If those boneheads wake up the Master, he'll burn them alive."

"They quiet now."

"They better stay that way."

"Maybe servant girl getting cheeky again."

"Master will burn her alive too. He's done with her games."

The second-floor door opened.

"What's going on here?" the first one yelled.

The two orcs ran through the door. It slammed shut behind them.

"Quick," Harvig said. "Before they come back."

They raced down the stairs, past the second and first-floor landings, taking the awkward-sized steps as fast as they could. Above them, they heard doors opening and voices shouting and feet running. When they reached the opening to the great hall under the citadel, they paused for a moment, looking for guards.

Only one guard stood below them. The same orc they had seen before. He stood next to the opening leading to the tunnels, looking around nervously.

"There's no way we'll get down these stairs without him seeing us," Randell whispered. "As soon as he sees us, he'll start yelling for help."

"What if just one of us goes down," Flyn said. "Maybe he'll think he can manage on his own and won't call for help."

"That might work," Harvig said. "But then it might not. And even if it does, one on one with an orc that's waiting for you would be a tough fight."

"I'll go," Brenna said.

The others looked at her.

"I'll go down with no weapons. He won't call for help. He'll come after me and try to catch me on his own. I'll lead him off to the side behind the pillars and while he's focused on me, the rest of you can sneak down and catch him off guard."

"That could work," Sigrid said.

"No," Randell said. "I can't let you do that. It's too risky. I swore to Gudbrant I would get you home safe, and that's what I'm going to do. Using you as bait to lure an orc away from his post isn't part of that goal."

Brenna frowned at Randell. "You aren't *letting* me do anything. I'm going. You don't have a say in it."

Before anyone could protest, she leapt down the first two steps and was gone.

"Fiery lass." Sigrid chuckled.

"You know better than to tell Brenna what she can't do," Harvig said to Randell.

Brenna made her way down the stairs without making a sound. The dim light on the upper half of the stairs must have helped as well. She was more than halfway down before the guard noticed her.

"Think you can sneak up on me?" The orc laughed. "Come on, little girl. Vorggak will take you back to bed."

Brenna raced the rest of the way down the stairs as the guard walked toward her.

"You don't need to run," Vorggak said. "I won't hurt you. Much."

"We have to help her," Flyn said. "He'll reach the stairs before she gets to the bottom."

Flyn stood up to start down the steps. Harvig grabbed his arm.

"Wait," he said.

As Vorggak reached the staircase, Brenna vaulted over the railing, jumping the last ten feet. She hit the ground and tucked into a roll. Vorggak cursed and raced after her.

"Now," Harvig said.

They rushed down the steps as quickly as they could. Flyn looked down anxiously each time he came around to the side where the guard was chasing Brenna. She was using the columns to keep him from reaching her. Whenever Vorggak lunged around one column, she would race back behind another. Flyn could see that she would run out of columns soon if they didn't hurry. He raced past Randell and Harvig, determined to get to the orc before he could catch Brenna.

Flyn was almost to the bottom when Vorggak caught her. Her back was against the wall, the orc standing in front of her.

"Nowhere to run now, little girl," Vorggak said, laughing.

The orc lunged at her. Brenna was ready. She ducked under his grasp and ran, but she was just a little too slow. Vorggak grabbed a handful of her hair and yanked her back. Her legs flew out from under her and she fell with a hard thud onto the marble tile.

Flyn jumped over the last few steps and charged toward the guard.

A low laugh echoed through the hall from behind him. Flyn stopped and turned.

"Flynygyn of the Andors," a familiar voice said from the shadows. "How nice of you to save me the trouble of tracking you down. Had you told me you wanted to visit the Master's palace, I would have brought you myself."

Out of the shadows appeared a large orc with dark red skin and large tusks protruding from his lower jaw.

"Ugglar," Flyn said.

CHAPTER 15

The orc commander turned toward the rest of the party as they reached the bottom of the stairs.

"Sigrid," Ugglar said. "So good to see you. But where is Gudbrant? I was so looking forward to speaking with him. We didn't get a chance to talk before you left."

"What do you want?" Flyn said. His face flushed with anger.

Ugglar laughed again, a deep rumbling sound that made Flyn's flesh crawl.

"I've come for you, Andor. And I've brought someone who wants to see you."

A smaller figure stepped out of the shadows.

"Kel!" Flyn said. He started toward his friend, then stopped. Something was wrong. The man standing before him looked like Kel, but the expression on his face did not.

"Hello, Flyn," Kel said. "I'm glad to see you."

"Are you okay?" Flyn remembered what Brenna had said.

"Of course. Why wouldn't I be?"

"The orcs captured you. They tortured you, Kel."

"An unfortunate misunderstanding," Ugglar said. "You see, we didn't know who he was. We thought he was one of those traitorous Ilfin. After all, we did find him near Garthset."

"Yes. A misunderstanding," Kel said.

"A misunderstanding?" Flyn shouted. "They almost killed you! And now you're their prisoner!"

"He's no prisoner," Ugglar said. "Are you, Kel?"

"No," Kel said. "I can leave anytime I want. But I like it here. You would like it here too, Flyn."

"Kel, what's wrong with you?"

"Don't listen to him, Flyn," Brenna yelled. "He's not the man you knew."

"Shut your mouth, girl," Vorggak said.

Brenna cried out as Vorggak smacked her.

"Come with me, Kel. Look. I brought your hat." Flyn pulled the battered hat from his belt pouch. "We'll go back home. You want that, don't you?"

"Of course I do. But you can't get me home. Lord Jarot is building a big ship, with a whole crew to take me home. *You* should come with *me*, Flyn. When I get home, everybody will be so happy with the new world I discovered that they'll make me Thane of Trygsted, Yarl of the Andors. You can be my commander, Flyn."

"What are you talking about? No one is going to make you Thane of Trygsted. Jarot is lying to you."

Ugglar laughed again.

"Bow before Thane Kel," Ugglar said. "Ruler of the Andors of Trygsted."

Flyn's eyes burned as sweat dripped into them. He tried to wipe his eyes with the back of his hand. The stinging persisted.

"Kel! How can you trust these orcs? They kidnap people, turn them into slaves."

"You have it all wrong, Flyn. Lord Jarot is the rightful ruler of Tirmar. The Ilfin are traitors. There was peace before they tried to over-throw Lord Jarot. The orcs capture the traitors, but instead of keeping them in prison cells, they let them atone for their treachery by working for Lord Jarot."

His head was spinning. That couldn't be true, could it? No, Jarot was the real evil.

"Kel, this is crazy. They've convinced you that they're the good guys."

"Flyn," Kel said softly. "I think it's you who has been deceived. Lord Jarot just wants his people to be happy and live long, healthy lives. Like any good ruler."

"Listen to your friend," Ugglar said. "He has seen the truth."

The truth? What was the truth? Gudbrant hadn't been a traitor. He had been a good man and a good friend.

"You've twisted everything around." Flyn's pulse pounded in his ears. He was having trouble breathing. "Jarot is the evil one. The only use he has for humans is as his slaves."

"Lord Jarot is kind and benevolent," Kel said. "These Ilfin want you to think he's evil so you will help them in their traitorous war against him. But you aren't one of them, Flyn. You're an Andor, like me. Join me and Lord Jarot will forgive you for your sins against him."

He was an Andor. He wasn't part of the Ilfin's fight.

Flyn's body was numb, floating in the flickering torchlight.

Kel stepped up to Flyn and grabbed his hands.

"Please, Flyn. I miss you. The only other humans here are the traitors. The orcs are okay, but they're pretty dull. Except for Lord Jarot and Commander Ugglar, there's no one here I can talk to about anything interesting."

"But..." Flyn couldn't think straight. The walls and pillars of the hall faded away, leaving only Kel's face. "They said Jarot can control people's minds. That he controls you."

Kel smiled at Flyn. "Listen to how silly you sound. Mind control. Lord Jarot isn't even here. What's more likely? That Lord Jarot is an evil magician controlling my mind? Or that the traitors lied to you to turn you against your best friend?"

Flyn turned to look at Randell and Harvig. Two more orcs had come down the stairs and were holding them. They had their hands over the militiamen's mouths. The two men struggled in vain in their captors' grasp. Vorggak had brought Brenna next to the staircase with the others. He had one arm around her waist, pinning her to his body. His other hand covered her mouth. The three Ilfin traitors were captured.

Flyn turned back to Kel.

"I was worried about you, Kel. I was afraid of what had happened to you. It's my fault we're here. If I had never built that boat, we would be home right now, safe. We would never have heard of Ilfins or orcs or Lord Jarot. I'm sorry."

Kel put his arms around Flyn. Flyn wept on his friend's shoulder.

"It's okay, Flyn. None of that matters anymore. We're both safe now. Lord Jarot will take care of you. He's looking forward to meeting you."

"Lord Jarot," Flyn said. "What's he like?"

"He's like a father. He's kind and caring and he'll help us both get back home."

"I'd like that. Will we be home in time for Matching Day?"

"When I'm Thane, I'll get rid of Matching Day. Why should we only get one chance to find a wife?"

"Good."

Flyn suddenly realized how tired he was. Weeks of climbing through the mountains and walking across open plains, fighting orcs and trolls and a vargolf. He was ready to rest. He sank to his knees.

"I've killed people, Kel. I've killed orcs and trolls. Will Lord Jarot forgive me?"

"It's okay." Kel put a hand on Flyn's shoulder. "Lord Jarot is kind and forgiving."

Flyn looked up at Kel and smiled.

"Take the prisoners to the stockade," Ugglar said. "I'll take the Andors to Lord Jarot." The orc commander laughed again.

"Over my dead body!" Sigrid leapt from the shadows, swinging her ax at the large orc, striking him in the arm.

Ugglar yelled in pain and anger. He swung his arm at the dwarf, knocking her back and sending her ax skittering across the floor.

"Kill that filthy mole!" Ugglar yelled.

The orcs holding the prisoners looked at each other. Finally, Vorggak shoved Brenna at the other two and ran toward Sigrid.

Kel stepped back, cowering behind Ugglar.

Flyn blinked. What was happening? He felt like his head was in a fog.

Vorggak reached Sigrid as she recovered her ax. She ducked as the orc swung his club at her head, then countered with her ax, striking at his legs, but her off-balance attack bounced off the leather armor covering his thigh.

A yell from the staircase distracted Flyn from Sigrid. Brenna had broken free from the orcs and picked up a dropped sword. She swung it in a wide arc at the head of the nearest orc, the one holding Harvig. The orc raised his arms to protect his face, releasing Harvig.

"Enough," Ugglar yelled. He pushed Kel out of his way and started toward the staircase.

Grunting and clinking metal and thudding of weapons filled the air. Flyn's head swam. He had almost let Kel talk him into joining Jarot. And now his friends were fighting for their lives. He pressed his hands to his temples trying to clear his head, trying to make sense of the commotion around him.

Sigrid was dodging Vorggak's club, her attacks falling short. Brenna had engaged one of the other orcs, while Harvig was freeing Randell from the other.

Flyn closed his eyes.

Jarot was evil. Kel was under Jarot's spell. The words Kel had spoken had been Jarot's lies. Jarot was his enemy, not the Ilfins, not Sigrid. Randell, Harvig, and Sigrid had risked their lives to help him find Kel. Gudbrant had died to help him. And Brenna. Even after finding out her love had died, she had still shown empathy to Flyn when she'd found out about his friend.

Those weren't the actions of evil people. Those were the actions of good people. Of friends. His friends. And now they needed his help.

Flyn opened his eyes.

Ugglar was almost to the staircase. Once he reached Randell and Harvig, they would be done for.

Flyn picked up his sword. He didn't even remember dropping it.

"No, Flyn!" Kel yelled as Flyn stood and turned. "Lord Jarot is your master now."

Flyn ignored Kel's pleas.

"Ugglar," Flyn yelled.

The orc commander turned to face Flyn.

"It's time we finish this."

"This time, you die, Andor." Ugglar scowled at Flyn. He reached down to his belt and pulled out the rod he had used to torture Flyn. Blue lightning bolts arced between the prongs. He moved toward Flyn, holding the rod up in front of him.

"Your magic doesn't scare me anymore, Ugglar." Flyn braced himself.

"I don't care," Ugglar replied. "I'll kill you just the same."

"Don't hurt him," Kel shrieked from behind Flyn. "He doesn't know what he's doing!"

"Your friend has chosen the wrong side and now he'll die."

"But Lord Jarot wants him alive!" Kel screamed.

"Jarot isn't here," Ugglar snarled.

Kel bolted past them. Flyn ignored him.

Clanging and yelling echoed through the hall. Flyn shut it all out. He stayed focused on the large orc advancing on him. He had to. If his larger opponent gained an advantage, the battle would be over. He raised his sword.

Ugglar snarled and ran toward Flyn, lightning flashing at the end of the rod. He thrust the rod at Flyn with a yell.

Flyn stepped to the left to dodge the strike and brought his sword down on the orc's arm, slicing through his leather gauntlet. Ugglar shrugged off the blow and spun back to Flyn, surprisingly quick for his size.

Again, Ugglar lunged at Flyn with the rod and again Flyn stepped to the side to avoid the strike. This time Ugglar expected the move and flicked his wrist at Flyn. The end of the rod struck his shoulder, sending a painful tingling up and down his side. He grabbed his sword with both hands to keep from dropping it as he twisted away from Ugglar's attack.

The combatants faced off against each other. Blood—red, Flyn noted, rather than blue like the other orcs—flowed freely from Ugglar's arm where Sigrid had cut him with her ax. Flyn's right side was going numb from Ugglar's rod. Flyn moved to his left, circling his larger opponent, looking for an opening. Ugglar turned to follow.

"You're no match for me, Andor. Your puny sword can't pierce my armor. I'll crush you like an insect!"

"My sword has already pierced your armor, orc. And I don't have to strike to defeat you. That wound in your arm will bleed you dry. I just have to wait."

Ugglar growled at Flyn, his eyes burning with hatred. Flyn tightened the grip on the hilt of his sword, waiting for the commander to strike.

With a loud yell that reverberated off the walls of the great hall, Ugglar lunged at Flyn, the rod spitting lightning as it drove for Flyn's chest. The attack was exactly what Flyn had expected. He easily side-stepped the thrust and brought his sword down on the rod.

Lightning exploded from the rod in a blinding flash that illuminated even the darkest corners of the great hall. A thunderclap, louder than any storm, reverberated off the marble. Sparks flew in all directions, striking the nearby columns and stairway and dancing along the blade of Flyn's sword.

Flyn and Ugglar were knocked back by the blast, landing on their backs. Flyn lay on the ground, stunned, his body tingling. Ugglar recovered first and with a scream of rage, pounced on his prone opponent, driving both fists down at Flyn's head.

Flyn raised his sword and braced himself. Too late, Ugglar saw the sword and tried to avoid landing on it. The sword pierced the side of the commander's neck and was buried to the hilt as the great orc's bulk smashed down on the smaller human. Ugglar collapsed, a final gasp escaping his mouth.

Smothered by the massive body of the dead commander, Flyn struggled to free himself, but the weight was too great. He couldn't move, couldn't see, couldn't even breathe. He heard the blood pounding in his ears. His lungs ached for air. He scraped and clawed at the body crushing him, trying to push it off of him, but it was too big.

Then the weight lifted from his chest, a blast of cool air hit his face. He gasped and felt the coolness rush into his lungs and relieve the aching.

He was alive.

He lay still, just breathing for a few seconds before opening his eyes. Gathered around him were his friends. Randell, Harvig, Sigrid, and Brenna looked down on him.

"Are you still alive, Andor?" Harvig asked.

Flyn nodded, still unable to talk.

With help from Randell, Flyn sat up and looked around. The other orcs were dead, two lying by the staircase, one off to the side.

"That was an amazing bit of swordsmanship," Sigrid said. "Well done."

"An amazing bit of luck," Flyn said. "I just remembered what Randell taught me. Use your opponent's size and anger against him."

"You learned that lesson well," Randell said.

"Where's Kel?" Flyn looked around.

No one knew. He had disappeared.

"We have to go," Harvig said. "More guards will be here soon."

"What about Kel?" Flyn said.

"He doesn't want to leave," Randell said. "He's completely under Jarot's control."

"And he almost had you, too," Brenna said. "If Sigrid hadn't attacked when she did, you'd be another one of Jarot's puppets. Kel knows your weaknesses and that gave Jarot a lot more power over you."

"I won't fall for it again," Flyn said.

"Probably not," Brenna replied. "But you won't get the chance. The whole citadel is bound to be on alert now."

As if to confirm her statement, the sound of orcs shouting drifted down from the stairwell.

Harvig started toward the tunnels, with Randell and Sigrid close behind. Flyn hesitated, looking up the stairs.

"I'll be back for you, Kel," Flyn said to himself. "I promise."

He turned and ran after the others.

Flyn looked over his shoulder as he entered the passageway to the tunnels. An endless line of orcs streamed down the stairs, the first ones almost to the floor of the great hall. Harvig stood at the doors, beckoning him to hurry. The shouts of the pursuing orcs echoed though the hall.

Once Flyn was through the door, Harvig slammed it shut and pushed Flyn ahead.

"No way to lock the door," Harvig said. "We'll just have to outrun them." He handed a torch to Flyn. "Run! I'll bring up the rear."

Flyn ran. Ahead of him, Randell and the others were exiting the room where they had stored their gear earlier. They waited for Flyn and Harvig with their packs and Flyn's bow and quiver.

"Go!" Flyn said, attaching the quiver to his belt. "I'll catch up."

The others ran, Harvig pulling on his pack as he went.

With his pack on, Flyn ran after his companions, the torch and quiver in one hand, his bow in the other. He slipped the bow over his head and reached for his sword.

It wasn't there. He remembered. He had left it buried in Ugglar's neck. He cursed himself for his carelessness, but there was nothing he could do about it now.

Behind him, the door to the great hall smashed open and the shouting of their pursuers filled the tunnel. He risked a glance over his shoulder.

The orcs were stopped in the doorway, shouting for torches. These orcs, dressed in black tunics with a red skull emblazoned on the chest, carried scimitars rather than clubs. The steel blades flashed in the torchlight from the great hall.

He turned back in time to see Harvig turn down an intersecting passage. Flyn raced to catch up with him. Reaching the intersection, he saw Randell's torch far ahead of him, bouncing and flickering as he ran. The others were just dark silhouettes in the torchlight. At each intersection, they were farther ahead of him than the last.

Flyn was already breathing heavy. His chest hurt where he had injured it escaping from the ogres what felt like years ago. The burning in his legs screamed for him to stop running. The orcs behind him kept him going. Gasping for air, he willed himself on as the sounds of their pursuers grew louder.

In front of him, Randell's torch disappeared down another tunnel.

He tried to run faster. His feet felt like blocks of stone.

He reached the intersection. There was no sign of Randell and the others. He checked the ceiling for his mark and, finding it, started again down the correct tunnel, no longer able to run. The orcs were less than a hundred feet from him now.

Flyn yelled with pain, forcing his legs to move faster.

Up ahead, Randell reappeared. He was at the next turn in the passageway. Harvig stood next to him, sword drawn.

"Hurry, Flyn!" Randell called.

Flyn could hear the footsteps of the pursuers gaining on him. Their torches cast his shadow on the wall, bouncing away from him into the darkness ahead.

Flyn reached Randell and Harvig, his head spinning. Harvig grabbed him and helped him turn the corner. He staggered forward, his lungs on fire. Harvig pulled him along the tunnel.

"Where's the key?" Randell asked.

Flyn couldn't answer. He reached into his belt pouch, pulled out the keys, and handed them to Randell. The militiaman took them and ran ahead.

"Don't give up now," Harvig said. "We're almost there."

Flyn nodded, the only response he could give.

They turned at another intersection. Ahead of them, Randell, Brenna, and Sigrid were at the steel doors that separated the citadel tunnels from the exit. Randell was holding one of the doors open. As soon as Flyn and Harvig ran through, he slammed it closed behind them. Sigrid was working the lock before the echoes faded.

Flyn fell to the ground, gasping for air.

"Got it," Sigrid said.

A loud boom echoed through the tunnel as the orcs on the other side smashed into the door.

"No time to rest," Harvig panted. He was bent over, his hands on his knees. "It won't take them long to find another key."

"They'll need more than a key." Sigrid chuckled. "I've jammed the lock. Unless those pig-faces are better at locks than I think they are, we don't have to worry about anybody following us."

Harvig looked up at Sigrid and shook his head. "There's no end to you, is there?" He sat down next to Flyn.

"How will the other girls get out now?" Brenna said.

"Maybe the pig-faces are so busy coming after us, they'll be able to sneak out another way," Sigrid said.

"I hope so," Brenna said. "I suppose we'll never know."

In spite of Sigrid's assurances, the group didn't rest long. Once they had caught their breath, they shouldered their packs and started up the tunnel. Brenna took a leather belt off one of the dead orcs, along with strips of cloth from his pants.

"When we stop again, I need to make something to cover my feet," she said.

The orcs were still pounding the doors as they started up the passageway toward the exit.

They rested again at the tunnel entrance. The fresh mountain air energized their spirits after the damp, stagnant air of the tunnels. Even Sigrid was glad to be in the open again.

"Those tunnels may have been built by dwarves," she said, "but they smell like orc."

"How long do you think it will take them to get here from the front gate?" Flyn asked.

No one could guess, so they didn't rest long.

"I'd rather not climb down that cliff at night," Sigrid said. "Especially with a bunch of novices."

"No choice," Flyn said. "We have to do it."

They walked to the edge of the small plateau and looked down. All Flyn could see below them was darkness.

"I remember being able to see clear to the ground where we came down earlier," Sigrid said. "We should try there."

Sigrid led them to the edge of the cliff where they had descended from the trail.

"I can't see any better here than over there," Flyn said, looking down.

"You'll just have to trust me, lad." Sigrid looped the rope around a tree.

"I'm not really dressed for climbing down a cliff," Brenna said, looking at her bare feet. "I'm not even dressed for a walk through the woods."

"Don't worry, lass," Sigrid said. "We'll lower you down first. You can take one of the torches so the rest of us can see where we're going."

Sigrid wrapped the ends of the rope around Brenna, fashioning a harness that allowed her to sit as they lowered her down. Harvig and Randell grabbed the rope while Flyn and Sigrid helped her over the side.

"Make sure you hold that torch away from the rope," Sigrid said. "Wouldn't want you to burn it through and fall."

"Important safety tip," Brenna said with a nervous smile.

Harvig and Randell lowered her down, Sigrid giving directions to them as Brenna descended.

"Who's next?" Sigrid asked after Brenna was safely on the ground.

Flyn volunteered and Sigrid reminded him how to wrap the rope and how to climb down. When he was ready, he eased himself over the edge, holding his breath.

He wasn't sure if not being able to see was better or worse. Brenna stood below him, holding the torch so he could see the ground, but looking down gave him the dizzy, tingling sensation again, so he focused on the cliff face in front of him.

Pausing after each step, he worked his way down. Ten minutes later, his feet touched the ground.

"That's an amazing trick," Brenna said after he had unwrapped himself from the rope.

"Sigrid taught us," he replied. "We wouldn't have been able to rescue you without her."

"I can see that."

Nearly an hour had passed before they were all safely on the ground below the ledge.

Flyn finally relaxed. They were free from the citadel and the orcs.

CHAPTER 16

Their journey back through the Nidfel Mountains was harder and slower. Except for a few torches in the distance on the first night, they saw no sign of pursuit. Even so, they didn't want to chance traveling the Yord Trail, instead finding smaller, less traveled paths. With the coming of summer, the spring rains had mostly ended, and with plenty of food from the supplies they had taken from Jarot's storeroom, they were in no particular hurry.

Harvig and Randell expected to be reprimanded for disobeying the Thane's orders to go after Kel and Brenna, even though he had only explicitly forbidden Gudbrant. Sigrid had a long journey in front of her, but she seemed content to accompany the humans at least as far as Inefel before departing to the south. And while Brenna talked eagerly of home, she couldn't hide how much the loss of Gudbrant weighed heavily on her heart. She confided in Flyn that she hoped the long journey to Garthset would bring her peace before facing Gudbrant's family and friends.

As for Flyn, his encounter with Kel had left him numb. Although the others tried to console him and convince him to let Kel go, he couldn't accept that his friend was gone forever. He vowed to search for a way to free Kel from Jarot's control, even if he had to search all of Tirmar for the answer.

Their first stop was Kaldersten. They needed to rest, resupply, and try to get a new mule. Brenna needed new clothes, not to mention shoes. The others had given her some of their spare clothing to replace the linen frock, but no one had spare boots. She had used the orc's belt and strips of cloth to fashion makeshift sandals to protect the bottoms of her feet, but they made for very poor hiking shoes.

On the afternoon of the tenth day after rescuing Brenna, the weary travelers arrived in Kaldersten and made their way straight to The Frozen Mug.

The main room was empty, except for the innkeeper sitting at a table eating a bowl of soup. When he saw who was walking in, he set down his bowl and clamored to his feet to greet them.

"By the gods, you're alive," he said, hurrying over to the group.

"We are," Flyn said. "You seem surprised by that."

"When Gunnulf came back alone, I feared the worst," Svendar said. "He told of how you planned to sneak into Uskleig."

"We did," Randell said. "We rescued Brenna." Randell introduced Brenna to Svendar.

"Well, that certainly calls for a celebration," the innkeeper said. He paused, looking at the group. "Where's the other one?"

"He didn't make it," Flyn said.

"I'm sorry. He seemed like a good man. Uskleig is a dangerous place."

"He never made it to Uskleig," Flyn said. "We were attacked by a vargolf."

"The Nidfels have many dangers," Svendar said, shaking his head.

"It would never have happened if that backstabbing Gunnulf hadn't stolen all our supplies and abandoned us," Randell said.

"He said *you* abandoned *him*." The innkeeper looked at them with a raised eyebrow. "He said he almost died trying to get back here on his own."

"If I ever get hold of that squeaky toad, he'll wish he had died out there," Sigrid said.

"Dear me. If I had known what he'd done, I would never have allowed him back in my doors, you can count on that." The innkeeper nodded his head to emphasize his words.

"It wasn't your fault," Flyn said. "Right now, we just need rest and a good meal."

"Of course, whatever I can do."

Svendar provided them with rooms and had fresh water brought in for them to bathe. He refused to take any money for the rooms, telling them it was the least he could do for letting them get swindled by Gunnulf, in spite of their assurances that it wasn't his fault.

That evening, freshly bathed and wearing new clothes, they met in the inn's dining room, much as they had almost three weeks earlier.

"I think I'm going to stay here," Flyn announced as they ate dinner.

"Why?" Randell asked. "You can't be thinking about going back to Uskleig alone?"

"What choice do I have? I can't leave Kel there. And if what he said is true, Jarot is planning on invading Trygsted."

"What we need to do is fight back," Harvig said.

"Mighty words from an Ilfin." Sigrid laughed.

"Not all Ilfin are afraid to fight," Harvig retorted.

"I've no doubt about you, lad."

"That's all good, but how do we fight back?" Randell asked.

"I'll talk to my father," Brenna said. "I'm sure he'll understand if I explain it to him."

"Your father is not a warrior. He didn't even want to let Gudbrant go to try to free you from Jarot."

"My father's concern is the safety of the citizens of Garthset. Once he understands that safety requires we fight back, he'll do the right thing. But Garthset doesn't have enough people to fight alone."

"What about the dwarves?" Flyn asked Sigrid. "Will they fight?"

"Aye, they'll fight, if Jarot threatens our cities. When I left home two years ago, no one even knew he existed. I'll try to convince them, but it would help if you came with me."

"Why me?" Flyn asked.

"You're an Andor. The return of the Andors to Tirmar would go a long way to convince them that times are changing."

"If they even believe me." Flyn still wasn't sure what the big deal was about being an Andor.

"They'll believe you."

"Even if you convince the Kirrs to help, I doubt it will be enough," Harvig said. "We must unite the Ilfin clan. We haven't been united as a single clan in decades."

"Can your father help do that?" Flyn asked Brenna.

"I don't know. All we can do is try."

"It still won't be enough," Randell said. "We need to unite all the clans."

"That hasn't been done since the Council of En was dissolved, four hundred years ago," Harvig said.

"Then perhaps it's time the council was reformed," Randell replied.

"What's the Council of En?" Flyn asked.

"After the Revolution, each clan settled in a different part of Tirmar," Sigrid said. "Before long, the leaders realized they needed a way to keep the peace between the clans, so they founded the Council. It was made up of representatives from each clan."

"Except the Andors," Brenna added.

"Aye, except the Andors, who had disappeared."

"Reuniting the clans," Harvig said, shaking his head. "How can we possibly hope to accomplish that?"

Sigrid sighed and looked around the table.

"There's something I should tell you," she said. "Me and Osgar weren't looking for gold when Jarot's beasties got us. We were looking for you." She looked at Flyn.

"Me?" Flyn said. "What do you mean?"

"A man named Rafin recruited us. He's some kind of wizard. Somehow, he knew you were coming. He told us that the Andor would arrive on the shores of the Mithar Ocean near Egrathwaite, where Andor himself left Tirmar. Of course, we thought he was crazy, but me brother talked me into it."

"But how would he know anything about us?" Flyn stared at the dwarf. "Or that our boat would wash up where it did? For that matter, why would he care?"

"An Andor coming back to Tirmar is a big thing, but according to Rafin, your arrival means more than that. He said you're the key to reuniting the clans."

"I don't understand," Flyn said.

"Can't really say I understand either. Me brother and me were just doing what we were paid to do. Rafin sent us to meet you and take you to Tralborg. When the orcs captured us, I figured we failed, especially after they killed Osgar."

Sigrid scowled.

"So your brother was killed looking for me?"

"Don't blame yourself, laddie. It was the orc bastards who killed him." She paused, frowning. "Anyway, when your friend showed up, we thought he must be the Andor we were sent to find. Osgar was killed trying to escape so he could free Kel before they sent him to Uskleig. I'd lost me brother and the Andor. I just wanted to get out and go home. Then you came along. After we escaped, I thought about trying to convince you to come to Tralborg with me, maybe get help there instead of heading off to rescue Kel yourself."

"I would never have done that. I had to at least try to rescue him."

"Aye, which is why I decided to go with you instead."

"I still don't understand how this Rafin knows about us."

"That's a question for him," Sigrid said. "But finding you, and now all this talk about reuniting the clans, makes me think that maybe the old wizard wasn't so crazy after all."

A stunned silence fell over the table. Flyn tried to make sense of what Sigrid was telling him. The others just stared at the two. Finally, Harvig spoke.

"If you hadn't already proved yourself to me, Dwarf, I would run you out of here right now for that story."

Sigrid nodded and sipped her beer.

"Isn't Tralborg where the Council of En met?" Brenna asked.

"It was," Randell said. He turned to Sigrid. "So, this wizard is a Ranjer?"

"Aye," Sigrid replied.

"What does that mean?" Flyn asked.

"It means that if anyone can help you rescue your friend, it's probably this Rafin," Harvig said.

"What do we do now?" Randell asked.

Flyn thought for a moment.

"I guess I'll go with Sigrid to see this Rafin. Maybe he can help, maybe not, but I don't know of any other way to save Kel."

"I'd like to go with you, but I need to return to Garthset," Brenna said. "Randell, Harvig, and I will try to convince my father, but whether he agrees or not, we'll do what we can to meet with the Thanes of larger Ilfin towns."

Randell and Harvig nodded in agreement.

"Well, I guess we have a plan," Sigrid said. She sat back and finished her beer.

Anxious to set out on their new journeys, the group left Kaldersten early the next morning. They traveled south together for as long as they could. With the fair weather, they reached Inefel less than three weeks after leaving Kaldersten.

Flyn spent much of the journey thinking of Sigrid's revelation and what Rafin might want with him. He asked Sigrid about Rafin and what he might be able to do to help him rescue Kel. Sigrid answered his questions as best she could, though she didn't seem to know a lot more about the wizard than what she had already told them.

After reaching Inefel, they spent one last night together. The next morning, each group set out to their own destination, Flyn and Sigrid south to Tralborg, Randell, Harvig, and Brenna east to Garthset. Flyn promised to return to Garthset once he rescued Kel. They wished him luck, then turned eastward, toward the Estlaeg Mountains, a thin, gray line on the horizon.

"Ready to go?" Sigrid asked.

Flyn nodded, but kept staring after his companions. He watched them until they disappeared over the crest of a small hill.

"I think I'm going to miss them," he said, still watching the road to the east.

"Aye, they're good folks. I'll miss them too."

As he and Sigrid set out from Inefel, Flyn thought about home, about his mother and father, and about his brother, and Kel's family. He wondered if they had given up hope for him and Kel. He wondered if he would ever see them again.

Flyn sighed and adjusted his pack.

"I will see them again," he said to himself. "And Kel too."

ACKNOWLEDGMENTS

Writing a book is simultaneously a solitary task and a group effort. A writer spends hours upon hours at his or her desk (or kitchen table) pouring a story onto paper or into a computer. Even those who write on the subway on their way to work are isolated from the world around them while they write.

But books aren't just the result of the author's efforts. Authors rely on many others to turn their work into something people want to read. While I can never mention everyone by name, you know who you are, and I thank you from the bottom of my heart. You don't know how much your help means.

There are, however, a few I do want to mention by name.

To my wife and kids for their love and support. I promise I won't make you read another first draft for at least a week. Love you guys!

As always, I want to thank my editor, Holly Atkinson. Once again, you've made me work harder than I wanted to, and kept me from getting lazy at the end.

A special thank you goes out to Jim Gillum, and his friend Tim Scheidler, for helping me with the lyrics to "The Last Ride." Jim is a wonderfully talented musician, and if you're into classic rock or country music, check him out at https://jimgillum.com/.

Liz, Ken, Jill, Michelle, and Shaina: Thanks so much for taking the time to read my early drafts and provide me with feedback on the story. This book is eminently better for your help.

And to all my readers, thanks so much for spending a little bit of your time in my imagination. If I've taken your mind off the world around you for a few hours, then I've done my job.

Until next time, happy reading!

Enjoy this book? You can make a difference!

Reviews are the most powerful tools in an author's arsenal when it comes to getting attention for his or her books. Not all of us have the financial muscle of a big New York publisher to take out full page ads in the newspaper or put posters up in the subway.

But we do have something much more powerful and effective than that, and it's something that those publishers would love to get their hands on.

A committed and loyal bunch of readers like you.

Honest reviews of my books help bring them to the attention of other readers.

If you've enjoyed this book, I would be very grateful if you could spend just a few minutes leaving a review (it can be as short as you like) on the book's page at the book retailer where you purchased it.

Thanks for reading. I hope you enjoyed reading it as much as I enjoyed writing it.

ABOUT THE AUTHOR

In addition to writing fiction, Mark Dame is a professional software developer and freelance commercial writer. He also works part-time as a flight instructor teaching people to fly small single engine planes. When he's not writing or flying, you might find Mark scuba diving in caves, camping, running, or biking. Mark lives in the suburbs of Cincinnati, Ohio with his wife and two sons.

Connect with Mark online:
Website: https://www.markdame.com/
Facebook: https://www.facebook.com/MarkDameAuthor
Twitter: https://twitter.com/MTDame
Goodreads: https://www.goodreads.com/markdame

Made in the USA
Las Vegas, NV
15 March 2022

45668242R00164